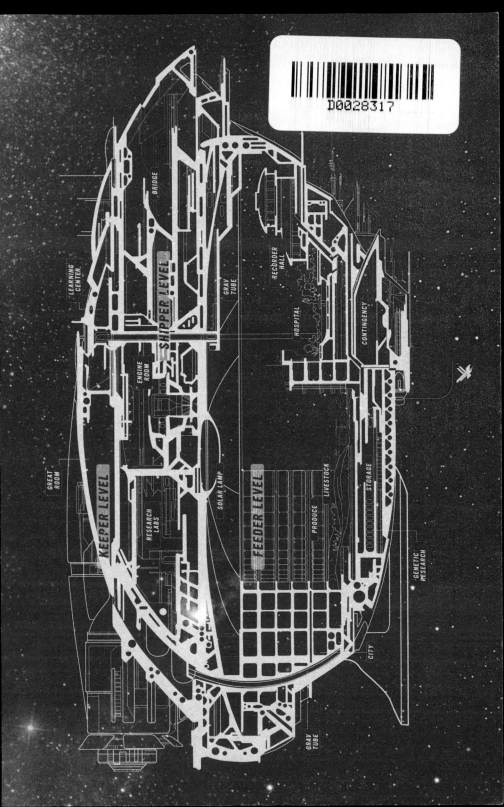

LEARNING CENTER

BRIDGE

SHIPPER LEVEL

GRAV TUBE

RECORDER HALL

ENGINE ROOM

HOSPITAL

CONTINGENCY

GREAT ROOM

KEEPER LEVEL

RESEARCH LABS

SOLAR LAMP

FEEDER LEVEL

PRODUCE

LIVESTOCK

STORAGE

GENETIC RESEARCH

CITY

GRAV TUBE

D0028317

BETH REVIS

razOr
bill

An Imprint of Penguin Group (USA) Inc.

Across the Universe

RAZORBILL

Published by the Penguin Group
Penguin Young Readers Group
345 Hudson Street, New York, New York 10014, U.S.A.
Penguin Group (USA) Inc., 375 Hudson Street, New York, New York 10014, U.S.A.
Penguin Group (Canada), 90 Eglinton Avenue East, Suite 700, Toronto, Ontario,
Canada M4P 2Y3 (a division of Pearson Penguin Canada Inc.)
Penguin Books Ltd, 80 Strand, London WC2R 0RL, England
Penguin Ireland, 25 St Stephen's Green, Dublin 2, Ireland
(a division of Penguin Books Ltd)
Penguin Group (Australia), 250 Camberwell Road, Camberwell, Victoria 3124,
Australia (a division of Pearson Australia Group Pty Ltd)
Penguin Books India Pvt Ltd, 11 Community Centre, Panchsheel Park,
New Delhi – 110 017, India
Penguin Group (NZ), 67 Apollo Drive, Mairangi Bay, Auckland 1311, New Zealand
(a division of Pearson New Zealand Ltd)
Penguin Books (South Africa) (Pty) Ltd, 24 Sturdee Avenue,
Rosebank, Johannesburg 2196, South Africa

Penguin Books Ltd, Registered Offices: 80 Strand, London WC2R 0RL, England

First published in hardcover by Razorbill 2011
Published in this edition 2012

18 17 16 15 14 13 12 11 10 9

ISBN: 978-1-59514-467-6

Library of Congress Cataloging-in-Publication Data is available

Printed in the United States of America

ACROSS THE UNIVERSE

For my parents, who found science in nature
and
For my husband, who found science in technology
because
They love me, who found science in fiction.

Dei gratia.

Images of broken light which dance before me like a
  million eyes,
That call me on and on across the universe . . .
                    . . . Nothing's gonna change my world.
                              —Lennon/McCartney

1: AMY

Daddy said, "Let Mom go first."

Mom wanted me to go first. I think it was because she was afraid that after they were contained and frozen, I'd walk away, return to life rather than consign myself to that cold, clear box. But Daddy insisted.

"Amy needs to see what it's like. You go first, let her watch. Then she can go and I'll be with her. I'll go last."

"You go first," Mom said. "I'll go last."

But the long and the short of it is that you have to be naked, and neither of them wanted me to see either of them naked (not like I wanted to see them in all their nude glory, gross), but given the choice, it'd be best for Mom to go first, since we had the same parts and all.

She looked so skinny after she undressed. Her collarbone stood out more; her skin had that rice-paper-thin, over-moisturized consistency old people's skin has. Her stomach—a part of her she always kept hidden under clothes—sagged in a wrinkly sort of way that made her look even more vulnerable and weak.

The men who worked in the lab seemed uninterested in my mother's nudity, just as they were impartial to my and my father's presence. They helped her lie down in the clear cryo box. It would have looked like a coffin, but coffins have pillows and look a lot more comfortable. This looked more like a shoebox.

"It's cold," Mom said. Her pale white skin pressed flat against the bottom of the box.

"You won't feel it," the first worker grunted. His nametag said ED.

I looked away as the other worker, Hassan, pierced Mom's skin with the IV needles. One in her left arm, hooked up at the crease of her inner elbow; one in her right hand, protruding from that big vein below her knuckles.

"Relax," Ed said. It was an order, not a kind suggestion.

Mom bit her lip.

The stuff in the IV bag did not flow like water. It rolled like honey. Hassan squeezed the bag, forcing it down the IV faster. It was sky blue, like the blue of the cornflowers Jason had given me at prom.

My mom hissed in pain. Ed removed a yellow plastic clamp on the empty IV in her elbow. A backflow of bright red blood shot through the IV, pouring into the bag. Mom's eyes filled with water. The blue goo from the other IV glowed, a soft sparkle of sky shining through my mother's veins as the goo traveled up her arm.

"Gotta wait for it to hit the heart," Ed said, glancing at us. Daddy clenched his fists, his eyes boring into my mom. Her eyes were clamped shut, two hot tears dangling on her lashes.

Hassan squeezed the bag of blue goo again. A line of blood trickled from under Mom's teeth where she was biting her lip.

"This stuff, it's what makes the freezing work." Ed spoke in a conversational tone, like a baker talking about how yeast makes bread rise. "Without it, little ice crystals form in the cells and split open the cell walls. This stuff makes the cell walls stronger, see? Ice don't break 'em." He glanced down at Mom. "Hurts like a bitch going in, though."

Her face was pale, and she was lying in that box, and she wasn't moving at all, as if moving would break her. She already looked dead.

"I wanted you to see this," Daddy whispered. He didn't look at me—he was still staring at Mom. He didn't even blink.

"Why?"

"So you knew before you did it."

Hassan kept kneading the bag of blue goo. Mom's eyes rolled up into the back of her head for a minute, and I thought she'd pass out, but she didn't.

"Almost there," Ed said, looking at the bag of Mom's blood. The flow had slowed down.

The only sound was Hassan's heavy breathing as he rubbed the plastic sides of the bag of goo. And whimpering, soft, like a dying kitten, coming from Mom.

A faint blue glow sparkled in the IV leading from Mom's elbow.

"Okay, stop," Ed said. "It's all in her blood now."

Hassan pulled the IVs out. Mom let out a crackling sigh.

Daddy pulled me forward. Looking down at Mom reminded me of looking down at Grandma last year at the church, when we all said goodbye and Mom said she was in a better place, but all she meant was that she was dead.

"How is it?" I asked.

"Not bad," Mom lied. At least she could still speak.

"Can I touch her?" I asked Ed. He shrugged, so I reached out, gripped the fingers of her left hand. They were already ice cold. She didn't squeeze back.

"Can we get on with it?" Ed asked. He shook a big eyedropper in his hand.

Daddy and I stepped back, but not so far that Mom would think we'd left her in that icy coffin alone. Ed pulled Mom's eyes open. His fingers were big, calloused, and they looked like rough-hewn logs spreading apart my mom's paper-thin eyelids. A drop of yellow liquid fell on each green eye. Ed did it quickly—*drop, drop*—then he sort of pushed her eyes shut. She didn't open them again.

I guess I looked shocked, because, this time, when Ed glanced up at me, he actually stopped working long enough to give me a comforting smile. "Keeps her from going blind," he said.

"It's okay," Mom said from her shoebox coffin. Even though her eyes were sealed shut, I could hear the tears in her voice.

"Tubes," Ed said, and Hassan handed him a trio of clear plastic tubes. "Okay, look." Ed leaned down close to Mom's face. "I'm gonna put these down your throat. It's not gonna feel good. Try to act like you're swallowin' 'em."

Mom nodded and opened her mouth. Ed crammed the tubes down her throat. Mom gagged, a violent motion that started at her belly and worked all the way up to her dry, cracked lips.

I glanced at Daddy. His eyes were cold and hard.

It was a long time before she became still and silent. She kept trying to swallow, the muscles in her neck rearranging themselves to accommodate the tubes. Ed threaded the tubes up through a hole at the top of the shoebox coffin, near Mom's head. Hassan opened a drawer and pulled out a mess of electrical wires. He stuffed a bundle of brightly colored wires down the first tube, then one long black cable with a small box at the end down the second one, and finally a small rectangular black piece of plastic that looked like a solar panel attached to a fiber-optic string down the last. Hassan plugged all the wires into a little white box that Ed fixed over the hole at the top of what I realized was nothing more than an elaborate packing crate.

"Say goodbye." I looked up, surprised at the kind voice. Ed had his back to us, typing something into a computer; it was Hassan who spoke. He nodded at me encouragingly.

Daddy had to pull my arm to make me approach Mom. This . . . this was not the last image of her I wanted. Yellow crusting her eyes, tubes holding wires crammed down her throat, a soft sky-blue sheen pumping through her veins. Daddy kissed her, and Mom smiled a bit around the tubes. I patted her on the shoulder. It was cold too. She gurgled something at me, and I leaned in closer. Three sounds, three spluttering grunts, really. I squeezed Mom's arm. I knew the words she was trying to get past the tubes were, "I love you."

"Momma," I whispered, stroking her paper-soft skin. I'd not called her anything but Mom since I was seven.

"'Kay, that's it," Ed said. Daddy's hand snaked into the crook of my elbow, and he tugged at me gently. I jerked away. He changed tactics and gripped my shoulder, spinning me against his hard, mus-cled chest in a tight hug, and I didn't resist this time. Ed and Hassan lifted up what looked like a hospital's version of a fire hose, and water flecked with sky-blue sparkles filled the shoebox coffin. Mom spluttered when it reached her nose.

"Just breathe it in," Ed shouted over the sound of rushing liquid. "Just relax."

A stream of bubbles shot through the blue water, obscuring her face. She shook her head, denying the water the chance to drown her, but a moment later, she gave up. The liquid covered her. Ed turned off the hose and the ripples faded. The water was still. She was still.

Ed and Hassan lowered the shoebox coffin lid over Mom. They pushed the box into the rear wall, and only when they closed it behind a little door on the wall did I notice all the little doors in the wall, like a morgue. They pulled the handle down. A hiss of steam escaped through the door—the flash freezing process was over. One second Mom was there, and the next, everything about her that made her Mom was frozen and stagnant. She was as good as dead for the next three centuries until someone opened that door and woke her up.

"The girl's next?" Ed asked.

I stepped forward, balling my hands into fists so they wouldn't shake.

"No," Daddy said.

Without waiting for Daddy's response, Ed and Hassan were already preparing another shoebox coffin. They didn't care whether it was me or him; they were just doing their job.

"What?" I asked Daddy.

"I'm going next. Your mother wouldn't agree to that—she thought you'd still back down, decide not to come with us. Well, I'm giving you that option. I'm going next. Then, if you'd like to walk away, not be frozen, that's okay. I've told your aunt and uncle. They're waiting outside; they'll be there until five. After they freeze me, you can just walk away. Mom and I won't know, not for centuries, not till we wake up, and if you do decide to live instead of being frozen, we'll be okay."

"But, Daddy, I—"

"No. It's not fair for us to guilt you into this. It'll be easier for you to make an honest decision if you do it without facing us."

"But I promised you. I promised Mom." My voice cracked. My eyes burned painfully, and I squeezed them shut. Two hot trails of tears leaked down my face.

"Doesn't matter. That's too big of a promise for us to make you keep. You have to make this choice yourself—if you want to stay here, I understand. I'm giving you a way out."

"But they don't need you! You could stay here with me! You're not even important to the mission—you're with the military, for Pete's sake! How is a battlefield analyst supposed to help on a new planet? You could stay here, you could be—"

Daddy shook his head.

"—with me," I whispered, but there was no point in asking him to stay. His mind was made up. And it wasn't true, anyway. Daddy was sixth in command, and while that didn't exactly make him commander in chief, it was still pretty high up. Mom was important too; no one was better at genetic splicing, and they needed her to help develop crops that could grow on the new planet.

I was the only one not needed.

Daddy went behind the curtain and undressed, and when he came out, Ed and Hassan let him use a hand towel to cover himself as he walked to the cryo chamber. They took it away when he lay down, and I forced my eyes to stare at his face, to not make this worse for either of us. But his face radiated pain, a look I had never seen Daddy wear before. It made my insides twist with even more fear, more doubt. I watched them plug the two IVs in. I watched them seal his eyes. I tried to retreat within myself, silence the scream of horror reverberating in my mind, and stand straight with a spine made of iron and a face made of stone. Then Daddy squeezed my hand, once, hard, as they crammed the tubes down his throat, and I crumbled, inside and out.

Before they filled his box with the blue-speckled liquid, Daddy held up his hand, his pinky finger sticking out. I wrapped my own pinky around his. I knew that with it, he was promising everything would be okay. And I almost believed him.

I cried so hard when they filled his cryo chamber up I couldn't see his face as it drowned in the liquid. Then they lowered the lid, slammed him in his mortuary, and a puff of white steam escaped through the cracks.

"Can I see him?" I asked.

Ed and Hassan looked at each other. Hassan shrugged. Ed jerked the lever of the little door open again and pulled out the clear shoebox coffin.

And there was Daddy. The translucent liquid was frozen solid and, I knew, so was Daddy. I put my hand on the glass, wishing there was a way to feel his warmth through the ice, but snatched it away quickly. The glass was so cold it burned. Green lights blinked on the little electric box Hassan had fixed to the top of Daddy's cryotube.

He didn't look like Daddy under the ice.

"So," Ed said, "are you going under, or are you leaving the party early?" He pushed Daddy's shoebox coffin back into its little slot in the wall.

When I looked up at Ed, my eyes were so watery that his face sort of melted, and he looked a bit like a Cyclops. "I . . ."

My eyes slid to the exit, past all the cryo equipment on the other side of the room. Beyond that door were my aunt and uncle, who I loved, who I could be happy living with. And beyond them was Jason. And Rebecca and Heather and Robyn and all my friends. And the mountains, the flowers, the sky. Earth. Beyond that door was Earth. And life.

But my eyes drifted to the little doors on the wall. Beyond those doors were my momma and daddy.

I cried as I undressed. The first boy who ever saw me naked was Jason, just that one time, the night I found out I would leave behind everything on Earth, and everything included him. I did not like the idea that the last boys to see me naked on this planet would be Ed and Hassan. I tried to cover myself with my arms and hands, but Ed and Hassan made me remove them so they could put the IVs in.

And, oh god, it was worse than Mom made it look. Oh, God. Oh, *God*. It was cold and it was burning all at the same time. I could feel my muscles straining as that blue goo entered my system. My heart wanted to *pound*, beat upon my rib cage like a lover beating on the door, but the blue goo made it do the opposite and slooooow down so that instead of *beatbeatbeatbeat*, it went *beat . . . beat . . .*

. . . *beat* . . .

. . .

. . .

. . . *beat* . . .

. . .

Ed jerked my eyelids open. *Plop!* Cold, yellow liquid filled my eyes, sealing them like gum. *Plop!*

I was blind now.

One of them, maybe Hassan, tapped on my chin, and I opened my mouth obediently. Apparently, not wide enough—the tubes hit my teeth. I opened wider.

And then the tubes were forced down my throat, hard. They did not feel as flexible as they had looked; they felt like a greased broomstick being crammed down my mouth. I gagged, and gagged again. I could taste bile and copper around the plastic of the tubes.

"Swallow it!" Ed shouted in my ear. "Just relax!"

Easy for him to say.

A few moments after it was done, my stomach tingled. I could feel the wires inside me being pulled and tugged as Hassan plugged the little black box to the outside of my very own shoebox coffin.

Shuffling noises. The hose.

"Don't know why anyone would sign up for this," Hassan said.

Silence.

A metallic sound—the hose being opened up. Cold, cold liquid splashed on my thighs. I wanted to move my hands to cover myself *there*, but my body was sluggish.

"I dunno," Ed said. "Things ain't exactly peachy here now. Nothing's been right since the first recession, let alone the second. The Financial Resource Exchange was s'posed to bring more jobs, wasn't it? Ain't got nothing now other than this P.O.S. job, and it'll be over soon as they're all frozen."

Another silence. The cryo liquid washed over my knees now,

seeping cold into the places on my body that had been warm—the crease of my knees, under my arms, under my breasts.

"Not worth giving your life away, not for what they're offering."

Ed snorted. "What they're offering? They're offering a lifetime's salary, all in one check."

"Ain't worth nothing on a ship that won't land for three hundred and one years."

My heart stopped. *Three hundred . . . and one? No—that's wrong. It's three hundred years even. Not three hundred and one.*

"That much money can sure help a family out. Might make the difference."

"What difference?" Hassan asked.

"Difference between surviving or not. It's not like when we were kids. Don't care what the prez says, that Financial Act ain't gonna be able to fix this kinda debt."

What are they yammering about? Who cares about national debt and jobs? Go back to that extra year!

"A man has time to think about it anyway," Ed continued. "Consider his options. Why'd they delay the launch again?"

Cryo liquid splashed against my ears as my shoebox coffin filled; I lifted my head.

Delay? What delay? I tried to speak around the tubes, but they filled my mouth, crowded my tongue, silenced my words.

"I have no idea. Something about the fuel and feedback from the probes. But why are they making us keep all the freezing on schedule?"

The cyro liquid was rising fast. I turned my head, so my right ear could catch their conversation.

"Who cares?" Ed asked. "Not them—they'll just sleep through it all. They say the ship'll take three hundred years just to get to that other planet—what's the difference in one more year?"

I tried to sit up. My muscles were hard, slow, but I struggled. I tried to talk again, make a sound, any sound, but the cryo liquid was spilling over my face.

"Just. Relax," Ed said very loudly near my face.

I shook my head. God, didn't they *know*? A year made the world of difference! This was one more year I could be with Jason, one more year I could *live*! I signed up for three hundred years . . . not three hundred and one!

Gentle hands—Hassan's?—pushed me under the cryo liquid. I held my breath. I tried to rise up. I wanted my year! My last year— one more year!

"Breathe in the liquid!" Ed's voice sounded muffled, almost indecipherable under the cryo liquid. I tried to shake my head, but as my neck muscles tensed, my lungs rebelled, and the cold, cold cryo liquid rushed down my nose, past the tubes, and into my body.

I felt the finality of the lid trapping me inside my Snow White coffin.

As one of them pushed at my feet, sliding me into my morgue, I imagined that my Prince Charming was just beyond my little door, that he really could come and kiss me awake and that we could have a whole year more together.

There was a *click, click, grrr* of gears, and I knew the flash freezing would start in mere moments, and then my life would be nothing but a puff of white steam leaking through the cracks of my morgue door.

And I thought: *At least I'll sleep. I will forget, for three hundred and one years, everything else.*

And then I thought: *That will be nice.*

And then *whoosh!* The flash-freeze filled the tiny chamber. I was in ice. I was ice.

I *am* ice.

But if I'm ice, how am I conscious? I was supposed to be asleep; I was supposed to forget about Jason and life and Earth for three hundred and one years. People have been cryo frozen before me, and none of them were conscious. If the *mind* is frozen, it cannot be awake or aware.

I've read before of coma victims who were supposed to be knocked out with anesthesia during an operation, but really they were awake and felt everything.

I hope — I *pray* — that's not me. I can't be awake for three hundred and one years. I'll never survive that.

Maybe I'm dreaming now. I've dreamt a lifetime in a thirty-minute nap. Maybe I'm still in that space between frozen and not, and this is all a dream. Maybe we haven't left Earth yet. Maybe I'm still in that limbo year before the ship launches, and I'm stuck, trapped in a dream I can't wake from.

Maybe I've still got three hundred and one years stretching out before me.

Maybe I'm not even asleep yet. Not all the way.

Maybe, maybe, maybe.

I only know one thing for certain.

I want my year back.

2 : ELDER

The door is locked.

"Now *that*," I say to the empty room, "is interesting."

See, there are hardly any locked doors on *Godspeed*. No need. *Godspeed* isn't small—it was the largest ship ever built when it was launched two and a half centuries ago—but it's not so huge that we don't all feel the weight of the metal walls crushing us. Privacy is our most valued possession and no one—*no one*—would dare betray privacy.

Which is why the locked door before me is so strange. Why lock a door no one would ever breach?

Not that I should be so surprised. A locked door just about sums up Eldest.

My mouth tightens. The worst part? I know that door is locked because of me. It has to be. This is the Keeper Level, and Eldest and I, as the current and future leaders of the ship, are the only ones allowed here.

"Frex!" I shout, punching the door.

Because I know—I *know*—on the other side of that door is my chance. When Eldest was called to the Shipper Level to inspect the engine, he rushed to his chamber for a box, went all the way to the hatch, then turned around and took the box back to his room. And locked the door before he left. Clearly, whatever is in that box is important and has something to do with the ship, something that I, as leader-in-training, should know about.

It's just one more thing Eldest is keeping from me. Because stars forbid he'd actually train me instead of giving me more mindless lessons and reports.

If I had that box, I'd *prove* to him I could . . . what? I don't actually know what's in there. But I *do* know that whatever it is has been making him spend a lot more time on the Shipper Level. There's a serious problem going on, something that's kept Eldest more preoccupied than I've ever seen him before.

And if they would just give me a frexing chance, maybe I could help.

I kick the door, then turn and fall against it. Three years ago, when it was time for me to start training, I didn't care for shite about whether or not Eldest trained me as he should. I was just glad to be off the Feeder Level. Even though my name is Elder, I'm the youngest person on the ship, and I've always known that I, as the one born in the off years, would be the Eldest of the generation born after me. I was never comfortable living with the Feeders and their obsession with farming. Moving in with Eldest felt like a relief.

But I'm sixteen now, and I'm tired of doing nothing but lessons. It's time for me to be a real leader, whether Eldest likes it or not.

Defeated by a locked door. No wonder Eldest doesn't bother to train me.

I bang my head against the wall and bump it against a piece of raised square metal. The biometric scanner. I'd always assumed it operated the lights to the Great Room. Most of the biometric scanners are there to interface with the ship—to turn on lights, start electronics, or *open doors*.

I turn around and roll my thumb over the biometric scanner bar. "Eldest/Elder access granted," the computer chirps in a cheerful female voice. As Elder, I always have the same security access as Eldest.

"Command?" the computer asks.

Huh. That's odd. Usually, a door opens automatically once access is granted. What other command does a door need?

"Um, open?"

Eldest's chamber door doesn't zip open like I expect it to. Instead, the ceiling moves. I spin around, my heart banging around inside my chest. Above me, the metal ceiling splits into two pieces and drops down slowly, exposing—

Exposing a *window*.

That shows the outside.

And the *stars*.

There are hatches in the ship, I know there are, but Eldest has never let me see them, just like he hasn't let me see the massive engine that fuels the ship, or some of the records of the ship before the Plague. I didn't even know the metal ceiling over the Great Room covered a window to the uni.

I've never seen stars before.

And I never knew they were so beautiful.

The entire uni stretches out before me. So big, so frexing big. My eyes fill with starshine. There are so, *so* many of them. The stars are abbreviated white dashes in the sky with streaks of faint colors— mostly reds and yellows, but sometimes blues or greens. And, seeing them all, I feel closer to planet-landing than I ever have before. I can see it: the ship disembarking for the first time, at night, with no moon or clouds, and before we set out to build our new world, we all stop and stare at the stars above.

"Access override," the computer says in its still-pleasant voice. "Screen lowering."

Screen lowering? What?

Above me, the stars glow brightly.

And then the window to the universe breaks. A thin line cracks right at the center of the window, splitting open, wider and wider.

Frex. *Frex!*

A rumbling sound fills the Great Room. My head whips left and right, and left and right again, looking for something to hold on to, but there's nothing here—the Great Room is just a wide-open floor. Why did I never notice how useless it is to have a room with nothing to hold on to? It's huge, sure, but there's nothing *here* except the vast floor and the walls and the doors—nothing that can save me from a broken window that exposes me to space. And what then? The ship will rip apart? And me? I'll explode or implode or something. I can't remember which, but it doesn't matter. The end result will still be the same. My tunic weighs heavily on my shoulders, sticking to my sweat, but all I can think about is how thin the material is against the ravages of space.

I'm going to die.

I'm going to be sucked out into space.

Implosion.

Death.

And then another thought hits me: the rest of the ship. If the Keeper Level is exposed, space won't just suck *me* out—it will rip through the Keeper Level, into the Shipper Level and the Feeder Level below it. They'll all die. Everyone. Every single person aboard the ship.

My feet slip on the tiled floor as I tear across the room. (For one tiny moment, my feet try to turn to the hatch door, the door that leads to life and freedom, but I ignore my feet. They're just trying to keep me alive; they don't care about the rest of the ship.) I throw myself at the big red lockdown button over the hatch. The floor shakes as the Keeper Level closes itself off from the rest of the ship. There's no going back now.

I turn toward the ceiling, toward the exposed universe.

Toward death.

3: AMY

The president called it the "epitome of the American dream."

Daddy called it the "unholy alliance of business and government."

But all it really was, was America giving up. Bailing out in order to join the Financial Resource Exchange. A multinational alliance focused on one thing: profit. Fund global medical care to monopolize vaccines. Back unified currency to collect planet-wide interest.

And provide the resources needed for a select group of scientists and military personnel to embark on the first trip across the universe in a quest to find more natural resources—more profit.

The answer to my parents' dreams.

And my worst nightmare.

And I know something about nightmares, seeing as how I've been sleeping longer than I've been alive.

I hope. What if this is just a part of a long dream dreamt in the short time between when Ed locked the cryo door and Hassan pushed the button to freeze me? What if?

It's a strange sort of sleep, this. Never really waking up, but becoming aware of consciousness inside a too-still body.

The dreams weave in and out of memories.

The only thing keeping the nightmares from engulfing me is the hope that there couldn't possibly be a hundred more years before I wake up.

Not a hundred years. Not three hundred. Not three hundred and one. Please, God, no.

Sometimes it feels like a thousand years have passed; sometimes it feels as if I've only been sleeping a few moments. I feel most like I'm in that weird state of half-asleep, half-awake I get when I've tried to sleep past noon, when I know I should get up, but my mind starts wandering and I'm sure I can never get back to sleep. Even if I do slip back into a dream for a few moments, I'm mostly just awake with my eyes shut.

Yeah. Cryo sleep is like that.

Sometimes I think there's something wrong. I shouldn't be so *aware.* But then I realize I'm only aware for a moment, and then, as I'm realizing it, I slip into another dream.

Mostly, I dream of Earth. I think that's because I didn't want to leave it.

A field of flowers; smells of dirt and rain. A breeze . . . But not really a breeze, a memory of a breeze, a memory made into a dream that tries to drown out my frozen mind.

Earth. I hold on to my thoughts of Earth. I don't like the dream-time. The dreamtime is too much like dying. They are dreams, but I'm too out of control, I lose myself in them, and I've already lost too much to let them take over.

Pressure on my pinky where Daddy wrapped his finger around mine, and a whisper of his words promising me I could stay with my aunt and uncle. The heaviness in my chest, where I thought about it, where I really thought about it. I push the dream-memory down. That happened centuries ago, and it's too late for regrets now. Because all my parents ever wanted was to be a part of the first manned interstellar exploratory mission, and all I ever wanted was to be with them.

And I guess it doesn't matter that I had a life on Earth, and that I loved Earth, and that by now, my friends have all lived and gotten old and died, and I've just been lying here in frozen sleep. That Jason lived and got old and maybe he married and had kids and everything, but it doesn't matter, because he's dead now. God, his *great-grandchildren* might be my age.

A splatter of rain on my skin, but it's bright and sunny under the blue sky. And Jason's there, and we almost kiss, but then everything changes and we're at that party where we met because dreams are like that: they go in and out of memories and scenes, but they're never real. They're never real, and I hate them because they aren't.

4 : ELDER

A cranking noise makes me lift my face up to the broken window, where the glass has split evenly in two. Why am I not dead yet?

Glass doesn't break like that, not in a perfectly straight line.

And . . . that's not the black emptiness of space beyond the glass.

That's metal. A metal ceiling behind the window?

The two halves of the window slide down, down, and the stars go with them. But that's . . . impossible. The stars are supposed to stay in place, not move with the window.

Wait . . . it's . . . it's not a window. It's, well, I'm not sure what it is. The Great Room's ceiling is domed, and the metal covering has folded up along the edge of the room at about chest height. The window— the thing I *thought* was a window—is really two halves of a giant glass and metal screen sprinkled with sparkling lights, held up by hydraulic arms that hiss and moan at me. The two folded halves rest on either side of the domed room at about shoulder height, and behind them is the real ceiling of the Keeper Level, more metal. More blank, empty, starless metal.

The stars, the beautiful shining stars, aren't stars at all. It's just glass and lightbulbs made to twinkle like stars. Fake stars on a screen sandwiched between two metal ceilings.

Why?

I reach up to touch the half of the universe that's closest to me. The tiny bulbs aren't quite hot to the touch, but warm enough to make me snatch my fingers away. The straggling remains of a spiderweb stretch from the base of a star-bulb to a tiny metal plaque on the bottom of the pane.

Navigational Tracking Chart
Patent No. 7329035
FRX—2036 CE

A navigational chart? Here? My eyes scan the section of screen in front of me, and, sure enough, I see a light blinking near the bottom of it, under the plaque, next to two close-together star-bulbs. A red light, triangular and pointing to the stars. I notice that the blinking red light isn't fixed like the star-bulbs; it's on a little track, and it's nearly at the end of its path.

My ship. Nearly at its new planet, its new home.

"Elder? Elder! What's happening?" Eldest shouts from the hatch connecting the Keeper Level to the Shipper Level. I can visualize him beyond the hatch door: angry face, blazing eyes, and long white hair brushing against his shoulders as he beats on the heavy metal door.

I turn back to the pieces of fake window. The stars are lies. I had them for a moment, but they weren't real.

Beep, beep-beep fills my left ear. My wireless communication device beeps, letting me know that someone is trying to link with me. Each of us has a wi-com implanted behind our left ear at birth—it's how we communicate with each other as well as the ship.

"Com link: Eldest," the computer says directly into my left ear through my wi-com.

"Ignore," I say, pushing the button under my skin.

The stars are lies. What else is?

Beep, beep-beep. "Eldest override," my wi-com says cheerfully. "Com link: Eldest."

"Elder!" Eldest's voice fills my ear, a low growl. "What happened? Why did you throw the Keeper Level into lockdown?"

"The stars are lies," I say hollowly.

"What? What happened? Is something wrong?"

Everything's wrong. "Nothing's wrong," I say.

"I'm going to release the lockdown." Eldest disconnects the link. A moment later, the floor rumbles and the hatch door opens. Eldest climbs up into the Keeper Level, slamming the hatch door behind him.

"What happened?" he demands.

I glance up at the biometric scanner by his door. "I scanned my access, and this—" I stop, indicating the two halves of the "window" still lowered.

"Why were you messing around with that?" Eldest roars. He strides across the room, and in his anger, he's forgotten to be gentle with his leg. It was wounded before I was born and never truly healed, but his limp has grown worse with age. His feet make an uneven beat against the metal floor: *stomp*, step, *stomp*, step, *stomp*. He'll be sore later, and he'll blame me for that, too.

When Eldest reaches the biometric scanner, he rolls his thumb over the bar. The glass rises first, pulling the stars up along the ceiling, the hydraulic arms sighing in relief. Then the grinding metal screen tucks them away, hiding their false light.

"You're loons! You put the Keeper Level into lockdown over *this*?" Eldest's rage almost makes me cower. Almost.

"I thought they were real! I thought the ship was being exposed to space!"

"They're just lightbulbs!"

"I didn't frexing know that! I thought those stars were real! What are they even there for?"

"They're not there for you!" Eldest bellows.

"Then who are they there for?" I shout back. "It's just you and me on this level!"

Eldest sets his jaw. A lump rises in my throat, but I swallow it down. I won't let Eldest think I'm nothing more than a little boy who throws a tantrum when he discovers the stars aren't real.

"You can't do this, Elder. You could cause the whole ship to panic!" Eldest looks both enraged and weary at the same time. "Don't you understand? You are Elder. When you take my role as Eldest, you must dedicate your whole life to this one idea: you are the caretaker of every single person on the ship. They are your responsibility. You can never show weakness in front of them: you are their strength. You can never let them see you in despair: you are their hope. You must always be everything to everyone on board." He takes a deep breath. "And that includes *not* panicking and throwing an entire level of the ship into lockdown!"

"I thought the ship had been exposed," I say.

Eldest stares at me. "And you put the ship into lockdown."

Does he have to remind me of that? I'm a frexing idiot, I get it.

"While you were still here." His voice is different now. Calmer. I meet his eyes, and I see something in them I've never seen before.

Pride.

"You were going to sacrifice yourself to save the ship," he says.

I shrug. "It was stupid. Sorry."

"No." Eldest drawls out the word. "Well, yes, it *was* stupid. But it was also noble. That took courage, boy. That took leadership. To be willing to sacrifice yourself for the rest of the ship? Shows you think. You thought about how the Keeper Level's on top, didn't you? That if the Keeper Level was exposed to space, the explosive decompression would affect the level below it, and the one below that. You thought before you acted. You thought of all the people below."

I look away. Maybe it had been noble, but all I can see is how the stars aren't real.

"I'm sorry," Eldest says. When he sees my confused look, he adds, "I've ignored you. It's my fault. You reminded me of the other Elder, and we . . . did not get along. When I trained him, I told him too much, too soon. And he acted foolishly, selfishly. But you're different. I forget that you're different, but you are."

Eldest has my full attention now. I know perfectly well there had been another Elder, one between me and Eldest. He died before I was born, but Eldest never talked much about him before.

"I'd already trained that Elder. He was supposed to train you, leaving me to care for the ship. When he died and I had to train you, too . . . I was never supposed to be saddled with another Elder, and I've lapsed in my responsibilities with you."

I search his eyes. When we're on the Feeder Level, Eldest is a kind grandpa. When we're on the Shipper Level, he's like an old king, commanding but attentive. But when it's just him and me, he lets his real self show—or at least what I take to be his real self—and his real self may be old, but it isn't kind and it isn't weak.

Something in the silence makes me realize Eldest has allowed me, and only me, to see this. And that, more than anything, makes me forgive his neglect.

"Well?" I demand. "Are you going to start training me properly now?"

Eldest nods once, then motions for me to follow him into the Learning Center. His uneven gait is more pronounced than usual, his leg already making him regret his stomping rage.

There are only four rooms on the Keeper Level: my and Eldest's chambers, the Learning Center, and the Great Room. The Learning Center is the smallest of the rooms, with only a table and the portal to the grav tube. The Great Room is the largest. It's big enough for everyone on board the ship to stand there at once, if they don't mind standing close together, but only Eldest and I are allowed on this level. It's leftover from before the Plague, before we used an Eldest system to rule. My and Eldest's chambers, as well as the Learning Center, were offices back then, for the crew, and, judging from the glowing star chart behind the metal screen, the Great Room was used for navigation.

After the Plague so many decades ago, the ship changed. It had to. The Plague Eldest renamed the levels, reserving this one for him-self and the Eldests who would follow.

Including me.

Eldest sits on one side of the table in the Learning Center. I sit on the other. The table is a rare antique from when the ship departed centuries ago, made of real wood, wood from Sol-Earth. I wonder at the life hidden in the wood: a tree that breathed Sol-Earth air, lived in Sol-Earth dirt, then was chopped down, crafted into a table, and thrown out into space aboard *Godspeed*.

"There are things you should know," he says. He picks up a floppy—a digital membrane screen nicknamed for its, er, floppiness— from the table and runs his finger over it, turning it on. When the screen lights up, he scans his thumb over the ID box.

"Eldest/Elder access granted," the floppy chirps. Eldest taps something onto the screen, then slides the floppy over to me. I can almost see the wood grain through the thin membrane, but then I grow distracted by what Eldest is showing me.

It's a floor plan of the Shipper Level—I recognize the main cen-tral hallway branching into the large rooms used for science and industry, manufacturing and research. Brightly glowing dots are scat-tered across the map, blinking and moving around.

"You know what this is?" Eldest asks, taking the floppy back.

"The wi-com locator map." The wireless communication devices implanted behind our left ears not only allow us to com with each other and the ship, but also serve as locators.

I lean over the table to better see the wi-com map. Eldest's long white hair brushes my face before he sweeps it behind his ear, and I can smell a whiff of soap and something stronger that bites at my nose.

"See all these dots? Each one is a Shipper. Each one has a very specific job: to ensure that the ship runs smoothly. The top Shippers are here." Eldest points to the energy room, then traces his finger beyond that, into the engine room I've never been in, then farther, into a room past that. "The command center is here. Although the ship runs by itself, if anything goes wrong—"

"You'll steer the ship?" I ask, awed. I imagine Eldest as the brave commander, almost like the captain of one of those ancient Sol-Earth ships that sailed across water, not the uni. Then I imagine me taking the wheel.

Eldest laughs. "Me? No. That's ridiculous. Elders are not trained to run ships; the Eldest's job is not to command the ship. An Eldest's job is to command the people. These Shippers"—he gestures at the blinking dots—"all receive training in specific roles of operating the ship in the event of an emergency." He glances up. His eyes are milky with age, but he can still see right through me. "You understand, don't you? The Shippers run the ship—not us."

The image of everyone cheering me as I sail the ship to Centauri-Earth fades and dies.

"The Shippers are here to take care of the ship, but the ship is just cold metal. You're the one who has to take care of the people."

He taps the zoom-out box, and for a moment, the three levels of the ship all light up at once, a dizzying maze of crisscrossing lines. The interior of the ship itself is mostly round. A tiny sliver on top is the Keeper Level. Below that, slightly larger, is the Shipper Level, all chopped up into offices and labs. By and far the largest part of the ship is the Feeder Level. There are two blinking dots for me and Eldest on the Keeper Level, fifty or more on the Shipper Level. Eldest taps on the Feeder Level. On the right side of the circle there are several dozen dots for the people at the Hospital, but none at all in the Recorder Hall. In the middle, dozens of dots are scattered around, each one representing the people living at the various farms. Eldest taps the left side of the screen, where the City is. There are so many dots there that it would be impossible for me to count. Not that I need to. I know everyone on board the ship, all 2,312 of them.

Each one of those 2,312 blinking red dots feels like a pounding weight on my shoulders, each one crushing me down just a little bit more. They're all, each one of them, *my* responsibility.

Eldest pulls the Shipper Level up again and rests his fingers on the level's largest room, just where the engine is. "Between the engine and computers and the nav system and everything else, there's a lot that can go wrong. This journey . . . it's long." He says this as if he's felt all 250 years of travel. "The builders of the ship knew this; that's why they named her *Godspeed*."

I mouth the name with him, tasting it like metal on my tongue.

"It's an old Sol-Earth expression for good luck." Eldest snorts. "They shot our ancestors into the sky, wished them all good luck, and forgot about us. We lost com with Sol-Earth during the Plague, and have never been able to regain it. We can't go back. They can't help us. All the people on Sol-Earth could give us was Godspeed."

I'm not sure if he means that they gave us luck or the ship, but they both seem a bit inadequate right now.

"But we need more than luck. The ship needs someone to protect the people, not just the ship itself. You will be that leader." Eldest takes a deep breath. "It's time for you to learn the three causes of discord."

I scoot my chair closer. This is new. Finally—*finally*—Eldest is *really* going to train me to be the leader after him.

"On *Godspeed*," he says, "do we all speak one language?"

"Of course," I answer, confused.

"Do we have any differences in race?"

"Race?"

"Skin color."

"No." Everyone on board has the same deep olive skin, the same dark brown hair and eyes.

"You've studied the myths of Sol-Earth: Buddhism, Christianity, Hinduism, Islam. Does anyone on *Godspeed* 'worship'?" He says the last word with dripping derision.

"Of course not!" I laugh. One of the first lessons Eldest gave me when I moved to the Keeper Level was about Sol-Earth's religions. They were magic stories, fairy tales, and I remember laughing myself silly when Eldest told me how people on Sol-Earth were willing to die or kill for these fictional characters.

Eldest nods once. "The first cause of discord is difference. There is no religion on *Godspeed*. We all speak the same language. We're all monoethnic. And because we are not different, we don't fight. Remember the Crusades I taught you about? The genocides? We will never have to worry about those types of horrific events on *Godspeed*."

I am on the edge of my seat, nodding, but inside I'm hoping Eldest can't see what a chutz I actually am. I remember those lessons. They were among my first lessons, when I was thirteen and had just moved to the Keeper Level to live with Eldest. Stars, I was such a kid then. I remember pictures on the floppies of people of different skin color and hair color, of people dressed in long gowns or loincloths, of the sounds of languages whose words I could not understand. And back then I thought it was all kind of brilly.

I slouch further down in my seat. No wonder Eldest has been slow to train me—clearly I never picked up the real lessons he's been teaching me.

"The second cause of discord," Eldest continues, "is lack of a strong central leader."

He leans forward, reaching his gnarled, wrinkled hands toward me. "Do you understand the importance of this?" he says, his eyes watery from old age or something else.

I nod.

"Do you really?" he asks more urgently, gripping my hands so hard that some of my knuckles crack.

I nod again, unable to take my eyes from his.

"What is the greatest danger of this ship?" His voice has fallen into a raspy whisper.

Um. Maybe I didn't understand. Eldest stares at me, expecting a response. I stare back.

"*Mutiny*. It's *mutiny*, Elder. More than technical error or ship malfunction or outside dangers, *mutiny* is the greatest threat to this ship. So, after the Plague, the Eldest system was created. One person, born ahead of the people he would lead, to act as patriarch and commander to the people younger than he. Each generation has an Eldest to lead. *You* will one day be an Eldest. *You* will be the strong central leader who prevents discord, who preserves every living person on this ship."

5: AMY

I am as silent as death.

Do this: Go to your bedroom. Your nice, safe, warm bedroom that is not a glass coffin behind a morgue door. Lie down on your bed not made of ice. Stick your fingers in your ears. Do you hear that? The pulse of life from your heart, the slow in-and-out from your lungs? Even when you are silent, even when you block out all noise, your body is still a cacophony of life. Mine is not. It is the silence that drives me mad. The silence that drives the nightmares to me.

Because what if I am dead? How can someone without a beating heart, without breathing lungs live like I do? I must be dead. And this is my greatest fear: After 301 years, when they pull my glass coffin from this morgue, and they let my body thaw like chicken meat on the kitchen counter, I will be just like I am now. I will spend all of eternity trapped in my dead body. There is nothing beyond this. I will be locked within myself forever.

And I want to scream. I want to throw open my eyes and wake up and not be alone with myself anymore, but I can't.

I can't.

6: ELDER

"So, what's the third cause of discord?" I ask Eldest as silence creeps around us in the Learning Center.

He contemplates me. For a moment, anger flashes in his faded eyes, and I wonder if he'll strike me. When I blink, though, that crazy idea is gone. Eldest puts both hands on his knees and pushes against them to raise himself, creaking, into a standing position. The Learning Center is small, and with Eldest standing, it feels oppressively so. The chair he's pushed back butts against the wall; the table feels like a chasm between us. Behind him, the faded globe of Sol-Earth looks miniscule, even smaller and more insignificant than me.

"I've told you enough," he says, heading to the door. "And I've got work to do. I want you to go to the Recorder Hall, do some research, see if you can figure out some of the reasons Sol-Earth had so much discord. You've got the first two reasons for their reign of blood and war; you should be able to figure out the third. It's not hard, not when you look at Sol-Earth history."

I recognize the challenge in this. Eldest is testing my ability to be a leader, testing my worthiness to follow in his footsteps as the next Eldest. He does this a lot, actually. Although the Elder who should have been between me and Eldest died a long time ago, Eldest didn't like him. The most I've ever heard Eldest speak of him was when he'd compare him to me. And the comparisons have never been positive. "You're slow, like him," Eldest would say. "That idea is something *he* would have said, too." I learned almost as soon as I started living on the Keeper Level to keep my ideas to myself and my mouth shut. Eldest still tests me often just to make sure I won't turn out as bad as that other Elder. I try to look confident, assertive—but it's wasted, because Eldest hasn't looked back at me once.

Part of me wants to call Eldest back and argue with him, remind him of his promise to tell me everything and insist he teach me the third cause of discord.

The other part of me, the part that could spend all day looking at vids and pics of Sol-Earth on the floppies, is relishing an assignment by Eldest to do just that.

On the far side of the Learning Center is the entrance to the grav tube Eldest and I use. This one is just for us, a direct link to the Feeder Level. The one that runs between the Shipper Level and the City in the Feeder Level is for everyone else.

I press my wi-com button behind my left ear.

"Command?" the pleasant female voice of my wi-com asks.

"Grav tube control," I say.

Beep, beep-beep fills my ear as my wi-com connects to the grav tube control. I roll my thumb over the biometric scanner on the far wall of the Learning Center, and a circular section of the floor slides open. There is nothing under it but empty space.

My stomach lurches—as it always does—when I step into the empty air of the grav tube. But the wi-com has linked to the ship's gravitational system inside the tube, and I bob gently over the air before sinking down like a penny dropped in a fountain's pool. Darkness envelops me as I slip down the tube through the Shipper Level, and then light floods my eyes. I blink; the Feeder Level is below me, distorted through the clear grav tube. The City rises up along the far wall, and the farms spread throughout the center, vast fields of green dotted with crops, cows, sheep, goats. From here, the Feeder Level is huge, a world in and of itself. 6,400 acres designed to support over 3,000 people looks like forever when you're gazing down at it. But when you're actually there, in the fields or the City, crammed up next to people whose eyes are always on you, it feels much more crowded.

The grav tube ends about seven feet from the ground of the Feeder Level. For a second, I bob in the air at the end of the tube, then *beep, beep-beep* fills my ear as my wi-com connects with the ship's gravity system, and I drop to the little round metal platform under the tube. I hop off the platform and begin walking down one of the four main roads on the Feeder Level. Only a few yards ahead is a tall brick building, the Recorder Hall, and beyond that is the Hospital.

As I stride toward the Recorder Hall, I think of how different my life is now from three years ago. Until I was thirteen, I lived on this level, passed from one family to the next. From a very young age, it was clear I'd never fit in. For one, everyone was very aware that I was

Elder. Perhaps because the Elder before me died unexpectedly, the Feeders were always overprotective. But more than that—we were different from one another. The Feeders *thought* differently. They were happy, content to plow fields and shear sheep. They never seemed to feel the walls of the ship cave in around them, to grow angry at time for passing so slowly. It wasn't until I moved to the Hospital in my thirteenth year, and met Harley, and talked to Doc, and then moved to the Keeper Level and started training with Eldest that I started to be happy on *Godspeed*. That I started to enjoy this life.

I don't always agree with Eldest, and his temper, shown only to me on the Keeper Level, can be terrifying, but I will always love him for taking me from the mind-numbing farms.

I bound up the steps toward the big brown doors that have been painted to look like wood. The Recorder Hall has always seemed too big to me, but Eldest assures me that most of the residents on *Godspeed* feel that it is too small. I suppose it's because when I go there, I go by myself, or with Eldest. Everyone else went with their gen, when they were younger and still in school. Since no one else on the ship is as young as me, there's no reason to have school. I just have Eldest.

Eldest watches me mount the steps to the Recorder Hall. Not the real Eldest, of course—a painting of him, done before I was born, when Eldest was about Doc's age. The painting is large, about half the size of the door, and hung in a little inset built into the bricks next to the entry.

Eventually, they will take Eldest's portrait down from here, and hang it in a dusty spot in the back of the Recorder Hall somewhere, with the portraits of all the other Eldests.

And my portrait will hang here, surveying my tiny kingdom.

The painted Eldest stares past me, past the porch on the Recorder Hall, looking out over the fields and, in the far distance, the City, a towering jumble of painted metal boxes where most of the Feeders and Shippers live. The painter has given Eldest kinder eyes than I've ever seen in his wrinkled face, and a soft curve of his lips that seems to indicate inquisitiveness, maybe even mischief. Or not. I'm reading too much into this painting. This Eldest isn't the Eldest I know. This Eldest looks like the kind of guy I could look up to as a leader. Not the kind of leader who rules through fear—the kind who listens to others, and cares about what they have to say, and gives them a chance. We have the same narrow nose, the same high cheekbones, the same olive skin—but this Eldest already has the authority in his eyes, the self-assurance in the tilt of his chin, the sense of power in his posture that I never have. That the real Eldest has sharpened and honed like a hunter does a knife.

I look behind me, to match the painted Eldest's line of sight, but I can't see *Godspeed* the way he clearly does. The painted Eldest is happy in ruling—that much exudes through the oil pigments. I can picture how the painting session went. I bet Eldest stood right here, where I am, looking past the railing. The painter stood on the lawn, below Eldest—of course below him—and gave shape to the paint with strong, broad sweeps. When Eldest looked at *Godspeed*, as I'm looking at it now, he saw the same things I see: an interior of a ship modeled like a county in Sol-Earth's America, but in miniature, trapped in a round bubble of ship walls. A city piled on one side, with neat, orderly streets laid out in a careful grid, the center of each block stacked with box trailers that served as homes and workplaces for trade. One block for weavers, like my friend Harley's parents. One block for dyers, one for spinners, one for tailors. Three blocks for food preservation: canners and dryers and freezers. Two blocks for butchers. Four blocks to house the scientists and Shippers who work on the level above this one. Each family, gen after gen, born and raised to work until death in the same block of the same city on the same ship.

When Eldest posed for his painting here, did he think of this? Did he look at the City and marvel at its smooth efficiency, its careful construction, its consistent productivity?

Or did he see it as I do: people boxed in trailers that are boxed in city blocks that are boxed in districts that are boxed in a ship, surrounded by metal walls?

No. Eldest never thought of *Godspeed* as a box. He never saw the City as a cage. You can tell that from his painted eyes, from the way he strides down the streets of the City now, like he owns them, because he does.

Even here, where fields and pastures and farms stretch out beyond the Recorder Hall porch all the way to the far wall, you can't escape the boxes. Each field and pasture and farm is blocked off in careful fences, each fence measured out centuries ago, on Sol-Earth, before the ship launched. The blocks of land are not all equal in size, but they are all square, all meticulously measured. The hills in the pastures are designed to be evenly spaced, exactly placed bumps of grass for sheep and goats who don't realize that their hills are just carefully organized, manufactured mounds of dirt and compost.

I've seen the landscape of Sol-Earth in the vids and maps. The land wasn't perfectly laid out in neat little squares. Even grid-like cities had alleys and backstreets. Fields were fenced off, but the fences didn't all go in perfect lines—they dipped around trees; they cut off at funny angles to avoid creeks or include ponds. Hills didn't make even rows of bumps.

When I look at the fields, all I can see is how fake they are, how poor an imitation they are of the pictures of Sol-Earth fields.

I bet when Eldest posed for his portrait, he was reveling in the one thing I can't stand about life aboard the ship: the perfect evenness of everything.

And that's why I'll never be as good an Eldest as he is.

Because I like a little chaos.

I push open the big doors to the Recorder Hall and smile at the topographical models that hang from the ceiling in the large entryway. Framed by the light pouring through the open doors behind me is a large clay Sol-Earth, thick with dust. A scale model of *Godspeed* shoots around Sol-Earth, designed to mimic the ship's departure so long ago. It looks small and insignificant compared to the planets beside it, a ball with wings and a pointed nose. I step into the hallway and crane my neck up. Directly overhead is the model of *Godspeed*'s goal: the big, round globe of Centauri-Earth. It's bigger than either of the two other models, and hangs in the center of the entryway. I'm not sure if the designers intended it or not, but the shaft of light pouring from the big entryway doors spills right across the surface of the Centauri-Earth model, illuminating it with a halo of light.

Striding forward, I reach my hands up so my fingertips brush Sol-Earth's Australia. I have always preferred the model of Sol-Earth to that of Centauri-Earth. While the model of Sol-Earth is detailed, with bumps for mountains and squiggly lines for waves on the oceans, Centauri-Earth is smooth, accurate only in terms of its relative size. We're not sure what we'll find there, mountains or oceans or something else entirely. We only know that the probe sent before us labeled Centauri-Earth as "habitable"—oxygen-based atmosphere, a significant amount of freshwater, and soil samples suitable for plant growth. Those are the only things we're sure of.

I want to touch it as well, but it's too high up.

Centauri-Earth always seems to be beyond my reach.

Eldest's words echo in my mind: my job is not to get the ship to Centauri-Earth, but to get the people there.

"Can I help you?"

I nearly jump out of my skin. "Oh, it's you," I say, laughing at my own skittishness.

Orion is a Recorder. Whenever someone invents something or writes something or does something brilly, the Recorders log it away and store it here. The last time I was here was to help my best friend, Harley, move some canvases. He's a painter—he's got a whole room of his art hanging up on the second story of the Recorder Hall. But I'm not here for that.

"Can you help me find some information on Sol-Earth?" I ask Orion.

Orion grins. I cringe—his teeth are stained and yellow. "Of course."

"I need to find out about . . ." I pause, thinking of how to phrase it. I can't just ask him if he knows what the third cause of discord is—he'd have no idea what I'm talking about. "Sol-Earth wars," I say finally. "Conflicts. Battles. Things like that."

"Anything specific?" Orion rushes toward me, excitement palpable on his face. I guess with school long over, there are very few visitors to the Recorder Hall. Come to think of it, I've never actually seen Orion outside of the Recorder Hall. His existence must be a lonely one.

"Whatever caused the problems on Sol-Earth."

"Oh."

"What?"

Orion doesn't say anything for a long moment, just contemplates me as if I were a puzzle with a piece missing. "It's an unusual topic for you to be studying, that's all. Bit grim."

I shrug. "Eldest needs me to figure something out."

"Ah, research for Eldest. Well, the easiest way to do this is with the wall floppies." He nods to the four long screens that hang from the walls of the entryway like tapestries, two on each side. Walking to the one closest to him, Orion taps the screen, and all four floppies turn on, filling the entire entryway with light.

Images flow in and out of each other: diagrams of a lead-cooled fast reactor, an irrigation map of the Feeder Level, paintings from Harley and other artists on board, digital representations of possible geographical features of Centauri-Earth.

"We'll need your access," Orion says, drawing my attention away from the wall floppies. When he sees my questioning face, he adds, "Feeders aren't allowed to view images of Sol-Earth."

Ah. I'd forgotten. These are images approved for everyone, but the information Eldest wants me to find is restricted. I step over to the biometric scanner against the wall and roll my thumb over the scan bar. "Eldest/Elder access granted," the computer's female voice chirps.

The images change. Now there is art from Sol-Earth, not just *Godspeed*. The people aren't monoethnic. Unlike the images of Centauri-Earth, those of Sol-Earth are not an artist's rendering. I stand back, staring into the paper-white face of a woman with a mountain of powdered hair and a dress so wide it borders each side of the screen. I wonder about the time and place she is in, the person she was. I am looking into the face of another world, one as unreachable to me as Centauri-Earth.

"Perhaps Genghis Khan's campaign is what Eldest wants you to learn about?" Orion mutters. He taps on the screen, and the woman's white-painted face melts into a screaming brown man with almond-shaped eyes and matted, dirty hair. "Or the Armenian Genocide?" A map of Sol-Earth replaces the terrifying man, and the outline of a small country flashes, inviting me to tap on it and learn more.

Before I can touch it, though, Orion taps something else on the screen. The map fades, replaced with a chart. I squint up at the tiny words and jumbled lines. A genealogical chart, tracing parents to children. My eye roams the chart, jumping from name to name, and it isn't until Orion murmurs, "Oops," and changes the screen to another map that I realize the name I was seeking on the screen was my own, even though I know that's silly—that chart was way too old.

I breathe deeply, ignoring whatever war or genocide Orion is now pointing out to me on the screen.

As Elder, I am not allowed to know my parents. It would make me partial and biased; it would lead to sentimental feelings that would impede my leadership and decisions as Eldest. I know this. I even *agree* with it.

But still.

I'd like to know who they are.

"Elder?" Orion asks, concern filling his voice. "Is something wrong?"

I shake my head. "Nothing."

Orion searches my face, but I'm not sure what he wants to find.

And then I find myself searching his face in return, and I know what I'm seeking. Is that *my* nose on his face? My eyes? My lips? I've never really noticed Orion before. He's always been in the background, fading into the records he keeps. But now that I really look at him . . .

Could *this* man be my father?

My breath catches, and I have to shake my head again before I can get a grip on myself. Sure, Orion reminds me of me. But on a ship where everyone's monoethnic, that's not hard to do. I can as easily see myself in Eldest as I can in Orion.

I just wish I could see myself in me.

Orion smiles at me, as if he understands what I'm going through, but he can't possibly. "So," he says, in such a fatherly tone that I flinch, "Eldest is having you do research? Sounds like he's really focusing on training you now."

"Yeah."

"Has he taken you below the Feeder Level yet?" Orion leans forward, his eyes eager.

"Below? There's nothing below the Feeder Level."

Orion's face slips into a blank mask. "Oh," he says, leaning back, disappointment evident in his down-turned mouth. "Well, let's get on with that research." He turns back to the screen.

"No, wait! Did you mean there's another level below this one?"

Orion hesitates. He brushes his long hair behind his ear, and I notice that the left side of his neck is marked by a peculiar spiderweb scar. "I'm not sure," he says. "I was going through the floppies recently, and I saw something. . . ." He taps his finger against the floppy, and the screen speeds through images. "I found some diagrams of *Godspeed*. But I shouldn't have been looking at them. Besides, surely Eldest will go over all that with you in your training, when it's time for you to learn about those sorts of things. I was just curious."

Of course he is. As a Recorder, his home and work is on the Feeder Level. Everyone's constrained to the Feeder Level except the Shippers, who have access to the Shipper Level, and Eldest and I, who also have the Keeper Level. Orion's probably spent his whole life on this one part of the ship.

"Can I see the diagram?"

Orion's hand twitches toward the screen, but he doesn't tap anything in. "Eldest would probably not want . . ." His voice trails off, indecision making him waver.

I smile back at him. "Let me," I say. "Then you can't be to blame." Orion looks a little guilty, but also eager and curious as I knock his hand aside and tap in "*Godspeed* ship diagram."

A list shows up instead of an image. Two options. Two different diagrams.

Before Plague
After Plague

"What does this mean?" I ask. "How did the ship change after the Plague?" I knew the Plague Eldest had renamed the levels, reallocated some of the rooms, and reserved the Keeper Level for the Eldest and Elder, but that's all. *Or at least I thought that was all. That hidden star screen must have been hidden for a reason . . . .*

Orion leans in closer. "See, that's what interested me, too. Look." He reaches up and taps the "After Plague" option. A diagram brightens the screen: a cross section of the ship, a big circle divided into levels. There's nothing unusual there. The top floor is marked "Keeper Level." It's simple and vague—there's just an outline of the rooms that Eldest and I occupy. Underneath that, the Shipper Level is more complicated, with space set aside for the engine room and the command center, as well as all the research labs used by the scientists. What is now the Feeder Level takes up more than two-thirds of the chart. The diagram is old; it shows the buildings that were a part of the ship's original design, including the Hospital and the Recorder Hall, where we are now. But it doesn't show the new additions made since launch— the grav tubes, developed two gens before Eldest, aren't on the diagram. Instead, there's a set of stairs connecting the Feeder Level to the Shipper Level, which were torn down when the grav tubes were made.

My eyes drift down. "Was this what you were talking about?" I ask, pointing to the unlabeled part of the diagram under the Feeder Level. "It's probably just electrical stuff, or pipes, or something."

"I thought that, too," Orion says. "But look." He taps the screen and goes back to the main menu, then taps "Before Plague."

The same chart shows up, but everything's labeled differently now. The Keeper Level is now labeled "Navigation," just like on the plaque I saw on the screen hidden under the ceiling. The Shipper Level is sectioned off into three portions: technological research (where the labs are now), the engine room, and something called a

"Bridge." That's not far off from what we have now, just different words for the same things. It's the Feeder Level where things really start to change. The left side, where the City is, is marked "Living Quarters (inclusive)" and all the rest of the Feeder Level is labeled "Biological Research." Biological Research? That's what they used to call goat herding and sheep shearing?

But it's what's under the Feeder Level that really fascinates me. What was blank space on the other diagram is now all filled in. It's like there really is another level of the ship below our feet, a level I never knew of, one that has, apparently, a genetic research lab, a second water pump, a huge section marked "Storage — Important" and a very small area labeled simply "Contingency."

"What is this?" I ask, staring at it. "I know they changed the names of the levels and moved some things around after the Plague, but this? This is more than just rearranging. There's a whole other *level*." What I don't say is: *Why didn't I know about this already? Why didn't Eldest teach me?* I already know the answer: because he doesn't think I'm ready or — worse — he doesn't think I'm worthy of knowing the secrets of the ship.

"They changed a lot of things after the Plague," Orion says. "There was no Eldest system then."

I know this much, at least. Everyone knows about that. After the Plague killed off around three quarters of the ship, dropping our numbers from over three thousand to little more than seven hundred, the Plague Eldest took control and remade the government into the peaceful, working society we have now. In the gens since then, we've rebuilt our population to over two thousand, developed new tech like the grav tubes, and maintained the peaceful society the Plague Eldest originally envisioned.

But I hadn't known just how much he changed the ship, or what all of those changes meant.

"Don't you want to know what's down there?" Orion asks, staring at the fourth level.

And now that he's said it—yeah, I really do. "Here, let me see that." I push Orion out of the way and tap on the wall floppy, searching. It takes me a few minutes, but then I find what I'm looking for. "Let's see what the designers put there," I say, grinning in triumph.

A blueprint flashes on the screen, but it's much more complicated than the diagrams of the ship's levels. I squint up at the lines, trying to trace pipes and electrical wiring and separate them from the walls and doors. The image is so big that I either have to zoom in and scroll, or zoom out and squint.

"I don't understand any of it," I say finally, throwing my hands up.

"I started with the elevator." Orion scrolls the blueprint up, and suddenly I recognize the building whose blueprints I'm seeing. The Hospital. He points to the fourth floor. "There's a second elevator."

"There's no second elevator!" I laugh. I've spent my share of time in the Hospital, and there's only one elevator there.

"At the end of the hall, there's another elevator. The blueprints don't lie."

"All the doors on that floor are locked," I say. I know. I've tried them all. And they're not locked with biometric scanners—I could get past those with a swipe of my thumb. No, those doors have old-fashioned Sol-Earth locks, made of metal. Harley and I once spent a week trying to break in until Doc caught us.

Orion's shaking his head. "Not the last door. That one's open. And there's a second elevator there."

I laugh again. "There's just no way. If there was some secret elevator leading to a secret level of the ship, I'd know."

Orion just looks at me. His silence is an accusation: Would I really know?

Eldest has kept things hidden from me before. Maybe there is another level.

7 : AMY

I hear something.

A creak. My door is open, my little morgue door is pulled open, and it's brighter here, I can see a tinge of light through my sealed-shut eyelids, and now something, someone is pulling out my glass coffin.

Something makes my glass coffin lift up; there's a sensation in my frozen stomach like being pushed on a swing, and I try to hold on to the feeling, assure myself it is real. Did they lift the lid off? I can hear—I can hear!—muffled cadences of speech through the ice. Growing louder! The sounds are not just vibrations through the ice, they're sounds! People are talking!

"Just a little more," a voice that reminds me of Ed says.

"The ice melts quickly."

"It's the—" I don't catch those words—a whooshing sound washes over me.

And warmth. I feel warmth for the first time in 301 years. Not ice—but a tingly sensation, crackling against the nerve endings in my skin, washing me with a feeling I thought I had lost forever. Warmth!

"Why hasn't she moved yet?" says the first voice again. It doesn't sound like harsh, careless Ed now, but gentler Hassan.

"Add more gel." Something is being rubbed into my skin. I realize that, for the first time in over three centuries, someone is touching me. Gentle hands knead my cold flesh with a goo that reminds me of the Icy Hot lotion I used on my knee when I twisted it at a cross-country race my freshman year. I am so happy I might explode.

And that's when I realize I can't smile.

"It's not working," says the gentle voice. It sounds sad now. Defeated.

"Try—"

"No, look, she's not even breathing."

Silence.

I will my lungs to pump air; I will my chest to move up and down with the rhythm of life.

Something cold—I never want to feel cold again—is pressed against the top of my left breast.

"No heartbeat."

I concentrate all my will on my heart—beat, dammit! Beat! But how can you tell your heart to beat? I could no sooner have told it not to beat before I was frozen.

"Should we wait?"

Yes! YES. Wait—I'm coming. Just give me some time to thaw, and I will rise from the ice and live again. I will be your frozen phoenix. Just give me a chance!

"Nah."

My mouth. I concentrate everything I have within me on my mouth. Lips, move! Speak, shout—scream!

"Just put her back in."

And the table bows under the weight of the lid lowering over me. And my stomach lurches as they shove me back into the morgue.

The door clicks shut.

I want to scream, but I can't.

Because none of this is real.

It's just another nightmare.

8 : ELDER

Doc is in the lobby of the Hospital, helping one nurse lead an old man toward the front desk where another nurse starts to check him in. When Doc sees me, he heads my way.

"Have you seen Harley?" he asks.

"No." I can't help but smile. Harley's famous for escaping Doc when med time rolls around.

Doc runs his fingers through his thick hair, then notices my smile and scowls. "It's no laughing matter. Harley needs to take his medication on a regular schedule."

I make an attempt to sober up my expression. Harley does sometimes get intense and dark, but I think that has more to do with how artistic he is than how crazy Doc thinks he is. Besides, he's my best friend; I'm not going to scamp him out to Doc.

"I ain't going!" the old man at the front desk yells. Doc whips around. The old man has shaken off the nurse who helped him walk in and is leaning toward the one sitting at the desk. "You can't make

me! I ain't going to no 'spital bed, I ain't sick!" He punctuates this
with a hacking cough and spits out a mouthful of phlegm on the floor.

"Now, now, calm down," Doc says, striding over to the man.

The old man turns his cataract gaze to Doc. "Where's my wife?
You got her?"

"Ms. Steela isn't here," Doc says, putting his hand on the man's
arm. "She isn't sick. You are."

"Ain't sick!" the old man roars, but immediately after he speaks, a
glazed expression falls over his eyes. His breathing calms, and he sags
under the weight of his own clothing. When Doc moves his hand, I see
why: Doc has slipped him a med patch. The lavender square of sticky
cloth on the old man's arm is already calming him into submission.

Doc shoots me a triumphant grin as he helps the man settle into a
wheelchair and then sends him and the nurse to the elevator. I swallow, hard. Doc is a good man, but his answer to everything is always
medicine. He doesn't like emotion, any emotion. He prefers things
quiet, controlled.

That's why he's so frexing close to Eldest. They think alike.

"So, what are you doing here?" Doc says once the old man is
safely ensconced in the elevator and on his way to treatment.

I scuff my shoes on the smooth tiled floor. There's no way I'm
going to tell him that I'm off to explore a secret elevator on the fourth
floor. I'm not even sure if I believe Orion enough to try it.

"Just thought I'd see Harley," I say finally.

Doc frowns. "If you find him, send him straight to me. It's long
past med time." He glances at the clock over the nurse's desk. "For
that matter, have you taken yours?"

I flush. I'm not proud of the year I lived here. On the third floor, the Ward. Where the mental patients are. I think living with the Feeders cracked me. It was fine when I was little, but the older I got, the more I felt like I was different from the rest of them. I couldn't make myself care about crops or cows the way they did.

(I remember, when Doc first made me start taking mental meds, I asked: Should I still be Elder? I was on mental meds, after all! I spent a year at the Ward! I was all ready to step down. But Doc and Eldest wouldn't let me.)

"I took them this morning," I mutter, my face hot. I hope the nurse at the desk hasn't heard. What would she think of a future leader who's on mental meds?

Doc scrutinizes me. "Is there anything wrong?" he asks.

Eldest lied to me about the stars, and there might be a secret level on the ship, and Orion looks more like me than I'd ever care to admit, but no, nothing's wrong, because if Doc thinks anything is wrong, he'll just give me more meds. I shake my head.

Doc doesn't look convinced. "I know it's hard on you. You're different."

"I'm not that different."

"'Course you are. You know you are."

I shrug. The elevator, now empty, returns to the lobby. I want to escape to it, and Doc, mercifully, lets me go.

Inside the elevator, my hand hovers over the round number four, then slides down to three. If Harley's off his meds, maybe I *should* check in on him before searching for the mysterious second elevator.

My spirits lift with the elevator. Despite Doc, one of my favorite places to be is the Ward. All my friends are here. The elevator bobs to a halt, and the doors slide open to the third-floor common room. I grin so hard it hurts. The Ward feels more like home than any other place on the ship, even if it's filled with crazy people.

Paint splatters onto my sleeve; I look up and see that Harley is attacking a canvas, letting his brush flick off the side of it. There's a ring of splattered red and blue paint all around where he's sitting.

"Hey Harley," I say. "Doc's looking for you."

"Haven't got time for him"—he spares a glance up at me—"49 and 267," he says before turning back to the canvas and attacking it with his paintbrush again. I grin wryly. You can count on Harley to know exactly when the ship's going to land. Most people—I mean, most people in the Ward—keep track of the time until the ship lands, but I bet if I asked, Harley would know not only the years (49) and days (267) before we land, but also the minutes and seconds.

I dodge the flying paint and peer around to see what he's painting. A koi fish floats in a sea of bright blue, but the light from the fish's scales and the sparkles on the water's surface intermingle, as if the fish is a part of the water and the water is a part of the fish. Harley's used these amazing colors—colors that no one else would think of. The fish's eyes are bright, bright green, almost yellow, like jade swirled with gold. The scales are shiny and bright, too, but they're all edged in blood red that looks like it should clash with the lighter colors, but it doesn't. The red makes it seem more real, somehow, as if the water could spill from the canvas and the fish could swim past our feet.

"I like this," I tell Harley after a long moment. "I mean it; this is frexing good."

Harley grunts. He's in his painting mood, and there's not really much point in talking to him. Doc will have a hard time giving him his meds, even when he inevitably finds him.

All around me, a subtle form of chaos flowers. This whole room is filled with creativity and art. It's actually a pretty brilly place to be. Except now, when everyone's all busy with their own stuff. I'm starting to feel like I'm a bit of a chutz just standing here while everyone's so intent on their own work.

"See you," I say, but Harley doesn't notice.

A pang of guilt bites at my stomach as I reenter the elevator and head to the fourth floor. Eldest wanted me to research the third cause of discord, and I'm definitely not doing that.

But lies are a cause of discord, too, I think sullenly as the elevator opens.

The fourth floor is silent. I go past the doors on the left and right, straight to the end of the hall. I put my hand on the doorknob. It'll be locked. All the doors on the fourth floor are locked. I've been here before, tried them all before.

But the knob twists under my hand, just like Orion said it would, to reveal a small room that contains a desk, a metal box, and, against the far wall—

Another elevator.

Above the call button is a biometric scanner. I half expect to be blocked. Eldest has banned me from his chambers and the engine room on the Shipper Level. Even though I have total access to the rest of the ship, I can't help but think that if he knew, Eldest would ban me from here, too. When I roll my thumb over the scanner, however, the doors slide open immediately.

There are five buttons inside—one for each floor, and another one labeled "**C.**" *C? What does C stand for?* I think back to the diagram Orion showed me. There was a section marked "Contingency," but this elevator doesn't go there; it goes to the area marked "Storage—Important." I put my finger on the C button, but I don't push it in, just feel the curve of the letter. How could there have been a whole other elevator, a whole other *level* of the ship?

I lean forward, letting my whole body weight push the button. The doors slide shut.

The little light over the doors blinks with every floor. Three. Two. One.

The light blinks out. I descend past the first floor. I start to count the seconds. I stare at the buttons by the door, but the "C" doesn't light up yet. The elevator keeps sinking. It's taken twice as long as it normally does to go from floor to floor in the Hospital . . . three times as long. A full minute passes. How big is *Godspeed*, really?

With a slight bump, the elevator stops.

The doors slide open.

I take a deep breath and step out onto a level of the ship that isn't supposed to exist.

It's dark. "Lights," I say, pushing my wi-com, but nothing happens.

The elevator door swishes closed, taking the dim glow of the elevator with it. I put my hand to the nearest wall so that I don't get too lost, and my finger brushes against a stubby piece of plastic.

A flickering fluorescent bulb switches on, then another, then another, like dominoes of light from the ceiling. Huh. A light switch. I've only seen them in floppies and vids of tech from Sol-Earth. The ship was rewired for wi-com control long before the Plague.

It's big, this place. Unusually big. It reminds me of the Keeper Level, actually—lots of space and no one filling it. Big enough for everyone on the ship to stand next to each other, just like the Great Room. There's a closed door to the left, and a hallway branching off to the right. It's all metal and hard edges. Apart from the vastness of it, there's an odd shape to it, almost egg-like and tapering at the roof, making a dome. I'm not sure why the roof rounds—the Feeder Level above is flat ground—but I can see heavy iron pipes extending through the curves.

This large room is filled with rows and rows of small metal doors. Like the old Sol-Earth bookshelves in the back of the Recorder Hall (locked away from the Feeders, of course), the rows stick out, ready to be browsed, but the contents are all hidden behind tiny square doors with heavily bolted hinges. The air feels cooler here, and the walls seem quieter. As if this is a place where only whispers are allowed, and few people.

I start down the nearest aisle, small doors on either side of me. The doors are numbered, scribbled with sloppy white paint. Lined along the bottom are little rectangles engraved into each metal door. I squint—they're flags, half a dozen of them, from Sol-Earth countries. At the end of the row of flags, three letters are engraved into the metal: FRX. The same letters on the star screen. This stuff is old. Part of the original design of the ship. I put my hand on a door—number 34—and start to turn the heavy lever when a flash of red catches my eye.

One of the doors is already open. A long metal tray extends from the mouth of the door like a tongue, and on that tray is a narrow clear box filled with frozen water speckled with blue glitter. Floating immobile in the ice, as still and silent as this empty room, is a girl.

It's her hair that pulls me forward. It's so *red*. I've never seen red hair before, not outside of pictures, and the pictures never caught the vivacity of these burnished strands tangled in the ice. Harley has a book of paintings he stole from the Recorder Hall, and one of the paintings is just a series of haystacks at different times of the day. He showed me the last painted haystack, the one covered in snow, the one at sunset. Harley went loons over it, saying how the artist was so brilliant to paint stuff with different light, and I said that was stupid, there's light or there isn't, and he said *I* was stupid, on Sol-Earth there were things like sunrise and sunset because the sun moves like a living thing and isn't just an overrated heat lamp in the sky.

This girl's hair is more brilliant than the rays of the sun on Sol-Earth captured by an artist Harley said was the most genius man ever to live.

I reach out to touch the glass that traps her inside, and only then do I realize how cold it is. My breath is rising in little clouds of white. My fingertips stick to the glass.

I stare down at her. She is the most beautiful thing I have ever seen, but also the strangest. Her skin is pale, almost translucent white, and I don't think it's just from the ice. I lay my hand on top of her glass box, above her heart. My skin is a dark shadow over the luminescence of hers.

This girl is definitely not monoethnic. She's not like anyone else on *Godspeed*. Her skin, her hair, her age — *my* age! — her very shape . . . short, but slender with an enticing curve to her breasts and hips.

How can this girl fit into the monoethnic no-differences-at-all world Eldest says provides perfect peace?

My eyes devour her body, then drift back to her breasts. The ice is a little foggy there, teasing me, but I can see enough to know they're lush, and even if they're frozen, I imagine that if they were warmed up . . .

"*Elder!*" I jump away from the clear box, as startled as I would have been if the beauty inside had suddenly awoken.

But it's just Doc.

"What are you *doing* down here? And how did you get down here in the first place?" Pause. "How did you even know about this place?"

"I took the elevator." I try to appear brilly, but my heart's banging around in my chest.

"You shouldn't be down here." He frowns. He touches the wi-com button behind his left ear. "Com link: Eldest," he says.

"No! Don't com Eldest! I'll go!" I say, but I don't want to go, I want to look more at the girl with sunset hair.

Doc shakes his head at me. "It's dangerous down here. Touch those buttons," he nods toward a little black electrical box at the frozen girl's head, "and you could wake her."

I look at the box. It's simple. On the top are three buttons: ELEC-TRICAL PULSE, CHECK DATA, and, under a clear protective case with a thumbprint scanner, a yellow button labeled "REANIMATION." Wires extending from it go back into the glass box; I follow the tubes with my eyes to her perfect cherry mouth.

"I won't touch it," I say, but Doc's already turned away from me.

"Elder's down here," he says, and I know those words aren't for me, but for Eldest, who must have connected to Doc's wi-com. "Yes," Doc says. Pause. "I don't frexing know." He eyes me again, a cold, evaluating look I have not seen since the days I was his patient. Doc touches the wi-com, and Eldest is disconnected. I know it won't be long before Eldest comes down here and drags me back to the Learning Center.

"Who is she?" I ask. I want to know all I can, while I can.

Doc narrows his eyes at me, but he bends down, looks at the front of the metal door. "Number 42. I was examining all the forties today, just a visual check that all is clear." He shakes his head. "I should have finished before going up to the Ward," he mutters to himself.

"The forties?"

Doc looks up at me. "They're all numbered."

"Yes, I can *see* that." I can't keep the impatience from my voice. "But what does it *mean*? Why are there numbered doors and frozen people here?"

Doc stares down at the girl with sunset hair. "You should ask Eldest that."

"I'm asking *you*."

Doc turns to me. "I'll tell you if you tell me how you got down here. All the doors that lead to that elevator are locked."

"Not the one on the fourth floor," I say. "It was unlocked."

He narrows his eyes. "And you just *happened* to come across an unlocked door on the fourth floor?"

I hesitate. "I found some blueprints of the ship in the Recorder Hall. I saw the second elevator there." I'm *not* going to scamp out Orion. It's not his fault I got caught.

I can tell Doc's thinking fast—his face has become blank and emotionless.

"So," I say, looking down at her again. "Who is she really?"

Doc walks past her glass box to a work desk on the far wall and comes back with a floppy. He slides a finger on it to open a program, punches in a code, and presses his index finger on an ID square. Then he types one-handed.

"Number 42, Number 42. Ah. She's nonessential."

"What?" I crouch down so that my face is even with her face. Her hair looks as if someone has poured yellow, orange, and red ink into a glass of water; the strands swirl around, pouring from her head, curling up at the ends at the bottom of the glass box. How could anyone say someone with sunset hair is nonessential?

"Her parents, apparently, put in a special request for her to be included," Doc continues, scrolling down the floppy. "They seem important enough—mother in biological engineering, father rather high up in the military. Lucky her. Not many nonessentials were allowed on. Not enough cargo space."

I blink. She's "cargo"? *Nonessential cargo*?

"Why is she here? Why are any of them here? Why is there a level full of frozen people?"

"That," Doc says as he puts down the floppy, "is for you to ask Eldest."

"I don't think I can trust Eldest," I whisper to the girl with sunset hair, but Doc doesn't hear.

I wonder what color her eyes are. I squint through the ice. I can see that her eyelashes are long and reddish-yellow—frex! I didn't know they made eyelashes like that!—but they are sealed firmly shut. All I know is if a girl can have skin that pale and hair that red and eyelashes that sunshiny, then who knows what colors live in her eyes?

"Elder."

I don't have to turn around to know it's Eldest speaking, but I do, one hand on the girl's glass box, as if I could protect her from Eldest's attention.

"How did you get down here?" Eldest's words are terse. He's angry, but maybe not at me.

Before I can speak, Doc announces, "I must have left the door unlocked. I got distracted when one of the nurses couldn't find one of the patients in need of meds; I wasn't careful."

Now that's a frexing lie. I know Doc didn't leave that door on the fourth floor unlocked because he hadn't known how I got down here. Still, you have to respect the man; it takes chutz to lie to Eldest.

"Come," Eldest says to me.

"I want to know why she—why there are so many frozen people down here," I say. "What's the point? Where did they come from? Why does she look so different?"

Eldest turns his cold stare to the girl with sunset hair. Then he looks back at me, slowly. "She looks odd because she is from Sol-Earth," Eldest says. "They all are. Now come."

"But—"

"Come." He turns and strides to the elevator. He's walking fast and has one fist pressed into the hip above his hurt leg.

I follow him, obedient as ever.

9: AMY

But there are also dreams.

Wonderful dreams. Beautiful dreams. Dreams of a new world.

I don't know what it will be like. No one does. But the nightmares rarely touch the new world, and in my mind, it is always paradise.

It is a place worth giving up Earth for.

Warmth. I always notice the warmth first.

And in my dream, I wake up, and I'm home.

My grandmother makes pancakes in the kitchen. She always mixes just a squeeze of syrup in with the batter, so the kitchen is already filled with a sticky-sweet smell that reminds me of home.

Grandma looks up at me and smiles —

And sometimes I'll lose the dream right then, because having Grandma again is the most unbelievable part of any dream—

She smiles, and it seems to make all her wrinkles disappear.

"Let's go!" Daddy says. He's dressed in sweats. He jogs a little in place, and his sneakers squeak on the linoleum. Then Mom runs up behind him in running shorts and a sports bra—

And sometimes I lose the dream there, because Mom never ran with me, it was always just me and Daddy—

And we start running.

And the new world spreads out around us as we run. It's always beautiful. It's the best parts of home made better. It's sandy beaches where the sand doesn't slip under our racing feet and the water's gold, not blue. It's cool forests with breezes that smell like lemons and honey, where strange woodland animals with soft fur play with us. It's deserts with towering sand sculptures that offer us sweet water to drink.

The new world is always beautiful, always perfect.

And if I'm lucky, the dream stays here.

I'm not always lucky.

As we run, the path curves around. We start to circle back. And I see our house, a mixed-up house that looks a little like our home in Florida where we lived when I was young, but it's brick like the one in Colorado, and Grandma's on the porch, waving and calling us in.

And Mom leaves the path and goes to the house.

"Come on," Daddy says, and he jogs up the steps of the porch.

But I can't quit running. My feet won't turn toward home.

I can't stop.

I have to race, round and round, in a world that's beautiful and serene and perfect.

I try to stop. I circle back to the house, and Mom and Grandma and Daddy are there, eating pancakes, and sometimes Jason's there too, and my dog from when I was little, and my friends from high school.

And I can't stop.

Because sometimes the dreams of the new world turn into nightmares.

10: ELDER

Eldest has apparently decided to punish me with lessons. He was silent during the long ride up the elevator, and did nothing but grunt at me in disdain when I tried to question him about the girl as he led me down the path from the Hospital to the grav tube. Now, in the Learning Center, he throws me into the hard blue plastic chair beside the faded globe of Sol-Earth.

I start to ask about the girl again, but Eldest collapses in the chair opposite me, shifting his weight uneasily. He grimaces as he props his leg up on the globe. His shoe covers Australia.

"Well?" Eldest growls.

"What?" I am unable to keep the whine from my voice.

"Well, did you figure out the third cause of discord?"

"No," I say, my eyes on the mountainous bumps on the globe.

"Oh, so you had *plenty* of time to go poking around places you don't belong but not to do the *one* thing I asked you to?" Eldest's sarcasm is cruel; he spits the words out at me.

"Why didn't you tell me about that hidden level filled with frozen *people?*" I shout back. "I'm the next frexing leader of this ship! I should know everything about it!"

"You should know everything, huh? Then why don't you tell me the third cause of discord?"

"I don't know!" I shout.

"Then stay here and learn!" Eldest roars, and he throws a floppy at me, its screen already flashing Sol-Earth history. Before I can hurl it back at Eldest, he tears from the room, knocking over the globe on his way out. Sol-Earth spins in his wake, a blue-green nothing, clattering against the table's leg.

Eldest's temper is worse because he's held it in until we were in private. I know that if we weren't here, in the Keeper Level, alone, he wouldn't have spoken like that.

Eldest leaves the Learning Center door open, and as he storms away, my eyes drift up to the metal screen, behind which are the twinkling lightbulbs I thought were stars.

Why lie about the screen, about the hidden level of the ship?

And what other lies has he been telling?

I tap my fingers on the table made from real Sol-Earth wood in front of me, trying to drum up new plans. If Eldest isn't going to tell me what's going on, I'll just find out for myself. My eyes drift to the metal circle covering the grav tube in the corner of the room. I could escape, take the tube back to the Feeder Level, see what else I could find. Maybe Orion knows something more. I can't think in this tiny room. I'd like to just walk about the fields a bit, visit the sheep pastures, wander aimlessly on a ship whose path was determined centuries ago. Gather my thoughts together so I can see them all in a straight line.

But to disobey a direct order from Eldest?

Even I don't have the chutz for that.

11: AMY

More than the sound of my own beating heart, I miss the sound of a ticking clock.

Time passes, it must pass, but I have no more assurance of moving through time than I have that I am moving through space. In a way, I'm glad: this means perhaps 300 years and 364 days have passed, and tomorrow I will wake up. Sometimes after a cross-country meet or a long day at school, I'd fall into bed with all my clothes on and be out before I knew it. When I'd finally open my eyes, it would feel like I'd just shut them for a minute, but really, the whole rest of the day and half the night was gone.

But.

There were other times when I'd collapse onto my mattress, shut my eyes and dream, and it felt like I'd lived a whole lifetime in that dream, but when I woke up, it had only been a few minutes.

What if only a year has gone by? What if we haven't even left yet?

That is my greatest fear.

Jason said, "When you get there, think of me when you look at the stars."
I said, "I won't limit myself to the stars."
A cool breeze, like the day we—

What was that?

—met, with the music from the party pounding so loudly that the ground under our feet vibrated. When I wore my heels, I was taller than Jason, but I was barefoot now, the cool grass a comfort to my tired feet as I looked up into his eyes.

Did I move?

The dream fades, the sensation of grass-breeze-Jason disappears. Darkness. Nightmares tickle my mind.

Something's happening.

No, no, no. Nothing's happening. Nothing ever happens. It's that nightmare again, that same nightmare. Ed/Hassan will unfreeze me, and I will be like now, and they'll throw me back in. Or the ship will crash, and I'll be stuck here, forever, never unfrozen. Or maybe this is the nightmare where—

Thunk.

—where they forget to unfreeze me at all, the ship lands and everyone's so excited they just leave me behind, and—

Something is happening.

No. The nightmares are getting more real, and they'll be so much worse because of it. I think I hear something. I can't hear anything. It's all in my mind. It's not real. Think about something better. Think about Jason. Think about Mom, about Daddy, think about—

Click.

No. I did not hear a click. A click did not vibrate through the ice. That did not happen. It's just the nightmares . . . it's another nightmare. It's as simple as that.

If I could, I would squeeze my eyes shut. Instead, I try to focus my mind, like I used to be able to focus my eyes in and out when I looked at something really close. Memories. Memories always kill nightmares.

My mind's eye flashes images, a slide show of memories. Hiking the Grand Canyon. The middle school trip to the beach. Gymnastics when I was a kid. The first time I drove. The first time I scratched the car (same day) and Daddy yelled at me, but got me ice cream afterward anyway, and we pinky-promised not to tell Mom. Baking Christmas cookies with Mom and Grandma the year before she went to the nursing home. Cross-country meets. Marathon training.

I feel something. I *feel* something. Warmth in my stomach. And I hear . . . the hum of electricity. I realize I hear it because it is coming from the tubes down my throat.

My body slips. Just a fraction of a millimeter, but it slips.

The ice is melting.

Oh, God.

Thump.

My heart.

Thump-thump.

Water leaks onto my left eye's lash-line. I twitch involuntarily. The yellow crust that has sealed my eyes for who knows how long cracks as—for the first time since I was frozen—*I move.*

OhGodohGodohGod.

12: ELDER

"What are you doing here?"

I jump, then grimace. Nothing could have given away my guilt more.

"It's almost dark," Doc continues. "Does Eldest know you're here?"

"Don't!" I say as Doc reaches for his wi-com button. "Look . . . I snuck out. I was tired of reading! C'mon," I add when Doc doesn't lower his hand. "I just . . . needed to get out for a bit. Don't scamp me out. Give me a break."

Doc's smirk tells me he's not happy with me, but at least he doesn't call for Eldest. I breathe a little easier.

For a moment, we both just stand there, me on the path that leads deeper into the garden behind the Hospital, Doc on the steps. I love this garden. When Eldest sent me to the Ward for that year, I spent a lot of free time here in the garden. Steela, an old woman who lived in the Ward long before I moved there, had made the garden blossom from a grass lawn with hedges around it into a veritable jungle of flowers and vegetables and vines and trees.

"So, looking for inspiration?" Doc nods to the statue in the center of the garden.

The Plague Eldest, his concrete face upturned and his arms spread wide, stands benevolent guard over the garden. Time and scheduled rain has smoothed the face and hands, blurring the details of our greatest ruler.

"Oh! Uh . . . yeah." I seize onto his excuse. "You know, Eldest wants me to learn leadership, and I figured, Plague Eldest did it the best. . . ." The Plague Eldest was the first and greatest Eldest. He's the only person I've ever seen my Eldest admire, and he's more of a leader than either of us ever will be.

"You just came here to look at the statue?"

I heave a sigh. "I wanted to see her."

"Don't go getting obsessed, boy. Not good, not good for anyone. She's frozen, and that's that."

"I know, but . . ."

"But nothing. Get her out of your mind."

A resounding low-pitched alarm fills the air. *Urk. Urk. Urk.* The warning tone that sunset is about to fall. A flash of green catches my eyes. On the other side of the ship, the Shippers are taking the grav tube from the offices and labs on the Shipper Level to the City here on the Feeder Level where they live. From here, they're tiny blurs of color zipping through the tube: brown, white, black, green. Doc raises his face to the center of the sky. That's not the sun there, it's an inertial confinement fusion container, a solar lamp providing both light and warmth to the Feeder Level, as well as the fuel for the ship's internal function. It flashes once—warning us that night is approach-ing—and then the tinted shield slides over the container. The world is dark now. We call it sunset, a word leftover from Sol-Earth, but this sunset is nothing more than turning off the light. There is no red-yellow-orange-gold in this sunset.

"Come on, boy," Doc says as he hangs his arm on my shoulder, pulling me down the garden path. "You need to get back to the grav tube before Eldest notices you're missing."

"But . . ."

"The doors are all locked, even the one on the fourth floor. Come on. There's no point obsessing."

I turn away, letting Doc's words drag me from thoughts of the girl with sunset hair. Eldest taught me about ancient religions that worshipped the sun. I never understood why—it's just a ball of light and heat. But if the sun of Sol-Earth swirls in colors and lights like that girl's hair, well, I can see why the ancients would worship that.

The path leading from the Hospital seems ominous in the shad-ows of dark-time. Doc's arm tightens around my shoulder, his fingers digging into my arm. "Who is that?" he hisses.

I squint into the darkness. A man walks down the path a few paces ahead of us. When he reaches the steps of the Recorder Hall, he bounds up them with jaunty cheerfulness. A snatch of a whistled tune—an old Sol-Earth nursery rhyme—flitters through the air.

"That's probably Orion," I say. Only a Recorder would know songs from Sol-Earth. Doc's grip on my arm doesn't relax. "A Recorder."

"The same Recorder who showed you the blueprints of the ship?"

I jerk my head around. Doc's still staring at Orion, who's

completely oblivious to us, just standing on the porch of the Recorder Hall. I tear myself from Doc's tense hold.

"How did you know a Recorder showed me the blueprints?"

Doc snorts, but his gaze doesn't waver. "You couldn't have found that on your own."

"Hello!" the man on the porch calls out as the path takes us closer to the Recorder Hall. His deep voice confirms that it's Orion.

"Hi!" I call back.

"It's a bit cold out tonight, isn't it?" Orion says, but I'm not sure why he'd point that out. Usually, the temperature is lowered by ten degrees after dark-time starts, but it's still too soon to feel it.

Doc, however, has stopped in his tracks, his face whitewashed. "Are you *sure* that's just a Recorder?"

"Yeah," I say. "Orion."

Doc sags in relief. "His voice reminds me of someone I used to know. I can't even remember the last time I was in the Recorder Hall. Hey, Orion!" Doc calls. "Think you could let us into the Hall?"

But Orion doesn't step out of the shadows.

Aroo! Aroo!

"The cryo level alarm," Doc mutters, spinning around toward the Hospital, from which a deep siren is screaming its warning into the dark. "Something's wrong!"

I tear down the path as if the void of space is at my heels, skidding on the plastic mulch that paves the trail. A pounding sound punctuated by cursing tells me that Doc is following close behind. The nurses in the lobby are looking around, panicked, unsure of where the siren is coming from, but Doc and I both ignore their shouted questions and dive for the elevator.

Doc wheezes as the elevator rises slowly. As it dings past the third floor, Doc raises his hand to his left ear.

"Wait," I say, pulling his hand away from his wi-com button. "Let's see what's going on before we com Eldest. Maybe it's nothing serious."

In the silence that greets my statement, I can still hear the muffled sounds of the alarm growing louder as we rise.

Doc shakes my hand away. The elevator dings, and the doors slide apart.

The door at the end of the hall is hanging open.

Doc breaks into a run down the hall, barreling into the room and going straight to the desk. He rolls his thumb over the biometric scanner on the metal box in the center of the desk. Nothing happens.

"Frex," he growls. "Scan in," he tells me, pushing the metal box toward me.

"But—"

"That box will only open with an Elder or Eldest security clearance. If the alarm's not turned off, the Hospital will go into lockdown. Scan. In."

I roll my thumb over the biometric scanner. The top of the box lifts and folds in on itself, revealing a control panel with a series of numbered buttons and a blinking red light. Doc punches in a code, and the *aroo! aroo!* fades into silence.

Doc turns to the elevator, scans in his access, rushes inside, and pushes the button for the cryo level before I even get all the way into the elevator. He's out of breath and tapping the floor of the elevator with his foot as we sink down, down. Doc doesn't talk the entire time we're descending. He clenches and unclenches his fists, as if he's keeping time with his heart. His face is tense.

The elevator stops, bouncing a bit as it rests on the cryo level floor. The doors slide open. We both stay in the elevator a moment, waiting to see who or what is on the other side.

The lights are all on. Doc steps out of the elevator, wary. His hands ball into fists.

"Non*ono*," Doc says all in a rush. He takes one step, pauses, then bursts into a run. I chase after him. Doc skids to a halt at the row of numbered doors in the forties.

Number 42 has been pulled out of her freezer in the wall; her glass box lies on the table in the center of the aisle.

The girl with sunset hair is inside. Her eyes are open—pale, bright green like blades of new grass—and panicked. She is thrashing in the water flecked with blue crystals. The box is too small for her now that she is awake and moving; her knees and elbows are beating against the glass. Her body bucks up—her stomach flattens against the top of the box; her head and feet slam to the bottom. She brings her hands to her face, and, for a moment, I think she is clawing at herself, but then I see she is yanking the tubes from her mouth, gagging and choking on them as she goes.

"Hurry up!" Doc shouts. "We've got to get the lid off before she pulls the tubes out!"

I don't bother asking why; I just rush to the other side of the box and help lift the heavy glass lid up. Inside, the tubes from the girl's throat encircle her head and neck, but she's still pulling at them; there's still more down her throat. She gags, and yellow bile mixed with pale red blood clouds the water around her face.

With a final heave, Doc and I lift the lid off the top of the box. Doc jerks back, yanking the lid from my grasp, and he half-throws, half-drops the glass lid to the cement floor. It breaks into two uneven pieces on the ground, too thick and heavy to shatter.

Under the blue-crystal-flecked water, the girl finally jerks out the last of the tubes, and I see little electronic devices attached to the ends. The girl's eyes are wide open, and she's staring straight up at us. Her mouth is open in a perfect circle, sucking in the water.

"What's she trying to do, drink it all up?" Doc asks, reaching into the watery mess for the girl.

I stand back, horrified. "No," I whisper. "She's screaming."

13: AMY

Pain.

Cold so cold it burns, but not with a burning that cauterizes, no, a burning that razes, decimates.

Pain.

Searing,
      pulling,
           freezing,
                 ripping,
                      bleeding,
                           breaking
                               pain.

My stomach muscles seize. Can't vomit empty.
Eyes see only blobs. Some bright. Some not. No focus.

Mucus slips down my nostrils, down the back of my throat. Choke. Gag. Cough.

Water sloshes in my ears, muffling the intonations of deep, male-voiced speech around me.

Hands lift me from the slush of my glass coffin, and it feels as if they are rescuing me from quicksand. The cryo liquid clings to me, pulling me back into my watery grave, dragging cold fingers across my skin.

They lay me on something cold, hard, and flat. A funnel-like mask is fitted over my nose, and air so warm it hurts blows into my nostrils, reminding my lungs to work. Hands press something sticky onto my skin, and shortly thereafter, my muscles cramp painfully.

Two gentle hands hold the sides of my head still, while two rough fingers rip open my eyelids. *No*, I think, *I don't want more eyedrops.* But *plop! plop!* The cold liquid falls onto my eyes. I blink painfully, my tears mixing with the goo they've put there.

The rough hands go for my mouth next. At first, I don't know what's happening, and I let my lips part easily. Then I realize that the person is doing *something*, and cold liquid drips down my throat, but I don't know what it is, so I clench my teeth and shake my head, but my neck isn't used to moving, so my head just sort of rolls around for a bit.

The gentle hands steady my head again. A face peers into mine. A boy—about Jason's age, but taller and broader and more mus-cly than Jason had been. Dark olive skin; milk-chocolate eyes with flecks of cinnamon that are narrow at the ends, almond-shaped. It's a handsome face, one I want to trust. As I stare at him, a sharp pain pierces my head; I am not used to focusing my eyes on anything.

The boy speaks, and while my ears are still too blocked to hear anything clearly, his tone is kind and reassuring as he taps my jaw. I let my chin drop—a nod, yes—and then part my lips for him. A warm, viscous syrup that tastes almost like peaches, but with an alcoholic bite, drips down my tongue, coating my throat. Some of the soreness fades.

The boy peers down into my face.

"Mmgnna gedyup," he says. I find that I can't understand him. He nods at me, like he's trying to tell me it'll all be okay, but that's not true—it won't be okay, how could anything ever be okay again?

The boy grabs my right hand; the rough hands grab my left. And before I can make my neck move—no!—they jerk me up into a sitting position.

I feel as if I am breaking in half.

Once, I was ice.

Now, I am pain.

14: ELDER

"**Momma?**" the girl whimpers in a raspy, unused voice. "Daddy?"

Her brilliant green eyes are shut again; her sunset hair sprawls across the metal examination table in a matted, wet mess.

"How long will she be like this?" I ask Doc.

"A day. Maybe more. She wasn't reanimated correctly. They are supposed to be removed from their cryogenic containment boxes before the process begins, and then they are supposed to be warmed in a reanimation bath, not left out on the table to melt. It's a miracle she's alive."

I swallow, hard. It feels as if a rock is moving down my throat.

Doc picks up the end of the box connected to the tubes that had been down the girl's throat. "Someone pushed the button," he says. "It's not supposed to be pushed until *after* the body's prepped for reanimation. This disconnects the power." He looks up at me. "She was unplugged. If we hadn't gotten here in time . . ." He glances at the girl now. "She would have died."

Shite. My stomach sinks to my shoes and stays there. "Just like that? Dead?"

Doc nods. "I have to com Eldest."

"No, but—"

"You won't be in trouble. You didn't do this. In fact, I'm glad you're here. Eldest told me you've begun learning about strong central leadership. This is the sort of thing that will teach you leadership."

The girl's chest moves up and down, but that is the only sign of life she's willing to give me. Funny how different her body looks outside the ice. She seems smaller, weaker, more vulnerable. The ice was her armor. I want to protect her now, cover her curves instead of run my fingers over them.

I put my hand on her shoulder, marveling at the differences in our skin tones. She opens her eyes.

"Cold," she whispers.

Doc stares down at the girl. "This is a frexing nightmare."

I want to say, how can this be a nightmare, with *her* here? But then she whimpers, a soft pathetic bleat like the lamb I once had as a pet, and the rock is back in my throat.

Doc gets the girl a hospital gown, the kind with no back, but she cries when we lift her arms through the sleeve holes. Then he covers her with a blanket. She keeps her eyes shut, and at first I think she's sleeping, but her breathing is rough, uneven, and I know she's keeping herself awake, listening to us.

We don't say much.

When Eldest storms into the cryo level, he brings all the fear back with him. He looks at her, he looks at me, and then he looks at Doc.

"Was it him?"

"No!" I protest immediately.

"Of course not," Doc says. Then, to me, "He's not talking about you." He turns back to Eldest. "It's impossible, and you know it. You're being paranoid."

"Who are you—" I start, but they both ignore me.

"It was a malfunction," Doc says. "The power glitched on her box." He holds up the electrical black box that had been on the top of Number 42's cryo container. Its light still faintly blinks red.

"You're sure of that?" Eldest asks.

Doc nods. "Of course I'm sure. Who would come down here, unplug a random girl, and leave? It was just a malfunction. The machinery's old. I'm constantly having to repair it. She got unlucky, slipped through the cracks."

More lies. I wonder how much of anything Doc says is true. After all, he had been checking her cryo chamber earlier today. And he was a lot more freaked out before Eldest showed up, when he told me someone pushed the button to unplug her.

The girl on the table moans.

"Who is she?" Eldest asks, his attention diverting to the girl.

"Number 42."

"Was she—?"

"Nonessential."

"Amy," the girl croaks.

"What?" I kneel beside her, close to her cracked lips.

"My name is Amy."

Eldest looks down at her. Amy opens her eyes—a flash of new-grass green—but shuts them again, flinching at the fluorescent light.

"Your name is immaterial, girl." Eldest turns to Doc. "We need to figure out who reanimated her."

"Where are my parents?" Her voice is a whisper, choked with pain. The others don't even notice her.

"Can we put her back in?" Eldest asks Doc. Doc shakes his head no. His eyes are sorrowful.

"Don't freeze me again!" Amy says, panic edging her voice. Her voice cracks from disuse, and she coughs.

"We couldn't if we wanted to," Doc tells Eldest.

"Why not? We have more freezing chambers." He looks past Doc's shoulder to a door on the other side of the room. I hadn't noticed it before, but I log it away in my memory, to explore later.

"Regenerative abilities deteriorate greatly across multiple freezings, especially when reanimation hasn't been done properly. If we put her in another cryo chamber, she might not ever wake up."

"I want Daddy," she whimpers, and even though I know that she is more woman than girl, she seems very much like a child now.

"Time to go to sleep," Doc says. He pulls a med patch from his pockets and rips it open.

Amy's eyes fly open. "NO!" she shouts, her voice cracking on the word.

Doc approaches her, and she flings her arm up gracelessly like a club, crashing into his elbow. The med patch falls to the ground. Doc picks it up and tosses it into the bin, then opens a drawer and pulls out another med patch. "It will make you feel better," he explains to the girl as he tears this one open.

"Don't want it." Her eyes are pinpricks of black in pale green circles.

"Hold her down," Doc tells me. I just stand there, looking at her. Eldest shoves me aside and pushes his weight against her shoulders.

"Don't want it!" the girl screams, but Doc has already slapped her arm with the patch, and the tiny needles prick her skin like sharp sandpaper, sending meds into her system.

"Don'twannagosleepagain." Her words slur together and are hard to understand. "Don' wan . . . na," she says, her voice dropping. A few small tears mixed with eyedrops linger on her lashes. "Not . . . sleep," she says, even quieter and slower. "No . . . no more . . . sleep." And her eyes roll back into her head, and her head sinks down amidst her sunset hair, and she loses all consciousness.

I stare at her, and even though her chest is moving up and down in steady breaths, she looks more dead now than she did in the ice.

I wonder if she dreams.

15: AMY

I am awake. But I do not stretch, yawn, or open my eyes. I am not used to doing any of that. At least, not anymore. So I lie here, becoming aware of my senses. I smell mustiness. I can hear someone breathing softly, as if asleep. I feel warmth, and it is not until I realize this that I remember I am no longer frozen.

My first thought: how much of the dreams and nightmares was real?

Even now, the dreams I had while frozen are fading, becoming fuzzy memories, like dreams do. Did I really dream for three centuries, or did I dream for the few minutes between fully waking and unfreezing? It felt like centuries, dream upon dream piling up in my head—but dreams are like that, time isn't real. When my tonsils were taken out, I had dozens of really detailed dreams, but I was only under the anesthesia for an hour or so. Besides, I *couldn't* have dreamt when I was frozen—that's impossible, dreams can't flit through frozen neurons.

But what about those stories of patients who are awake during surgery, even though the anesthesia is supposed to knock them out?

No. Ignore that. It's not the same. I could only have dreamt in that small time when my body was melting but my soul hadn't yet. If I start thinking about time, and how much passed, and how aware I was of it passing, I'll drive myself crazy.

I force my eyes open. I can't be haunted by dreams—whether they're centuries old or not—if I am awake.

The crinkle of my eyelids feels new to me, and I revel in opening my eyes.

And then—*oh*—I strrrrretch. My muscles burn. I can feel them all tightening, the muscles at the small of my back, the ones running along the sides of my calves, the slender muscles wrapped around my elbows.

The blanket slips down my legs. I sit up, my abdominal muscles pulling me forward with relish. I am bare from the tops of my thighs down, and above that all I am wearing is a blue-green hospital gown, the kind that doesn't close in the back.

A boy sits beside my bed, breathing in a slow steady way that drifts in and out of snoring. I pull the blanket all the way up to my shoulders. He fell asleep while sitting in the chair and is slouched over in a way that looks uncomfortable. He must have been watching me. I hate the idea that he was there, awake and conscious, while I slept. It creeps me out.

It's the same boy who was there when I first woke up inside the glass coffin. His face is soft but has an edge to it that belies the innocent appearance he has while sleeping. I'm not sure what race he is— not black, but not white; neither Hispanic nor Asian. It's a nice color, though—dark in a creamy sort of way that compliments his almost-black hair. The high cut of his cheekbones and the strong curve of his forehead make him look instantly trustworthy, maybe even kind.

"Who are you?" I say loudly. For the first time since I woke from my centuries-long slumber, my voice does not crack. They must have done something to my throat. A dull, throbbing ache fills my body.

The boy jumps, a look of guilt or wariness on his face when his eyes focus on me. He looks around as if he's surprised I'm talking to him, but he's the only other person in the room.

"I'm uh . . . I'm Elder. I'm the future, um, leader. Of the ship. Um." He stands up, but I don't, so he sits down again awkwardly.

Future leader of the ship? Why does the *ship* need a future leader? "Where am I?"

"You're in the Ward," he says, but I can barely understand him. There's a strange clipped quality to his words, and they're inflected with a singsongy intonation. His short speech sounds like this: "Yar in-tha Wart," with a lilt at the end of each word.

"Where's the Ward?" I ask.

"The Hospital." ("Thas pital.")

I look around. This isn't what I expected. "Why am I in a hospital? What are you doing here?"

I'm not fully concentrating on what he's saying, and I don't really catch everything he says in reply. The room suddenly feels colder, and I clutch the blanket tighter to me. Something about being a future leader, again, like that has any weight to it. Future leader of the ship. Well, of course he is. I inspect him closer. He's got wide, broad shoulders with just enough muscle that it isn't too obvious under his shirt-tunic thing, although I can see the hard corners of his biceps.

Tall—much taller than me, but a few inches taller than most people, even though he's probably about my age. He slouches, though. His face is narrow but inviting, with almond-shaped eyes that pierce. All of this adds up to a certain *something* that makes him just look like the kind of guy who could lead a ship. It's almost as if God had known Elder was going to be some sort of leader or whatever, so He gave him the right face and body for it.

I turn in the bed so that my feet touch the floor. The floor's cold, though, so I raise my knees to my chin—under the blanket, of course, since the hospital gown does little to cover me. "What's it like?"

"What's what like?" ("Waz-wa lick?")

"The new planet." And even though I didn't want to come here in the first place, and even though I hated every moment of my frozen years to get here, there is a little awe in my voice that even I cannot hide. A new planet. We are finally on a new planet. A planet no human being has ever been on before.

The boy stands up. He's so tall, it doesn't feel fair to call him a boy, but at the same time, he's got a bit of a baby face, as if he's never seen or done anything to make him grow up, to make the angles of his face sharpen with the harshness of age. He walks to the far wall, his back to me. He is towering in this small room; it can barely contain him. He reminds me, in a small way, of Jason. Not in how he looks— this boy is darker and more muscular than Jason—but in the way he stands and walks, as if he knows his place in the world with absolute certainty. He leans against the wall, facing a rectangular piece of metal hanging there. Light peeps out from around the edges of the metal. It must be some sort of window covering.

"Ware na onnda plant yeah," he says. I had not realized how confusing his accent was until he was facing away from me, unintentionally shielding his lips from my view.

"What?" I ask.

He turns to me; this time when he speaks, I am able to decipher his words. "We're not on the planet yet."

"What . . . do you mean?" Cold, the coldness of ice and hell, fills my empty stomach.

"We've still got about fifty years before we land."

"*What?*"

"I'm sorry; 49 years and 266 days. I'm sorry."

"Why did you wake me up early?"

"I didn't!" the boy protests, flushing deeply. "It wasn't me! Why did you accuse me?"

"I just want to know why we were all woken up 49 years and 200-some days early! And where are my parents?"

The boy lowers his eyes. Something in his look makes the ice pit in my belly churn.

"You weren't all woken up early," he says. His eyes beg me to understand what he means, to quit asking questions.

"Where are my parents?" I repeat.

"They're . . . below."

"I want to see my parents. I want to talk to my parents."

"They . . ."

"*What happened to my parents?*"

"They haven't been reanimated yet. They're still frozen. Everyone else down there is still frozen but you."

"When will they wake up? When do I get to see them?"

The boy edges to the door. "Maybe I should get Eldest to come explain?"

"Eldest who? Explain what?" I am shouting, but I don't care. The blanket has slipped from my legs. My brain is racing, falling into place, crashing against the words I think the boy will say, the words I dread hearing, the words I must hear him speak aloud before I will believe them to be true.

"Er . . . well, uh . . . They're not going to be woken up until we get there."

"Fifty years from now," I say hollowly.

The boy nods. "Forty-nine years and 266 days from now."

I have been frozen in ice for centuries. And yet, I have never felt more alone than I do right now, at this moment, when I realize that I am alive and aware and awake, and they are not.

16: ELDER

She starts crying. Not soft, sad tears, but the angry sort, like she hates the whole world, or at least the ship that's now her world. So, I do what any reasonable person would do when faced with a crying girl.

I get the frex out of there.

A familiar *beep, beep-beep* fills my left ear. "Com link: Eldest," says the soft female voice of my wi-com.

"Ignore."

Eldest had left the Hospital as soon as Doc had begun administering post-regenerative meds to Amy. He hadn't helped set up the IV bags or watched as they slowly dripped three full bags of nutrition and fluid into her. He wasn't there to help us lift her onto the new bed in the Ward that Doc made up for her. He wasn't there when she woke up, having stayed by her side for more than seven hours just so she wouldn't have to wake up alone.

I don't really care what he has to say right now.

What I care about is Amy. Maybe if she sees more of *Godspeed*, she won't cry so much. If I can bring her a piece of her home, something that reminds her of Sol-Earth, maybe she'll . . .

I head straight to the garden just behind the Hospital. The garden is full of blooms right now, but I know what I want—the large yellow and orange flowers growing near the pond, the ones with streaks of color almost as brilly as Amy's hair.

It takes me a moment to find them; there're only a few blooms left, their big heads drooping toward the pond water. I kneel, ignoring the muddy stains seeping into my trousers, and break the stems of half a dozen flowers. The petals are as long as my fingers, curling at the ends, and their honey-like scent drifts lazily to my nose.

"Elder."

Shite. I turn to face Eldest, my fingers tightening around the stems.

"You ignored my com." His voice is low, monotone.

"I was busy."

His cold eyes drop to the flowers in my hand. "Clearly."

I start back toward the Hospital. Eldest follows me.

"You're forgetting your duties. You have yet to complete the assignment I gave you yesterday."

"It can wait."

I start to climb the steps leading back to the Hospital, but Eldest grabs my shirt collar and drags me back.

"Being leader of the ship is more important than any girl."

I nod. He *is* right.

"She shouldn't even be here in the first place," Eldest mumbles. "What a nuisance."

I crush the flower stems into my palms.

"A nuisance?" Now *my* voice is a low monotone.

"Her presence is bad for the ship. Difference. The first cause of discord."

Something roars in protest inside me. This is not the kind of leader I want to learn to be—one so coldly indifferent to Amy. Yesterday, Eldest told me that it was my job to protect the people. I didn't know he just meant *our* people.

"Now go back to the Keeper Level and work on that assignment."

"No."

Eldest's eyes widen, then narrow. "No?"

"No." I rip myself from his grip and head to the Hospital elevator. Before the doors slide shut, Eldest steps inside with me.

"I don't have time for your childishness. I'll tell you once more. Go back to the Keeper Level."

"No," I say, still smiling, but it's all a front to hide my fear. Eldest cannot stand rebellion, and I've never pushed back at him this hard before. Part of me wants to take it all back, apologize, and obey him like I always have. Part of me wishes he'd take a swing at me so I could punch him back.

Eldest raises his left hand to his wi-com button.

"Keeper override; Eldest clearance," he says, and my stomach lurches. This can't be good. "Command: apply noise modification enhancer to wi-com Elder. Vary tone and pitch. Intensity level: three. Cease at subject's entry to the Keeper Level."

Immediately, a low-pitched buzz fills my left ear. I clap my hand over it, but the noise isn't coming from outside; it's coming from inside my ear, in my wi-com. The buzz rises into a screech for a second, dips back into a buzz, then makes a grating, teeth-jarring scratching sound against my eardrum.

I jab my finger into my wi-com. "Override!" I say. "Command: stop all sounds!"

"Access denied," the female voice of my wi-com says over a sound worse than the squelching noise of a cow giving birth. Augh! This isn't like the biometric scanner where I have the same clearance as Eldest. Wi-coms are different, unique to each of us. The only thing that can stop mine from bugging out is Eldest's.

"Make it stop," I say to Eldest. A burbling sound pops in my ear, which isn't too bad on its own, but each burble is punctuated by a short high-pitched *eep!* that makes me jump a little with surprise every other second.

The elevator doors slide open and we step into the common room.

"The noise will stop as soon as you enter the Learning Center prepared to learn and listen," Eldest says pleasantly. He pushes his wi-com again. "Command: increase intensity to level four." The sounds grow louder. Eldest smiles at me. Then he turns and strolls out of the common room toward Doc's office.

I try sticking my finger down my ear, but it's no good. The wi-com is wired directly into my eardrum. Something that sounds like glass shattering over a crowing rooster crackles in my ear.

"Nice flowers."

"Orion?" Any surprise at seeing the Recorder here in the Ward is replaced by the cacophony vibrating through my left ear. I'd even forgotten the flowers clutched in my right hand. Green plant blood oozes between my fingers from broken stems.

"I needed to get more supplies." Orion shakes a small plastic bottle, and pills rattle inside it. He must have swiped them. No one's supposed to have a store of mental meds—even if you don't live in the Ward, the Inhibitors are delivered daily, one pill at a time.

"Don't want Eldest or Doc to catch me." Orion pockets the pills.

I clap one hand over my ear in a feeble attempt to stifle the noise, but it's no good.

Orion smiles grimly. "That old trick. There's no point trying to stop the noise. It'll just get worse the longer it goes." He watches as I beat my fist against my ear. "Just do whatever he told you to do, or you'll go mad from it."

"How do you know?" The words come out harsh and angry, but only because I am having such a hard time concentrating on anything beyond the braying in my ear.

"I just wanted to give you a bit of advice—there's no point in standing up directly to Eldest. Won't work. He's an old king, too used to power. You can't face him directly. You'll have to be a bit sneakier than that." Orion tucks a piece of his long, straggly hair behind his ear, and I notice again the spiderweb white scars creeping down the left side of his neck, as if his flesh had been ripped open and the pieces didn't quite fit back together again.

"I'll do what I want," I say as I push past him, one hand clutching my ear.

I stagger across the common room. When I pass Harley, I knock into his canvas as another high-pitched tone starts an unnatural staccato in my ear, throwing me off balance.

"Elder?" he asks, jumping up in concern.

I ignore him as I open the hall door and head toward Amy's room.

I'm going to give her these frexing flowers if it kills me. I won't let Eldest push me around.

"What's wrong?" Harley's followed me. He leaves a koi-colored handprint on my arm as he reaches for me, but I shake him off.

I stop at Amy's room and knock on the door.

No answer.

"What are you doing here?" There's a hitch in Harley's voice that I notice through the loud crowing that's started up in my left ear. I remember now—this was his former girlfriend's room before it was given to Amy.

"A new res," I say, wincing. My voice sounds loud to my pained ear.

Harley puts his hand to the wall, leaving behind a smear of orange-yellow on the matte white finish. No one will care; it's just another mark of many. Ever since Harley moved into the Ward permanently, spots of color follow him everywhere he goes, like a trail of rainbows.

The wi-com is doing its best to distract me—the sounds and tones are cycling through at a dizzying pace. Part of me wants to bash my head against the door, just to make the noise stop. It's driving me insane, the sort of insane that Doc's mental meds can't fix. My left hand grips my ear so hard that blood trickles between my fingers— I'm afraid I'll rip it off. Instead, I punch the wall with my right hand.

The flowers I'd so carefully chosen from the garden—the big, bright blooms I'd selected specifically because they reminded me of Amy's hair—crinkle against the force of my fist meeting the wall. Petals fall in a shower of reds and golds. I unclench my fist. The stems are a stringy, gooey mass. The leaves have been crushed beyond recognition. The flowers themselves are pitiful remnants of the natural beauty they held on the pond's edge.

An undercurrent of clicking sounds adds itself to my tonal torture. I let the flowers drop at Amy's door, slap both hands around my ears, trapping the noises inside my skull as I run from the Hospital to the grav tube to the Keeper Level and silent tranquility.

17: AMY

The man in front of me has long fingers. He weaves them in and out of one another, then rests his head upon them while he stares at me as if I am a puzzle he cannot solve. He seemed polite, almost sympathetic, when he'd fetched me from my room, but now I wish he'd left his office door open.

"I'm sorry you're in this situation." Although he sounds sincere, he just looks curious.

Even though that boy had explained everything to me, I still feel the need to have this "doctor" confirm it.

"We're really fifty years from landing?" My voice is cold and hard, like the ice I am beginning to wish I was still encased in.

"About 49 years and 250 days, yes."

It's 266 days, I think, remembering what the boy said. "I can't be refrozen?"

"No," the doctor says simply. When all I do is sit there, staring at him, he adds, "We *do* actually have a few more cryo chambers—"

"Put me in one of them!" I say, leaning forward. I will face a century of nightmares if I can wake up with my parents.

"*If* you had been reanimated correctly, that *might* have been an option, and even then, it would have been dangerous. Cells are not meant to be frozen and refrozen. The body deteriorates with multiple reanimations." The doctor shakes his head. "Refreezing might kill you." He struggles to find a way to describe it to me. "You will become like freezer-burned meat. Dried out. Dead," he adds when that gross image does not deter my eagerness.

For a moment, I'm crestfallen. Then I remember. "What about my parents?"

"What about them?"

"Are they going to be unfrozen early, too?"

"Ah." He unwraps his fingers and straightens the objects on his desk, making the notepad parallel to the desk edge, the pens in the cup all lean to one side. He's wasting time, avoiding eye contact. "You weren't meant to be unfrozen. What you must understand is that your parents, Numbers 41 and 40, are essential. They both have highly specialized skills that will be needed when we land. We will require their knowledge and aid at Centauri-Earth's developmental stages."

"So, basically, no." I want to hear him say it.

"No."

I shut my eyes and breathe. I am so angry—so frustrated—just so pissed off that this has happened and that I can't do anything at all about it. I can feel the hot, itchy tears in my eyes, but I do *not* want to cry, not now in front of the doctor, not ever again.

The doctor pushes the bottom right corner of his big notepad so that it is perfectly square to the edge of the desk. His long, twitchy fingers pause. There is nothing out of place on his desk. There is nothing out of place in his whole office. Except me.

"It's not so bad here," the doctor says. I look up. There's a blurry film fogging my vision, and I know if I'm not careful, I'll cry. I let him continue. "In a very real way, it's better that you are here now, instead of there later. Who knows what Centauri-Earth will be like? It may not even be habitable, despite the probes sent before *Godspeed* left Sol-Earth. It's not an option we like to consider, but it's possible. . . ." His voice trails off as his eyes meet mine.

"What am I supposed to *do*?"

"I'm sorry?"

"What am I supposed to do now?" I say, my voice rising. "Are you just saying I've got to sit around? Waiting until the ship lands before I can see my parents again?" I pause. "God, I'll be so *old* by then. I'll be older than them! That's not *right*!" I pound my fist on the desk. His pencils rattle in their neat little cup, and one of them does not settle back in line with the others. He reaches up to place it neatly against its fellows. With a roar of frustration, I grab the cup and hurl it at the doctor, who dodges just in time. The pencils fly like freed birds, then clatter to the floor like dead ones.

"No one cares about your stupid pencils!" I shout as the doctor jumps to pick up the fallen pencils. "No one cares! Why can't you see that?"

He freezes, gripping his pencils, his back curved away from me. "I know this is difficult for you. . . ."

"Difficult? *Difficult?* You don't know what it's been like! You have no idea how long I've suffered—only for it to amount to nothing! *NOTHING!*"

The doctor throws the pencils into the cup so violently that two pop back out again. He does not replace them, but lets them sit, disorderly and random, on the desk. "There is no need to react violently," he says in a calm, even tone. "Life will not be so bad for you on the ship. The key," he adds, "is to find a way to occupy your time."

I clench my fists, willing myself not to kick his desk, not to throw the chair I am sitting in at him, not to pull down the walls that surround me. "In fifty years I'm going to be older than my parents, and you're telling me to find a way to *occupy my freaking time*?!"

"A hobby, perhaps?"

"GAH!" I screech. I lunge for his desk, about to sweep everything on it onto the floor. The doctor stands, too, but instead of trying to stop me, he reaches for the cabinet behind him. There is something so calmly disturbing about this action that I pause as he pulls open a drawer and, after rummaging around for a bit, withdraws a small, square, white package, similar to the hand wipes I used to get from the Chinese restaurant Jason took me to on our first date.

"This is a med patch," the doctor says. "Tiny needles glued to the adhesive will administer calming drugs directly into your system. I do not want to spend the next fifty years medicating you just so you stay calm." He sets the white package in the center of his desk, then looks me square in the eyes. "But I will."

The med patch lies there, a line in the sand that I do not want to cross. I sit back down.

"Now, do you have any hobbies or skills that you could put to use on the ship?"

Hobbies? Hobbies are something ninety-year-old men have as they piddle around the garage.

"I liked history in school," I finally say, although I feel like a dork for thinking of school before anything else.

"We don't have school here." Before I can contemplate life without school, the doctor continues. "Not now. And besides, at this point, the life you lived is, well . . ."

Oh. I see his point. My life, my *former* life, already is history. What will it be like to see the things I loved and lived in a history book? What if I flip through the pages and recognize someone? What if I recognize myself, staring up at me from the pages of a history tome older than I am?

"I was on the cross-country team," I say. The doctor looks at me blankly. I realize the phrase "cross-country" means nothing to him, here on a ship where there is no country to cross. "I ran. It's a sport where you run."

The doctor looks skeptical. "You can, of course, 'run' whenever you'd like. But . . ." His gaze roves over me. "It may not be advisable. You will stand out on board this ship . . . I cannot vouch for your safety when you leave the Hospital."

My stomach clenches. What kind of people are these? And what does he mean by "safety"? Does he think I'll be attacked?

The doctor, however, seems oblivious to my uneasiness. "What other activities could you do?"

"I was on the yearbook staff. I like photography," I say, still a little distracted by thoughts of how I'm going to be treated when I go outside.

"Hmm." The doctor sounds disapproving. "We do not actually allow photography on board the ship outside of scientific uses."

Even though I'm determined to prove to the doctor I can be calm without medication, I can't help but show my disbelief. "Are you serious? Photography's banned?"

"What other activities do you enjoy?" he says, completely ignoring my question.

"I don't know," I say, throwing my hands up. "What do most of the teenagers around here do? Clubs? Parties?"

"We do not have school or parties or anything of that sort," the doctor says slowly, replacing the two stray pencils on his desk into the cup, "because we do not have children aboard the ship. Not currently."

"What?" I ask, leaning forward, as if by doing so I will actually understand what he is saying.

The door behind me slides open.

The doctor stands to greet the man walking through the door, but I don't. He's old, but he walks into the office as if he owns it, despite a slight limp.

"This is Amy." The doctor sounds out my name as if he's unsure of its pronunciation, even though it's only three letters long.

"Obviously," the man replies. He remains standing, sneering down at me. "Tell me what you know about *Godspeed*."

"Is that the name of this ship?"

He nods impatiently. It seems so weird to me, that this ship has a name with "God" in it. This too-neat office that smells of disinfectant and something soured doesn't remind me of God at all.

"They called it Project Ark Ship before I was frozen. All I know about it is that I'm on it. We're heading to a planet in the Centauri system that NASA discovered a few years before I was born. It's a generation ship—you all are supposed to have been born on the ship, keeping it running and all, until we get there and my parents and the rest of the people from the mission can terraform the new planet."

The man nods. "That's all you need to know about *Godspeed*," he says. "Although you should also know this. I am Eldest."

Good for you, I think. *Congrats on being old.*

He takes my silence as a cue to continue. "This ship does not need a captain. Its path was determined long ago, and the ship was designed to operate without need of human interference." The old man sighs. "But while the ship doesn't need guidance, the people do. I am the oldest. I am their leader." The old man picks up a round paperweight from the doctor's desk. He contemplates it as if he's holding the world in his hands, and I realize that to him, the world is this ship.

"Okay."

"As such, everyone follows my rules."

"Fine."

"Including you."

"Whatever."

Eldest glares. He slams the paperweight back on the doctor's desk—but not in the same place it had been originally. The doctor's hands twitch as if he'd like to move it to its proper place, but he restrains himself.

"To that end," he continues, "I cannot let any disturbance disrupt the lives of the people. And *you* are a disturbance."

"Me?"

"You. You don't look like us, you don't sound like us, and you are not one of us."

"I'm not some kind of freak!"

"On this ship you are. First," he says, before I can protest, "there's your physical appearance."

"Huh?"

"We're monoethnic," the doctor says, leaning forward. "We all share the same physical features—skin, hair, and eye color. It's to be expected on a ship where there's no new blood; our features have genetically merged."

I glance down at my red hair falling over my shoulders, at my pale, pale skin that always freckles too much. It's a long-shot difference from the dark olive skin and graying hair that still holds traces of deep brown on the doctor. Eldest's hair is mostly white, but I can tell it, too, was once dark to match his skin and eyes.

"Not only are you freakishly white with weird hair," Eldest adds, "you're also abnormally young."

"I'm seventeen!"

"Yes," the doctor says slowly, as if even my age disgusts him. "But, see, we regulate mating." He's attempting to speak with a calm, kind voice, but he keeps looking nervously at Eldest.

"Mating?" I say, incredulous. They have rules about sex?

"We have to prevent incest."

"Oh, ew!"

Eldest ignores me. "And control is more easily maintained with set generations. The younger generation, which applies to most of the people in this Ward, are in their twenties and on the cusp of their Season. Doc's generation—the older generation—are in their early forties."

My brain whirls. "You're telling me that there are two generations on the ship, and everyone is either twenty or forty?"

The old man nods. "There's some variation; some children are born a little late or early, some families have multiple children. We're still recouping our population loss from when a great Plague hit several gens ago."

"A plague?"

"A devastating one," the doctor jumps in. "It killed over three-quarters of the ship's population, and we still haven't recouped our losses."

I think back to my last year on Earth. Daddy took me to the observatory in Utah to celebrate the completion of Project Ark Ship. They had built the ship primarily in space, using a series of several hundred shuttle launches to take materials and people to the build site in orbit around Earth. It was the largest space project ever attempted by any nation.

But it just looked like a bright round blob in the telescope to me.

"About twenty-five years ago, the International Space Station took over a decade to complete and was around three-hundred-feet long. Now we have a ship that took less than four years to complete and is larger than the entire island of Iwo Jima," Daddy had said, pride ringing in his voice.

I didn't like associating a ship I would be on for three centuries with an island known for a bloody battle in a bloody war.

Now, staring up at these two men who have lived their whole lives on this ship, who have in their history a plague that nearly decimated it—now the comparison seems apt.

"But as we were saying," the doctor continues, "most of the people on board are either in their early twenties or early forties."

I look up at the old man. "You're not in your early forties," I say. The statement comes out much more obnoxious than I'd meant it to.

The old man's eyes bore into me with a look of either speculation or revulsion—I'm not sure which.

"I am fifty-six." I hold back a snort; the old man looks way older than fifty-six. "I am the Eldest of the ship—the oldest person, and the one with the right to rule. Before each generation, an Elder is born to be that generation's leader."

"There's no one on the ship older than fifty-six?" I ask.

"A few grays still exist, all sixty or so, but they won't last much longer."

"Why not?"

"Old people die. It's what they do."

This doesn't seem right to me. I mean, yeah, sixty is way old . . . but it's not like people reach a certain age and just die. Lots of people are older than sixty. My great-grandma was ninety-four before she died.

"What about that boy?"

"What boy?" Eldest asks.

"She's talking about Elder."

Eldest grunts.

"Amy," the doctor says, "Elder was born between the generations. He is sixteen years old. When the Season starts and the young generation begin to mate, the children born from that will be the generation that Elder rules after Eldest passes to the stars. The boy you met is the next Eldest."

"Where's the other one?" I ask.

"Other what?" The doctor weighs his round paperweight in his hands and carefully puts it back where it was before Eldest picked it up.

"Other Eldey-thingy. There's you," I say to Eldest. "You're in charge of the doctor's generation. And the boy I met will be in charge of the new generation. But what about all those twenty-year-olds? Who's in charge of them?"

The doctor and Eldest exchange a look.

"That Elder died," Eldest says. His face is dark, set. I glance up at the doctor. His face is downcast, the folds of his crow's feet crinkling deeper.

I wonder just how that Elder died.

"Clearly," Eldest says, a tone of finality in his voice, "you are different. Freakish appearance, abnormally young."

"So?"

"I do not like differences. Differences cause trouble."

The doctor twitches nervously. He starts rearranging his desktop again.

"Gee, I'm real sorry about all that. But, you know, it's not like I wanted to be here."

"Regardless. The easiest thing to do would be to deposit you among the stars."

"Eldest!" The doctor steps forward, a look of shock and concern on his face.

"What do you mean?" I ask.

"We have release hatches." Eldest speaks slowly, as if talking to someone stupid. "They open up to the outside."

The meaning of his words sinks slowly into my skin until I have absorbed it with all that I am.

"You want to just dump me in space?" My voice is low, but not for long. "It's not like I've done anything wrong! I didn't wake myself up, you know!"

Eldest shrugs. "It would be by far the simplest solution. You are, after all, nonessential."

"We can't do that," the doctor says, and I totally forgive him for being creepy and threatening me with drugs. At least he doesn't want to let me implode in space.

"No, Doc," Eldest says. "It's very important that you understand, that *she* understands that yes, we could just dump her in space. We could," he repeats, gazing at me.

"But we *won't*," the doctor says firmly. "She can stay here in the Ward. That will keep her away from the general population. She won't cause as much of a disturbance if she stays here."

"You think so?" Eldest says, his voice soft but doubtful.

"I'm sure of it. Besides, the Season will begin soon. That will distract the others."

Eldest narrows his eyes at the doctor. Something the doctor said there has struck the wrong chord with him, that much's for sure. He opens his mouth, notices me watching him avidly, and glares at me. "Come outside with me, Doc," Eldest commands.

The doctor looks nervous. Guilty.

"Oh, don't go on my account," I say, leaning back in the chair. "Go ahead and say whatever it is you want to say in front of me."

Eldest turns to the door. "Doc," he orders.

The doctor scampers up and follows Eldest out.

As soon as the door zips shut behind them, I leap from my chair and press my ear against the metal. Nothing. I go back to the doctor's desk, dump out his pencils, and put the cup against the door, like they do in those old Disney movies. More nothing.

"—last time!" Eldest roars so loudly that I almost drop the cup. I cram my ear against the metal door, straining for sound.

"It's *not* like last time," the doctor hisses. He must be standing closer to the door—his voice is softer, but I can hear him better. I wonder if he's moved closer just for my benefit.

Eldest, meanwhile, has lowered his voice, and I only catch snatches of what he says. "*Really?*—The Season starting . . . someone unplugged—again—and you . . ."

"You know it can't be *him* again," the doctor says. There's some mumbling, a deep rumble of a voice, but I can't discern it. I catch one word: "Impossible."

"Whabout *you*?" Their strange accent isn't helping my eavesdropping, either.

"Me?" the doctor says.

"You." I catch the sneer in Eldest's voice, even through the metal door. "You were sympathetic to him last time, don't try to deny it."

"—posterous," the doctor mumbles, " . . . could as easily say it was *you*."

Another low grumbling. It sounds almost like Eldest is actually growling.

"Well?" the doctor exclaims. "Elder told me you were teaching him about discord. How am I to know this isn't all some sick trial you've devised to test the boy!" *Something, something*—stupid door makes it impossible to hear properly—"like last time."

Eldest's voice deepens and grows gravelly. There's some sort of scuffling, and before I have time to move, the door zips open. The doctor bumps right into me, and I do drop the cup this time. It rolls across the floor, the only sound as the three of us stare at one another.

Eldest's face is hard, harsh. "I'll be keeping a close eye on this . . . situation," he says, but he's looking at Doc, not me. He straightens his tunic-like shirt and turns to leave. Then he pauses and looks back at me. "Don't leave the Hospital grounds. I haven't decided what to do with you yet."

"I'm not some sort of prisoner!" I shout at him.

"On this ship, we all are," he says, and then he's gone.

"Don't worry about him," the doctor says, reaching over to pat my shoulder. I shrug him away. "He won't put you in a release hatch."

"Humph." I didn't quite believe that.

"I have set you up in a room with all the appropriate necessities. You will be living here, at least for now. Do you have any questions?"

Is he really going to pretend like nothing happened? Like I couldn't hear what they were arguing about? All right, I *didn't* hear most of it, but I heard enough.

"What happened last time?" I ask.

"What do you mean?" the doctor says, sitting down at his desk. He waves graciously at the chair across from him, and I slump down in it.

I give him a look, but he ignores it. "Come on. Really?"

The doctor starts straightening the pencils I dumped on his desk. He's seriously OCD. But . . . I wonder how much of him is real. He's as expressionless with me as he is with Eldest. I doubt he likes me—but he did stand up for me when Eldest threatened to throw me out the hatch. As for how the doctor feels about Eldest . . . I thought he respected him, maybe even feared him, but he seemed to move closer to the door when I was trying to listen in on his conversation with Eldest. Did he do that on purpose? Now—is he trying to get me to ask the right questions? Or am I just playing mind games with myself?

"Last Season," the doctor says, "we had some trouble. But it has nothing to do with this."

"It might. How do you know?"

"Because the person who caused trouble last Season is dead," the doctor says. "Anything else?"

He's getting angry, maybe already regretting that he promised not to throw me off the ship. He likes things organized, and I've already proven more than once just in this little office that he can't organize me like he can his pencils.

"Yeah," I say, unable to keep the aggression from my voice. "Why was I woken up early? What happened?"

The doctor frowns. "I'm not sure," he says finally. "But it appears as if someone . . . disconnected you."

"Disconnected me?"

"The cryostasis chambers are attached to a very simple electrical device that monitors temperatures and life support systems. You were simply . . . disconnected from the power unit. Turned off. Unplugged."

"Who unplugged me?!" I demand, rising. The doctor's hand twitches, inching closer to the med patch on his desk. I sit back down, but my heart is racing, my breathing shallow. Between that conversation in the hall and this revelation, it's clear that something's going on. And I'm stuck in the middle of it.

"We are not sure. But we will find out." Then, so low I almost don't hear it, he adds, "But it had to have been someone with access." His eyes shoot to the door behind me, and I know he's thinking of Eldest. Which is stupid: Eldest didn't want me dead until I was unfrozen. But . . . why would *anyone* unplug me? To kill me? But why me? I am, as the doctor so kindly pointed out, nonessential.

And then another question, one much more important, rises above everything else. "What about my parents? Is whoever unplugged me going to unplug my parents?" I remember choking on cryo liquid; I remember believing that I would drown in that box. I don't want my parents to feel the same thing. I don't want to run the risk of losing them forever if their boxes are opened too late after the ice melts.

"Go back to your chamber to rest. Try not to think these disturbing thoughts. You can rest assured that your parents—and all the rest of the frozens—are protected. Eldest will see to that."

I narrow my eyes. I doubt very much that old man will do anything to help anyone else. He'd probably think setting guards around the cryo chambers would be too much of a "disturbance." And with his callousness, I wouldn't be too surprised to find out that he unplugged me just to see if it would kill me.

But I cannot think here. I cannot figure out what to do. Even though I don't want to rest, I do need to be somewhere alone with my thoughts. So, I leave.

A pile of crushed flowers rests beside my door. I bend and pick them up. The blooms remind me of tiger lilies, but they are bigger and brighter than any tiger lilies I remember from Earth. Even though they're ruined, a part of me wants to set them in a bowl of water— they're beautiful and their fragrance is sweet. In the end, though, I stand up and leave the broken flowers in the hall. They remind me too much of me.

18: ELDER

"Oh, here you are," Eldest says casually as he climbs up the hatch that connects the Keeper Level to the Shipper Level.

I lie on the cool metal floor below the metal screen hiding the fake stars. My head is pounding from Eldest's little noise trick. I have never in all my life had a headache this bad before. Every time I let my head roll on the floor, it feels as if a ton of weight is crashing around, slamming against my skull, flattening my brain into useless mush. I try to stay still.

"That was a frexing dirty thing to do," I mutter, pressing the palms of my hands into my forehead.

"What? Oh, the tonal thing. Well, next time don't ignore my com."

"I can if I want to!" I know it sounds childish, but I can barely frexing *see* with this headache. I stare up at the dull metal ceiling, grateful the star screen is blocked from view. Just thinking about the tiny pin-pricks of the lightbulb stars makes my head ache more.

Eldest walks across the Great Room to his chamber, goes inside, and returns a few moments later with something in his hand. He tosses it at me. A lavender-colored med patch. I rip it open and apply it directly to my forehead, the tiny needles catching on my skin like hook-and-loop tape. I breathe deeply, willing the medicine to take effect and ease my pulsing, throbbing head.

"Let this be a lesson," Eldest says. His voice rings out across the Great Room. There's no need for him to shout—it's only us in here. I wonder if he's speaking so loudly just to aggravate my headache more. "The job of the Eldest is to prevent discord. Through the centuries, we have perfected the prevention of the first main cause of discord by eliminating differences."

"I know," I moan, rubbing the med-patch on my forehead deeper into my skin. Did I really need a lesson *now*?

Eldest starts to squat down next to me, but his knees creak, so he stands up and hobbles around instead, pacing. "Don't you see?" he finally says, exasperated. "That girl could not *be* more different!"

"So?"

Eldest throws up his hands. "Chaos! Discord! Fighting! She is nothing but trouble!"

I cock my eyebrow, grateful that the med patch is already making me feel normal again. "Being a bit dramatic, aren't you?"

Eldest drops his hands and glares at me. "She could ruin this ship."

"She's just a girl."

Eldest growls.

"Wait . . ." I say, leaning up and staring at him. "That's it, isn't it? She's a girl, and she's my age. You're afraid we'll . . ." My face burns at the thought. If Eldest is afraid of what Amy and I could do together, well, to be honest, that's a possibility I'm rather hoping for.

"Don't be such a chutz." Eldest laughs, and my face grows even hotter. "I'm not worried about that at all."

I splutter as I jump up. Does he think that I couldn't? I know I'm not old enough for my Season yet, but I also know that I'm more than capable. When I look at Amy . . . I know what I'd like to do with her, and I know that I could. How dare he think I couldn't! I am not the child he thinks I am!

"You're losing focus," Eldest says, snapping his fingers in front of my face. "This is all beside the point. The point is, that girl is going to cause trouble."

"Well, what are you going to do about it?" I ask, sinking back to the floor.

Eldest appraises me. "You'll be the next Eldest. What would *you* do about it?"

"Nothing." I tilt my chin up at him. "She's not hurting anything. She'll be fine."

"An Eldest can never do 'nothing.'" Eldest is wearing this smug little smile on his face that makes me want to just punch him. Before I can think of anything snappy to say back to him, Eldest holds a finger up to me and turns away, pressing his wi-com button.

"Mm-hm," he says to whoever has linked to him. "I see. Yes, of course."

He turns back to me. "I'm going to the Shipper Level. Stay here and read more about the leaders of Sol-Earth. I've left a floppy for you in the Learning Center."

"But—" Eldest is on the Shipper Level these days far more than he used to be. "Is everything okay?"

Eldest gives me an appraising look. Weighing whether or not I'm

worthy of hearing his thoughts, sharing his problems. And I see it
there, in the hunch of his shoulders, the uneasy way he carries his leg,
the one he limps on. He can feel the weight of the ship on him, just like
I can. No—he feels it more. He's carried the weight longer than me,
and he's carried it not just for himself, but the Elder before me who
died and couldn't take over.

For just a moment, I see Amy through his eyes: as a problem.

"We need to have a talk when we get back." Eldest's tone now
is serious, uncomfortable. He shifts on his feet, but does not head
toward the hatch.

"What about?"

"The Season is coming soon. . . ."

"Oh." I knew about the Season already. While I was living on the
Feeder Level, it was easy to learn about what happened between a
male and a female. I saw it with the cows when I lived on the ranch;
with the goats on the farm; with the sheep near the fields. I'd have
been stupid not to notice what the animals did. Several of the women
who kept me during my time on the Feeder Level explained reproduction to me. At the time, it seemed a bit uncomfortable and gross,
but they all assured me that when my Season came, I'd be ready,
and a woman from Harley's gen would have a second Season with
me. Since meeting Amy, I think I know what they mean about being
ready.

"During the Season, you will see, er . . ." Eldest voice trails off.

"I know what the Season is," I say. I am as uncomfortable as he. It
was bad enough to learn about mating from a matronly farmer, worse
yet to hear about it from Eldest.

"Still, we should talk—" This time, Eldest is interrupted by his wi-com. He presses the button and says something softly, so I don't hear it.

"Hey," I say. "HEY."

He raises one finger, telling me to give him a second, and mumbles more into his wi-com.

"Quit ignoring me," I say loudly.

Eldest sighs and disconnects the wi-com. "I've got to go."

"Aren't you going to tell me what that was all about?"

Eldest heaves a sigh, as if I'm a child pestering him.

"Look," I say, "I'm getting sick of secrets."

"Fine," Eldest says, already walking to the hatch with his uneven gait. "You study; we'll talk when I get back." Before I can protest, he's gone.

The med patch has worked its wonders: My headache is mostly gone. I don't like the idea of how easy it would be for Eldest to do that again, though. Maybe I should keep some med patches with me.

My first thought is to go to the Hospital, where all the meds for the ship are stored. Doc keeps them locked up, but if Orion can get extra mental meds, it shouldn't be that hard for me to get some med patches. But, then again, that's what got me in trouble in the first place. Then I think about Eldest's chamber. I know he stores extra med supplies there.

But to do that would mean sneaking into Eldest's room, breaking the unspoken law of privacy.

I may have tested the door handles on the fourth floor of the Hospital (okay, fine, I broke in), but I've never gone into someone's private space without permission first.

But then I remember Orion's advice. With Eldest, to get what I want, I'll *have* to be sneaky.

I tell myself as I stand and walk toward Eldest's chamber that I am only going to turn the knob, not even push the door open, but even as I mentally relay these words, I recognize that I am lying to myself so I don't lose my courage.

My hand trembles as I reach for the knob.

"Com link: Harley," chirps the pleasant female voice of my wi-com.

"Hey, Harley," I say, hoping the quaver on my voice doesn't carry through the wi-coms.

"What was wrong with you earlier?"

"I'll tell you later."

"Who's the new girl? Where'd she come from? I thought Doc already ID'd all the loons."

"I'm busy, Harley."

Harley crows with laughter. "Busy! Ha! You just want to keep her to yourself!"

That's too close to the truth, so I disconnect the link.

Eldest's door stands in front of me, mockingly.

This time, my hand doesn't shake. The door swings open. Although there's an old-fashioned Sol-Earth lock built into the door, Eldest has—luckily—forgotten to lock it.

I look around. This is not what I expected. Eldest is something of a slob. Like me. I smile. Stepping over a pile of dirty clothes, I make my way to the neatest area of the room—the desk. There are only three things on the top: a small, dark plastic bottle like the kind Doc uses for meds, a large glass bottle filled with clear liquid, and a box. A box that I recognize: the one that Eldest came to fetch the other day, just before I opened the ceiling and revealed a canopy of false stars. This is the box I was trying to look at then—this is the box that I had thought held all the answers to my leadership.

I rip the top of the box off expecting . . . something brilly at least. But all that's inside is a scale model made of resin that resembles an engine, but it's more cylindrical than the ones the tractors use on the Feeder Level. The replica is fascinating in its level of detail. When I push a button on the side, the engine breaks in half, exposing its insides. I poke at the pieces. From my studies, I'd guess this is a lead-cooled fast reactor, the same kind of engine *Godspeed* uses. But if so, this is the closest I've ever been to the heart of the ship I will one day lead.

I snap the engine closed, perhaps more forcefully than I should have.

This is just one more secret Eldest is keeping from me.

I examine the bottles on the desk. The big one is filled with liquid that smells like fumes—the drink some of the Shippers make. Eldest has never let me taste it. When I sip it, though, I nearly spew the stuff all over Eldest's unmade bed. The back of my throat burns, and all the little hairs in my nose shrivel. When it hits my stomach, I gag.

The small bottle contains twenty or so mental meds.

Well, now I know why Doc and Eldest didn't let me step down from being Elder after I started taking the Inhibitor pills. Eldest is as crazy as I am! I crush the bottle against my hand. Eldest knew how upset I was when Doc made me stay in the Ward for the year. I used to fight so hard against taking the pills.

Why wouldn't he just admit that he was on mental meds, too?

I *hate* his secrets and lies.

I slam the door behind me and head to my own room for a drink of water—an old Feeder wives' remedy for nerves.

Good thing, too—a moment later, Eldest bursts through the hatch, calling for me.

"Come with me," he says. "We've got a situation."

19: AMY

Everything about the room I have been given by the doctor is an odd mixture of personal and industrial. The colors are bland—gray and white—but someone has stenciled in a peeling green ivy chain around the doorframe and hand painted a vine of flowers along the baseboards. The attached bathroom is cold and decorated with plain white tile and chrome, but the towels smell of lemons and lavender.

The best way to clear my head of all these disturbing thoughts is to take the hottest shower I can stand. I peel off the clothes the doctor gave me earlier. They are shades of brown, a pale taupe tunic and chocolate pants. I think they are homemade. Although the stitches are even and clean, they're not machine made. The cloth is smooth and not itchy, but there are tiny pricks and flaws in the fabric that imply craftsmanship, not manufacturing. It's so weird. I kind of expected space suits and shiny material. The weekend before we were frozen, Mom and Daddy and I stayed up all night watching ancient sci-fi movies—*Star Trek* and *Star Wars* and *Star*-something else. I envisioned everyone wearing uniforms or with crazy hair or something, but I'm wearing stuff that could have been made for a Renaissance fair.

It takes me a moment to figure out the shower. There are buttons, not knobs, and more steam than water pours from small mesh squares embedded in the walls of the shower stall. Two bars of soap line a tiny shelf near the top of the shower. There are no shampoo or conditioner bottles, but the round bar of soap lathers in my hair when I test it.

I mash buttons, trying to figure out how to get real water—the steam's not rinsing the suds from my hair. Suddenly, I hit the right one, and a jet of cold water shoots out of a nozzle near my face. I sputter, and for one horrible moment, the shower reminds me of when Ed and Hassan filled the glass box with cryo liquid before I was frozen. I have to remind myself I'm not drowning, I don't have to breathe in the liquid, I won't be frozen again. It happened centuries ago, but the memory is still fresh to me. My knees wobble. I have to lean against the warm tile for several minutes, breathing deeply, before I can stand on my own again.

When I leave the shower, I stand in the room, a towel wrapped around my body, my hair dripping. It feels very quiet and alone. I think back to the boy who was here when I woke up, Elder, and I'm surprised to realize that I actually miss him. Now that he's gone, this room makes me feel like a trespasser.

I wrap the towel tighter around me. Nothing here is personal, other than the ivy decorating the baseboards in chipping green paint. No books, no TV. There is a desk, and on it is a floppy piece of plastic about the size and thickness of a legal-size sheet of paper. When I was on the yearbook staff in high school, I took the drama club picture. They all posed with these things called color gels—really thin pieces of plastic they could attach to the stage lights to change the color. This piece of plastic on the desk is just like the color gels, but clear, and when I touch it, a screen flashes on, requesting my ID. This is a computer?

On the opposite wall is a shelf and, to the right of it, the door. Beside the door, where a light switch should be, is a small metal square inset with a bar. I push it. Nothing happens, but the bar spins in place.

"Identity unknown." A tinny female voice emanates throughout the room. "Voice command."

"Umm," I say.

"Command unknown," the computer voice says. "Prompt command: lights, door."

"Lights off?" I try.

The lights in the room flick off.

I roll my finger over the bar again. "Identity unknown. Voice command."

"Lights on," I say, and the lights turn back on.

Beside the rolly-bar that controls the lights are two rectangles of metal built into the wall, one about the size of a Post-it note, the other larger, roughly the same size and shape of an envelope. As I get closer, I notice a small button under each rectangle. I push the button under the small rectangle, and the metal disappears, showing a cavity just large enough for me to fit two fingers into it. It's empty. When I push the button under the larger rectangle, though, the door doesn't slide open. I push again, harder. A small *beep!* echoes through my silent room. I have just enough time to panic—have I done something stupid? Have I set off an alarm?—when the door zips open.

Behind the door is another cavity, just like the smaller one. But it's not empty. Inside is a fat, steaming roll of bread that oozes a bit at the side. It reminds me of a Hot Pocket, but no Hot Pocket ever smelled this good. I reach inside, my mouth already watering. The bottom of the cavity peels away under my touch—a napkin. The pastry is warm, and I can't resist—I eat three or four bites of it before I really taste it.

But once I do taste it, it becomes hard to swallow. It's a meat pie, filled with gravy and some vegetables I can recognize. But the round green things that look like peas are larger and chewier than any peas I've ever had. And the chunks I took for potatoes aren't potatoes at all. They're something like tofu, but thicker, and when I suck the gravy off a chunk, it feels like rubber on my tongue and tastes about as appealing. There is very little spice in this meat pie—definitely salt, and something sort of sweet, like cinnamon, but no pepper, nothing with kick.

And the meat . . . it's not any meat I know. Red meat, but no fat on it at all. Each piece is a perfect cube, and I can't help but wonder—is it that way because of some skillful cook who cut it, or is it that way because it's not really meat? I imagine ice trays filled not with water, but red gooey meat-like substitute, and I gag and drop the remains of the pie into the small canister by the door that looks like a trash can. As soon as it lands in the trashcan, the bottom of it zips away, revealing a long, black tunnel that sucks the meat pie and napkin away.

Nothing remains but a waft of steam from the rectangle metal by the door and a scent of unseasoned gravy in the air that is both strangely familiar and deeply alien.

I shake my head. This technology is better than anything on Earth. Another sign that I don't belong here.

I wish I had someone to share all these discoveries with. My eyes drift to the chair, and I can almost see Elder sitting there. Elder, with his kind eyes. The only person on this ship who doesn't seem to wish I was off it.

I think about my parents. They are on this ship too, but they are still fifty years away.

I screw up my eyes and will myself not to think anymore.

And then I think about how I was unplugged, and how they might be too.

I shiver, and I tell myself that it's just because it's chilly in here. A wardrobe stands against the far wall, beside the large piece of metal hanging from the wall that I think covers a window—light creeps in around its edges. The clothes inside smell musty, but when I shake some of them out, they seem to be clean and in good shape. I cannot find a bra in any of the drawers, but one drawer is filled with cotton panties. I am a little grossed out, putting on panties when I don't know where they came from, or if they once belonged to someone else, but they don't look old or used. I let the towel drop to the floor and wiggle into a tan tunic and dark pair of pants, both of which have been decorated at the hems with tiny painted yellow flowers. When I drop the towel inside the hamper by the wardrobe, the lid snaps shut. A puff of steam emerges from under the lid, and then the hamper pops open. The towel inside is dry and clean.

There is too much about this ship I don't know. That will be what I do first: find others, learn about the ship, and figure out what to do to protect my parents from whoever unplugged me. Because even though I want them more than anything right now, I don't want them to wake up cold, alone, and drowning under glass.

A crack of light lines the carpet under the square piece of metal hanging on the wall beside the wardrobe. When I touch the thin raised metal, it whirrs away, revealing a smudged, dirty window looking out onto bright green fields.

So this is where I will spend the next 49 years and 266 days.

It's not ugly. It's not what I expected. There *is* green here. Rolling hills spread out from the lawn of the Hospital down a dusty dirt road. The pastures and fields are divided by dark green hedges or brown fence posts. The cows are the closest, and I assume the white fluffy dots further down are sheep or goats. Neat rows of vibrant verdant plants spread out like a crazy quilt. And there, on the edge, is something that looks like oversize stacked LEGOs—train cargo cars or the trailers on big rig trucks stacked upon each other in rows, each painted a different bright color. The jumbled stack of colors reminds me vaguely of Walt Disney World. When I was little and lived in Florida, my parents took me there every summer. It seemed massive then, giant, like a whole country in a theme park, but I realize with a shock that Cinderella's castle would fit in this metal bubble, and that this level is easily fifty times bigger than the whole Magic Kingdom.

I try to count the trailers, but can't. Just how many people live on this ship? There's room there for at least a couple thousand.

I wonder if Elder lives in one of the colored boxes.

My eyes drift toward the horizon.

There is no skyline. Because there is no sky. Cool gray metal rises over the brightly painted boxes. The metal curves over the city, arching over everything. Near the top, a sickly shade of blue replaces the gray. I suppose they were trying to make it look like a sky, but they didn't do a good job of it.

Smack in the middle is a bright yellow-orange ball of light. It doesn't hurt to look at it like it hurts to look at the sun, but it's still painful. Maybe if I'd never seen the sun, I would be impressed by this glowing source of light and heat made by man. But I *have* seen the sun, and it is not this tiny false thing, it is so much grander than that. I stare at it until my eyes prick with water, and when I blink away, I keep my eyes shut longer than I need to.

Images of broken light dance behind my eyelids. How could this giant lamp compare to the sun?

Everything is wrong here. Shattered. Broken.

Like the light.

Like me.

I never thought about how important the sky was until I didn't have one.

I am surrounded by walls.

I have just replaced one box for another.

20: ELDER

Eldest and I don't talk as we descend in the elevator to the cryo level. We particularly don't talk about how the alarm on the table on the fourth floor lay open and smashed, its guts spewing from it and spilling out on the floor. Broken. Useless.

When the doors slide open, the lights are already on.

"Back here!" Doc's voice calls.

Eldest's strides are long, although uneven with his limp, and I have to rush to keep up as we go down the aisle with the numbered doors. I seek out Number 42, but we're going too fast for me to find it without stopping.

We round the corner and start down the aisle numbered 75–100.

One of the little doors is opened. The tray table has already been extended, and a cryo box lays on it. Doc is standing in front of it, his back to us, bent over the box, but even though he blocks our view, I can tell that something is wrong.

Eldest doesn't hesitate as we approach.

I do.

The man inside the box is dead, floating in water with blue spar-kles. His arms are bent, his fingers curled into claws, and I know he died trying to escape the box as the cryo liquid melted. I know because his eyes are open, and his mouth is a gaping maw, and his face is twisted in anger and defeat. There is a pool of blue-specked cryo liquid on the floor underneath him, and red marks around his too-pale throat.

Eldest and Doc lift the lid together. The dead man inside bobs, his fingers and nose and knees pushing up at the viscous layer of the water.

"Who was he?" I ask.

"Number 100." The last box in the row, the last person cryogeni-cally frozen.

This means nothing to me, but Eldest sucks in his breath. Doc nods at him in a knowing way.

The dead man's head jerks and I jump back, startled. But Doc is just pulling at the tubes in the man's mouth. With each yank, his body twitches violently. Water splashes from the box. I step back, but it still splatters on my boots. I go over to the table at the end of the aisle and pick up Doc's floppy, running my finger along the edge to turn it on. The screen glows. I rest my thumb on the scanner square, and a mes-sage flashes: "Eldest/Elder override: full access granted." The screen fills up with images—icons, folders, notes. I search for Number 100, and after tapping around a bit, I find it: the dead man's folder.

NAME: WILLIAM ROBERTSON
NUMBER: 100

Occupation: Leadership specialist

Status: Essential to offensive organization

Prior Experience: United States Marines, active duty in War of—

Eldest snatches the floppy from my hands. With a swipe of his finger, he blacks the screen.

"Pay attention," he growls. He jerks his head toward Doc, who is finally reaching the end of the tubing. A small electrical panel pops out of the dead man's mouth, and he sinks further beneath the cryo liquid.

"Well?" Eldest says. "Was it a *malfunction*? Another one?"

"Give me a minute." Doc is bent over the electrical box. He pushes a button, and a door springs open. He pulls out a tiny round metallic object that rests on his fingertip. Eldest hands Doc the floppy he had taken from me, and Doc presses the computer chip into it.

"*Well?*"

" . . . It was turned off." Doc's voice is hollow.

"Turned off?"

"What are you talking about?" I ask.

"This." Doc points to the blinking black box near the head of the glass coffin. The light flashes red. "Someone opened the cover and flipped the switch." He shoots Eldest a look. "Someone with access."

"This was done on purpose?" I ask, but I suspect the answer already.

Doc glares, and I hope that the anger in his eyes is not directed at me. "Someone came down here. Pulled this drawer out. And flipped this switch. Then walked away as the cryo liquid melted, walked away as the man inside slowly revitalized, slowly died, drowning in his own liquid."

I want to look away from Doc, but what else should I look at? Eldest, whose rage is burning behind his stony face? Or the dead man with unblinking eyes that shimmer under the blue-speckled cryo liquid?

"Who would do that?" I ask.

"Who *could* do that?" Eldest asks, his deep voice rumbling behind me like the roar of the centrifugal machine in the labs.

"Few people know about this level," Doc says. He looks away, and I can already see him slipping into his scientist-doctor mask, the one that's cool and calculating, the one he wears when he diagnoses in the Ward. "Us," he says, looking at both me and Eldest in turn. "But also some of the scientists. The ones who have worked in the"—he pauses, flicks his eyes from Eldest to me—"in the *other* lab, they know, of course."

Other lab? I think, shooting Doc a look. I bite back the question— I've got to be careful what I say, or they won't tell me anything. "*Why?*" I ask instead. "Who cares who knows about this place—why would anyone want to do this? Why would anyone *intentionally* kill someone frozen?"

Silence.

Then: "Why it happened doesn't matter. What's important is to find out who—and to take it from there." Eldest's voice is cold and horrible.

"But—"

Doc steps in front of me, drawing Eldest a few steps away.

"Promise me," he hisses. "Promise me this isn't some sort of sick test you've devised for Elder."

Eldest gives Doc a quelling, disgusted look, as if he's affronted Doc would even think it.

But he doesn't answer.

"Let's take care of this," Eldest says to me. He shoves past Doc and fiddles with a latch near the table that I'd not seen before. The table breaks away from the little door that had held the dead man's box, and Eldest wheels the table down the aisle. The cryo liquid sloshes back and forth with his pace, spilling bubbles of sparkling liquid onto the ground. I can hear a soft *thump, swish, thump* over the thuds of Eldest's feet, and I know it's from the body hitting the glass, muffled by the liquid.

"Come on," Doc says. We follow the splatters of liquid like bread-crumbs in that Sol-Earth children's tale.

Past the rows and rows of little doors. Past three rows of narrow metal lockers, each with a simple combination lock on the door. Past a series of tables with papers and diagrams on them. Down a hall-way. And at the end of the hallway: a hatch door, made of thick metal painted a dull yellow, with a round bubble glass window in the center.

The lock on the door looks old—it's a keypad, not a thumb swipe. It must be original to the ship; we've upgraded a lot over the years. I watch as Eldest types in the code. It's simple enough to remember: *Godspeed*.

Eldest swings open the door and pushes the table inside.

"What are you—" I start, but Eldest has already lifted the edge of the table and let the thick glass coffin and the body inside it crash to the floor. Mr. William Robertson, Number 100, bounces as half the liquid sloshes out. His body hangs over the edge of the box, twisted around in a position that would have hurt if he were still alive. His open eyes stare at the ceiling, and both his hands curl up from the floor.

Eldest shoves me back out into the hallway and slams the hatch door shut after him.

"What are you doing?" I say again.

Eldest pushes the button on the keypad, the big red one without any markings on it.

Through the bubble glass window, I see the hatch door on the opposite wall fly open, and then Mr. William Robertson, Number 100, is sucked out into the stars. And I see them—the stars—real stars, millions of pinpoints of light, like glitter thrown into the air by a child. Now that I have seen these, I can never be deceived by lightbulbs again.

These stars, these real stars, are the most beautiful things I have ever seen. The stars make me believe there is a world out there beyond this ship.

And for just a moment, I envy Mr. William Robertson, Number 100, who is floating in a sea of stars.

21: AMY

The walls of the room cave in around me. Without realizing it, I have begun to pace, back and forth, back and forth, but this room is too tiny to contain me. The window is solid, thick, and cannot be opened. I begin stretching my calf muscles without realizing what I am doing. My body has decided for me: I need to run.

I wasn't kidding when I told the doctor I liked running. I joined the cross-country team as a freshman, but what I really wanted to do was run marathons. Jason used to laugh at me—he could never understand why anyone would want to run when there are video games to play and TV to watch. The closest he came to exercise was VR games.

I smile, but almost as soon as the corners of my mouth curve up, they sink again.

I can't let myself think about Jason.

I need to run.

The clothes I am wearing are wildly inappropriate for running:

loose trousers and a looser tunic paired with thin moccasin-like shoes. I smile. My mom, at least, would be happy. I always ran in these really short, tight running shorts and a sports tank, and it drove her mad. She would say it was like I was inviting the wrong sort of attention, but I just did it because I ran better in those clothes. We had a fight about it, once, a real screaming, yelling fight. It got so bad that Daddy had to jump in the middle and say I could run naked if we'd both just shut up about it. It was such a stupid thing to say that all three of us just laughed and laughed.

It hurts to think about that now.

On Earth I had short socks and Nikes. I always ran with a wide hair band on my head and music plugged into my ears. This wardrobe has only more of the same handspun clothes. I stretch my foot—the moccasins are certainly not $200 running shoes, but at least I have flexibility. It would have to do. I braid my hair and wrap the end with a bit of string I yank from one of the more raggedy pairs of trousers.

It takes me a couple of wrong turns to find my way out, but I soon discover a large room with glass walls and a pair of heavy glass doors. It's a common room of sorts; there are tables and chairs scattered casually around the room. There's only one person in the room, a tall man with biceps as big as my head. His gaze devours me, and his eyes pause too long in places I don't want him looking. I glare back at him until he turns back toward the window, but I can tell he's staring at my reflection. I don't breathe properly until the elevator doors close.

Seeing the way the tall man looked at me reminds me of the doctor's warning about leaving the Hospital.

No. I won't be a prisoner.

The elevator has buttons for four floors, and I am on the third.

I force myself to remember this, to map out where my room is in my mind. I don't want to be lost and have to ask anyone for directions.

The elevator doors open to a lounge-like room, where a heavyset nurse sits at a desk tapping information on a thin screen. My muscles are taut, ready to go. I am already running before I reach the door, my moccasins making soft *pat pat pat* noises on the cold tile floor.

The air hits me like a wall, and I stop a few feet from the door. It smells processed, cool against my nostrils, just like the air-conditioned hospital. I'd expected mechanical, industrial-cold air inside. That air felt natural, because it was just like every other air-conditioned house back on Earth, with that falsely cool, slightly stale feel to it. But outside . . . the air is still the same. This is not air that has ever felt a breeze. This is air that has been used and reused for centuries. I breathe deeply, but cannot get over how it still tastes inexpressibly like indoor air.

I look around me. The hospital opens up to a flower garden. The path under my feet is not made from natural mulch, but some sort of rubbery-plastic. I step over to the grass and jog a bit in place, warming up. Out of the corner of my eyes, I can see the steel-gray metal of the walls that curve over this level of the ship, trapping us inside a metallic bubble.

I run with my back to the closest wall, straight out into the green fields. This ship's level is vast, but not so wide that I cannot see the wall on the other side. Maybe three or four kilometers in diameter, less than the 5K track I ran for cross-country. Still, it's small enough to make me claustrophobic, but large enough to make me marvel at its size.

A road winds around the area, but I ignore it. I run through rows of corn that are as tall as my shoulders; I race along the fence dotted with white puffs of sheep and goats who keep their distance from the low fence surrounding the pasture. I startle a group of fat chickens that have wandered onto my path. They flutter up, chattering at me, but when I turn my head to look back at them moments later, they've already forgotten me.

A sheen of sticky sweat films over my arms, pooling in the creases of my elbows and at my neck. I suck in the cool, recycled air. I can almost imagine that I'm just in an elaborate gym, that when I'm done running, I can leave, and Mom will be there, waiting for me in the car, and we can go home. The thought of it makes me stop, almost brings me to my knees. I breathe deeply, not because of running now, but because if I don't, I'll start sobbing.

They're so *close*.

And so, so far away.

I run again. I cannot let myself think about anything. I can only run.

My legs pump up-down, I force myself to take longer and longer strides, to use my arms to make my entire body fall into the race. My muscles strain and burn, but I revel in the pain. Although the doctor must have done something to make my muscles not atrophy, they still feel unused, not as well-oiled as before I was frozen.

I turn a corner and see someone kneeling on the ground, hunched over some plants. I slow down, and the man looks up.

"'Lo," he says in greeting.

"Um," I say.

His eyes rove up and down, soaking in my pale skin, red hair, green eyes, and he instantly turns wary. I can see it in his face—his eyes narrow in suspicion, his mouth tightens. His grip on the trowel shifts, and it's more a weapon than a gardening tool.

I nod and continue running. When I turn back, he's still watching me, still clutching the trowel.

Run. Run harder.

When I reach that moment—when everything in my body is focused only on racing forward—that is when my mind is finally silent, when I can forget about everything the doctor said, when I don't have to remember all that I've lost and will never have again.

It's the zone. It's why I run. That feeling of being nothing but movement. I tried to explain it to Jason once. He even went on a jog with me. He didn't get it, but he got that I like it, and that was good enough. We walked back to his house after jogging less than a quarter mile. We didn't talk, we just held hands, and even though I hadn't broken a sweat with that baby run, my heart was still racing when I looked at him—

Don't think of that.

Don't think at all.

Run.

My thick braid swishes against my neck. I am aware of a trickle of sweat down my face, nothing else. I stop when the fields fade to gravel, then pavement. This is the city I saw from my window, although it is significantly smaller than any city I've ever seen on Earth. Mom once gave a speech to the biological engineering department at North Carolina State University, and they took us on a tour of the campus. This city is about the size of the old part of the campus, with stacked up metal trailers instead of dorms and college buildings. A thin tube of plastic hugs the curving metal wall behind the city. I stare at it curiously, panting from my run, then gasp aloud as I see a figure zooming up through the tube. A second later, another zooms up. People—*people!*—are being sucked up from that tube into another level of the ship, like the tubes of money sucked up in the drive-through bank teller line. How cool! It must be like flying! So much better than an elevator! I stare at the tube, open-mouthed, for so long that I don't notice how close I have come to other people, not until I start to hear their whispers.

My gaze drops from the people-tube to the people who are slowly starting to gather around me. A dozen or so. My eyes flick to the trailers. There are at least a couple hundred people on the streets of the makeshift city. I feel vastly outnumbered.

They're all a little older than me; this must be the twenty-year-old generation. They have dark skin, dark eyes, dark hair. And they're all staring at me. I reach my hand up to my sweaty, braided red hair, bright under this false sun. My pale skin flashes white. I am different from them in every way. I am shorter, younger, paler, brighter. I am from another world.

Even from here, I can tell that their first reaction is wariness, too—but there are more of them than me. I want to speak. But none of them even smile at me. They just stare, mutely, eerily.

My heart seizes with a deep, primal fear.

"Hello," I say, hating the quaver in my voice.

"What are you?" one of them, a man, asks. Not who. What.

"I—I'm Amy. I, uh, I live here now. Not here, I mean, at the Hospital." I point to the white building in the distance behind me, but I don't feel comfortable turning my back to them.

"What's wrong with you?" the man asks. A few of the others nod, encouraging him to ask what they're all thinking.

Goose bumps prickle under my cold sweat. I stare at them. They stare at me. I have never felt more different, more of a freak—more alone—than now. I bite my lip. These people are nothing like Elder. Elder may stare at my skin and hair, but he's not staring out of fear. He didn't look at me like I'm a sideshow.

"What's going on here?" a gruff female voice calls. A woman emerges from the fields toward the City. She scans the crowd, her eyes lingering on me. She's older than everyone else here, older even than the doctor at the Hospital, but there's a spark in her missing from the others.

She swings her basket as she walks. It's filled with broccoli as big as melons.

The old woman stops a few feet away from me, glaring at the crowd. She looks at me once, slowly, from head to toe, then faces the man who spoke to me. "All right," she says in a soft, drawling voice. "Nothing to see here. Go on, get back to your work."

And they do.

They don't protest. They don't argue. They just accept what she's said, and they all leave. They don't even talk to one another as they go. They just turn and wander away.

"Now," the old woman says, turning back to me, "You're living in the Hospital, I hear that right?"

I nod. "Yes, I mean—I—" I trip over my words. This world is crazy. Earlier, a man was going to attack me with a gardening trowel. Now, a little old lady is able to single-handedly disperse a group of people who looked like they were about to grab some pitchforks and turn into a proper mob.

The woman raises her hand to stop me. "I'm Steela," she says. "Don't know who you are or where you came from. But looks to me this is some of Eldest's doing. Most of the strange stuff that happens here starts off on the Keeper Level."

Does she . . . does she not like Eldest?

"I don't want to get mixed up with none of that. Had enough of Eldest's experiments when I lived in the Ward. Worked as head agri-culturalist for three decades." Despite herself, there's a note of pride in Steela's voice. She pauses, inspecting me. "You don't look stupid."

"I'm . . . sorry?"

"You're weird-looking." She says it bluntly, and I flinch. "You might be okay in the Hospital. The Ward's used to weird. But you be careful out here. Most Feeders don't know how to react to something strange."

"But you—all you did was tell them to go away, and they did."

Steela shifts her basket of broccoli to her other arm. "Thing is," she says, "I'm one of them. You're not."

"So?"

Steela looks at the backs of the people who had crowded around me as they fade into the town. "You've got to understand. The Feed-ers are simple people. If you complicate their world, they'll get rid of you just to eliminate the problem. Why do you think they round up every person with a shred of creativity and jam them in a building clear on the other side of the ship?"

My first instinct is to protest, but then I remember the man in the fields. The way he clutched his trowel, the blade of it turned to me.

"You best head back to where you came from," Steela says. Without glancing back at me, she continues on her way into the town. She walks briskly, and quickly overtakes the man from the crowd who spoke to me. He turns as she passes, and he catches my eye.

Then he starts walking back to me.

I take three steps behind me, almost stumble, turn around, and race away faster than I've ever run. This is not my measured run from before. I am not pacing myself, counting my breaths, conscious of my strides. I race like a monster is chasing me; I race as if they were chasing me. I cannot go fast enough. I tear through the tall grass of the fields, the thin blades slicing my skin like paper cuts. I break corn stalks as I pound through the field.

I run and run and run.

Past the hospital, through the garden, past a pond.

And to the cold metal wall.

I stop, gulping at the air, my heart racing in my ears. I reach up with one hand and touch the wall. My fingers curl into a fist, but it falls weakly to my side.

And that's when I realize the most important truth of life on this ship.

There is nowhere to run.

22: ELDER

The hatch door slams shut. Behind me, Doc and Eldest are talking in low, frantic whispers.

"Do you think it was—?"

"That's not possible."

"Does *he* know?"

Pause.

"Of course not."

"Did *you*—?"

"Of *course* not."

But I can think of nothing but the stars.

It is like a piece of my soul had been lost, empty, and it is now filled with the light of a million stars.

They are all that I had ever dreamed of; they are nothing I ever expected.

How could I have *ever* thought the lightbulbs in the Great Room were stars?

I will never, *never* be the same.

I have seen stars.

Real stars.

23: AMY

My face is pressed against the metal, breathing in the dust that clings to the rivets curving around the interior wall. My eyes burn; my vision is so blurred all I can see is the grayness of the metal world.

Something inside me snaps.

I. Can't. *Do* this. I can't. It's too much. This—all of this—*living*—I can't. I just can't. To have given it all up, and be left with nothing but this metal wall—

I slide down its slight curve, leaving a trail of sweat and tears and snot, but I don't care. As I fall to my knees, the damp earth seeps wetness through the knees of my pants. My fists clench the dirt. It *feels* like dirt—real, honest dirt.

But it's not.

"Are you all right?"

A man is standing on a path that connects the Hospital to a big brick building farther down.

I lift my filthy hands in front of my face, dirt falling in clumps from my fingers. I try to wipe the tears and snot from my face, but I'm pretty sure I'm just a muddy mess.

I press against the wall to stand. "You must think I'm crazy," I choke out, attempting a half-laugh.

"I think you're very upset," the man says, rushing forward to help me stand, "but not crazy. What's wrong?"

I snort. "Everything."

"It can't all be bad."

"It really can."

The man stands there, totally ignoring the mud I've smeared on his sleeve.

"I'm Amy, by the way."

"Orion."

"Nice to meet you." As I say it, I realize it's true. This is the first person on the whole ship who either didn't creep me out, threaten to kill me, or both. He's older, almost as old as my father, and although the thought feels like a splinter in my heart, it's also a little comforting.

Orion starts leading me toward the brick building, away from the Hospital. "Let's clean you up before I send you back on your way. What were you doing at the wall, anyway?"

"Looking for a way off this ship," I mutter.

Orion laughs, a sincere, real laugh that makes me smile, too. His eyes light up, reminding me of Elder. Not so much because of the way he looks—everyone looks like they're related to everyone else on this ship, with the same skin and same hair. No—it's the kindness in his eyes that reminds me of Elder.

I pause at the steps of the brick building. RECORDER HALL it says in big, white-painted letters. Next to the big doors is a painting of

Eldest. His cold eyes follow me as I mount the steps, and I try to avoid his painted gaze. Orion rushes ahead, saying something about a towel.

I push the door open after him, and it takes a moment for my eyes to adjust to the dim interior light.

Then I see it.

Earth.

Not the real Earth, obviously, but a big clay model.

I rush forward, my fingers reaching for the huge clay globe of Earth that hangs in the center of the giant entryway. There's America, there's Florida, where I was born, there's Colorado, where I met Jason. My hands tremble as I stretch up to touch the dusty, bumpy clay, even though it's far beyond my reach.

Orion snatches my hands away and scrubs them with a steaming hot, slightly damp towel. It feels almost as if he's scrubbing away my skin, and when I pull away and look at my hands, they're red, but clean. Before I can say anything else, Orion shoves the towel in my face and scrubs it as well. He's laughing, and so am I—I haven't been treated as if I was a child in need of a bath for a very long time.

"Clean again!" Orion says cheerily, tossing the towel behind him. He hands me a glass of cold water, and I drink it greedily. My muscles seem to relax, and I finally start to feel calm again. "So," Orion says, nodding to the replica, "you found our model of Sol-Earth."

By Sol-Earth, I guess he means my Earth.

"And here," Orion adds, "is *Godspeed*."

I hadn't noticed the little model of the ship made to look as if it were flying from Earth before. It's about the size of my head, whereas the model of Earth is so big my arms wouldn't reach around it.

I flick the model with my hand. It swings on its wire, chaotically off-course. Then settles back, as if nothing has happened. It's a ship. It can't be bothered to care.

"Everything better now?" Orion asks, as if a warm towel is enough to solve any problem.

"I'll be okay," I say, but we both know I'm lying.

24: ELDER

"Come," Eldest demands, and I know by the way he says it, as if he's a master speaking to a slave, that he means me and not Doc. I tear my gaze away from the closed hatch door and follow Eldest. Doc comes, too, but his steps are measured, an ominous drum beat on the floor.

When Eldest gets to the table against the wall at the end of the rows of cryo chambers, he stops and looks at me expectantly. My eyes are on that table, remembering how Amy huddled on its cold metal top, and how there was nothing I could do to help her.

"Well?" Eldest demands, his voice a short bark.

"What?"

"As leader, what would you do in this situation?"

"Um . . ." I say, wrong-footed. Typical Eldest. Just like him to throw a lesson at me when I'm least ready for it.

"Um, um!" Eldest mocks. "Be a leader! What should we do?"

"Uh—we need to see the vid records. And!"—I add when Eldest shows signs of derision—"we could check the wi-com locators, too."

Eldest harrumphs, but does not insult my plan, just hands me a floppy. I press my thumb against the access login, and the floppy flashes into life. I tap in a few commands, searching for the video recordings of the cryo level. But when I find them, they show nothing but black.

"Something's wrong with the vid screens," I say, trying again and getting nothing but black.

Eldest grunts. "The vids were out the first time, too. I thought I'd taken care of that, but clearly he's found a way around it. Try the wi-com locator."

I tap more commands, this time accessing the map of *Godspeed*. Hundreds of blinking dots shine up at me: one dot for each person, each traced through the locator in the wi-com. I've done this before— it's a good way to cheat at hide-and-seek, and it took Harley a full six months before he realized how I was so good—but I've never tried to use it for anything else. Now that I know what I'm looking for, I see an access dot on the fourth floor of the Hospital, and when I tap the screen there, the map shifts to the cryo level. Three dots blink on the cryo level now: one for my wi-com, one for Doc's, one for Eldest's. I press the time slider and move it back an hour. The wi-com map shows no one except—

"Doc," I say, handing the floppy to Eldest for his inspection. "It was only Doc down here."

"Some of the scientists have been in the secondary lab with me. They could have come out here, too. It would be easy. It's not like I escorted them out. Any of the scientists could have been here earlier today." Doc's voice is emotionless and analytical. "I know what you're thinking, Eldest, but you're jaded. It could be any of them. They all have access to this floor; they all know about the cryo chambers and how they work."

"Or it could be *him*," Eldest says.

Doc's face is like carved ice. "He's dead," he says, with such finality that whoever Doc is talking about, I'm convinced he's not alive.

"Yes, he is," Eldest growls, staring at Doc, hard. "But I'm not sure his influence is."

Doc's jaw juts forward, biting back whatever chutzy thing he was going to mouth off to Eldest.

"Either way," Eldest says, "we're going to have to figure out a way to fix the vids. And as for the wi-com locators—" He pauses mid-sentence, cocking his head as he listens to his wi-com.

He keeps his voice low, but I can still hear him say in a low growl, "She's doing *what*?"

25: AMY

When I get back to the hospital, I breathe deeply. It's almost a relief to smell the harsh, stingy scent of disinfectant in the air—at least there's one difference between the air inside and the air outside.

I pass a family checking in their elderly father. The old man mutters to himself under his breath, too low and with too thick an accent for me to understand, but I can still tell he's upset.

"What's wrong with him?" the nurse at the desk asks in a bored voice as I wait for the elevator.

"He is having strange memories." The young woman's voice is empty, monotone. I pause, staring at them. If I were checking my father into the hospital, I think I'd be a little more emotional.

The nurse checks something off on a thin piece of plastic-like stuff. "We've seen a lot of this recently in the grays."

The young man nods. "It's their time." The elevator doors open, but I just stand there, staring at them. Does he mean it's the old people's time to die? Surely not.

"Come with me," the nurse says to the old man. He takes her arm and walks with her toward the elevator. The young couple leave the old man without saying goodbye.

"Please hold the elevator," the nurse says. I jump out of my distraction and throw my arm out, catching the elevator doors.

"She has odd hair," the old man says, staring at me, but he's got very little emotion behind the words.

"Yes, I know," the nurse says. She glances at me as she steps inside the elevator. "Doc has told us a strange girl would be taking up residency in the Hospital."

"Um, yeah." How am I supposed to respond to that? I press the third button, where my room is.

"The fourth floor, please," the nurse says. She glances at the glowing screen on the elevator. "It's almost time for meds; if we hurry, we'll get you to your new room in time." She pats the old man on the hand.

The elevator doors slide open to the third floor and I move to step out, glad to be breaking free from them. The old man seems as if he should have been checked into a nursing home years ago, even though he doesn't look *that* old. But his eyes are vacant, his expression slack. It reminds me of Grandma, when her Alzheimer's was bad enough that Mom put her in a nursing home. We visited her the Easter before she died, and she gave me a decorated egg. She called me by my mother's name and didn't know where she was, but she gave that egg to me.

I give the old man a watery sort of smile that's mostly an apology.

When I had left earlier, there was only the tall man in the common room. But, as the nurse said, it is now time for medicine. The common room is crowded, and two nurses walk among those gathered inside, passing out big blue-and-white pills. I can tell by the uncomfortable silence that this room had once been buzzing with noise and activity—the dying strains of guitar music are still on the air—but it is as if I'd pushed pause. As soon as everyone turns my way, they freeze.

"Yeah," says a friendly-looking guy with a grin, "this is gonna get good."

Standing behind him, leaning against the big glass window, is the tall man who saw me this morning. His lips spread in a smile, but his grin is more malicious than the friendly guy's.

Hostile stares follow me as I take a few steps into the room.

"I'm Harley," the friendly guy says. "You must be the new res!"

One of the nurses fussily hands him three pills—one of the big blue-and-white ones, and two smaller ones, one green, one pink. The man swallows them in one big gulp and bypasses the nurse, striding toward me with an even bigger grin than before. "What's wrong with everyone?" he calls over his shoulder. "This is the new res Elder told me about!"

Some girls near the elevator twitter nervously, then turn to whisper to each other. A wave of words and whispers washes over the crowd. I can't distinguish what most of them are saying—really, that accent is hard to figure out sometimes. Still, it's not like it's hard to know what they're talking about. It feels very much like high school lunch for the new girl: seeing everyone staring, hearing everyone talking, and knowing that everyone's staring at and talking about *you*.

"What's wrong with her?" I hear someone nearby whisper.

"Nothing's *wrong* with me," I say, loudly.

"Her hair . . ." says someone else behind me. When I whip around, my red hair spinning out behind me, I cannot tell who spoke, but they are all staring with brown eyes in dark faces framed by darker hair.

The tall man licks his lips at me. He doesn't even pretend not to stare.

"Nice to meet you!" says Harley, interrupting the uncomfortable silence. When he shakes my hand, he leaves behind a bright stain of color on my palms. Harley's skinny and lanky, with hair that sticks up everywhere, some of it streaked with paint. His face is bright and open. He reminds me a little of Elder that way.

"Everyone, this is the new girl. Elder knows her. New girl, this is everyone." A few people look up politely; some actually smile. Most, however, look wary at best, disgusted at worse. The nurse closest to me jabs her finger behind her ear and starts whispering to nobody.

"What's wrong with her?" I ask Harley as he leads me to the table he was sitting at.

"Oh, don't worry, we're all mad here."

I giggle, mostly from nerves. "It's a good thing I read *Alice in Wonderland*. I definitely think I've fallen into the rabbit hole."

"Read what?" Harley asks.

"Never mind." All around me, eyes follow my every move.

"Look," I say loudly. "I know I look different. But I'm just a person, like you." I hold my head up high, looking them all in the eyes, trying to hold their stares for as long as possible.

"You tell 'em," says Harley with another Cheshire grin.

"Where did you come from?" asks the tall man who keeps watching me, smirking.

"Who are you?" I demand, annoyed.

"Luthe." His voice is low and gravelly.

"Well, quit staring at me like that, *Luthe*." I cross my arms over my chest. Luthe's smirk widens, and his gaze doesn't leave me.

"Where *did* you come from?" a woman near Harley asks.

I sigh. There's no real point in demanding that Luthe not stare at me; they're all staring at me. "I came from Earth," I say. "A long time ago."

There are looks of disbelief—from most of them, actually—but a few glance up with a light in their eyes that makes me know that they, too, are very aware of how their sky is painted metal.

"Will you tell us about it?" Harley asks.

So I sit down in the seat he offers, ignoring how the woman closest to me scoots away. What can I tell them about Earth? How can I describe how the air smells different, how the earth feels richer, how you yourself are different, just from knowing the entire world is at your disposal? Should I start with the mountains always hidden in clouds and snow—or do they even know what those words are: *cloud* and *snow* and *mountain*? I could tell them about the different kinds of rain, pouring rain that's perfect for when you want to stay inside and watch a movie or read, or piercing rain that feels like needles on your skin, or soft summer rain that makes your first kiss with your first love all the sweeter.

They look at me eagerly, waiting to hear about the planet I called home.

I begin with the sky.

26: ELDER

"That frexing girl has gone into the Ward common room and is telling them all about Sol-Earth," Eldest growls. "Didn't we tell her about what would happen if she created more of a disturbance? Didn't we?"

"Now, Eldest," Doc says in a placating tone. "The Season will begin any day now. They'll be distracted enough to forget anything she says."

Eldest punches the nearest cryo chamber door. I jump back, wary of him, unsure of what or who he will strike next.

"Fine," Eldest says. He turns his burning gaze to me. "The first cause of discord?"

A pop quiz? Now? "Difference," I say.

"Exactly. Discord will follow that girl everywhere she goes on this ship like dirt a child tracks across the floor. And the second is lack of leadership. Boy, when differences cause discord, the only thing that can maintain control is leadership. Learn from this."

He jabs his wi-com button. "All-call com link," he says.

"What are you doing, Eldest?" I ask as a familiar *beep, beep-beep* fills my ear.

"Attention all residents of *Godspeed*. I have a very important announcement."

My stomach drops. Eldest is talking to every resident on the ship through his wi-com link. And I think I know what he's going to say. My mind races. There's no way he'd tell everyone on *Godspeed* about the cryo level, the frozens, where Amy really came from. He would never tell them that.

"Eldest, don't do this," I say.

He ignores me.

"Some of you, particularly those of you on the Feeder Level near the Hospital, may notice a new resident on board."

"Stop." I lunge at Eldest. I'm sick of his lies.

Doc pulls me back, his long fingers gripping my arms. I try to shake him off, but he's too strong.

"This new resident is a young female with strangely pale skin and bright hair. She is the result of a Shipper science experiment attempting to develop physical attributes of the body to withstand the possible harsh nature of Centauri-Earth. The girl is harmless, though simple, and prone to lying. She is easily confused and poorly suited to labor; therefore she will remain in the Ward. You are not required nor expected to interact with her at all. She is a freak, and should be treated as such."

My fists clench. A freak, is she? The result of a crazy Shipper science experiment? Well, that is believable—the Shipper scientists spend most of their time coming up with new things that will protect us in whatever kind of environment Centauri-Earth provides. Still, it's clear Eldest is trying to cover up Amy's real origins and keep her away from most people.

I shake with anger as Doc releases me, but there's no point. Eldest is done. I turn and head back to the elevator, back to Amy.

27: AMY

"What I don't understand," I say, "is why you're all here."

"What ya mean?" one of the men says. He has a guitar on his lap, an old acoustic relic.

"Harley said you all were crazy. He said this was a mental hospital."

"Ah, we're not crazy," the guitar player says. His accent is thicker than the others; I can barely understand him.

"We are." This is the woman who had originally scooted away from me. Harley called her Victria, said she wrote stories. She has an ancient-looking book in her hand—a real book bound in leather, not an electronic thing. I wonder where she got it. "The only thing keeping us close to sane is the mental meds," Victria adds.

"You might be crazy," says the guitar player in a joking tone, "but I'm not."

"You are," says Harley. "She is. I am. We all are here."

"But you're not," I insist.

"Speak for yourself."

"No, I mean it! You're not. You don't act crazy. None of you do."

Harley smiles. "I'll count that as a compliment. After all—" he starts, but then he cocks his head to the left, as if he's listening to something.

"What?" I ask.

"Shh," says Victria.

I look around the room. All of them, they've all got their heads tilted, each appearing to listen deeply to something.

"An all-call," the guitar player says under his breath. "Eldest hasn't done one since our Elder died."

"*Shh!*" Victria hisses.

My eyes bounce from person to person. Each one in the psych ward, patient or nurse, is listening intensely.

It's eerie, the way they've all stopped to listen to something I can't hear. Everyone around me is still and silent, but I jump up and pace around the crowded room, waiting for the spell to break, waiting for everyone else to return to my world.

"Load of shite," Harley says in an offhand manner. They all start to straighten up, readjust their focus. Whatever they'd been listening to is gone now.

"What is?" I ask.

Harley looks at me, and for the first time, there is no smile in his eyes.

"Nothing," he says.

Victria mutters a word, a single syllable, but I can't hear it.

"What?" I say, an unbidden edge to my voice.

She looks me square in the eyes. "Freak."

"Victria!" the guitar player says.

She whirls around on him. "You heard Eldest! She is a freak! And here she's been lying to us all this whole time, *lying*. Saying she's from Sol-Earth! Telling us of wide spans of land, of an unending sky! She's madder than all of us—why do you think Eldest brought her here? With her *lies*." She spits the word out. "Telling us she's seen Sol-Earth! How dare she? How dare you!" She turns on me, cold hatred in her eyes.

"Calm down, Victria. She's simple. Damaged. She doesn't know what she's saying," says the guitar player.

"What are you talking about?" I back away.

"Don't tell me about a sky that never ends," she says, her voice low. "Don't ever tell me about that sort of thing. Don't even talk about it. There is no sky. Only a metal roof."

I flinch at the harshness of her words, but just before she whirls away from me and runs down the hall, I see that there are tears glistening in her eyes.

"What is going on?" I ask. I turn in a circle around the room. With the exception of Harley, they all stare at me with the same contempt and bitter anger that Victria spewed forth.

"Come on," Harley says, standing up. "Let's go back to your room."

"Why? I don't understand. What's going on?"

"Come on," Harley says, and he leads me through the silent stares and out of the hostile room.

28 : ELDER

When I get off the elevator, the talking drops to a whisper. It's not hard to guess what they're discussing. I leave them with their whispers and lies. I don't care what they think. I want to know what Amy thinks.

There is a brown stain just outside her door: the crushed remains of the flowers I'd left for her.

I knock. "Come in," a deep male voice says. Harley. My stomach lurches. I run my finger on the door release button, and the door slides open.

Amy sits before her window, gazing out. The light shines on her upturned face, spilling over on her red-gold hair, making her clear green eyes sparkle. I stare, unable to tear my gaze from her.

"Beautiful, huh?" Harley says. He's rearranged the desk so that it's not leaning against the wall; instead it is cockeyed in front of Amy, with his table-easel propped on top. A small canvas leans against the easel, and Harley has already sketched out the scene before him with charcoal.

"You quit painting the fish?" I ask, hoping the bitterness doesn't sound as obvious to them as it does to me.

"Yup!" Harley chirps. He dabs a tiny bit of blue on Amy's painted face, giving her a hint of a shadow under her lips. "Funnily enough, I'm using almost the exact same colors on her as I was on the koi. Hey!" he adds, peeking from behind the canvas to Amy, "that's your new name: from now on, you're my Little Fish!"

Amy laughs cheerily at her new nickname, but I am glowering at Harley for calling her "his." It's true, though: her red-gold-orange-yellow hair is the same color as the scales on Harley's koi fish.

"So, Little Fish, ignore the boy and tell me about the sky."

My back stiffens at how Harley calls me "boy." I want to punch him. I *really* want to punch him, even if he is my best friend.

"The stars were my favorite, ever since I was little and my parents would take me to the observatory."

I'm not sure what an *observatory* is, but I do know this much: Amy's first memory of seeing stars is with her family, and mine is with a dead man.

Amy looks at me, and I'm glad she can't tell what I'm thinking. She picks at the meat pie on a napkin in her lap, and pops a piece in her mouth. She swallows it quickly, then drops the rest of the pie in the trash chute. She and Harley must have eaten here, instead of in the Ward cafeteria. Good. I can only imagine how the Ward residents are treating her after Eldest's all-call. She takes a sip of water from the glass beside her and winces.

"What's wrong?" I ask.

"Headache," she says. "So, will you tell me what happened to make everyone think I'm a freak?"

"You didn't tell her?" I ask Harley.

"Of course I didn't," Harley growls, stabbing his canvas with his paintbrush. "Why would I insult her with such lies?"

Part of me is very glad that Amy doesn't know what Eldest has said. But Harley has always been this way, for as long as I've known him: he thinks ignorance is the best way to protect someone, and he doesn't understand that what we imagine is often worse than the truth.

"Will you tell me?"

I look up, and Amy's eyes draw me in. "It was Eldest," I say. "He sent out an all-call to everyone about you." I pause. *Does she know what an all-call is?* "A, er, message. He sent everyone a message. About you." I pause again, unable to meet her big green eyes. "It was mostly lies."

Amy senses my hesitance to continue. "What kind of lies?" she asks.

"That you're the product of an experiment gone wrong, and you're, uh, simple. Slow." I pause again. "A freak."

Amy's face scrunches as she absorbs this information. I can tell, from the distaste curling her lips, that she has met Eldest and can probably guess what it is he said. "Ah," she finally says, and turns back to the window. Harley straightens up, stares at her face again, and then turns back to his canvas. He is shaping her sadness onto the painted image of her face.

"So, there were lots of stars in the sky?" Harley asks, turning to the nighttime sky in the background of the painting. The word "stars" is heavy on his tongue, as if he's not used to the idea of them.

"Millions," Amy says. "Billions." There is longing in her voice.

Harley flicks silver paint on the canvas.

"But," I say, leaning over Harley's canvas, "they're scattered about, not so clustered together. Spread them out more. And they're different sizes. Some are bigger; some are just tiny specks."

It is as if I have done something foul in the room. Harley turns slowly toward me. Amy's eyes are wide.

"You've seen the stars?" Harley's voice accuses me.

"I . . . er . . ."

Amy's eyes search mine, and I know she's looking for starshine in them.

"Just once," I say.

"*How?*" Harley breathes.

"There's a hatch door. For the dead."

Amy's head snaps toward mine.

"Where is it?" Harley asks, an eager tone in his voice that reminds me of the last time he had what Doc called a "downward spiral."

"It's not on the Feeder Level."

Harley sinks in on himself. He's not one of the select few with access to the other levels and has spent his entire life here, on the Feeder Level.

"Can we see it?" Amy asks. "Can we see the stars?"

And, oh, I want to show her. I want to show her, but not him, not now, not with her. I want to be the one to give Amy back her stars.

But what would Eldest say? What would Eldest do? To me? To her?

"No," I say. "Eldest wouldn't like it."

Amy's eyes narrow into pinpricks of jade. "I met Eldest," she says, disgust dripping from her voice.

Harley snorts, and Amy turns her glare on him. Eldest is not a laughing matter to her.

"What in the uni could he have said to make you not like him?" He laughs.

"You know that hatch Elder was talking about?" Amy holds back the rage in her voice, like a man holding back a snarling dog on a leash. "He wanted to throw me out of it, just so I wouldn't create a 'disturbance' on the ship."

Harley laughs. "He wouldn't do that!"

Amy doesn't crack a smile.

"Yes, he would," I say. Harley's laughter dies and he looks at me.

"Maybe he said something as a threat, but he'd never—"

"Yes," I say as firmly as I can. "He would."

Harley attacks the canvas with paint again, a frown creasing his forehead.

"He doesn't like 'disturbances,'" I tell Amy. "He doesn't like anyone to be different at all. Difference, he says, is the first cause of discord."

"He sounds like a regular Hitler to me," Amy mutters. I wonder what she means by that. Eldest has always taught me that Hitler was a wise, cultured leader for his people. Maybe that's what she means: Eldest is a strong leader, like Hitler was. The turn of phrase is unusual, another difference between us, another difference I'm sure Eldest would hate.

Amy hops up from her seat at the window. She twirls her hair into a quick bun and secures it with two dry brushes she snatches from the desk before Harley can protest. She paces the room, an animal unsatisfied with the smallness of her cage.

Harley snorts again, but images flash in my mind: Eldest, walking throughout the Feeder Level, showing all the farmers and workers his kind-grandfather face, and then going up to the Keeper Level with me, and snarling with distaste at their stupidity. Eldest, pounding lessons into me that stressed control above all else. Eldest, revulsion souring his face when I first came to the Keeper Level and did anything out of the ordinary. In my mind's eye, Eldest's face is growing twisted, just like I suspect his soul has become.

And I realize that, yes, this man who I have lived with for three years, who is leader of this entire ship, whose control over everyone on board is absolute . . . this man is capable of killing whomever, whenever.

He *could* have. "But why would he?" I ask.

"Dunno. And—why *me*? I'm not important. Why try to kill me?"

Harley's brush is paused midair. Silence permeates the little room.

"You weren't the only one," I say, my words like arrows slicing through the air. "A man was killed. That's where I saw the hatch—I was helping Doc and Elder send the body to the stars."

"Who?" Amy breathes, terror in her voice.

"Mr. William Robertson."

"I didn't know him." Amy sounds relieved. It is only then that I realize she was afraid it was one of her parents floating dead amongst the stars.

29: AMY

"What kind of security is there on this ship?" I ask, turning to Elder. "Do you guys have cops or anything?"

Elder and Harley look confused. "Cops?" Elder asks.

I nod. "You know, policemen. Cops." They stare blankly at me. "People whose job it is to keep the bad guys under control."

"That's what Eldest is for," Harley says, turning back to his canvas.

Great.

"We don't have a need for 'cops' like on Sol-Earth," Elder says. It takes me a moment to remember that the "Sol-Earth" he's talking about is *my* Earth. "On Sol-Earth, there was more discord, because there were more differences. There aren't differences on *Godspeed*, so there aren't problems."

I bristle. "The problems on Earth didn't stem from people being different—"

"Slavery. The Crusades. Genocide. Civil rights violence.

Apartheid. Differences were the main source of all of Sol-Earth's greatest man-made disasters."

My mouth hangs open, but I can't refute the blemishes of my world's history.

"Look at you being so smart," Harley says. He winks at me. "Elder gets more education than the rest of us. Our education on Sol-Earth was mostly just farming methods and science. Elder's the smart one."

Elder flushes deeply.

I don't have time for this. "What's being done to find the murderer?"

Both guys look up at me, blankly.

"Is there a guard over the cryogenically frozen people? Is Eldest investigating the crime? Are there suspects? Is there any kind of security or surveillance there? *What's happening?*"

Neither of them have thoughts on any of this, and it infuriates me. "You never even gave any of this a second thought, did you? Someone's *died*, and you're just going to sit back and let this happen? I thought you were the future leader of this ship," I shout, pointing at Elder. "And you're going to ignore this and hope it goes away? Some leader!"

"I . . . I . . ." Elder splutters.

"Don't you realize that my *parents* are down there? Helpless? Frozen in a little box? You weren't there. In the box. When it was unplugged. *You don't know what it felt like.* That moment, when you're finally awake, and you know you're awake, and you want to vomit out those tubes, but you *can't*, and you want to get out of that box, but you *can't*, and you want to *breathe*. But. You. *Can't.*"

"Okay, okay," he says. "Calm down. Drink some water." Elder uses this as an excuse to refill my empty cup from the bathroom tap.

"I don't need water!" I say. Why is it so difficult for them to see what's important?

Elder keeps thrusting the cup toward me anyway. I take it and gulp down a swallow. An odd bitter taste stays on my tongue. I wonder how often this water has been recycled and processed. Thinking that, my anger fades and I do actually feel calmer.

"How would you feel if it were your parents?" I ask Elder quietly.

Harley looks up at us both, then slowly puts his paintbrush down. He is more intent on Elder's answer than on my ranting.

"I never knew my parents," Elder says.

"Did they die?" The words come out harsher than I'd intended, but this world seems intent on making me more callous.

Elder shakes his head. "No. I just never knew who they were. An Elder isn't allowed to know. He must feel as if he is a child of the ship."

He speaks as if he's reciting from a textbook, but there is also a sadness to his words that I am not sure even he recognizes. He seems very small and alone. His shoulders have hunched down, as if he wants his body to swallow him.

"Is that why you're here?" I ask Harley.

"Nah. I know my parents. They're weavers, in the City. My whole family has been weavers, ever since the Plague. I'd say my parents were disappointed that I didn't uphold the family tradition, but I'm not even sure they noticed when I left. They couldn't make me care about cloth, and I couldn't make them care about anything else. So I moved here. It's only Elder here without proper parents."

"As it should be," Elder says in a low voice without looking at either of us. "But right now," he says, "if we can't figure out *who* killed Mr. Robertson, let's start with *why*."

I stride across the room to Harley and his art supplies and take up his biggest brush and the cup of black paint.

"Hey!" Harley says, but before he or Elder can do anything, I scrawl my name in big letters across the wall beside the window.

"What are you doing to your wall?!" Elder sounds shocked.

"It's not my wall," I say. Nothing on this ship is mine.

Under my name, I add everything that I can think of that might make me a target for the killer. *Girl*, I write. *Seventeen. Red hair. White. Average appearance.*

"You're beautiful," Elder says quietly, but I ignore him.

Not part of any mission, I add.

"Okay," I say, turning around. "What about Mr. Robertson?" I write his name on the wall next to my own.

Elder picks up the thin sheet of plastic off my desk that I'd wondered at before. When he runs his finger across it, it lights up like a computer screen. He starts tapping on it, and images flash across the screen.

"Eldest/Elder access granted," a female voice says from the computer.

"Mr. William Robertson," Elder reads from the screen. "Male. Fifty-seven years old, Hispanic, 212 pounds. Leadership specialist. Experience with United State Marines. Mission: offensive organization. Funded by the FRX. FRX?" He pauses. "I've seen that before. On a plaque in the Keeper Level . . ." His voice trails off.

"Financial Resource Exchange," I say as I write the details about

Mr. Robertson below his name. "Everyone in the military was funded by the FRX. It's how Daddy got to join the mission."

Elder rolls his finger on the screen. "That's all there is."

I look at that weird computer thing. "Does that say anything about me?"

Elder hesitates.

"What?" I say. "What does it say about me?"

"Er—"

Harley, who's been watching us silently, snatches the computer thing from Elder. He scans it quickly, the laughter dying from his eyes.

"Oh."

"What?"

"It's nothing." Harley moves to touch the screen—to turn it off, I'm sure. Before he can, I grab it from his hand.

There's the picture they took of me a few days before I was frozen, during the health screening. My date of birth, blood type, height, weight. And, in tiny letters at the bottom: NONESSENTIAL CARGO.

Oh, that's right. I'd forgotten.

I'm just extra baggage.

I drop the computer thing on the desk and turn back to the wall with my paintbrush. Under my name, I add *nonessential*.

"You're not—" Elder starts, but I silence him with a look.

Stepping back, I look at my handiwork. I painted the lines too thick; trails of black trickle down from the letters, some of them making it all the way to the baseboard, streaking over the peeling old painted vines on the floor, made by whoever once lived in this room.

Harley's eyes are on the trailing black, watching the drips race one another over the hand-painted flowers.

"So," I say, scanning the lists, "what's the connection? Why would someone want to kill both of us?"

Silence.

"We're missing something," I say, smoothing my hair down with both hands. "There must be some connection."

But whatever it is, none of us can see it.

I throw my hands down to my sides. "We're getting nowhere this way. Let's just go down to the cryo chambers and see what we can see."

"Go down there?" Elder asks, surprised.

I nod. "Maybe we'll find some clues."

Harley laughs, like this is a game. "Clues?!"

I just stare at him, and his laughter dies.

"Okay," Elder says. His eyes meet mine, and I don't remember why I used to think his face looked innocent. He's determined now, ready for a fight, prepared to back me up.

"Okay?" I ask.

"Let's go."

30: ELDER

Amy ignores the cold stares from the people in the Ward common room as we make our way to the elevator. She keeps her chin raised and avoids eye contact, and to me she looks like a queen, but I can tell from the whispers that follow her that the people around her view her as something very different. My jaw clenches. Eldest did this.

The elevator dings as the doors slide open on the fourth floor.

"Did you hear that?" Amy asks as we walk down the empty hall.

"Hear what?" Harley asks.

Amy shakes her head. "Nothing. I guess it was just my imagination." Still, she looks at the doors as if she's a little skeeved out.

I open the door at the end of the hall—still unlocked—and cross the room to get to the second elevator. The smashed alarm box is gone. Eldest has probably taken it to the Shippers to see if they can fix it.

"So, what are we looking for?" Harley asks as the elevator descends.

"I'm not sure." Amy shifts on her feet. "A clue. Something."

I think about the last time I was on the floor with the cryo chambers. The only evidence that I remember seeing that proved a murder had taken place was the body of Mr. William Robertson. There were no other clues.

But I don't tell Amy that.

When the elevator doors slide open, Harley strides out, looking around eagerly. I follow. Amy doesn't step out until the doors start to slide shut again.

"Where's the hatch with the stars?" Harley asks eagerly.

Amy steps forward. She grabs my sleeve and tugs at it until I turn to face her. "Where are my parents?" she asks very, very softly.

"I don't know," I say. "But I can look up their location for you."

Amy bites her lip, shakes her head. "No . . . that's okay." She looks around her with wide, round, scared eyes. "Not . . . not this time. Later."

"Can we look at the stars first?" Harley asks eagerly.

"There's a hatch down there," I start to say, but before I can finish, Harley takes off down the rows to where I've pointed. I turn to Amy. "But he doesn't know the code to open the door."

She throws me a half-smile. "Let him figure it out. Why don't we try to find something here that can help? Can you show me where Mr. . . . er . . . Robertson was?"

We go down the aisle of cryo chambers marked 75–100, and stop at Number 100.

Amy reaches toward the empty tray with shaking fingers. I wonder if she's imagining her parents on that tray, or herself. Before her fingers actually touch it, though, she snatches back her hand and holds it against her.

"So, what should we be doing?" I ask, trying to distract her from whatever thoughts she's having that are making her draw into herself.

Amy steps back, looks at the ground. Her eyes scan the bare, clean floor, then rove over the clinically neat room.

"I don't know what I expected to find," Amy says. "I guess I thought this was like a cop show, and I'd come down here and find a fiber that I could match to Eldest's shirt, or a blood drop we could DNA test, but I don't even know if you have DNA testing here—"

"The biometric scanners read DNA," I interject, but she's not listening to me.

"Or maybe a giant fingerprint . . ." Her voice trails off. "Harley's art supplies," she says. She looks me fully in the face. "Harley's art supplies!"

"What?"

"Harley has brushes. And he sketched me with charcoal before he started painting me. He's got everything I need."

"I don't know what you're talking about!" I say, but I'm smiling too, because she's gotten back that spark of life she'd lost when she first got off the elevator.

"Harley!" she calls, jumping up and heading toward the end of the aisle. "Harley!"

I have no idea why she needs them. I just know that I'd face another Plague to get them for her if I had to. Fortunately, it's a lot easier than that.

"Com link: Harley," I say, pressing my wi-com.

"What?" Harley's voice asks impatiently in my ear.

"Get your art box."

"Where's the hatch with the stars? There are a lot of doors and hatches and things down here, but they're all locked."

"Go get us your art box first."

"If I do, will you tell me which hatch leads to the stars?"

"Yup."

"Done," Harley says, and he disconnects the com link.

"What is that thing?" Amy asks me after a moment, when she's sure I'm done talking with Harley. "I thought you all had tiny headsets or something, but that's actually embedded in your *skin*, isn't it?"

I brush my wi-com button with my fingers. "It's a wi-com. Wireless communication link."

"Does it hurt?"

I laugh. "No."

"So cool," Amy exhales, leaning in. Her soft, warm breath tickles the hairs near my ear. "It's like a phone built into your ear."

Her fingers brush the raised skin over my wi-com. My breath catches. She's right in front of me, tantalizingly close. Amy bites her lip, and all I want to do is seize her, crush her against me, feel her lips with mine.

Then she steps back, dropping her hand, an unreadable expression on her face.

"Doc can, uh, get you one if you like," I say, trying to ignore how much I want to grab her and pull her back to me.

Amy's hands fly to the side of her neck, below her left ear. Her fingers smooth the skin. "No," she says. "I don't think I'd like one yet."

Harley shows up a few moments later. He dumps his art box at our feet. I can tell part of him just wants to run off and open the hatch to the stars, but he's also curious about what we'll do with his art stuff. For that matter, so am I.

Amy rifles through the box, bypassing jars of paint, nubs of pencils, and scraps of paper. She finally pulls out a pile of charcoal wrapped in thin cloth. Then she smashes it on the ground.

"Hey!" Harley shouts. "I have to make that myself."

"I need the powder," Amy says, pulverizing the black bits of charcoal.

"Why?"

Amy grins. "Just watch."

After selecting one of Harley's loosest, biggest brushes, she runs the bristles through the black powder, and then twirls the brush over the surface of the morgue door.

"Please work, please work, please work," she chants as she dusts the metal with a fine coat of powder. Her breath catches.

The powder reveals the whorls and swirls of a fingerprint.

Amy laughs. "Now if there was only a simple way to tell whose fingerprint this was!"

I'm one step ahead of her. "Try this," I say, kneeling beside her with the floppy from the desk at the end of the aisle. I hold the digital membrane over the fingerprint and press scan. The print shows up on the display in seconds.

"Now," I say, tapping on the screen, "all I have to do is match this with the biometric scanners. . . ."

"Wow," Amy says under her breath. I grin at her.

The floppy beeps.

"Well?" Harley asks, leaning over my shoulder.

"Mine. I was down here with Doc; that's my print."

"It says 'Eldest/Elder,'" Harley says, pointing to the screen. "It could be Eldest."

Amy looks up eagerly, but I shake my head. "We have the same access in the computer—it always shows both our names on biometric scans. But I checked the wi-com locator map earlier, and he wasn't down here. That has to be my print."

"Try some more," Harley tells Amy, and she eagerly turns back to the door with her brush and powder. I scan every print she finds, but the only ones clear enough to scan are four of Doc's and twelve of mine. Most of the prints are smudged or overlapped to the point of uselessness.

"Found another one," Amy says, brushing charcoal dust over the top of the cryo chambers. "Is this you?"

"I don't remember touching there," I say.

Amy's eyes glisten. "Maybe this is the murderer!" she says, excitement creeping back into her voice.

I hold the floppy over the print and scan it in. The print is wide and fat—a thumb. A thin jagged line slices its way through the whorls.

"What's that?" Harley asks as the floppy zooms in on the print.

Amy looks over my shoulder at it. "Maybe nothing—but it looks kind of like a scar, doesn't it?"

Beep. Beep-beep. The scan is done.

"Eldest/Elder," flash the words over the thumbprint.

"Another one of yours." Amy sighs, her face falling. She turns back to the cryo chamber, but she brushes the charcoal dust across the surface as if it were achingly heavy.

"You have a scar on your thumb?" Harley asks.

I inspect my thumbs, even though I know there is no scar there connecting the ridges of my thumbprint.

"He could have just had something on his thumb when he touched the cryo chamber," Amy says without looking up. "Something that got between the surface and his thumb."

But I hadn't touched there.

I know I hadn't.

Amy picks up the floppy. "Are you sure, absolutely *sure*, that it couldn't be Eldest?"

"Positive. Right after we found Mr. Robertson I checked the wi-com locator map. He wasn't down here."

Amy blows air out her nostrils like an angry bull. "I still think he could have—"

I'm already shaking my head, and Amy stops. There's just no way. Even though Amy's right about his cruel personality, Eldest simply wasn't here when the murder happened.

Amy throws the brush down in disgust. "So much for fingerprinting."

"Sorry," I say absently, more distracted by who could have left the print if it wasn't Eldest and it wasn't me.

Harley snatches the floppy from my hand and throws it on the desk at the end of the aisle. "Can I see the hatch now?" He picks up his art box, and I notice that he's also brought along a fresh—albeit small—canvas.

"If I open the hatch for you, will you spend the night down here and make sure no one messes with the frozens?"

Amy's smile is more than enough reason to ignore the voice in my head warning me that Eldest won't like me leaving Harley here, alone.

"Sure," Harley says.

I tell Harley the location of the hatch and the access code as I retrieve the floppy he'd tossed away. Tapping quickly, I set up access approval for both him and Amy so they can come and leave the cryo level as they please, and I add in access for Amy to use floppies. Harley runs straight to the hatch as soon as I scan his thumbprint, not bothering to hide his eagerness. Amy's still laughing at him when I press her thumb into the scanner on the floppy. When she stops laughing, I realize I've been holding her thumb down for a full minute.

"Sorry," I say, snatching my hand back.

Amy smiles at me.

"Wannagogardenwime?" I ask all in one breath. My eyes grow wide. What came over me? Why would I blurt that out like that?

"What?" Amy asks, her smile widening. She leans against the metal table behind her.

"Want to see the garden?" I ask, speaking much slower than my heart is pounding. "With me?"

She bites her lips, and although she doesn't look away from me, her gaze grows distant and unfocused. Her hands grip the edge of the table, and she looks as if she's afraid I'm going to drag her from this cold, dark place against her will. It's not hard to guess why. She wants to stay close to her parents. Her eyes flick to the right, where Harley ran off. She wants to see the stars, too.

My heart sinks. How can I compete with that?

Then her eyes focus on me again, and she smiles. "Sure," she says.

And in her smile I see something more beautiful than stars.

31: AMY

Elder takes me to a sprawling garden behind the Hospital, the one I ran through this morning during my jog. I hadn't noticed its beauty—before, I'd only ever seen the walls surrounding it. But really, it's lovely. It has a chaotic feel to it, like it has grown wild, but there are paths and clusters of plants and no weeds, all indications that a true gardener has had his hand in the development of this contained beautiful mess.

"What's that?" I ask.

"A statue of the Eldest during the Plague."

"So everyone who's leader around here is called Eldest?" He nods. "That's a stupid way of doing it. It gets confusing who's who. How many Eldests have there been, anyway?"

"I . . . er . . . I don't know."

I look up at the face of the statue. It's not carved from stone. I think it was made of concrete, or something very similar to it. Makes sense. Where would they get stone? It's not like they could just dig into the ground to extract some.

A drop of water splashes on my head. I glance up, expecting for one crazy moment to see rain clouds. I have always loved rain, but, looking up at the plain metal ceiling, I think I will not like this ship's version of rain. It reminds me, once again, of how false *Godspeed* is. There are no rain clouds, no dark sky punctuated by lightning. Here on *Godspeed*, when it rains, water just falls from the sprinkler system attached to the ceiling. I taste a drop of it on my tongue. It's cool, like real rain, but there's a slightly stale, recycled taste to it, and it smells very faintly of oil.

The "rain" is not heavy now, though, just a few drops sprinkling down, so I continue down the path, closer to the statue.

"I'm surprised you have rain," I say.

Elder smiles at me, a sort of half-smile that looks like a smirk.

"What?"

"You talk funny," he says, which is ironic since his words sound like "ya tal-funnae" to me.

"Ha! You're the one with the weird accent!"

"Wee-urd axe-scent," he mocks. I stick my tongue out at him, but I'm laughing, too.

A few raindrops fall on the statue's head, and they snake down his face like tears, leaving behind dark trails. I squint. The face is not as detailed as I'd expect. In fact, it looks weatherworn.

"How long ago was the Plague?" I ask.

"I'm not sure," Elder says, strolling away from the statue. "I'd have to look it up. Why were you surprised we have rain?"

"Well . . ." I drawl the word out, emphasizing the accent Elder says I have. His smile broadens. "It's just that—it's not rain. Why make it look like it? You could just water the plants yourselves with sprinklers."

Elder shrugs. "It's in the ship's original design." He pauses, then mutters to himself, "Biological Research . . ."

"What?"

"I saw some old plans of the ship at the Recorder Hall. Originally, the Feeder Level was labeled 'Biological Research.' I didn't think of it at the time, but . . . Eldest engineers the weather patterns. To emulate different conditions that Centauri-Earth may have. He changes the pattern every five or so years. Last time . . . last time the rain was scheduled to fall only once a month. The scientists had to help the farmers develop different irrigation methods. And . . . " He's thinking now; he's practically forgotten I'm there, listening. "When I was a kid, it used to rain *a lot.* I helped dig a drainage ditch. The sheep pastures kept flooding. Eldest has us change the soil sometimes, too, adding or taking away different minerals."

He looks up at me now, but he doesn't really see me. "The Feeder Level really is biological research—researching conditions of what Centauri-Earth might be like. There are records in the Recorder Hall of all the different methods we've come up with out of necessity. No . . . not necessity. It's what Eldest does. It's part of Eldest's job. . . ."

"That means it's part of your job, too, right?" I say. "You're the next Eldest." I want to ask, *Why didn't he teach you all this?* But it doesn't seem like the kind of thing I should say aloud. Elder can see the question in my face, though. He turns down the path toward the pond, but I can tell he doesn't have an answer for my unspoken question. He's just got more questions, too.

I follow him down the path. Hydrangeas with big, blossoming heads spill out onto the walkway.

The rain picks up. It has a steady, methodical way of falling, but it's close enough to real rain that I tip my head back and let the water splash on my closed eyelids and pretend.

"This whole Eldest thing . . . I don't see how it works."

"Why not?"

We stop near a pond about the size of the swimming pool in my high school. A man and woman, laughing in the rain, collapse on a bench further down the path.

"He's not a peaceful man. He must scare everyone into obeying him." I don't want to admit that he's got me scared, too, but I think Elder can guess it.

"Eldest is a great leader. I don't always agree with him, or his methods, but they *work*. You can't deny that."

"That old man's a dictator—that's how it works," I mutter. I catch Elder smirking. "What?"

"I like how you call him an old man. Most people around here worship at his feet."

"He seemed like a jerk to me. More than a jerk. He was pretty much King Asshole to me. I mean, I know he's your leader and all, but he did want to basically kill me."

"Maybe he wouldn't really throw you out of the hatch."

"Really?"

Elder stares at the flowers at our feet. "He might have. Yes. He probably would have."

I kick at the big orangey-red flowers, like tiger lilies, that line the edge of the pool.

The couple on the bench are really going at it. The man's got one hand up the woman's shirt, another hand down her pants. Elder follows my gaze and stares at the couple.

"Eldest said that the Season would start soon."

"This is the Season? People don't act like that in public." At least, they didn't used to. Is this what happens when you coop people up together on a ship, or am I just a prude compared to their evolved standards?

Elder doesn't watch the couple on the bench; he's watching me. The rain is pouring harder now, and I think about going in, but in a strange way I like how the rain makes me feel as if I am grounded, connected to this place. Even though I know the rain is fake, it *feels* the same as real rain, and I desperately need that.

32: ELDER

Across from us, the man and woman on the bench are using the rain as an excuse to remove their clothing. The man rips the woman's shirt off, and she arches her back, pushing up against him.

"That's disgusting," Amy says.

I don't want to talk about the Season, though, even if the couple is giving me some ideas. I want to know if her hatred for Eldest is limited to the man, not the title. "He's not all bad," I say. "Eldest is actually quite a good leader." I take a step closer to her. "I mean, I know he can be forceful, but he's really kept everyone on board working together and happy."

Amy snorts. "So, are you going to hate people because they're different, too?"

"I would never hate you!"

It is her differences—her red hair, her Sol-Earth background, the way she doesn't blindly follow Eldest—these are the things I like best about her.

The rain is pouring now, but neither one of us cares. Amy looks at me expectantly, as if she's waiting for me to prove to her I'm not Eldest.

Instead, I reach around and pull out the paintbrushes holding up her hair in a knot. A flash of red as her hair cascades down, then the rain drenches her heavy locks, darkening them so much that her hair almost looks brown like mine. Almost. I reach up and tuck one orange-gold strand behind her ear. She flinches as my fingertips brush her skin.

"Eldest is a great leader," I insist, my voice soft. "But," I say before Amy can protest, "we disagree on the issue of differences. I happen to like differences. Quite a lot." I swallow, hard. My mouth feels too wet, my throat too dry.

And then—I'm not sure how it happens—but she takes a step closer and I take a step closer, and then we're both just entirely too close.

And there is nothing between us but rain.

Then there is nothing between us at all.

My lips melt into hers. A drop of rainwater slips around the edge of my mouth, and then her lips part, and so do mine. The raindrop falls on my tongue, and then it's lost on hers.

My body is drenched; I should be cold. But the warmth of her fills me.

My arms snake around her body, pulling her hard against me. I want to crush her into me.

I never want this to end.

And then—

—She's pulling away.

She's stepping back.

Her fingers are on her swollen lips.

Her eyes are wide and sparkling.

Raindrops drip down her cheeks, but it's not rain, and for the first time, I taste salt on my tongue.

"It's always in the rain," she murmurs. "With Jason, too."
And whoever this Jason is, I want to kill him.

"I'm sorry," she says, taking another step back. "I never meant to—"
And no, *no*, it's not supposed to be like this.

I shouldn't have kissed her. She has too much else in her mind and heart to bother adding me.
"I'm sorry," I say.
I reach for her, but she pulls back.
And then she's gone.

Water pours from the metal ceiling overhead. In my hand, forgotten until they were all I had left, are the paintbrushes Amy had used to keep her hair in place. Harley's paintbrushes.
I snap them in half and toss them into the pond.

33 : AMY

A splatter of rain on my skin. And Jason's there, and we almost kiss. But it's not rain, it's my steamy shower, and it's not Jason, it's Elder.

My head thunks on the tile of the shower stall, warmed by the steam.

I don't know what to do.

I wrap a towel around myself as I leave the bathroom. The chart I painted on the wall grabs my attention, and I stand, dripping shower water on the matted carpet as I stare at it. It doesn't help. I still can't see any connection between me and Mr. Robertson.

I have never felt this lost—this alone—before in my life. All the people who should be with me—my parents, Jason, my friends—are gone. Without them, the ship feels empty and small—*I* feel empty and small.

I should go to the cryo level and guard my parents. I shouldn't have left Harley there. It's my parents down there, not his. He has no ties to this.

But I saw the longing in his eyes when we left, and I don't want to be the one to pull him from the stars.

And I don't want to be the one alone down there, in the coldness of death.

I sit on the edge of the bed, unwilling to lie down.

I cross the room to the chair by the window. I glance back at the bed, the covers wrinkled but not pulled back. My first night here, Elder sat in this very chair while I slept there.

I pull my feet up into the chair and wrap my arms around my knees. I fall asleep facing the window.

There is no sunrise. The big yellow lamp in the center of the ship's roof flicks on like a light, and it is day.

My head feels fuzzy, like I can't wake up all the way. I grab a glass of cold water from the bathroom, but it doesn't help. If anything, the world is fuzzier. I'm so *tired*. Of thinking, of worrying. There's only one way I know to stop the babble in my head.

Luthe, the tall man who watches me too closely, is the only person in the common room when I go through it to the elevator. Does he ever sleep? It almost feels as if he stays in the common room just so he can stare at me and make me feel uncomfortable. I want to turn around and tell him to keep his eyes to himself, but he'd probably like the attention. He scares me a little, anyway.

The day is only a few minutes old. Without a proper sunrise, it doesn't feel like early morning, just regular daylight, the same it will be at noon or a few minutes before dark. Still, even though it looks like nearly the entire level is sleeping, I stick to the rural areas, jogging past the cows and through the rows of corn with tassels that tickle me as I brush by. After ten minutes or so, I pick up the pace, willing my body to enter the zone.

"Why do you like to run, Red?" Jason asked me after our third or so date, after we had started kissing, but before I'd worked up the courage to tell him I despised the nickname "Red."

"I told you. I love that moment when you get totally focused on running, when all you are is pounding feet."

Harder. I have to run harder.

"I guess I can get that." Jason leaned in for a kiss, but I was already focused on tying my shoestrings, and all he got was a cheek.

I looked up at him. "And I want to win."

"Win?"

I can outrun these memories. I just have to go faster. The cornfield stops against a low fence. Sheep stare at me from the other side. I skid in my turn, racing along the fence.

"Yeah. Win the New York City Marathon. It's kind of my dream." I was avoiding his eyes now not because I was focused on adjusting my socks, but because I'd never told anyone about this before.

"The New York City Marathon?"

"Yeah. It's a big deal. One of the best marathons in the world. Over twenty-six miles, through all the boroughs. But to run it—I mean really run it, not just show up and get to the end—well, you have to be good."

"How good?"

"The best time is like in two and a half hours."

"Two and a half hours? For twenty-six freaking miles? Dude!"

"I know. I'm nowhere near that. But . . ." I glanced up at him now. He wasn't joking, like usual; he was taking me completely seriously.

"You can do it."

"I can barely do ten miles in two hours."

"You can do it. For real. You never give up. I've watched you. One day, you're going to win that marathon, and I'll be at the finish line, waiting for you. With a surprise." He grinned now, mischievous again.

"Lemme guess," I said. *"Is the surprise this?"* And I kissed him, pressing all the love I had for him and his faith in me from my lips to his.

I stop when it hits me, gulping at air that tastes like ozone.

It's not just that there is no Jason. There is no marathon. There is no New York. New York—*New York!* It's huge. There are—there *were* so many people there. No New York. Whatever New York exists now, it's not the way it was. It's not subways and Central Park, marathons and Broadway. By now it's something else entirely—flying cars and teleporters for all I know. I'll never see it, and it will never be what it was. For me, forever, there is no New York.

But, my heart whispers, *there is Elder.*

I run harder.

When I start seeing people outside, awake and beginning their days, I turn back to the Hospital.

I can't lie to myself.

I know I want to hide.

I slow down when I see the cows up close.

They're not normal cows.

I haven't, you know, grown up on a farm or anything, but still, I know what a cow is supposed to look like. And these cows—well, clearly they're supposed to be cows, but I've never seen any cow like these before.

For one thing, they're shorter. A lot shorter. Their heads barely reach my shoulder. The males have horns like cows are supposed to have horns, but they're mushroom shaped and blunted, not because they've been cut off, but because they've grown that way.

They seem as curious about me as I am about them. I stop at the fence and lean over it, panting and sweaty, and a few of the cows wobble in my direction. They have more muscle on them than normal cows, meat bulging under their hides, making them bowlegged and slow. They chew on cud in even, measured movements, smacking a little each time, releasing a whiff of dirt and grass that almost reminds me of home.

One of them moos, but it's not a regular moo; it ends with a squeal like a pig. *Moo-uh-eeee!*

I back away from the fence.

The cow-pig-things watch me as I go, their silent big brown eyes somehow ominous.

Next is a field of plants, at least twice the size of the other fields I've run past, the corn and wheat and green beans. Rows and rows and more rows of bright green leafy plants grow in neat, long lines. I bend down and pluck a round leaf, delicate and a little fuzzy, but it tastes bitter. The stem is thick and hard; I guess the plant is like a carrot or potato—the food part of it is underground.

Then I hear something.

Beep! "Number 517, inoculated." A clatter of something like hard plastic, a scurry of feet.

A low fence made of thick chicken wire encloses the field behind me. Squatting near the edge, bent down so low I didn't see her at first, is a girl a few years older than me, about Harley's age. She's just released a fat, short-legged oversize rabbit, and it's hopping away, shaking its back left leg every few hops. Its fluffy white tail is flashing, and I can hear it chattering its teeth angrily as it bounds off.

I start to say something, but the girl rises up on her knees. Another rabbit nibbles on clover a couple of feet away. Without making a sound, the girl lunges at the rabbit, grabs it by its back legs, and pins it to the ground before it can so much as twitch. She reaches behind her for one of those thin plastic computer things I've seen Elder use, and waves it behind the rabbit's ears, like a cashier at a grocery store checkout. The computer thing beeps, and she glances at it, then tosses it to the ground beside her.

"Hello," I say.

I expect her to be surprised—she hadn't acknowledged before that she'd noticed me—but the girl just glances up and says, "Hello."

She does do a double take when she sees me, though. I remember what Elder said about me, and how easy I'd be to recognize. My hair is sweaty from my run and plastered to my skull, with flyaways escaping my hasty braid. I smooth my hands over it anyway, not that it will do any good; there is no hiding who I am on this ship.

"You're the genetically modified experiment," the girl states. I nod. "Eldest has said we don't have to speak to you."

"Well you don't have to," I say, unable to keep the growl from my voice, "but you could at least be polite."

The girl tilts her head, considering. She reaches behind her and grabs a small basket full of hypodermic needles. About half are empty; the other half contain golden-yellow liquid that looks like honey swirled with butter.

"What's that?" I ask.

"Inoculations," the girl says, turning to the rabbit she still holds pinned to the ground. The rabbit doesn't seem to have any fight in it. It twitches its heavy back legs occasionally but doesn't really struggle against her grip.

"Are these your pets?" I ask.

She looks at me, and I can tell she's thinking about what Eldest said, how I am supposedly slow and stupid. "No," she says. "They are food."

Stupid question. The field is fairly large, and I can see about twenty rabbits nearby, and dozens more in the distance. On the far side of the field is a house—the girl's home, I suppose—and lined around the house are wired hutches for more rabbits. There must be hundreds of people on *Godspeed*; it makes sense that they'd need a source of protein that reproduces as quickly as rabbits.

"I saw you running," she says, her attention on the rabbit. "What were you running from?"

"Just running," I say. She's watching me silently and intently, like a cat.

"Why?" she asks.

I shrug. "Why not?"

"It's not Productive." She says it like productivity is holy, the only thing worth having.

"So?" I say.

Instead of answering, the girl just cocks her head to the left, then turns away from me. She picks up one of the full needles in the basket, jabs it into the rabbit's back leg, and lets the rabbit go. "Number 623, inoculated," she says. The computer thing flashes a wavy line and a green light, and the words she's spoken show up on a chart on the screen.

"What are you inoculating them against?" I ask. How many rabbit diseases could there be on a contained ship?

"It makes them stronger. Healthier. Better meat." She squats on her heels and stares at me. "You live in the Hospital, right?"

I nod.

"My grandfather was taken to the Hospital," she says.

"Is he better now?"

"He's gone."

She says this matter-of-factly, without a hint of emotion, but her eyes are glistening. "I'm sorry," I say.

"Why?" she asks simply. "It was his time."

"You're crying."

She wipes one dirty finger under her eye, leaving a smudge of dirt and green grass stains on her cheek. She looks at the tear on her finger, confused that such emotion should leak from her eyes. "I have no reason to be sad," she tells the evidence dripping down her fingertip. Her voice is even, monotone, and I know she believes she's not sad, even though her body tells her differently.

The girl picks up her basket and then reaches for the computer thing. It's further away than she'd thought, and it slips out of her hands, floating toward me. I catch two words on the top of the screen: GENETIC MODIFICATION.

"What's that say?" I ask, pointing.

She obeys me without question, which surprises me a bit. "Genetic modification to manipulate reproductive genes and muscle mass," she recites in her same even monotone. "Projected increased productivity: 20 percent, with increased meat production at 25 percent."

"Those shots aren't inoculations," I say, searching her blank eyes.

"They're something to do with gene manipulation. I know. My mom was a genetic splicer back—" I pause. She still thinks I'm a freak, a by-product of a science experiment on board the ship. "Look, I'm not who Eldest said I was. I'm from Earth. Sol-Earth, I mean. I was born there. I was cryogenically frozen and I woke up early. And my mother, back on Ear—on Sol-Earth, she was a genetic splicer. That stuff you're injecting the rabbits with—that's not a vaccine. That's genetic modification material. You're changing the rabbits' DNA."

She nods like she's agreeing with me, following every word, but she says, "Eldest said you were simple and didn't understand things."

"I *am* from Earth—but that's not the point! Look, the point is, that stuff is dangerous. Genetic modification material isn't something to play around with, not even with rabbits, especially if you're going to eat them. Don't you know what you're doing?"

"Eldest said it was an inoculation," the girl says. She starts to walk away from me.

"Hey, wait—hold up!" The fence keeps me back.

The girl stops—but only because she is positioning herself to lunge at another rabbit.

"Look, you read that stuff on the computer thing. It says *right there* that you're injecting them with genetic mod material. Right. There." I point at the screen. She looks down at it, curiously, like she's looking for what I'm talking about, even though the chart she's been working on is clearly labeled. "Look at that. There. Do you even see the word *inoculation*?"

She shakes her head slowly, her eyes scanning the words on the screen.

"So . . ." I say, waiting for her to realize my point. When she doesn't, I add, "So you're not inoculating the rabbits. You're modifying their DNA."

She looks back up at me, eyes wide, and for a moment I think she's understood. "Oh, no," she says. "You're wrong. Eldest told me. Inoculations." She holds out the basket of needles for me to inspect. "They make the rabbits healthier. Stronger. Better meat."

I start to protest, but her wide, innocent, and empty eyes tell me it would be pointless. I shiver, but it has nothing to do with how cold I feel as my sweat dries on my skin. Eldest's control is absolute. I don't know why this girl is so vacant that she won't believe what's right in front of her face when it contradicts what Eldest has told her. I don't know for sure if it even *is* Eldest behind the unpluggings. But I do know one thing: if it *is* him, and he's got the entire ship blindly following him like this, there's no chance I can stand against him.

34: ELDER

Starlight trickles under my door the next morning. When I emerge from my chamber, yawning and stretching, I see that Eldest has lowered the metal screen over the navigation chart, exposing the lightbulb stars.

"Hey," Eldest says. He's leaning against the wall by his room, staring up at the false stars. He scoots over when I sit down, and I hear glass clattering on the metal floor. A bottle of the drink the Shippers make. Eldest moves to hide it, but he's too late.

We stare at the lightbulbs.

"I forget sometimes," Eldest says. "How hard it is. I've been doing it . . . for so long." He sighs. Although the sharp, stinging scent of the drink lingers in the air, Eldest isn't drunk. I glance at the bottle—it's been opened, but no more than a swallow or two are missing. Trust Eldest not to let go of control even in this.

"I know it's hard," I say.

Eldest shakes his head. "No, you don't. Not really. You're just starting. You . . . haven't had to make the decisions I've had to. You haven't had to live with yourself afterward."

What does he mean by that?

Just what has he *done*?

And another part of me, the part that's felt what it's like to be Elder for sixteen years, not Eldest's fifty-six, that part of me asks: What has he *had* to do?

Because I know Eldest, and what's more, I know the job. And I know why we do the job. Why we live the job. Why we have to.

"It'd be easier, if the Elder before you was still alive. He could take care of you and the Season, and I could take care of—"

"Of what?" I ask, leaning forward.

"Of everything else."

Eldest stands now, the light of the false stars speckling his body. He looks very old. Much older than I've ever seen him before. It's not years that age him, though.

"I *hate* the Season." Eldest's disgust is apparent in his voice.

I start to ask why, but he's not looking at me, and something stays my tongue. I wonder—does he hate it because he has no one to mate with? I've never seen him look at a woman the way Harley used to look at his girlfriend . . . the way I look at Amy. Maybe he had a woman before me, for his Season, but she died. Maybe . . . I swallow. I can't say I haven't wondered before, wondered if Eldest was really my—

"Don't get proud," Eldest says, interrupting my thoughts.

"Sir?"

"Don't get proud. You do what you have to do, whether you like it or not. There's nothing to be proud of, not as Eldest. There's never a right answer. Just keep them alive. Doesn't matter how. Just keep the frexing ship alive."

He picks up his practically full bottle and locks himself in his dark room. The metal screen covers the false stars, and I'm left in darkness too.

An hour later, it's time for the day to begin. Eldest emerges from his chamber. His clothes are pristine, his eyes are clear, and his breath is fresh. I guess the bottle's still full. The conversation beneath the lying stars feels like a dream.

Eldest walks to the hatch that leads to the Shipper Level. The clatter of his steps across the metal floor—uneven from his limp—is the only sound filling the silence.

"You spent all yesterday with that Sol-Earth girl," he says finally, lifting the hatch door.

I shrug.

"I don't have time for lessons right now. The ship comes first. But you've completely ignored my assignment, haven't you? To discover the third cause of discord?"

My head sinks. I had forgotten. It seems so long ago. When I glance up, Eldest is looking over his shoulder, not meeting my eyes. I can't tell what he's thinking, but I doubt it could be good.

"Fine," he says finally.

"Fine?"

"Spend your time with her," Eldest says. "You will see firsthand what sort of trouble she can cause."

Then he descends down the hatch, leaving me with questions I know he won't answer.

I head straight for the grav tube and the Feeder Level. If Elder's giving me permission to abandon his assignment and spend time with Amy, who am I to question it? Orion's on the Recorder Hall porch (leaning with his back obscuring the portrait of Eldest, which makes me grin), and I wave as I pass.

The garden is more crowded than I've ever seen it before. The only sounds drifting through it are the pants and grunts of the people mating, rutting behind the bushes, at the base of the trees, at the foot of the statue, right in the middle of the path. I have to step over squirming, sweaty bodies to enter the Hospital.

The elevator, thankfully, is empty. But it doesn't smell as if it's been empty for long.

In the Ward, there is some semblance of sanity. Yes, Victria and Bartie are kissing in the corner, and several of the acting troupe are pressed against the glass wall, but most of them are mostly clothed.

I half expect Amy to be like the rest of them when I knock on her door—I half hope it—but she's not. She's dressed, looking out the window.

"Why are they doing that? In public, everywhere . . ." she whispers as I walk into her room.

"It's the Season."

"This . . . isn't normal. People don't act like this. This is . . . mating, it's not love."

I shrug. "Of course it's mating. That's the point. To make a new gen."

"Everyone? All at once? Everyone decides to have sex *now*?"

I nod. Maybe her parents never told her about the Season, but surely she was old enough to know. All animals go into heat. People have a Season just like the cows, the sheep, the goats.

Amy snorts. "Must be something in the water," she says with a weak laugh, as if it were a joke. Her face grows dark again, though, and she says in a low whisper, mostly to herself, "But it's not *natural.*"

I don't answer. I'm too busy thinking about how when we're twenty, we'll be in Season. Together. Just us.

She's said something. I shake my head to clear it from the thoughts invading my brain.

"Will you?" she asks.

"Will I what?"

"Will you go with me to see my parents?"

I take a deep breath, let it out slowly. "Amy . . . they're still frozen."

"I know," she says in a calm, even tone. "But I still want to see them. I don't think I can stand watch on that floor without first seeing them properly."

So I go with her.

The lights are already on in the cryo level. Amy steps out first and looks around at the rows and rows of square doors.

I follow her as she silently goes down one aisle. Her fingers bounce on the metal doors. At the end of the row, Amy turns to me.

"I don't even know which one is them." She sounds lost.

"I can look that up," I say. I go around her to the table at the end of the row and pick up the floppy on it.

"What were their names?" I say.

"Maria Martin and Bob—Robert Martin."

I tap their names onto the on-screen keyboard. "Numbers 40 and 41," I say. Before I can put the floppy down, Amy's running up the rows, counting under her breath. She stops in front of the two side-by-side doors labeled with her parents' numbers.

"Do you want me to open it?" I ask.

Amy nods her head, yes, but when I step forward with my arm outstretched, she grabs my hand. "I'll do it," she says, but she doesn't, she just stands there, looking at the closed doors.

3 5 : AMY

I want to see them.

I want to trace Mom's laugh lines with my eyes. I want to touch Daddy's scruffy beard with my smooth cheek.

I want to see them.

But I don't want to see them as frozen meat.

36: ELDER

"Amy?"

Amy and I both whirl around. Harley is standing at the end of the row.

"What have you been doing down here?" I ask.

Harley yawns as he walks over to us. "Standing guard. Like we said we would. No one's been down here but you two."

"I'll stay tonight," I say guiltily, looking at the dark circles under Harley's eyes.

"Nah, you won't." Harley grins at me. "You can't. Eldest would notice. I don't mind it down here. It's quiet and gives me a chance to paint." I know Harley. I know how obsessed he can get. He's probably spent more time looking at the stars than guarding the frozens.

I lean in closer, so Amy won't hear. "But your meds—"

I'm not just talking about the blue-and-white Inhibitor pill we both take, that everyone in the Ward takes. Harley's been on more meds than that, for his "episodes," ever since—

"I'll be fine," Harley says and even though I'm not sure I believe him, I can tell from the way he's looking at Amy that he doesn't want to discuss this issue in front of her.

"Why don't you come with us? Amy's finding her parents," I say.

Harley hesitates—he wants to return to the stars. But when he sees me staring at him in concern, he changes his mind.

"Okay," he says, even as he glances toward the hallway leading to the hatch. There is something in the empty hollow of Harley's eyes, a greedy sort of longing, that makes me worry about him. It's the same sort of obsession he fell into last time.

"I'm done here," Amy says from behind me.

"Are you sure?" I ask. She nods.

"But . . . don't you want to get your trunk?" I ask her, glancing at the floppy.

"My trunk?"

"The one you packed before you were frozen? It's recorded here that you and your parents each have a trunk."

37: AMY

My heart thuds as Harley and I follow Elder past the rows of little metal doors to a wall lined with lockers.

I never packed anything for this. Mom and Daddy never told me that I could take anything with me.

Elder pulls open a locker; a stack of ten suitcase-size trunks lines the inside.

"Here you are," he says, pulling out three trunks.

Harley and Elder stand over me as I push the button on the first trunk. The lid opens with an audible pop—the airlock preservation seal breaks.

This one must be Mom's trunk. Her perfume wafts up as soon as the lid opens. I breathe deeply, eyes closed, remembering how her clothes smelled of this same perfume when I played dress up so many years ago. I breathe again and realize that all I can smell is the bitter preservation gas they must have filled the trunk with, and Mom's perfume is nothing but memory.

I pick up the clear preservation bag filled with pictures.

"What's that?" Harley asks.

"The ocean."

He stares at it, open-mouthed.

"And that?" Elder asks.

"This was our family trip to the Grand Canyon."

Elder takes the picture I hand to him. He traces the stone carved by the Colorado River with his finger. He looks incredulous, as if he doesn't quite believe that the canyon behind my parents and me is real.

"This is all water?" Harley asks, pointing at the picture of me making a sand castle on the beach when I was seven.

I laugh. "All water! It's salty, which is gross, but the waves are always going up and down, in and out. My daddy and I used to jump in the waves, see how far out we could go, and then ride them back to the shoreline."

"All water," Harley mutters. "All water."

The other pictures aren't as exciting. They are mostly of me. Me as a baby. Me as a toddler, in my grandparents' garden, among the pumpkin vines. First day of school. Me at prom in my black slinky dress, standing next to Jason, accepting his cornflower corsage.

I root around deeper in the trunk. There's something I know Mom wouldn't have left on Earth. When my fingers close on something small and hard, my heart gives a little lurch. I withdraw the round-topped velvet box from the trunk and hold it in my palm.

"What's that?" Elder asks. Harley is still staring at the ocean.

Inside the box is a gold cross necklace. My grandmother's cross.

Elder laughs. "Don't tell me you're one of the ones who believed in those fairy tales!"

His laugh dies as I put the cross around my neck, never once breaking eye contact with him. "This ship is named *Godspeed*," I say, adjusting the cross to lie at the center of my chest.

"*Godspeed* just means luck."

I turn from Elder, stare out at the frozen morgue doors. "It means more than that."

I swallow and put the pictures back into the trunk. Except for the one of my family and me at the Grand Canyon.

The cross swings forward as I reach for Daddy's trunk. It's filled with mostly books. Some I recognize: the complete works of Shakespeare, *Pilgrim's Progress*, the Bible, *The Hitchhiker's Guide to the Galaxy*. Ten or twelve books on military tactics, survival, and science. Three books filled with blank paper and a pack of unopened mechanical pencils. I set one notebook and three pencils aside.

I hesitate, then reach back in the trunk for Sun Tzu's *The Art of War*. I've never read the book, but I'm judging by the title that it'll give me some pointers on what to do with whoever's unplugging people. I tuck it away under the notebook, hoping Elder didn't notice the title. Somehow, some way, I'm sure his mentor Eldest is at the bottom of all this, and I'm afraid that if it comes down to it, I might have to wage a war against him all by myself.

And then I see it.

My teddy bear.

I lift her up. The big green bow at her neck is lopsided and the felt is worn off her nose. The fur on her right paw is almost gone, because when I was a baby, I used to suck on it instead of my thumb.

I hug Amber to my chest, longing for something I know felt and stuffing can't give.

"Last trunk," Elder says, pushing it toward me as I close Daddy's trunk.

I take a deep breath. I squeeze Amber.

But that trunk is empty.

"Where's your stuff?" Harley asks, leaning over my shoulder.

Tears prick my eyes.

"Daddy didn't think I was going to go," I said. "He didn't pack anything for me, because he didn't think I was really going with them."

38: ELDER

"But it's okay," I say. "We've got everything you need here on the ship. You won't have to worry about clothes or anything."

Harley punches me in the arm.

"What?"

Amy hugs her stuffed animal and picks up the notebook, pencils, book, and photograph she's selected from her parents' boxes. "I'm done here," she says in a hollow voice.

Harley helps me load the trunks back into the locker. He keeps shooting me these looks and waggling his eyebrows at Amy, but I have no idea what he means by it.

Click. Whoosh. Thud.

Amy drops the stuffed animal and books, the pencils clatter on the floor, and the photograph drifts down. "I know that sound," she breathes, and she's off, running down the aisle toward the rows of frozen bodies.

"Amy, wait!" Harley calls, but I just chase after her. She skids around the corner in the row of sixties.

"Hurry up!" she screams.

I round the corner. Fog is rising from a glass box resting in the center of the aisle.

"Did you do this?" I ask, even though I know the answer.

"Of course not!" Amy says, her voice raspy, as if she's trying to say everything at once. "Is she going to wake up like me?"

I glance at the box—there is a woman inside, a taller, heavier woman than Amy with dark kinky hair and darker skin than mine. The light at the top of the box blinks red. I look at the black electrical box. The switch inside has been flipped.

I jab my finger into my wi-com button. "Com link: Doc. *Now!*"

"What is it?" Doc's voice fills my wi-com.

"Doc! There's been another one! There's another box out here! Come quick!"

"Wait, what?"

"Down in the cryo level. One of the other frozens. She's been pulled outside. *The light is red!*"

"I'll be right there."

Doc disconnects the link. I hope he's close. If he's in the Hospital, he'll be here in minutes—if he's in the City or on the Shipper Level, it will be longer.

"What's going on?" Harley asks.

"Someone's done to this woman what they did to me," Amy says. "Someone just unplugged me, left me here to die."

"So will she wake up?" Harley asks.

"I don't know. I think if we flip the switch back, put her back in . . . but I don't know. I'm afraid to mess with it. It looks so simple, but . . ."

"Don't let her wake up," Amy says softly. "It's bad, being frozen, but it's better than waking up alone."

My heart jerks. She still thinks of herself as alone.

"Elder?" a voice calls.

"Here!" I call back. "Number . . . " I glance at the open door. "Number 63!"

Doc races down the aisle. He shoves Harley aside as he bends over the glass box. He wipes away the fog blurring the glass. "She's not been out long," Doc says. "She's hardly melted at all."

"That's good, right? Right?" Amy's fingers press against the glass box, like she's trying to reach through the ice and hold the woman's hand.

"Good," Doc says. He bumps into me. I step back. Doc leans over the glass, looking at the electrical box. He plugs a floppy into a wire on the box and reads the numbers that pop up on the screen. He grunts, but I can't tell whether it's a good grunt or a bad grunt. He taps some more numbers onto the floppy, then unhooks it before flipping the switch. The light fades from red to green.

Doc shoves the glass box into the cryo chamber. He slams the door shut and pulls down the latch. A trace of cold swirls up around us, the only evidence that Number 63 was out at all.

"She's fine," Doc says. "You caught her in time."

"Guys?" Harley calls. I look behind me in surprise—Harley has walked down the aisle and away from us, on the other side, out of sight.

"How did you know she was here?" Doc asks.

"I heard it," Amy says.

Doc's face scrunches in concentration. "That means whoever did this was down here when you were. Why were you down here, anyway?"

"I wanted to show Amy her parents' trunks," I say before Amy can mention how we were going to look at her parents. I somehow think admitting we were going to mess with the cryo chambers may not be a good thing to do now.

"Uh . . . guys?" Harley calls from two rows over.

"I don't like this," Doc says. "Whoever was down here when you were must have known you were here, must have known you would hear what was happening. Other than you three, did anyone else come?"

Amy and I glance at each other. "Not that I know of," she says.

"Me neither."

"Guys!" Harley shouts.

"*What?!*" I shout back.

"Come to the twenties row. Now!"

Doc starts walking, but Amy and I know better: we run. The urgency in Harley's voice wasn't false. Something is wrong.

When we round the corner, it's clear what Harley was shouting about.

Another box lies in the center of the aisle. But this one has melted. And the man inside is already dead.

39: AMY

"Oh."

I hadn't meant to say it out loud.

But I know this man.

Mr. Kennedy had worked with my mom, and I'd always thought he was a little creepy. He was one of those old men who never got married but who thinks that because he's old, he can be a pervert and get away with it. He was always looking down my mom's shirt or getting me to pick up something off the floor whenever I came to the lab to visit my parents. Mom always laughed it off, but I wondered what Mr. Kennedy did at home with his memories of my mom's wrinkled cleavage or my panty line.

And now he's dead, floating in the cryo liquid with his eyes opened and his irises milky. His skin is sallow, as if soaked with water like a sponge. His mouth is slack, and his cheeks sag, creating tiny water-filled balloons at his jaw.

"Number 63 was a distraction," Elder says.

"I don't think so," Doc says. "This one has been out for a while." He lifts the lid of the glass box up, and Harley and Elder help him set it down on the floor. Doc dips his finger into the liquid Mr. Kennedy floats in. "The water's cool, but not cold. He could have been unplugged yesterday, last night at the latest."

Elder catches my eye. While we were running through the rain, laughing, Mr. Kennedy was drowning. As that couple made love on the bench by the pond, Mr. Kennedy was dying. As I stripped off my wet clothes and stood in the steamy shower, as I fell asleep gazing at the dark fields, Mr. Kennedy was swimming in death.

Another thought: Harley was here the same time the killer was.

"Why?" I ask.

Doc taps on his thin computer thing. "Number 26. A man named—"

"Mr. Kennedy," I say.

"Yes." Doc looks at me, surprise on his face.

"I knew him before."

"Ah. I'm sorry," he says, but in an offhand manner, as if he's just saying it to be polite. "Number 26—"

"Mr. Kennedy."

"*Mr. Kennedy* was a weapons specialist."

"Really?" I ask. Even though Mr. Kennedy worked in the same department as my mother, I'd never known that he had anything to do with weapons. My mother didn't. She worked on genetic splicing. She dealt with DNA, not weapons.

Doc nods. "He was well learned in bio-weaponry. It says here he worked with the government to develop eco bombs."

"Who is doing this?" Elder asks. "Who is unplugging all these people? First William Robertson, then the woman, Number 63, now this guy."

"And me," I add.

Elder's brow furrows as he stares at me.

"Two victims—two near misses," the doctor says.

"And no reason why." I stare at the empty cryo chamber, where Mr. Kennedy once was. And past it, to the rows and rows of little doors with numbers scrawled on them. How many cryo chambers will be empty before we can stop the killer?

40: ELDER

Harley and I wheel Mr. Kennedy to the release hatch for Doc. Amy says she'll wait for us. But I know she wants to go to the other row, to see her parents' doors, to make sure they're still sealed shut.

Doc opens the hatch door, and Harley and I dump the body inside. The door slams shut, protecting us from the maw of open space. Harley peers through the bubble glass window, eyes wide, relishing in one more chance to see the stars. But I only see Mr. Kennedy's bloated body.

And I look at Harley, and the billions of stars are in his eyes, and he's drinking them up, pouring them into his soul. He raises his arms to the window, and for a moment I have a crazy vision of Harley trying to open the door, to fly after Mr. Kennedy and reach the stars. The hatch closes. But the light of the stars is still in Harley's eyes.

"They're more beautiful than anything I've ever seen," Harley whispers.

"Yeah, I'm sure Mr. Kennedy agrees," I say, but Harley doesn't notice my sarcasm.

"Come on, boys." Doc's worried expression deepens the lines at his eyes.

Amy is wiping her face when we get back. She's retrieved her stuffed animal, photos, pencils, and books from where she'd dropped them by the lockers. Doc looks at them, but he doesn't comment. He picks up a floppy and fiddles with it. Wasting time. Preparing to say whatever it is he means to say.

And I know then: he's thinking about how he is going to contact Eldest and tell him about this. And I know that the reason why he's fiddling with the floppy is to give himself time to think of something to say to me so that I will acquiesce.

I stand a little straighter. Before, Doc would have just called for Eldest without thinking of me, without even consulting me.

"Elder," Doc says, "I know you understand the gravity of the situation. But Amy, Harley, it is vital that you do not tell anyone else about this. Not about Mr. Kennedy, not about the hatch"—he glares at Harley—"not about the people down here, not about the fact that there is even a level below the Hospital. You *must* keep this secret."

It's coming. I can feel it. That niggling doubt Doc has that he still needs to refer to Eldest.

His hand inches toward his wi-com.

Ah. There it is.

"You don't need to com Eldest," I say. "I vouch for Amy and Harley." I shift my weight so that I'm between Doc and them. I've always been tall, but I don't let myself slouch now. Instead, I make Doc look up to meet my eyes.

He hesitates, but finally nods. "You're the Elder." He means, I'm the one who will have to answer to Eldest.

"Little Fish and I will be fine," Harley says, throwing an arm around Amy. "You don't have to worry about us."

Doc's doubt returns. "Maybe I should com Eldest anyway, just see what he thinks."

"No," I say.

"What?"

"I've got just as much authority as he does. The Season is in full swing up there, and my gen is coming from that. Doc, you've got to learn to trust me, not just Eldest. I say Amy and Harley are fine knowing this, and that we can trust them. And I say it's time to go. But first," I add before Doc can say anything else, "let me see your floppy."

"My . . . ?"

"Your floppy." I take the digital membrane computer from his still fingers. The scanner reads my thumbprint and grants me Eldest/Elder access. I tap quickly, with the back of the screen black. I don't want any of them to see what I'm looking for.

I'm trying to find out who has been here in the lower level. The scanners on the doors read thumbprints; it shouldn't be that hard to find a trail of thumbs leading to this level, this aisle of cryo chambers, this murder of a helpless frozen victim. And it isn't hard to find. When we checked before, we didn't have a time frame—Doc had been down to the cryo level, and so had Eldest and a handful of Shipper scientists.

But since then, there's only been one person on the cryo level other than us.

I stare at the name on the screen.

Eldest.

41: AMY

Elder doesn't get on the elevator.

"I've got something else to do," he says. There is a dark, serious manner in the way he stands now. I never noticed how much he slouched until he stood up straight. Before, I knew he was the destined leader of this ship merely because Doc and Eldest told me he was. Now I look at him, and I can see the determined leader within.

A part of me wants to stay here, on this level, and protect my parents from whoever is clever enough to unplug the frozen people while we're all down there on the same level, but I can see that Elder needs to be by himself down here, for whatever purpose, and I trust him to guard my parents.

"Elder, I think you should come back with us, meet with Eldest," Doc says.

"Oh, I'm going to meet with Eldest," Elder says, and he reaches over, pushes the elevator button for Doc, and stands back as the doors slide shut. Before they close all the way, he turns away from the elevator and strides purposefully down the hall.

"I think his chutz is up, don't you?" Harley says in a conversational tone. He's awfully cheerful for someone who's just dumped a body out into space.

Doc harrumphs.

When the elevator stops, Doc storms off. I watch him, waiting for him to push that little button behind his left ear and snitch on Elder, but he doesn't—he just keeps walking.

"Wanna go back to the Ward?" Harley asks, holding his arm out in mock chivalry.

"Let's go to that garden Elder showed me," I say.

"Oh, he showed you the garden?" A lopsided grin smears across Harley's face. He starts to head down the hallway.

"It must be weird for him," I say. "He's the youngest one on the ship, but he's also something of a leader. I don't know if I could tell someone older than me to do something and expect them to do it."

Harley looks at me out of the corner of his eye. "You're a strange one, Little Fish."

"How so?" I grin back, willing to play along.

"You're thinking about how weird it is for Elder on the ship. But you're the fish out of water."

I snort. "It's easier to think of Elder than myself." Unexpected tears prick my eyes. I had not meant to say something so close to the truth.

When we get to the doors in the lobby, Harley holds them open for me, and I step out into fresh sunlight and the smell of grass after a light rain.

And the sweaty, musky smell of sex.

"Frex. Forgot about the Season for a second," Harley says as a half-naked couple bump into him, so distracted by their passionate groping and kissing that they don't even notice Harley standing there. "Let's go back inside."

"Come on, we'll just go away from the crowded areas. I don't think I can stand being inside anymore." I think I will never like enclosed spaces again. When I was younger, before the freezing, I never felt claustrophobic. Now, even here, on the edge of a garden, outside, tight bands squeeze the air from my lungs, and my vision lingers on the walls that seem to constantly be pressing down on me. I close my eyes. If I let myself think about it, it's so, so much worse.

"The light is good out here," Harley says as we start down the path away from the Hospital. "Shite, I wish I had my paints!"

I laugh. "Go ahead. Get them. I'll wait here."

Harley hesitates. "It's not safe. Not now."

I think of the crowd of people I ran into on my first run. Now seems like the perfect time to be out—none of the people are going to care about me. They're way too busy with each other.

"Seriously," I say when Harley looks wistfully back up at the Hospital. "I'll go to that wheat field. No one's over there; they're all in the garden or on the road."

"Come with me," Harley says. He grabs my wrist and starts to pull me to the Hospital, but I wriggle out of his grip.

"I really need to not be in a building. I need some fresh air. Go on!" I laugh, shooing him down the path. "I'll be fine."

Harley hesitates again, but the pull of his paint is too much. "Be careful, Little Fish," he says seriously. I nod, smiling. He sprints up the path to the Hospital. I stroll the opposite direction, toward the field.

I was right: the further I get from the garden, the fewer people are around. The path is practically empty, and it is only from the moaning and sighs that I know there are people further out in the fields, behind the trees, in the ditch beside the path. I try to ignore them. It creeps me out to see people so loose. I know that when I lived on Earth, I must have seen people having sex on TV a million times. But it's not the same when people are having sex right in front of you.

"It's her."

My first instinct is to freeze; my next one is to run. I know from the tone of voice that whoever spoke was talking about me. I risk glancing back. There are three men, all about Harley's age, all follow-ing me. I don't recognize two of them — Feeders who do some kind of heavy labor judging by the size of their muscles.

My stomach drops.

I do recognize the third one.

Luthe, who's always staring at me, always watching me in the Ward.

"Hey, freak!" Luthe calls when he sees me looking. He wiggles his fingers at me in a mock hello, and the other two men laugh.

I start walking faster. I wonder if the moaning, sighing masses of sweaty people in the fields will look up if I call for help. I somehow doubt it.

I can hear their heavy footfalls behind me. Their stride is longer than mine; they've already set their pace quicker.

"Don't think I wanna freak," one of them says.

"I do," Luthe responds.

I quit caring about what I look like. I *run*. My legs pump high and hard, and I have panic to fuel me. One of them curses, and I realize the chase is on. I cut into a field, but the wheat slows me, and my wild race leaves a clear trail right toward me. I leap over a pair of lovers in the field who do not even notice my presence, let alone my plight. I turn around to see how close the men are.

Too close.

And I am too stupid. I trip over a pair of heaving bodies and land in the wheat, rolling over tall, sharp stalks. The girl, who is on top, looks at me with love-hazed eyes, then grins in an inviting sort of way. I scoot back, feeling the wheat bend and break under my body, struggling to regain my footing.

But I'm not quick enough.

One of the big Feeder men is on top of me first.

I struggle to get up, but my squirming only excites him. I still my body, but jerk my hands. He pins my wrists to the ground under his meaty fists, and now the other two men have caught up. The other Feeder grabs my ankles. Luthe drops to the ground beside me, leaning over my face. Grinning.

I thrash against the men. They all laugh, a deep, guttural sound that isn't humorous at all.

I jerk my head to the naked couple I tripped over. "Help me!" I say.

The woman arches her back, digs her hips against the man she's riding.

"Help me!" I scream.

The man beneath her stares back at me, but his eyes are glazed. He smiles dreamily. The woman notices, and turns to look at me. "It only hurts the first time," she says, and then she thrusts against the man, and he moans, and she moans, and they have forgotten all about me.

Luthe straddles me and rips my tunic off, curses at the undershirt I've been wearing in place of a bra, and rips it off, too. The tattered remains of my clothes pool at my arms, but my breasts are exposed. And even though I've seen half the crew of this ship walking around naked in a lovemaking haze, I am ashamed of my nudity. And terrified.

Luthe bends over me and buries his face in my breasts. I try to wriggle away, but he moans in desire and grinds his pelvis harder against my hips. One hand fumbles with his trousers while the other twists my breast, hard. The Feeder man holding my arms makes a noise deep inside his throat, and bends down, licking my arms, nibbling my skin playfully at first, then harder bites that were they to have come from my boyfriend Jason, I would have liked.

The Feeder looks up at me as I start to cry. There is blank nothing in his gaze, vacant emptiness. He is lustful in the way an animal in heat is lustful. Luthe, however, is not. His huge smile exposes all his teeth. He's been watching me from the moment I first entered the Ward.

And he *knows*.

I can tell it in his eyes. Most of the people—the Feeders—they're acting like animals. But this guy's not acting at all. He knows what he's doing.

And he likes it.

It's hopeless.

The man holding my ankles starts to tug at my pants.

I kick him, and I'm fairly certain that my heel connects with his teeth. He shouts, and his shout is not one of lust but of pain. But Luthe has gotten hold of his idea and starts yanking at the waist of my pants.

I open my mouth to scream, and the man holding my arms presses his mouth against mine, his tongue delving deep into me, rooting around against the soft palate of my mouth.

I bite until I taste blood. I bite even as he tries to jerk his tongue away. When he finally escapes, I spit his blood from my mouth, and scream.

"Little Fish! Amy!" Harley's voice is panicked.

"*Harley!*" I scream with all my might. "HARLEY!"

And then he's there, and he bangs his easel against the man straddling me, and his easel breaks apart, and now he's pummeling the men with his fists. And I curl up into a ball, holding myself with myself, and choking back my tears. The Feeder men run away, but Luthe stands to fight. He and Harley circle each other like vultures circling a carcass, and I know I'm the carcass. Luthe hits first, but Harley hits harder. Luthe sprawls down, but he's not knocked out. Harley grabs my wrist.

"Come on. Come *on*," he says, yanking me up. My pants are loosened and they slip over my hip. I hold them with one hand, I hold Harley with the other, and I run and run and run, and I can hear the man's heavy footsteps behind me, and then I don't hear them anymore, but still I run and run and run, and I'm holding onto Harley like he's the rope pulling me from the undertow.

42: ELDER

Orion told me that the only way to get around Eldest was to be sneaky. I have never had a reason to be sneaky before now.

But it's not like I don't know how.

As soon as the elevator doors close, taking Amy, Harley, and Doc back to the Hospital, I turn the floppy over in my hand.

First I check the biometric scan logs. The elevator opened to Harley's biometric scan last night, and he spent all night here on this floor. Doc was down here and back up again early in the day, just before the solar lamp turned on, and he was only here for a few minutes. But another name is logged between his name and mine.

ELDEST/ELDER, 0724 HOURS

I wasn't down here at 7:24 a.m. That just leaves Eldest.

Now to find out where he is.

It's a simple enough thing to do. Override the access with my thumb scan and upload the wi-com receiver locations.

I zoom in on the screen. There's Doc, in his office. Bartie and Victria are in the Ward common room, close together. Harley's going down the path toward the fields—from his speed, I guess he's running. Wonder why. Amy's not on the screen—she doesn't have a wi-com.

"Find Eldest," I command. One of the dots starts blinking blue.

He's here. On this level. Past the aisles of frozens, behind the door on the far wall. Doc's "other" lab.

The door is closed, and I'm not sure Eldest would let me in if I knocked. Orion had told me that the rules don't apply to Eldest, that he doesn't follow the rules. So why should I?

A sterile disinfectant smell greets me as I enter the cramped room. Rows and rows of refrigeration tubes line one side of the wall. Inside the clear tubes, I see more cryo liquid with bubbles of goo and solid masses floating inside. Although I know I should be looking for Eldest, I cannot help but get a closer look at the gelatinous material. The chunky stuff inside each of the bubbles looks like curled up, malformed beans.

"They're embryos."

Eldest has found me. But he isn't glowering at me. He actually looks a bit pleased to see me. If anything, that just puts me more on edge.

"When we land, we'll artificially birth them."

"Embryos of what?" I ask. I slip the floppy into my pocket. No reason for Eldest to know I was looking for him, not when he found me first.

"Animals. You're looking at the cat tube. Cougars, I think, maybe bobcats. I'd have to look it up."

I struggle to remember what a cougar is. I think it's something like a lion, but the pictures I've seen on the floppies in the Recorder Hall all run together.

"What are they here for?"

"When we land. We don't know what animals from Sol-Earth we'll need. There may be animals on the planet that are detrimental, and we'll need predators to eliminate them. We'll introduce ones from Sol-Earth. Or there may be animals that are good, but require new traits to make them useful to us. We'll attempt crossbreeding or genetic splicing."

I'm not interested in big lion-cats. I want to know why Eldest was the last one in the cryo chamber room, just before another frozen person drowned.

Before I can speak, Eldest strides past me to a table on the other side of the room. There is only one glass tube on this side, halfway empty. The embryos float in the cryo liquid like bubbles in gel, scattered throughout the tube. I lean in closer to look at one, examining the little bean-shaped fetus inside the amniotic sac. When I look up, I see Eldest watching me intently, a furrow of concern creasing his brow. His gaze doesn't waiver when our eyes meet.

"What have you come here for?" he asks finally. "I didn't think you even knew about this lab. Did Doc tell you?"

I shrug, unwilling to scamp out either Doc or myself.

"It doesn't matter. I should have brought you here sooner. You'll only have this one Season to prepare, then you'll have to teach the Elder after you what to do."

"What to do?" I ask.

Eldest picks up a big needle from the table beside the refrigeration tube. The actual metal part of the needle is nearly a foot long, and there's at least twenty ounces of liquid inside the cylinder.

"You know that one of the biggest concerns on a generation ship is incest." Eldest puts the needle down in a basket, picks up another one, and places it in the basket next to the first. "It is inevitable that, with a limited population of people, eventually the bloodlines will become too intermingled."

He selects a needle from another stack this time. There is a tiny black-and-yellow label near the plunger of each needle. The one in Eldest's hand now states simply "visual art."

"I know all this," I say. "It's why the Plague Eldest developed the Season. So that you—we—could monitor reproduction."

"Yes, that's part of it." Eldest is distracted as he selects more needles to put into the basket. "But another problem isn't just preventing mental and physical handicaps from incest. Another problem is that this ship's mission is so important, we cannot afford a generation that has no genius or talent."

Now the needles he's selecting are from another stack, one labeled "mathematics." He takes five of these needles for the basket.

"The founders of the ship never intended us to be just idle farmers while we waited to land. We need inventors, artists, scientists. We need people who can think and process and develop whole new things for the ship and the new world."

Three "audio arts" go into the basket, followed by ten "science: biological."

"We have gained so much during our centuries of travel. Wi-coms were developed here. So were floppies. We modified the gravtube when I was younger than you."

Eldest grabs a handful of "science: physical," and puts five or six into the basket. He thinks for a moment, then takes two out of the basket and places them back on the table with the rest of the stack.

"Okay, so we need smart people on the ship. What's that got to do with anything?" I ask.

Eldest holds up a needle labeled "analytical."

"In each of these needles," he says, waggling the one he's holding at my face, "there is a special compound that combines DNA and RNA, a chimera. It makes a bond with the DNA of the fetus in an impregnated woman and ensures that the child born has certain desirable characteristics."

I open my mouth to speak, but Eldest interrupts. "When you are Eldest, you must analyze the needs of your ship. Does your generation lack scientists? Make more. Do you need more artists? Ensure that more are born. It is your responsibility to make the people of this ship not only survive, but *thrive*."

My stomach squirms. I'm not sure if I agree with Eldest or not—I don't like to think of a ship full of inbred idiots, but I also don't like how Eldest thinks he can just engineer genius.

Eldest places the last needle in the basket and looks up at me. His face is very serious, but he looks tired, too, as if he is made of wax and slowly melting. "I don't say this enough. But I believe in you. I think you'll be a good leader. One day."

I want to smile and thank him—I don't even remember the last time Eldest complimented me like this—but at the same time, I cannot help but wonder if the reason Eldest is so sure I'll be an okay leader is because I was injected with some "leadership" goo before I was born.

And if I have been, I wonder if it was enough.

43 : AMY

I am curled on my bed, my legs tucked under my chin, my arms wrapped around my knees. My teddy bear, Amber, is tucked between my chest and my knees. Her button eyes and nose dig into my ribs, but I don't care.

Harley hands me a glass of cool water.

"I'm sorry," Harley says. An angry purple-red bruise the size of my pinky finger underscores his left eye.

He touches my hand, and I flinch. I want to cry, I want to scream, I want to hide, but all I can do is flinch because a man came close enough to touch me.

"I'm sorry," Harley says again. He backs up and sits at the desk chair, all the way on the other side of the room. He sits on the edge of his seat, as if ready to jump up and protect me again. But he holds himself back. His hands grip the armrest, making sure he doesn't touch me again.

I raise my head. "No . . . I mean . . . Thank you. You saved me."

Harley shakes his head. "I left you. That was stupid. I knew the Season was full on. I've seen it getting worse since yesterday. And I left you alone."

"Why were they like that?" I ask. In my mind's eye, I can still see the glazed look of the couple having sex beside me, of how they turned away from my screams. I press Amber closer into me, relishing the feeling of her buttons grinding into my ribcage, wondering how the bruises she makes will compare to the ones already blossoming on my wrists.

Harley shrugs. "That's just the way the Season is. Wasn't Sol-Earth like that? People are animals. No matter how civilized we are, when our mating season arrives, we mate."

"Not you. Not Elder. Not everyone's acting like they're insane with lust."

Harley's brows knit together, a ridge of flesh forming between his eyes. It reminds me of the deep, heavy brow of the man who was on top of me, who held me down, who ground his hips against mine. I bury my face into Amber's fake brown fur, and I breathe in her musty smell. My arms tense around my knees, and my hands grip my legs, and I'm glad, because if I wasn't holding on to myself, I think my body would all fall apart like a puzzle lifted at the corners.

Harley has not noticed that I'm quivering under my hard exterior. "Actually, a lot of the people in the Ward are fine. Some are using the Season as an excuse to act . . . recklessly . . . but most of the Ward patients aren't quite so . . ."

"Crazy?" My voice cracks.

"Ironic, huh? The crazy people are less affected by all this than any of the others. Maybe it's our mental meds. They're called

'Inhibitors.' They're supposed to inhibit the crazy, but maybe they inhibit lust as well."

Didn't seem to inhibit Luthe's lust. He knew what he was doing. But the Feeders hadn't, not really. I wonder if it's because the Feeders are so brainless. Whatever's making them want to screw, the Feeders just do it, like how that girl with the rabbits just believed what Eldest had told her, even when she read the truth. People like Harley and Luthe, who aren't mindless idiots, have more control over themselves. They can choose to be kind, like Harley.

Or they can choose to be like Luthe.

Harley's still talking, trying to distract me from everything. He talks like talking will make everything okay again, but it isn't, it can't be, it won't be. I just want him to go.

Harley stands up. "Let me get you some more water."

"No." I want to be alone. I want him to go and let me shrink into myself.

"But I think—"

"NO!" I scream. My hands slip down my sweaty arms. My fingers scrabble back up to my elbows, and my fingernails dig into my flesh so I can't lose my grip on myself again. "No," I whisper. "Please. Just leave me alone. Let me be alone."

"But—"

"Please," I whisper into Amber's fur.

Harley goes.

I lie curled on the bed for a long time, my eyes shut but my vision still achingly clear.

My arms grow tighter and tighter, pulling my knees so hard against my chest that it hurts. It doesn't help. I am tired of hugging myself. I want my daddy to hug me and tell me he'll kill anyone who hurts me. I want my momma to kiss me and stroke my hair and tell me everything will be okay. Because the only way I can believe anything will ever be okay again is if I hear one of them say it.

I let my knuckles relax. They are white on the edges, and my fingertips tingle as the blood returns to them. The insides of my elbows are slick with sweat. Creaking, popping sounds escape my knees as I stretch my legs fully out.

For a moment, I lie flat on the bed, but that reminds me of lying flat on the grass in the field, and I jump up so quickly that I make myself dizzy.

I cross the room to the door in three long strides, but when I reach for the button to open it, my hands are shaking.

They're still out there.

With their sweating, pulsing bodies, with the up-and-down rhythm, with their hungry eyes and clutching hands.

I have to, I whisper to myself.

But my hands won't stop shaking.

I let my head fall against the cool wall. I am panting from the effort of standing close to the barrier between me and them. I want to call Harley or Elder to me, but I don't have that ear button they use to communicate. And besides, Harley can't save me every time.

I punch the button. The door zips open. Before it has cleared the doorway, I punch the button again, and the door slams back shut just as quickly.

I plan the route in my mind. I imagine myself running, running, running so fast no one can catch me. I can see the path so clear before me that I think I could run it without opening my eyes at all.

My hand slips over the button, and the door flies open. The hall is, thankfully, free of people. I rip open the glass common room door, and hold my breath as I race past the people who are too distracted to notice me streaking by them. My neck screams at me for the number of times I whip it around, looking for danger over my shoulder. I slip inside the empty elevator. And for the first time since I left my room, I allow myself to breathe again as I push the button for the fourth floor.

That hallway is deserted, too, and I send a silent prayer up for that. Still, I run past the locked doors, part of me fearful that they will swing open and reveal rooms full of eager men hungry for something other than food. I don't relax until I'm in the other elevator, sinking down below the madness of the ship, into the deathly quiet of the cryo level.

I want to see where they are. That's all. I tell myself, that's all.

I run, first. But as I get closer and closer, my steps drop off to a walk, then a slow, rhythmic *thud* . . . *thud* . . . *thud* of each individual step on the hard floor.

I come to a complete stop at the row. I stare at their numbered doors: 40 and 41.

And then I run to the doors. I fall to my knees, and my hands are uplifted, one on each door. And I'm sure it looks as if I'm in rapturous praise of something holy, but all that's inside me is a scream ricocheting around my hollow body.

For a long while, I stay on my knees like that, with my arms up and my head down.

I just want to see them. *That's all*, I tell myself, *that's all*.

I stand. I wrap my hands around the handle of the door labeled 40, and I shut my eyes and grip the handle and pull it open. Without looking at the block of ice exposed, I spin on my heels and jerk open number 41, too.

There they are.

My parents.

Or . . . well, at least their bodies are there. Under the blue-flecked ice.

The room is cold, so cold, and I shiver. My arms prickle with goose bumps. The glass coffins are cold and dry. My fingertips skid across the top as I run my hands over my mother's face.

"I need you," I whisper. My breath fogs the glass. I wipe it away, a sheen of wet sparkling on my palm.

I squat, my face parallel to hers. "I need you!" I say. "It's so . . . strange here, and I don't understand any of them, and—and I'm scared. I need you. I need you!"

But she is ice.

I spin to Daddy. Through the ice, I can see the stiff bristles of his beard. When I was little, he'd rub his face against my bare stomach, and I'd scream in glee. I'd give anything to feel that now. I'd give anything to feel anything but cold.

The glass is fogged and the ice isn't crystal clear, but I can see where Daddy's hand is. I rub my pinky against the cold glass, pretending that his finger will wrap around mine in a promise.

I don't realize I'm crying until the tears splash on the coffin. "Daddy, I couldn't do anything. I couldn't get up, Daddy. They were too strong. If it wasn't for Harley—" My voice cracks. "Daddy, you said you'd protect me! You said you'd always be there for me! I need you *now*, Daddy, I need you!"

I pound my fists against the cold hard glass surrounding the ice. My hands crack and bleed, smearing crimson across the glass.

"I NEED YOU!" I scream. I want to break through the glass, to rub life back into his bristly-bearded face.

My body falls limp. I curl up under their cold, lifeless forms, draw my knees to my chest, sob dry, empty sobs, and scrabble to fill my lungs with air that is too thin and weak.

One giant droplet of condensation slips off the glass and plops onto my cheek.

I rub it, and the warmth of my hands brings life back to me.

It doesn't have to be like this. I may be awake, and it may be impossible to put me back inside a cryo chamber . . . but that doesn't mean I can't see my parents.

I stand. This time, I don't look for my parents' faces in the ice. This time, my eyes seek out the tiny black box at their heads, the one with the blinking green light. The one with the switch under the cover.

It can't be that hard. Flip the switch. That's all I have to do. I will stand here and wait. I will pull them from the box when it melts so that it won't drown them. I will help them climb out of their coffins. I will wrap them with towels, and I will hug them, and they will hug me. Daddy will whisper, "Everything will be okay now," and Mom will whisper, "We love you very much."

They're essential, a small voice whispers in my mind. I see the row of flags on the bottom of the door, the symbol for the FRX, the Financial Resource Exchange. They are a part of a mission that's greater than me.

Mom's a genetic splicer, a biological genius. Who knows what life we'll see on this new world? She's needed.

But Daddy—he's with the military, that's all. He's a field analyst. He's sixth in command, let the five in front of him be essential, not him. They can take care of the new world; Daddy can take care of me.

"I'm the failsafe." I can hear Daddy's strong, proud voice in my mind, just like the day he told me we'd be a happy frozen family, wasn't I excited? "That's my mission—if anything goes wrong, I'll be there."

A glorified backup plan. They needed him in case something went wrong. But what if nothing went wrong?

If I leave them Mom, maybe they won't mind that I take Daddy back. He's not *really* needed.

My hand is already on the box over Daddy's head. I run my finger across the biometric scanner at the top. The light blinks yellow. Access denied. I don't have high security clearance; I'm not important enough to be able to open up the box and flip the switch and wake Daddy up.

But I can smash it. The whole idea plays out in my mind—my eyes wild and my hair swinging as I beat the box with my fists until it shatters and I can press the button and melt Daddy.

It's such a ridiculous image that I laugh. A high-pitched hysterical laugh that breaks with a dry sob.

I can't wake up Daddy. He's needed. I know he is, even if I don't want to admit it. I'm proof enough that he's needed—they wouldn't have let me come if he weren't. He and Mom knew what it meant when they signed up for the ship. I remember that first day. They were both willing to say goodbye to me so they could be on this ship.

Daddy had already arranged it so that I could walk away from them. When he hugged me before he was frozen, he was hugging me good-bye. He never expected to see me again. He didn't even pack me a trunk. He gave me up so that he could wake up on another planet.

I can't take his dream away.

If he can say goodbye to me, I can say goodbye to him.

Besides, I'm not so selfish as not to remember my status. I was the nonessential one, not them. If food won't grow or animals won't live, Mom will make it happen. If there's a bunch of evil aliens already on the new planet, Daddy will take care of them.

Either way, they're the difference between a whole planet of peo-ple living and a whole planet of people dying.

I can't take them away from that. I can't kill their dreams, and I can't kill the future inhabitants of the planet I won't reach until I'm older than them.

I can wait. I can wait fifty years until I see them again.

I slide their trays back into their cryo chambers and push the doors shut, then head silently back to the elevator and my lonely room.

I can wait.

44: ELDER

"What's that noise?" I ask, only now noticing the churning sound.

Eldest glances over his shoulder, where the room makes a hard right angle. "The water pump's back there."

I frown. The water processor is on the Shipper Level, not here. But then I remember the blueprints Orion showed me before Amy woke up. There *was* another water pump on the fourth level in the diagram.

"This is old," I say.

"How do you know that?" Eldest asks sharply, but I ignore him.

I step forward, inspecting it. It's nowhere near as big as the pump on the Shipper Level. There's a control panel and, above that, a nozzle. The pump on the Shipper Level is used to recycle, purify, and distribute water. This pump is just designed to mix something into the water. An empty bucket rests beside the pump, a thick, syrup-like substance coating the inside.

"What's that water pump for?" I ask.

Eldest looks at me like he can't believe my stupidity. "To pump water."

"No. That's what the pump on the Shipper Level is for. What's this one for?"

Eldest smiles, and it actually looks genuine. Like he's proud of me for seeing through him. "It was a part of the ship's original design. *Godspeed* is only so big. By adding nutritional supplements to the food and water, we can maintain a population rate of up to one person per two acres. Even with that, though, the ship can't support much more than three thousand people. We've always had to enforce population control." He notices my confused face. "Birth control."

"Through here?" I ask, pointing to the nozzle.

Eldest nods. "We use this water pump to distribute contraceptives and vits to everyone. Mix it directly into the water supply, keep everyone healthy. Why do you think the Feeder wives say to drink water when you don't feel well? And, at the start of the Season, we take out the contraceptives and add in hormones. To increase sexual desire. It works particularly well on the Feeders."

I remember Amy's words, how the Season wasn't natural. She was right.

"I'm glad you're asking these kinds of questions," Eldest says. "Glad you're finally starting to think like an Eldest." He grips the basket in his hands. "It's important for me to know that you are willing to do whatever it takes to make this ship and its people prosper. Whatever. It. Takes."

"Are you?" My voice cracks over the words.

"I always have been." Eldest speaks with such sincerity that I don't question him. "Every moment of my life is spent making this ship a better place for the people on it to live. I know you don't always agree with me, but it *works*."

"Every moment, huh?" I ask. I can feel my chutz rising at Eldest's cocky attitude. I know he's implying that I'm not as dedicated as he is.

"Every moment."

"Then how were you ensuring that the ship prospers when you were in the cryo chambers earlier? What great leadership action were you taking then?"

Eldest straightens up. "I do not have to answer to you, boy."

I know how Eldest operates; I know how to make him talk. "I thought the second cause of discord was lack of one strong central leader. How can you be a strong central leader without disclosing important information to your successor?"

I hear a creak. Eldest is crushing the sides of the basket of needles under his hands. "Why don't you just tell me what you think I should have been doing." It's not a question, it's more of a threat.

"Why not just say what I think you shouldn't have been doing? Like how maybe you shouldn't have been ripping more people from cryo chambers. The man died. The woman would've, if Amy hadn't found her."

Eldest shoves the basket away from him. The needles clatter inside it. "Are you accusing me of opening the cryo chambers, of killing another one of the frozens?"

"All I'm saying is that you've been awful close every time one of them dies."

"I do not have to listen to this drivel from the likes of YOU!" Eldest roars. He heads to the door, but his bad leg makes him stumble.

He crashes into one of the big cylinders of goo, and the bean-shaped things wobble in the bubbles.

"Some leader," I mutter.

Eldest straightens up, glaring at me.

"The third cause of discord," he says in a terrible monotone, "is individual thought. No society can thrive if a single individual can poison its members into mutiny and chaos." He turns now, glaring. "And if the individual thought is coming from the ship's future leader, and if the ship's future leader is spewing forth such vitriol and stupidity that he'd accuse *me* of killing the frozens, then I *pray* to the stars above that he puts something more intelligent in that empty head of his before I die and he takes over!"

"That's just like you, to try to turn this into a lesson about how shite of a leader I'll be!" I shout. "But you haven't told me what you were doing down here, or how Mr. Kennedy ended up drowned just on the other side of this door!" I fling my arm toward the door, hitting the tube of cryo liquid and embryos so hard that the embryos inside jiggle like fruit in gelatin.

"You are a fool," Eldest spits out at me. He storms from the room, slamming his foot against the door when it rises too slowly. The needles clatter with each of his steps.

"I might be a fool," I mutter, "but you haven't told me that you didn't do it."

45: AMY

I have one regret.

I don't know why I'm thinking about this, now. But it's think about *this* or think about *that*.

It was our last date.

I'd already told Jason by then. Told him how I'd be gone soon. Gone forever. We'd said goodbye earlier that night, alone in his bedroom. Together. *Really* together. For the first—and last—time.

After, he took me to this overpriced Italian place called Little Sienna. And it was so wonderful that all I wanted to do was cry, because I knew it would end. And of course I hadn't worn waterproof mascara, and of course it smudged all over the place, so I excused myself. There was only one toilet, and a line of women waiting.

"Are you here with Jason?" the girl in front of me asked. I nodded. Her name was Erin, and she was a senior, and that's about all I knew of her.

"He broke my heart last year. I don't know how he does it."

"Does what?" I was still smiling, but the smile was starting to feel plastic.

"Keep up with all his girls." My smile disappeared. "I swear," Erin said, "I thought I was the only one, all those months we dated, but I never knew about Jill and Stacy, not until after we broke up."

I felt like I had swallowed boiling lead.

"He cheated on you?"

"Oh, yeah," she said. Then she laughed. "But that was last year. I'm sure he's not like that now. You two look really cute together. I'm glad to see you were able to reform him. Your name's Kristen, right?"

"No," I said hollowly. "Amy." Who was Kristen? Why'd she think my name was Kristen? Was Jason seeing Kristen on the side?

"My bad," Erin said.

Was that *pity* in her eyes?

I left the line. Screw smudged mascara.

But when I sat down at the table, Jason laughed and passed me a napkin, and then he licked the corner of it and wiped my eye himself, and he brushed my cheek with his fingers, and his eyes lingered on my lips.

And I remembered saying goodbye to him, earlier that night.

Part of me wanted to demand who Kristen was. To find out who he'd been texting, earlier, when he wouldn't let me see his phone. What his friends had meant about "big plans" next Saturday. After I'd be gone.

But another part of me said it was too late. We'd already . . . said goodbye.

Wouldn't it be easier to believe Jason was *my* Jason, not a cheater, not a scumbag?

At the time, I didn't think it would matter.

But now, my only regret is that I didn't demand the truth.

46: ELDER

"She's not here," Harley says. He's sitting in the Ward common room, staring out the window at the wheat fields in the distance.

I head to the door that leads to the private chambers. "Don't bother," Harley snarls. "She wants to be left alone." I open my mouth to ask why, but he adds, "For that matter, I want to be left alone too." He rubs the side of his face, and I notice a dark bruise under his eye.

I make a mental note to check with Doc about the last time Harley took his meds. It's not the standard mental meds I'm worried about— it's the other pills Doc gives him, the ones that hold back Harley's dark moods, make him less loons.

So I leave the Hospital alone. I pass the statue of the Plague Eldest, but I don't pause. I don't want him looking down on me, too.

Instead, I head up the path to the Recorder Hall. I see the people, still in full swing of the Season, and it makes me feel sick to my stomach, knowing that all of this is just contrived through Eldest's water pump.

When I get to the Recorder Hall, I have to step over a pair of intertwined bodies to get up the stairs. Victria sits on a rocker on the porch, watching them, occasionally writing something in her small leather-bound book. I'm surprised she's not with Bartie, not doing what the couple on the steps are doing, but Eldest did say the hormones affected the Feeders more than others.

Orion stands with his back to me, facing the picture of Eldest that looks out over the vastness of the Feeder Level. Before I can say anything, however, he lifts the picture from its nook on the wall and leans it against the floor of the porch.

"What are you doing?" I ask, shocked. The wall of the Recorder Hall looks naked without Eldest's falsely welcoming face peering down from it.

"Time for an updated picture," Orion says, picking the painting up and heading back inside the Hall. That makes sense. The painting of Eldest is at least a decade old. In the painting, his hair is still mostly brown, his eyes still clear, only a hint of wrinkles on his brow. I wonder what the new picture will show. Long white hair? Stooping shoulders that slope more because of years of limping? Maybe I'm off entirely. Maybe his age will make him regal.

"Hey," Victria says without looking up at me from her book. She's not talked to me much since Amy arrived, although we were really close before, when I lived in the Ward. She looks meaner now, more bitter than three years ago, when she was seventeen and I was thirteen. She was my first crush, then, but I don't know why anymore.

"Hey. Writing another book?" Victria has authored nearly a dozen books and uploads them to the floppy network. They're great—I don't know how she does it. Really amazing stories about heroes during the

Plague. Tragic stuff. My stomach sinks. I guess Eldest gave her "writing" goo before she was born.

"Not exactly." She snaps her book closed and tucks it into the large pocket on her jacket. She doesn't turn to me, though, she just stares out at the perfectly square and measured fields in front of her, dotted with couples.

I follow her gaze. "Hey, be careful out there. The Season's pretty wild right now." I'm glad Amy's safe with Harley.

Victria doesn't look at me. "Luthe walked me over. Orion's here now; he can walk me back."

Shrugging, I turn back to the wall and am surprised to see that the old painting of Eldest hid a plaque.

Hall of Records & Research
Built 2036 CE
Funded by FRX

Underneath that are letters I don't recognize—from the Cyrillic or Greek alphabet, I'm not sure which. Then, beneath that:

"If you would understand anything, observe its beginning and its development."
—Aristotle

There are eight other lines of text, each in a different language, two of which are nothing but unrecognizable symbols, but it's not hard to guess that it's the same quote in other languages.

"This is old," I tell Victria, who doesn't seem to care. "Really old. This has been here since the ship's creation."

She grunts to acknowledge that she's heard me.

I think about the plans of the ship Orion showed me a few days ago. How once, the Feeder Level was focused on "Biological Research" and this "Hall of Records & Research" was its hub. The couple I had to walk over to get to the Recorder Hall are moaning, loudly.

This can't be the kind of records and research the ship builders intended.

Eldest talks so much about how we've progressed, how much better we are with monoethnicity and our strong system of leadership. But right now, it seems to me that the austere words of this Aristotle sneer down at us, at how our research isn't more than fornication.

I wonder at the timing of the new painting. This is twice now that Orion has led me to discover something new about the ship. How much do I know about him, really? I've hardly ever seen him anywhere except for the Recorder Hall, and even there he mostly stays hidden behind books and shadows, a ghost among words and digitized information. I may know everyone aboard this ship—their names, even their faces—but do I *really* know any of them? He could be anybody.

"You think they love each other?" Victria's voice cuts through my thoughts. She's not looking at me—she looking at the couple finishing on the Recorder Hall steps.

"No," I say.

"It's disgusting," Victria mutters. "Can't they control themselves?"

No, I think. *They really can't.*

"Orion says it's human nature." *It's not*, I think.

"It's not," Victria says.

I look at her, surprised.

"If it was, I'd be like them," she says, nodding at the couple by the steps. Well, frex. She's right. "But I'm not. I have no . . . desire to be like that. Not with anyone I don't — "

She cuts herself off, but I can guess what she's going to say. Not with anyone she doesn't love.

A week ago, I would have snorted at those words. Love was no more real than the "god" Amy worshipped. I'd heard of "love" in the same context that I heard of those religious fairy tales — as stories Sol-Earth people used to tell to make themselves feel better about the imperfect world they helped to create.

But now . . .

"'Tis better to have loved and lost than never to have loved at all," Victria says.

"Is that from your new book?"

Victria snorts. She shifts in her seat, and I notice a stack of books — real books, from Sol-Earth — sitting on the porch floor beside her rocker. I frown. Orion, as a Recorder, should know better. Even Recorders are forbidden from messing with the ancient books. If Eldest catches him . . .

On the lawn in front of us, the woman's hand rests on her bare belly, her fingers curling against her skin, as if she were clutching something invisible but precious.

"Do you think they're happy, at least?" she asks, nodding her head at the couple. Before I can answer, she adds, "Because I never am."

"Okay, let's get this brilly painting hung!" Orion says cheerfully as he emerges from the Recorder Hall. The canvas he's holding is so new that I can still smell the paint on it—it reminds me of Harley.

Orion twirls the canvas around to position it on the hook over the plaque, and I gasp. He looks up at me and smiles knowingly.

It's not Eldest on the canvas.

It's me.

"This Season is the start of your gen," Orion says, sliding the wire on the back of the canvas over the hook and straightening the picture. "It's almost time for Eldest to step down. For you to be the new leader."

Painted me looks out on *Godspeed* from exactly where painted Eldest had looked. Harley's done this—I recognize his style—although I never sat for a painting. He must have done it by memory—which would explain why he's added all sorts of things into painted me that just don't exist. The same confident tilt of the head that Eldest has, not me. The same clear eyes, the same assured posture. It doesn't look like me at all. Is this how Harley really sees me? It's not me at all.

"It looks exactly like you," Victria says. She's abandoned her rocker and stands behind me, peering over my shoulder to look at the painting.

"It looks like a leader," Orion says.

A leader? No. A leader would know what to do.

47: AMY

The next morning, I shower—then shower again. But I cannot scrub away the bruises on my wrists or legs, and I cannot wash away the memory from my mind.

Fewer people populate the fields. Almost none.

People are animals, Harley had said.

They are. Luthe and the two Feeder men proved that. And that man and woman, who were right beside me, who didn't even notice, or care . . . .

Elder kissed me in the garden, just as the Season began. Was that a real kiss—or would any female lips have done in my place? My face burns. It had been real to me. But probably not to him.

I don't care what sort of plague happened on the ship, or what sort of rules Eldest has made: the Season is *not* normal human behavior. There has to be some reason for it. Something in what they eat, or a chemical in the recycled air—maybe even a disease to make people act like rutting animals.

Then it occurs to me: the doctor. He should know this isn't normal, he should know how to isolate—and stop—whatever trigger makes the people so barbaric.

I jump up and stride to the door, but my hand shakes as I reach for the button to open it. In here, I'm safe. Out there . . .

No.

I will not stay in my hidey-hole like a scared rabbit. The whole point of finding the doctor is to prove people aren't animals. I can't hide like one.

The doctor, however, can. He's not on the third floor, or the fourth. A nurse in the lobby directs me to the second floor.

"But he's busy," she calls after me.

Dozens of women line the hallways on the second floor, some wearing hospital gowns and sitting by doors, apparently waiting for a room to open up, some wearing their plain tunics and wide-legged pants, holding neatly folded hospital gowns and waiting to change. This entire floor looks like a gynecologist's office. In each room, there is a bed with stirrups, and nearly every bed is occupied. My steps slow. Why is a gynecologist's office so crowded now? These women can't think they're pregnant already, can they? Not after just one day. I shake my head. I can't be sure of that. On a ship where phones are built into your ears and paper-thin plastic is a whole computer, it's not that crazy to think that maybe you can know if you're pregnant as quickly as this.

None of the women talk.

"Get in line," a nurse says, handing me a folded hospital gown.

"Oh, but I'm just here to see the doctor . . . " I start, my voice trailing off. Obviously I'm here to see the doctor—obviously all the women here are. "I mean," I add at the nurse's impatient look, "not the, uh, gynecologist, but the other doctor, the one who's usually on the third floor."

"Only got one doctor," the nurse says. She eyes my red hair and pale skin a little closer. "I take it you're not here because of the Season?"

"No!"

She sighs. "Follow me."

The nurse leads me down the hall, weaving in and out of clusters of women. Many of the women look up and stare at me with a surprised sort of curiosity, as one would look at a strange person on the bus. None of them speak; they don't seem too greatly bothered by me.

"Only one doctor, with this many patients?" I ask the nurse.

"He's got us nurses, and he's got assistants—several of the scientists have been working under him directly for years." The nurse sighs again. "But Doc won't pick any as his apprentice. Not the trusting type."

I wonder what trust has to do with hiring more help, but there's no time to ask. The nurse stops by an open door and jerks her head for me to go in. I enter. The doctor is sitting at a chair between the stirrups of a bed, with a woman's legs propped up in the bed's stirrups. Everything the woman probably doesn't want me to see is right there.

"Oh my gosh! I'm sorry!" I cover my eyes and turn to go. Why did the nurse let me in the room in the middle of an examination, a very personal, private examination?

"It's okay," the doctor says. "What did you need me for?"

"I don't think she wants me here. . . ."

"She doesn't mind. Do you mind?" he asks, peering up at the woman over her knees.

"No, of course not," she says. She sounds bored.

All I know is that if I were lying on a stirrup bed with my legs in the air and my private bits just out there for everyone to see, I'd be *mortified*. My mother made me go to the gynecologist after I first started getting serious with Jason, and I have never had a more uncomfortable half hour in my life. I didn't want anyone in the room with me, up to and including the doctor, the nurse, and my mother, let alone some stranger.

But this woman couldn't care less. I risk opening my eyes, and she meets my gaze with a calm look. She doesn't seem bothered in the least by my presence.

"I, um . . ." I try to ignore what the doctor is doing with that clear goo and that metal thing that looks like a torture device. "I wanted to ask you about the Season."

"Ah," the doctor says. He's just going right on with his examination. I mean, couldn't he stop for a second?

"Does it change people?" I say it all at once, trying to get it over with as quickly as possible.

"What do you mean?"

The doctor's metal thing slips. The woman grimaces, but doesn't say anything. She's staring at the ceiling blankly.

The glazed look in her eyes, the passive way she's lying there, it all reminds me of the way that couple acted when I was attacked. Those people's apathy wasn't normal . . . but neither is this woman's. In fact, all the women I saw in the hallway were a bit off. They were all sitting so patiently, so quietly . . . so *blankly*. With that many women all lined up to take a gynecological exam . . . they should be impatient, they should be talking, they should be nervous or disgusted or anxious or a thousand other things than nothing.

"What's your name?" I ask the woman. Her face shifts downward so she can see me, and I can tell that she'd forgotten I was there but isn't entirely put out about it.

"Filomina," she says in an even tone, even though the doctor's doing something to her now that would have made me squirm with unease.

"Are you happy?" I know it's a weird question, but it was the first thing I could think of.

"I'm not unhappy."

"Amy, what do you want?" the doctor says.

"It's like she's not even human," I say. "Can't you tell? You're a doctor! You should know this isn't normal!"

"What's not normal?" the doctor asks as the woman lets her head slide back to the center of the pillow. She stares blankly up at the ceiling, her eyes blinking but otherwise showing no sign of life.

"This," I say. "Her."

The doctor squirts clear lube jelly on the woman's stomach, then rubs a flat-bottom handheld instrument across it. I think, at first, that he's doing an ultrasound, but there's no screen to show a fuzzy black-and-white picture of a fetus. Instead, a small monitor on top of the handheld device beeps.

STATUS: HORMONE LEVELS OPTIMAL

GENETIC LIKELIHOOD OF PHYSICAL DEFORMITIES: MEDIUM

GENETIC LIKELIHOOD OF MENTAL DEFORMITIES: MEDIUM-HIGH

INCESTUOUS INFLUENCE ON GENETIC SEQUENCE: HIGH

"Well, Filomina, looks like you are pregnant!" the doctor says as he puts away his device.

She sighs with contented delight—the only real emotion she's had the whole time.

"How do you know?" I say.

The doctor turns to the table by the bed. "What do you mean?" he asks.

"They've only been doing it for like a few days. Don't you have to wait a couple weeks before you can tell someone's pregnant?"

The doctor wipes off the lube jelly from Filomina's bare stomach, then rubs her skin with something that smells of rubbing alcohol. He reaches down and opens a drawer from the cabinet beside the stirrup bed and pulls out a syringe as long as my forearm. The long glass cylinder is filled with amber liquid. Near the plunger is a tiny label; I can tell words are written on it, but I am too far away to read them.

"Her hormone levels indicate that she's got a good chance at fertilization. And if she wasn't pregnant before, she will be after this. This will sting a little," the doctor adds to Filomina, who doesn't seem to care.

Then he stabs her with the needle, ramming it deep inside her—into her uterus, I'm guessing.

I shrink back in horror, my own stomach clenching at the sight, but Filomina just gives a tiny *uh!* of pain, and then it's over. The doctor pushes down on the plunger, and the amber liquid shoots into Filomina.

"That stuff is there to change the baby," I say in a choked whisper.

The doctor looks at me, still depressing the plunger. "It makes the baby stronger, better."

My mouth is dry. I remember what the girl in the rabbit field said about the "inoculations."

"Is that why all these women are so odd? Because you changed them before they were born?"

"All I did," the doctor says as he starts to pull the needle from Filomina's abdomen, "is give this baby additional DNA sequencing, so that the part of its DNA that's weaker because of incest can be remade. I'm not affecting its personality."

"If you change it, you are."

The doctor pulls the needle out. I can't stop staring at the tiny jewel of blood rising from the puncture.

The doctor drops the needle in a waste bin and finally turns his full attention to me.

"This is all perfectly normal," he says, stressing each word. "There is nothing wrong here. This is the way normal people are."

"Oh, yes," Filomina says in a flat monotone. "This is normal. I'm normal."

I back away, fumbling with the doorknob. I spill out of the room and run down the hall. The women stare at me silently as I race past. And even though I know their eyes aren't interested in me, the soullessness of them fills me with a dread I cannot explain.

48 : ELDER

"Twinkle, twinkle, little bat. How I wonder what you're at."

"Pardon?" I ask, smiling.

"Just a text from Sol-Earth," Orion says, turning back to the floppy in his hand.

I didn't expect to see Orion in the Ward's common room again, but I'm glad he's here. A friendly face. Harley commed me yesterday to say he took my shift in the cryo level. I've been stuck with Eldest most of the day.

"Have you see Harley or Amy?"

Orion shakes his head.

"What are you doing here, anyway? I thought you didn't want Eldest or Doc to see you."

Orion laughs. "Oh, no worries. They're both quite busy, I'm sure." I almost think he's trying to tell me something secret with his eyes, but whatever it is, I can't figure it out. Sighing, Orion turns back to his floppy. "These Sol-Earth texts are just so fascinating." He taps on the screen, flipping through different texts.

"You should be careful. If Eldest finds out you gave Victria a Sol-Earth book . . . You're a Recorder. You know the Sol-Earth books aren't supposed to leave the Recorder Hall and aren't meant to be seen by Feeders." I try to peer over his shoulder to see what he's reading. "What is that?"

Orion holds the floppy out to me, and I see a line drawing of a winged man with three faces. "It's a story about hell. The bottom layer's all ice."

I'm not looking at the floppy anymore—I'm looking at Orion.

"Oh—access?" he says. "Don't worry. I have access."

Something about the casual way he speaks of access makes me pause. "What do you know?" I ask, my voice low so the others in the common room can't hear. Orion's the one who showed me the blueprints that led me to Amy. Now he's talking about hellish ice.

Orion stands. Too close. I take a step back, but he leans in next to my face. "What do *you* know?" he asks. "Do you know you have a friend in me?"

49: AMY

When I get to my room, the first thing I do is punch the button that operates the blind over the window. The room dims. Good. I want darkness.

Someone knocks on my door.

I ignore it. Who on this ship would I want to talk with?

"Amy?" Harley says. "I saw you come in. I wanted to check on you."

"I'm fine," I call through the door.

"No, you're not. Open the door."

"No."

"Doc has the master code. I'll go get him if I need to."

I jump up and press the button to open the door. The doctor is the last one I ever want to see.

Harley steps inside and surveys the room.

"What?" I ask.

"Nothing. I just thought . . . someone would be in here with you."

I snort. "Who?"

Harley steps over to the desk and sits in the chair. "I thought Elder might be here."

"Why would he come to see me?" I sit on the bed.

"Because he likes you."

I stare at Harley, but I see no sign that he's not sincere. "I don't think anyone here likes anyone else." Not like *that,* anyway.

"Why do you say that?" He looks truly surprised.

"Didn't you see those men yesterday? That wasn't 'like'! That was—*ugh!* And just now—" I stop. I don't want to talk about Filomina.

"I'm sorry about yesterday," Harley says, and I know he means it. "But the Season is over now. It won't happen again." I can hear the threat in his voice. I hope I'm there when he sees Luthe again. "But what happened today?" he adds. "Where were you?"

"On the second floor." Harley waits for me to go on. "The women there—"

"Oh!" Harley smiles. "The Feeder women! They were here for their examinations."

"They were creepy."

"Oh, no, they're normal." I shudder at his choice of words.

"They were *not* normal," I spit out. "That is *not* the way normal people act. People are not mindless drones!"

Harley shakes his head. "You're only saying that because you've been in the Ward since you were unfrozen. We're the ones who aren't normal. People are supposed to be like that: obedient, calm, working together. It's us—who can't focus, who can't work together, who can't do the Feeder or Shipper jobs—we're the ones who aren't normal.

We're the ones who have to take the mental meds just so we don't go loons."

I stare at him. I don't know what's going on, but everything is twisted here. The normal people are "insane," while the ones who've lost any capacity for real thought are "normal." And the Season . . . Luthe's mocking eyes flash in my memory, and I choke down bile.

"Don't people around here have emotions?" I ask finally.

"Sure. Take now for instance. Now, I'm hungry. Do you want to go to the cafeteria with me?"

"No, I'm serious. Do you have love, or just the Season?"

Whatever laughter had crinkled Harley's eyes is dead now. "The Season wasn't our finest moment, but I wish you would appreciate the fact that I didn't act like that."

"And why didn't you?" I ask, frustrated. "What is it with this ship? Why were some people rutting in the streets, and some not affected at all?"

Harley fiddles with the pencils lying on the desk next to the notebook I got from my daddy's trunk. "Maybe you don't know as much as you think you do."

"Then tell me!"

"I was in love. Once."

It is the "once" that stops me. Because I was in love once, too. And we're both talking in the past tense.

"That's probably why I wasn't affected by the Season. Why would I want to be with any other woman?" His eyes drift to the peeling painted ivy that swirls around the doorframe. "I painted that for Kayleigh."

I don't even dare to breathe. I'm afraid anything—movement, a sound—will silence Harley's confession.

"It's been three years. I was a little older than Elder is now. Kayleigh and I . . . we matched. We couldn't have been more different, but we matched. I liked art; she liked machines and mechanical things. Whenever I'd paint, she'd tinker with stuff."

"What happened?" I ask as Harley grows silent.

"She died."

The words hang in the air. I want to ask how. But I don't want to make Harley look any sadder. The rough wool of my clothing feels uncomfortable on my skin. I think about how I found her clothes here, that first night. I remember touching the ivy around the door, tracing the delicate petals, and I can picture a younger Harley painting them for a laughing Kayleigh whose face I cannot see, but who is wearing these clothes.

"She wasn't meant for a false sun. Kayleigh needed a real sky, like the one you told us about. She felt trapped by the walls of the ship. We all knew we'd land one day—we'd be the generation that would leave this ship and live in the new world." Harley picks up my bear from the desk and holds it against him, like he's remembering the feel of Kayleigh. "But she couldn't wait that long."

And I know without being told that she killed herself. And I totally understand why.

50: ELDER

I pound on Amy's door harder than I'd intended to, my mind stuck on Orion's words.

Harley opens the door.

"Where's Amy?" I push past him into her room.

She's on her bed. I wonder what the two of them have been talking about. Alone. In her room. On her bed.

"What do you want?" Amy asks, and even though she doesn't sound impatient, in my mind I wonder whether she's trying to get rid of me in order to be alone again with Harley.

Harley steps into the bathroom and returns with a glass of water.

"Why are you upset?" I ask.

"It's nothing." Amy gulps down the water.

I sit down in the desk chair. Harley sits beside Amy on the bed. I wish I had left the chair open for Harley. "Why would anyone want to kill the frozens?" I ask. Harley and Amy seem surprised by the abruptness of my question, but I've had enough beating around the bush with Orion. "Two are dead now. *Dead*. For no reason at all."

"What did Eldest say when you found him?" Harley asks.

I leave the question hanging long enough for the two of them to realize there's something wrong. It's not like I'm trying to be mysterious. It's just that I don't know what to say. That I don't think I can trust Eldest? Harley's only ever seen the grandfatherly-kind version of Eldest; to him, Eldest is his wise leader. How am I supposed to tell him that out of everyone on the ship, the one I most suspect of murder is Eldest?

"I think we've got to figure out *why* the frozens are being attacked," I say finally. "That's the key; that's what we need to focus on. Meanwhile, I have an idea." Taking the floppy from Amy's desk, I tap in my access and bring up the wi-com locator map. "This is the cryo level," I say, handing the map to Amy. Our fingers brush together, and I can feel the heat of her touch on my hand long after she moves away.

"What's this?" Amy points to the glowing blue dot.

"Tap it."

When she does, a name pops up on the screen. "Eldest/Elder? But you're here."

I nod. "That means Eldest is down there. We've got the same access to everything, so the computer always labels us alike, remember?"

Amy's fingers clench, crushing the edge of the floppy.

"I know what you're thinking," I say. "But he's in the lab. The cryo chambers are over here."

Amy doesn't look comforted.

"Look." Harley points as Eldest's dot moves across the map and disappears.

"What happened?" Amy asks, surprised.

"That's where the elevator is. He'll show up on the Feeder Level now. But I thought you'd like to keep this. I set it up to work with your fingerprint when I scanned you in earlier. Then you can watch who's coming and going."

"Thank you," Amy says. "But . . . that's not good enough. We need to be down there. All the time. We should go now." She stands up, but looks lost. "Right now. If we're not there to protect them—that's why people are being murdered! Because we aren't protecting them!"

"No." My voice is calm and sure. "People are getting murdered because there's a murderer."

Amy opens her mouth, probably to insist on going to the cryo level, but Harley thrusts another cup of water in her hands. I'd been so intent on Amy that I'd not noticed him get up and get water from the bathroom tap. Amy snatches it from his hand.

"Go easy on the water," I say, thinking about the second water pump Eldest has hidden on the cyro level. Amy chugs the entire glass, though, and when she sets it on the table, her skin's no longer red-and-white splotchy, and her breathing's back to normal. Harley hesitantly sits down at the very edge of the bed, ready to leap up and run for more water at a moment's notice.

"I'll still keep guard when I can," Harley tells Amy, a distant look in his eyes. I wonder if he's only offering so he can be close to the hatch that leads outside to the stars. I wonder how many times he's opened it, just so he can get one more glimpse.

A shadow crosses my mind. Harley was down there all that night. He could have slid open Mr. Kennedy's tray and let him melt. I can see it in my mind's eye: Harley standing over a melting man, watching him die. He *could* have done it.

But why?

Another shadow whispers to me, reminds me of Harley's dark moods, of the extra meds Doc feeds him, of how he's probably missed a week's worth of those meds in all this chaos.

I take a deep breath to clear my mind.

Harley's no killer.

Right?

No—*no*. Harley would never—

"And—" Amy starts.

Beep, beep-beep.

My hand jumps to my wi-com button just as Harley's does. We glance at each other. It's rare to get a com-link at the same time as someone else.

"What is it?" Amy asks, her eyes darting nervously between us.

Then that deep, aged voice fills my ear.

"Attention all residents of *Godspeed*. I have a very important announcement."

51: AMY

"What is it?" I ask again. Both boys have their heads cocked to the side, listening. I'm reminded of the last time an all-call went out, the time when the people in the common room all turned on me. My stomach drops, and I feel my muscles tense. What if Elder and Harley turn on me after this? They're all I've got.

"What is it?" I ask again, more urgently. Elder waves at me like I'm a bothersome fly. I turn to Harley, but he's got his face all scrunched up in concentration, as if he's hearing something direly important. I grab his elbow, but he shakes me off. Elder glares at me.

I can't let them hate me now. I don't know what they're hearing, but I can tell it's bad. They look very serious. And now Elder's staring at me, with this darkness in his eyes. I can't let them hate me. I won't let them hate me.

I grab Amber from the desk and squeeze her into me. I taste copper before I realize that I'm biting my lip.

I snatch the empty glass of water, run to the bathroom, and refill it.

I drain it in five seconds flat. Fill it up again. Then gulp it all at once.

There's something to Harley's mothering; the water does actually calm me down a bit. It's like taking a deep breath just before lining up for a race.

I go back into the bedroom.

Elder and Harley's heads straighten. They both look at me.

I knew it. They hate me.

Whatever that ear button said, it said to hate me. And now they hate me, and they're going to turn on me just like the other people in the Ward. The space between my eyes at the bridge of my nose feels tight. I can't breathe.

"What is it?" I say, unable to bear it any longer.

"It's not good," is all Elder says.

"You don't know that," Harley says.

Elder turns to him. "It can't be good."

"What is it?!"

"Eldest did an all-call announcement. Another one. We're all supposed to go to the Keeper Level." Elder's mouth turns down, crinkling the skin into a deep, concerned frown.

"I'm kind of excited." Harley jumps up and starts heading to the door. "I've always wondered about the Keeper Level." I remember then that most people are restricted to this level—it's bad enough to be trapped on the ship, but to not even be allowed to go to different parts of it seems ridiculous.

Harley pushes the button to open my door and bounces out. I start to follow him, but when Elder doesn't move, I stop.

"I've got a bad feeling about this," Elder says.

"Come on!" Harley calls.

Eldest and Harley argue with each other as they lead me down the path behind the Hospital, past the Recorder Hall, and to the metal wall that surrounds the Feeder Level.

"She can't ride the grav tube; she doesn't have a wi-com," Harley says.

"Then how can she get to the Keeper Level?" Elder asks.

"I guess you could leave me here," I say. Maybe that would be best. My head *aches*. My skull feels as if it's stuffed with cotton. Something about what Harley said, about the wi-coms, is nagging at me, but I can't think through this fuzziness.

"No way." Elder's hand twitches, like he's going to reach out for me but at the last second changes his mind.

"She could ride with you," Harley says, doubt drawing out the words.

"Ride?" I ask.

Harley grins. "You just have to hold on to Elder, and he'll carry you up the grav tube."

"But—" Elder's face is flushed.

"Here." Harley grabs me by the wrist and pulls me close to Elder. "Wrap your arms around him—like this. Good. Get in close. Closer. And Elder, you need to hold her around the waist. No, you'll have to actually touch her. Here." Harley pushes Elder's hovering arm against my waist. We're close. I can smell earth and grass on Elder's skin. It's nice.

"Are you okay?" Elder asks.

I smile weakly at him. I can't tell if it's nerves or something else that's making me feel as if I've got a bucket of water sloshing around in my stomach. Heck, I probably *do* have a bucket of water in there, considering how many glasses I drank earlier.

"Give the grav tube order," Harley says in a matter-of-fact way.

Elder's hand shakes as he pushes the button behind his ear. "Keeper Level," he says. "You'll have to take the grav tube in the City; you don't have access for this one. Eldest must have opened up the hatch in the Great Room for everyone else," he adds. Harley just nods impatiently, waving for us to go on.

"And off you go!" Harley says. He pushes us straight under the big clear tube.

I have one second to look up at the swirling winds inside, feel it lift my hair, and breathe the compressed air—and then we start to rise.

Elder's arm clenches, and he instinctively pulls me closer. I close my eyes and let him hold me, trusting him, feeling safe in his strong grip. For a moment, we hover on the winds blowing around us, bobbing like buoys in the ocean, as if the whirlwind swirling around us is testing our weight. I should be scared, but I glance at Elder's smiling eyes and can't help but smile back.

The winds grow stronger. My stomach lurches as we're pulled up, headfirst, speeding faster and faster, zipping through the clear tube, the wind plastering our hair against our scalps.

"What's happening?" I scream, struggling to raise my head from Elder's shoulders and look at him properly.

"Don't worry!" Elder calls down. His words flit past my ears like hummingbirds.

The wind is so quick and loud that it would be pointless for him to say anything else. His arms tighten around me, and I press my face against his chest.

And through it all—the rushing winds, my hair whipping around me, the flap of our clothes—I can hear his heartbeat.

The tube curves against the wall and we rise, a single arrow soaring through the heart of a hurricane. I can see the blur of green pastures below. I struggle to pull my head up, my neck muscles straining against the pressure, and as I do so, I can see the dotted colors of trailers falling away from us, far on the other side of the level.

And then with a jerk that leaves me nauseated and light-headed, the tube angles up sharply. There is darkness for a few seconds as we shoot through an opening in the floor of the level above us. Finally, we stop.

My eyes are bleary, watering. I feel strange, like I'm sick. I try to swallow the odd feeling down. I'm dizzy, but I can't tell if it's from the grav tube ride or something else. I feel slow and tired.

"Welcome to the Keeper Level," Elder says. "This is where I live."

52: ELDER

Her cool fingers wrap around my hand. She is holding me so hard that my fingertips, already cold from the grav tube, are now numb, but I don't mind. I don't mind at all. She is breathless and smiling, and I wish that we could stay alone in the Learning Center, and that I could tuck that stray strand of hair behind her ear, and that I could kiss those laughing lips. But I can already hear people's voices on the other side of the door as everyone else enters through the hatch from the Shipper Level.

When I meet her eyes, there's a glazed film over them, as if she's just woken up. But when I smile, she smiles back. We hold hands as we cross the Learning Center and enter the Great Room. I'm surprised—I didn't think she'd let me hold on to her that long—but she's just smiling away, almost as if she's forgotten that I am holding her hand.

People pile into the Great Room. I never realized it was so big—but everyone's here, and still more people climb up from the hatch. I see Harley finally arrive, followed by Bartie and Victria. He stands

with them, near the hatch, but he winks at me when he sees how
Amy's trailing me. Her eyes are wide, taking in all the new faces she's
seeing. The Feeders cluster together, clucking like chickens. The
Shippers all stand stoically around the edges of the room. I wonder
what they know. Eldest surely wouldn't have revealed his intentions
to them, but the way they're standing, huddled together, makes me
think they know something I don't.

Maybe Doc knows. I scan the crowd, but I don't see him.

Nearly all the people have their faces upturned. The "stars" from
the metal screen shine and twinkle. The red dot that indicates our
ship blinks. Just 49 years and 264 days away from the still light that
represents Centauri-Earth. Home.

"Look at the stars," I hear a farmer from the Feeder Level say to a
woman standing next to him. They move a little closer, their shoulders
touching as they gaze upward. The woman snakes her arm around
her belly, splaying her fingers over her abdomen. The two whisper to
each other, still staring at the burning lightbulbs they think are stars.

It feels like every person in the Great Room is pairing off into couples, and more than one woman has her hands over her belly. I lean in
closer to Amy, let our arms touch, but she doesn't pick my hand back up.

The ebb of people rising from the hatch slows, then stops. We're
all here. Waiting.

A few Shippers gather near Eldest's chamber door. Their backs
are straight; they shoot furtive looks at the crowd. The people from
the Ward cluster together, their voices rising over the crowd. When
I glance back at them, though, I see that Harley is silent. He stares
up, and I guess he's figured out that these stars aren't real. How could
anyone who had seen the real stars be deceived by this light show?

I open my mouth to ask Amy what she thinks about the false stars, but before I can speak, Eldest's chamber door opens.

He steps out wearing his official Eldest garb, a heavy woolen set of robes embroidered with silent, still stars on the shoulders and bountiful green crops on the hem—the hopes of everyone on board the ship.

"Friends," Eldest says in his very best grandfather voice, "nay, *family*."

The Feeders around me sigh, and the women rub their bellies and smile at their men.

"I have invited you all up here for a very specific reason. First, I wanted to show you the stars." He sweeps his hand up high and every face follows it, every eye turning to the brightly burning "stars."

"Do you see the trails that follow the stars?" As Eldest continues, the Feeders nod their heads. "They show how fast our ship is traveling as we soar through space to our new home."

I glance at Amy, but she's just staring blankly up at them. I don't think she's realized yet that these stars aren't real. I turn to Harley. Across the room, he's staring right at me, a deep frown creasing his forehead. He knows this isn't right.

"As you know, you young ones are the generation that is to land on the surface of Centauri-Earth." Eldest pauses, gives a dramatically deep sigh. "But, alas, that is not to be."

Murmurs rise from the crowd. The little red light that indicates *Godspeed* moves backward on the track, away from Centauri-Earth.

"The engines of our dear *Godspeed* are tired, friends, and the ship can only go so fast. We were due to land in fifty years."

"In 49 years, 264 days," a voice shouts, interrupting him. As one, we all turn to face Harley, who stares at Eldest. His face is pale, the bruise under his eye dark in contrast.

Eldest smiles graciously. "As you say. And within your lifetime, friends. But, I fear, this may not be the case. Planet-landing is beyond the reach of fifty years."

"When?" Harley says, his voice now softer, scared.

"We must hope, friends, that science lies, and that Centauri-Earth is closer than we'd believed."

"*When?*"

"Seventy-five years before we land," Eldest says simply. "Twenty-five more than we thought."

Silence permeates the Keeper Level. Twenty-five *additional* years? I will not be an old man at planet-landing—I'll be dead. I clutch Amy's hand without realizing it. She presses against my fingers so lightly that I can barely feel her touch.

"*Twenty-five* more *years?!*" Harley shouts, pushing people apart to go through the crowd toward Eldest. "Twenty-five *more?!*"

Bartie and Victria hold Harley back. He swallows, hard, like he's going to be sick right there in front of us. I can hear him muttering: "74, 264 . . . 74, 264 . . ."

"Twenty-five more." Eldest speaks over Harley. "I'm sorry, but I cannot help it. It will be too late for you to see land . . . but your children . . ."

Around me, all the women's hands curl around their bellies. "Our children," the woman closest to me says to the man beside her. "Our children will see land."

The words spread like fire, and all the Feeder women are murmuring to the babies inside them. Whispering words of hope, words of comfort. They don't care about themselves. They care about the children forming inside them, about the future.

"To have miscalculated a centuries-long voyage by only twenty-five years is not so great a thing, friends," Eldest says, and already I can see some of the Feeders nodding in agreement.

"It is!" Harley roars. He breaks free from Bartie and Victria's grasp. "You promised us land, you promised us a home, you promised us *real* stars, and now you say we'll die before we have a chance to taste air that's not been recycled for so many frexing centuries?!"

"But our children," one of the Feeder women says. "Our children will have the Earth. That is enough."

"It is *not enough*!" Harley shouts. He's almost at the front now; he's almost at Eldest. "It will never be enough, not until I can feel real dirt beneath my feet!"

Eldest steps forward, and then he's in front of Harley. He crooks his finger, and Harley, despite his rage, leans down to hear what Eldest whispers in his ear. Harley's face becomes ghostlike, and his eyes fill with sorrow and death. When Eldest is done whispering, Harley straightens, looks out at the crowd of us, and runs from the Great Room. He clambers down the hatch. We are all silent, listening to his pounding footsteps below, until the sound fades to nothing.

I glance at Amy, expecting her face to be filled with similar rage. She was certainly angry enough when I told her she'd have to wait fifty years before landing—how does she feel now that it'll be seventy-five years before we take our first steps onto our new planet? My heart thuds. When her parents are finally reanimated, their daughter will probably be dead. And Amy will never have gotten to say goodbye.

Amy's face is pale, but there is no flash of anger in her eyes, no defiance in the tilt of her head.

"Amy?" I say under my breath. She turns toward me. "What do you think of this?"

Pause. "It is sad," she says, but there is no sadness in her voice. "I regret that it must happen. But I guess it will be okay." Her tone is even, flat.

"What's wrong with you?" I ask.

"Nothing is wrong with me," Amy says. She blinks; her eyes are unfocused. "The stars are pretty," she adds.

"They're not real stars!" I hiss into her ear. "Can't you see that?"

"I like how they have little tails, like comets."

I lean in closer. "You have seen *real* stars! You know these aren't real! They just added the tails to make it look like we're going fast!"

"Oh, we *are* going fast," Amy says. She points to Eldest. "He told us we are."

I step back and inspect her. Her body slumps a little. Her shoulders sag. Even her hair looks limp. "What is wrong with you?" I ask again.

She blinks. "Shh," she says. "Our Eldest is speaking."

I gape at her. Our Eldest? *Our* Eldest?!

"Friends," Eldest says, "I know this is hard news to bear. But I wanted to bring you here, to see the stars, so that you can tell your children, when they are born, about the sky that awaits them! About the world that will be their home!"

And the people cheer. They actually cheer.

Even Amy.

53: AMY

I feel funny.

Not funny ha-ha. Funny weird.

Run, my body tells my brain. *When something's not right, run. Running makes you feel better. Normal.*

But why run? Run where? What's the point?

Seems silly, running.

May as well stand here.

And wait.

The world seems slow.

Like walking through water.

Like drowning.

The cheering washes over me, like a warm wave of joy, and I join in, raising my voice in happiness, becoming a part of the crowd. Elder looks at me funny (not funny ha-ha, but funny weird), and he doesn't cheer. I don't know why.

"Why don't you cheer?" I ask.

Elder takes a long time to answer, and when he finally does, I've nearly forgotten the question. "I've got nothing to cheer about."

Why do you need a reason to cheer? Why not just . . . cheer?

Everyone starts to leave the Keeper Level. I stand still, watching them go. Their walking makes the floor rumble a bit, like ripples when you throw a pebble in the water. I close my eyes and feel the world through my feet.

For a moment, I remember Earth. Remember ripples in ponds.

The memory fades. I am here. Now. Not there.

Why think about Earth?

Elder touches my arm. I open my eyes. Everyone else is gone. But not Elder or Eldest. And not me.

Elder starts to stride toward Eldest. He turns around and looks at me. "Come on," he says. "Aren't you going to come with me?"

Oh, yes. Of course. I follow him.

Eldest looks at me, and my body reacts before my mind, my stomach clenching and my gut twisting in nausea. I stumble—why don't my feet want to go closer to Eldest? Why is my breath catching, my heart racing?

Why don't I like Eldest?

I shake my head to clear my mind. Of course I like Eldest. Why would I *not* like him? He is my leader.

A loud noise makes me jump. The noise came from Elder.

I have missed part of their conversation. I squint and focus my attention on them. It seems very important that I understand. I feel like I *should* understand, should care.

"What did you *do*?" Elder shouts.

Why is he shouting?

"Nothing more than what *you* will do." Eldest's voice is a snarl.

"I will *never* be like you! Never! This is all a lie!" My gaze follows his arm up, to the stars. They are so pretty. Sparkly. Glittering. Not like the stars at home.

My heart misses a beat, and my breath is gone for a moment. Home? This is home. Why think about other stars? I have these stars. These stars are enough. They're pretty. Sparkly. Glittering.

"What are you playing at?" Elder shouts, and I realize I've forgotten to pay attention again.

I should pay attention.

But . . . why? This has nothing to do with me.

It does, a voice whispers in my head.

How? I ask it.

But there is no answer.

"You frexing chutz," Eldest says, leaning in close to Elder. "They need hope, don't they? They need to look at the pretty sparklies—"

I look up at the pretty sparklies. They are pretty. And sparkly.

I blink. Where did the sound go?

Elder and Eldest stare at me.

Should I say something to them? They look like they want me to say something.

But what should I say?

"Amy?" Elder asks, quietly.

Eldest grins with all his teeth showing. My stomach clenches again, bile on my tongue, but my lips curve up, matching his smile. Eldest leans forward. He strokes my cheek. As he reaches for me, I have a sudden urge to flinch. But that's silly—why should I flinch? I stand there. He wraps both hands around the sides of my face and draws me closer.

"Get your hands off her," Elder snarls.

"Don't you see?" Eldest says. I think he's talking to Elder, not me, but I'm the one he's looking at. "The people of *Godspeed* have simple needs, simple wants. Give them some sparkly lights and they call it hope. Give them hope, and they'll do anything. They'll work when they don't want to. They'll breed when the ship needs it. And they'll smile the whole time."

Eldest smiles, his lips curling up. His eyes stare into mine, so warm and brown and comforting.

I smile back.

54: ELDER

Something's not right. Amy's not right.

"What's wrong?" I ask her.

She blinks. "Nothing."

I have to get her to Doc. I don't know if I can trust Doc, but I don't know of anyone else who can help. I sure as frex can't trust Eldest.

I get Amy off the Keeper Level and away from Eldest as fast as I can. The fear and exhilaration she showed when we first went up the grav tube is gone, replaced with mild disinterest. She follows me down the path to the Hospital garden like a dog. Her eyes stare straight ahead, not at the flowers, not at the statue of the Plague Eldest, just straight ahead. I wonder if she's even really seeing anything at all.

At least a dozen people litter the ground floor of the Hospital.

Half of them are elderly, and the other half are their younger coun-
terparts, sons and daughters who have brought in their mothers and
fathers.

"She's gone," a man says, leaning in close to the flabby-armed
nurse who runs the ground floor emergency room. "She's too old to
travel through the grav tubes, but I told her about the meeting—you
know, the meeting on the Keeper Level. And it's left her completely
baffled. She's gotten all confused."

"Not confused," the old woman behind him says in a cracked
voice. "I remember it, clear as day. Those stars that trailed with light.
Only time I ever saw stars."

I pull Amy along behind me, as if she is a distracted child, but in
truth, I'm more distracted than she is.

The flabby-armed nurse nods at the young man. "It's not your
fault. Many elderly get confused in their old age. We've got rooms for
them on the fourth floor. I'll send her there and have Doc look at her."

"Thank you," the young man says, a sigh of relief floating among
his words. He turns to talk to his mother, then hands her over to a
nurse who leads her to the elevator where Amy and I are waiting.

"You're the Elder. The one who didn't die," the old woman says as
she sees me. "And that's the freak girl Eldest told us about."

"Hello," Amy says with a smile, holding out her hand to the
woman. If I had any doubt about something being wrong with Amy,
it's gone now. Amy—the normal Amy I'd come to know—would not
have put up with an old lady calling her a freak girl.

"They say I'm sick," the old lady tells Amy.

"This is the Hospital," Amy says. Her speech has a childlike
cadence to it, simple and factual.

"I didn't know I was sick."

"You're just confused, dear," the nurse says. "You're getting the past and the present mixed up."

"That's not good," Amy says, her eyes wide.

The doors slide open and we all step inside. I push the third button. The nurse reaches over and pushes the fourth.

"What's on the fourth floor?" I ask. I've noticed that Doc occasionally takes patients—usually the grays—there, but never really noticed anything special about it other than the secret elevator.

"It's where we've got rooms set up for the elderly," the nurse says. "Sometimes, they get to the point where they can't take care of themselves, so we give them rooms there. They need rest and peace, and we have some meds for that on the fourth floor." She pats the old woman's hand, and the woman smiles up at the nurse, her smile shining through the deep wrinkles of her face.

My brow creases. Why were the doors on the fourth floor locked if they merely contained old people relaxing?

The doors slide open to the common room of the Ward. I step out.

"Aren't you forgetting something?" the nurse calls.

Amy is still standing in the elevator, staring vacantly up at the numbers above the doors.

"Three," she says solemnly, reading the lit number.

"Yes," I say. "Come on." I grab her wrist and pull her into the common room. Many of the mental patients are inside, dark looks on their faces, anger in their eyes.

Amy grimaces. I look down at her wrists and see greenish-purple bruises staining her pale skin.

"Did I do this?" I ask, gently lifting her wrist up for closer inspection.

"No," Amy says simply.

The bruises are old, anyway, at least a day or more. "What happened?"

"Some men pinned me down," Amy says. "But it's okay."

My heart thuds. "Some men *pinned you down*? And it's *okay*?"

"Yes."

"B-but—" I splutter.

Amy blinks up at me, as if she cannot fathom why anything is worth this much emotion.

"You don't care, do you?" I ask.

"About what?"

"About . . . about *anything*."

"I care," Amy says, but her voice sounds bored.

"Do you remember when you got these bruises?" I wave her limp wrist in front of her face. Her eyes focus on them, then drift away. She nods. "Think about how you felt afterward. What did you do?"

"I remember . . . crying? But that's silly. It's not worth crying about. Everything's fine."

I cannot help it. I drop Amy's wrist, grab her by the shoulders, and shake her. Her head bobbles on her neck. It's like shaking a doll. And no matter how much I shake, I cannot bring the life back into her eyes.

"What happened to you?" I gasp, letting her go.

"Nothing. I'm fine."

"I'm going to find a way to fix you."

"I'm not broken," Amy says in a voice as empty as her eyes.

I lead her down the hall, deposit her in her chamber, and tell her not to leave. I have no doubt she will follow my order.

I eventually find Harley on the other side of the pond, tossing rocks into the water.

"What did Eldest whisper to you?" I ask, standing next to him.

He doesn't look up. "I'm not telling you," he snarls.

I don't have time for Harley's bad mood. "There's something wrong with Amy."

Harley's head whips up. "What is it?"

"She's . . . she's acting like the Feeders do."

Harley turns back to the pond. "Oh." Then: "Maybe it's better that way."

"What do you mean?"

"They were all okay with not landing, didn't you notice? It's only the mental cases like us who were bothered."

I had noticed. Only Harley, who had seen real stars, protested, but the others at the Ward were abuzz with the news, and they certainly weren't happy about it.

"It's to be expected," I say. "It's typical that we're the only ones bothered. It's why we're in the Ward, isn't it? Because we can't take direction, follow leadership. It's why we take the Inhibitor meds." Even as I say it, though, I'm thinking about the couple on the lawn in front of the Recorder Hall, about how they didn't know love and clearly don't know grief, either.

"Amy might be happier that way," Harley says. "I think I'd be happier if I didn't care about getting off this frexing ship."

I want to say not to worry, that we'll land someday, but I know the words are hollow, and no amount of false hope in my voice can fill them up.

"But Amy didn't start that way. She started out like us. And now she's like one of the Feeders."

Harley shrugs. "So? That just means she's normal. Good for her."

"But I liked her so much more before," I say, more to myself than to Harley.

He stands and heads down the path. "I'll go to the cryo level and stand guard anyway."

I watch him leave. His words sting because they're true. I forget sometimes, since I spend so much time at the Ward or alone with Eldest, that most people on the ship *are* calm, complacent—not insane. Not bothered by things like false stars and delayed landing times. Happier.

Would Amy really be happier if she stayed hollow inside?

Would I be happier if I didn't have to live with the idea that I'd live all my life encased in a ship?

It doesn't matter. I know that if Amy was given the choice, she'd never choose this blind ignorance, even if it is bliss. Something— *someone*—has done this to her, and I'm going to find out who.

55: AMY

I am sitting in my room.

The door opens.

"What are you doing?" Elder asks.
"I am sitting in my room," I say.
"What are you looking at?"
"The wall."
"Why are you looking at the wall?"

Elder asks so many questions.

Elder walks to me. He picks up my hand. His fingers trace my bruises.

"Come with me," Elder says. I stand up. He walks. I follow.

We walk until we stop.

Elder pushes a button. The door opens. I follow him inside. He takes me to a chair.

I sit.

"Amy," a deep voice says. I look up and see the doctor. We are in his office. He is sitting at his desk. "What seems to be the problem?"

I blink. "Nothing. Everything is fine."

"Everything is *not* fine!" Elder shouts.

I look at him. "Everything is fine."

The chair I am sitting in is blue. It is made of hard plastic. The desk is interesting. Everything is placed so neatly on the desk. The pencils are all straight in their cup.

"What happened to you?" Elder shouts.

I jump. I had forgotten he was there. I stare at him.

Elder growls, like a dog, and it is funny, and I smile.

"There is nothing wrong with her, Elder," the doctor says. "I think you've become too accustomed to being around the mental patients. Perhaps it would be better for you to spend more time with normal people. I recommend . . ."

The doctor is still talking. I know because his mouth is going up and down and sound is coming out, but the words just jangle around in my head, cluttering it up. The notepad on the doctor's desk has such neat, even edges. I reach out and run my finger along the edges. They are smooth — so smooth that the paper slices my skin. A tiny line of red sprouts on the end of my finger. Look, the doctor has another notebook on the other side of his desk. That's nice. Symmetrical. I like symmetrical. *See-met-tree-cul*. That's a nice word. I say it out loud.

"See-met-tree-cul." Yes. That sounds nice.

Elder is staring at me as if I'm crazy, but that's crazy, ha ha, because he's the one who hangs out at a mental hospital for fun.

The walls are painted a nice shade of blue. So nice. Like a foggy sky.

Something rattles. I look. The doctor places a brown bottle of pills on his desk. I cock my head, staring at them. The pills lay chaotically on the bottom of the bottle. Piled up like little candies.

The doctor and Elder speak.

"You're right," the doctor says. "Her condition *is* unusually severe. Has she had any shocks recently? Trauma? Increased heart rate? These will sometimes make the reaction more severe."

"Reaction to what?" Eldest says, his voice loud.

The doctor has a funny look on his face.

"To the ship. You've got to understand, things are different now from when she lived on Sol-Earth. We have different meds, different food, take more nutritional supplements and vits."

"Vits," Elder says, jumping on the word. "Like the ones Eldest puts in the water?"

"Yeess," the doctor says, drawling the word out in a funny way.

I giggle at him.

Elder turns to stare at me. I giggle at him, too.

"And hormones. Eldest puts hormones in the water. For the Season."

The doctor shakes his head. "They wouldn't affect her. It takes time for the hormones to build up in one's body. They need several weeks, over a month to be effective."

"She's been drinking a lot of water lately, though." Elder looks at my wrists. "And maybe there's something to that trauma you mentioned."

I blink, and realize that time has passed, and for a moment I wonder what happened in that time, but it doesn't matter, nothing's changed, I'm still here, they're still talking.

. . .

I blink. I was gone again.

. . .

Blink.

Really, it's easier when I stay gone. It's too hard to keep up with
the words Elder and the doctor say. They are too intense. Why are
they so worked up?

Everything is fine.

Elder snaps his fingers in front of my face.

"Amy, Doc thinks you need medicine," he says loudly.

"She's unbalanced, not deaf," the doctor says.

Elder reaches over and grabs the bottle on the doctor's desk.
"These are Inhibitor pills, mental meds. I'm going to give you one,
okay, and we'll see if that fixes you."

I open my mouth. The pill sits on my tongue, a bitter taste seeping
into my mouth.

"Swallow it," the doctor reminds me.

I swallow.

"Do you remember the night we met?" Elder says. "You were
thrashing around in that cryo liquid, and you fought us every step
of the way. I had to hold you down so Doc could give you the
eyedrops that made you not go blind. And now you just sit there,
swallowing the pill like an obedient dog. Don't you see how that's
just sad?"

"No," I say. What was there to be sad about?

"How long will it take to work?" Elder asks the doctor.

"I'm not sure," the doctor says. "Like I said, her mental state is more extreme than many other Feeders. *If* it will work at all, it should only be a few hours."

"If?" Elder asks, choking on the word.

His voice drones on and I fade out.

56: ELDER

I left her with Doc for the night.

Believe me, I didn't want to. But Doc wanted to give her some meds intravenously, and they knocked her out. She was just sleeping; it wouldn't do me any good to watch her sleep. I walk around for most of the night, drifting off once in the garden by the pond, but I'm just avoiding the inevitable.

I need to see Eldest.

I take the grav tube up before dawn. The Keeper Level is empty now, but it still smells crowded. Sweat and dirt linger in the air.

Eldest is on the floor, leaning against the wall by his door, staring at the false stars.

"Feeling proud?" I snarl, remembering the last time I found him here, like this.

Eldest doesn't look at me. "No," he says simply.

"How can you stand to do it?" I shout. "Lie to them like that?"

"Shaddup," Eldest snarls, standing up to face me. And then I smell it. That harsh, stringent smell. I don't see the bottle, but I know it's got to be somewhere—and it's probably empty now. But why? Why get drunk now? He's told his terrible truth, and the people still love him. This is his moment of triumph. What does he have to mourn with liquor?

"Ya don' know what iz like. But ya will. Ya will." He leans in close, and his breath burns my nose hairs.

I don't have time for this drunken stupidity. "What happened to Amy?" I say, leaning in even closer to him. I don't intimidate him, I can tell, but I don't back down, either.

Eldest snorts, a great honking wet noise that he'd never allow himself to make when he was sober. "Amy, Amy, Amy," he mocks. "Throw one pale-skinned freak your direction and your chutz shoots up to tha stars! You've forgotten 'bout the ship, 'bout your 'sponsibil- ity!" He stresses every syllable of the last word, jabbing a finger into my chest each time.

"What's wrong with her?" I roar.

"What's wrong with you?" Eldest says, still mocking. "What's wrong with me? What's wrong with this whole frexing ship?"

"Just tell me. Did you do it?"

"Do what?" he asks warily.

"Did you give her something to make her sick?" He's not above it. I know that much. He gave the Feeders extra hormones before the Season to make them lusty. He gives babies goo to make them who they are. What did he give Amy? And *how*?

Eldest throws back his head and laughs at me.

So I punch him.

He stops laughing, a red mark already blossoming on his cheek.

"You'd do it too," he hisses, the stink of his breath making me gag. "You're more like me than you think."

I leave. There are no answers to be had from this drunk fool.

When I get back, Amy's awake.

Sort of.

She lies on her bed with her back perfectly straight, her arms to her side, her toes pointing up, her eyes staring at the ceiling.

I wonder how long it will be until the mental meds kick in.

I don't use the word Doc used. *If.*

Tapping the bottle of pills against my leg, I pace around the small room. Finally, I sit at the desk and pick up the floppy on it. The wi-com locator map only shows Harley on the cryo level, standing still in the hallway where the hatch is. Part of me wants to com him and tell him to guard the frozens, but I don't feel like having another fight. They'll be fine.

It worries me, though, how obsessed he is with the stars. He hasn't been this way since Kayleigh died, since Doc upped his mental meds.

I glance at Amy, wondering when the mental meds will fix her.

If.

I turn my back on her, and look at the wall Amy painted the list of victims on. She's updated the roster, adding Number 63, the woman who didn't die, and Number 26, the man who did. She's only been able to add what information she knew at the time — Number 63 is female, black, survived. Number 26 is Theo Kennedy, male, white, bio-weaponry specialist, from Colorado. And dead.

After looking up their files on the floppy, I grab the brush and paint on Amy's wall to add more details. Number 63 was named

Emma Bledsoe. She was thirty-four and worked in the Marines as a tactician. I add Mr. Kennedy's age—sixty-six—and that his spot aboard *Godspeed* was funded by the Financial Resource Exchange.

I step back and examine the wall. Lines snake from one victim to the other, but no line connects them all. Mr. Robertson and Mr. Kennedy are both male, but Amy's not. There's at least a decade in each of their age differences. None of them were born in the same month. The similarities that are there are weak. I add a line from Emma Bledsoe's Marine experience to William Robertson's. Both Amy and Mr. Kennedy are from Colorado. I hesitate at Amy's chart, the thick black paint dripping from my brush and down the wall before I can make myself draw the line connecting them. It feels wrong to paint this line. It's weird to see Amy's name connected to the dead man's. But nothing connects all four victims. From the scribbles and crossings out that Amy has streaked the wall with, I can see she's come to the same conclusion I have, that it all might just be random. There is both too much and too little. Too many insignificant details line up, but nothing important enough for murder.

I turn to ask Amy what she thinks.

But she's still staring at the ceiling.

I'll ask her when she's better.

If.

Replacing the paintbrush on Amy's desk, a flash of blue catches my eye: the notebook Amy took from her father's trunk. Bells jangle in my mind when I reach for the book. Privacy is valued on this ship of limited space, and I've never consciously violated someone's privacy before. I smirk. Except when I broke into Eldest's room.

Amy seems to inspire me to be all kinds of different.

Eldest's lesson reverberates through my mind: Difference is a cause of discord. Fine. This ship could do with some discord.

On the first page of the book is a list of names. At the top is Eldest's. She's written over that name repeatedly, making it stand out in bold, and she's underlined and circled it dozens of times. Under it is "the doctor" and a question mark, followed by several tiny streaks on the paper, as if she tapped the end of the pencil against the page while thinking. Beneath Doc's name, a hasty list of names and descriptions of people is scribbled: me, Harley (although his name has been crossed out), Luthe (underlined so hard that her pencil ripped through the paper), "that mean girl" (surrounded by question marks and a doodle of a frowny face), and Orion (also crossed out).

I stare at the list of names, wondering at their importance and why Amy would bother writing them down in her special notebook.

Then it hits me.

This is her list of suspects.

My lips tighten as I stare down at it. She's eliminated Harley and Orion, and seems unsure about "that mean girl" (Victria? Maybe). But she hasn't marked me off. She still thinks I might be a suspect, or at least she did when she wrote her list.

I wonder what Harley's done to get his name marked off, what I need to do to have that same honor.

When she wakes up, I'll prove my worth to her.

If.

This is just another test, one which I have failed. I have proven myself, somehow, as unworthy in Amy's eyes, just as Eldest always sees me as unworthy to be a leader.

"Uhr . . ." Amy moans.

I drop the book and pencil onto her desk and rush to her. Her fingers pinch the bridge of her nose between her eyes, and when she drops her hand, I can see that the light has returned to her eyes.

"I've got a killer headache," Amy groans, shutting her eyes. There is more expression on her face now than I've seen from her all day.

"What happened?" she asks.

"What do you think happened?"

"Lord, I don't know. I remember when you got that all-call. And we rode in that tube thing. That was fun. But by the time we got to that big room with the lights, I was starting to feel kind of . . . woozy."

"Doc said that you've had a reaction to the ship. He's put you on ment—on the Inhibitor pills."

"Inhibitor pills? The same pill you and Harley and everyone 'crazy' takes?" Amy pushes me aside to sit up straight.

"Well—yes."

"Gah!" Amy screeches. She leaps off the bed, pacing, her hands curling into fists. "This ship is so effing messed up! I'm not crazy! You and Harley aren't crazy!"

I don't say anything because I half believe her. She takes my silence, however, for contradiction.

"What happened to make you and everyone else on this stupid ship think that things like—like screwing around with anything that walks, like being mindless drones—what made you think that— *that*—was *normal*!?"

I shrug. It's the way it's always been. How can I explain to this girl, who was raised among differences and lack of leadership and chaos and war that this is the way a normal society is run, a peaceful society, a society that doesn't just survive, as hers did, but one that thrives and flourishes as it hurtles through space toward a new planet?

Amy marches to the desk and picks up the floppy. "How do you make this freaking thing work?" she demands, fiddling with it. "This thing is like a computer, right? Doesn't it have information on Earth? Let me show you what real people, normal people, are like! Let me show you how weird this place is!"

She's not doing it right — she's swiped her finger across the screen and brought up the wi-com locator map I showed her before, but she doesn't know how to access anything else. She taps it, then jabs it, then balls her hand into a fist and pounds it against the table. I stand, walk to her, and gently take the floppy from her hands. There are tears in her eyes.

"I can't stand it," she whispers. "I can't stand these people, I can't stand this 'world.' I can't live here. I can't spend the rest of my life here. I can't. I *can't.*"

So. Enough of Eldest's speech on the Keeper Level penetrated into her mind. She knows how trapped she — all of us — are.

I want to take her into my arms and hold her tight. But at the same time, I know that is the exact opposite of what she wants. She wants to be free, and all I want to do is hold her tight against me.

"I think I know something that will help," I say.

57: AMY

As we walk along the path leading away from the Hospital, Elder is very mysterious. He won't tell me anything, and I suppose that's what really lifts my mood—he is like a little kid, eager to show his friend a new toy. That alone is enough to make me forget about the weird, fuzzy, slogging-through-water feeling of the day.

A couple sitting on the bench by the pond wave at us as we pass. The woman's face is aglow, and she leans against the man's chest with a look of utter bliss. Her right arm is wrapped around her stomach, and the man's arm cradles hers.

The woman bends her head down, and I realize she's talking to her unborn baby, not the man she's leaning against. "And the stars all had streaks of light chasing them, all shining down on us, on you."

"Eldest told me it wasn't for me," Elder says under his breath as the couple's chatter fades behind us.

I give Elder a confused look.

"The star screen in the Great Room. Eldest told me it wasn't there for me when I found out they weren't real stars, just lightbulbs." He looks away from me and says in a very small voice, "That was the day you woke up." His words hang in the air between us. It feels like a long time ago, for both of us.

Elder motions back at the happy couple on the bench. "Eldest said the fake stars were for them."

"Oh, I see." Typical that Eldest would want to control even the stars. He used them to manipulate the people of the ship, so that when they were told they would not be alive at planet-landing, they could at least have a taste of the stars to tell their children about. I look behind me at the woman sitting on the bench, holding her stomach with gentle hands and whispering to her unborn child about the stars they saw, promising it a lifetime under the heavens.

"It's cruel," I say. "To tantalize them with the outside, and then to take it away."

Elder shakes his head. "It's not like that. It gave them a story to feed their children. It's the way hope is passed down."

I stare at Elder. "You sort of agree with Eldest, don't you?"

"Sort of."

I want to argue. Eldest is like a spoiled child throwing his toys around. Waiting for an excuse to break us, watching for any sign that we don't want to play his game. Always watching, with eyes that remind me of Luthe's. He's not helping people, like Elder almost seems to think—he's twisting the situation to make no one really care about the fact that we'll all be dead or super-old before we land on the new planet. But before I can say anything, Elder announces, "We're here!"

He's so proud of himself that I don't have the heart to tell him I've been to the Recorder Hall before. Then again, the last time I was here,

I was a mess, covered in mud and tears. I remember the man who helped me then, Orion. His kindness kept me sane.

One of the rockers on the porch moves slowly, as if someone has just left it, but there's no other sign of life. Elder reaches to open the door for me. I see eyes then, and I smile, expecting Orion, but instead, Elder's painted face peers up at me from the brick wall.

"Oh!" I say, leaning over to inspect the new portrait by the door. Elder's face has replaced Eldest's dour one.

"Yeah." Elder sounds sheepish. My first thought was that he was going to show off with the painting—that's what Jason would have done, hammed it up—but I can tell he wishes I hadn't noticed it.

"Come inside," Elder says. The Recorder Hall is empty except for us, silent and dark. Elder shows me the big model of Earth and the ship that I saw earlier. I pretend to pay attention, but I'm distracted by the flashing images on the walls. The last time I was here with Orion, these were blank; I'd barely noticed them.

"Wall floppies," Elder says when he notices my distraction. "This is what *Godspeed* has been doing while you slept."

He grins at me, but I barely notice. I'm fascinated by all that's flashing in front of me: a diagram of how wi-coms work, and more of grav tubes. Art: I can pick out several scans of Harley's artwork— several of them koi fish, which seems to be his favorite subject—but there's more: sculptures, pottery, drawings, hand-sewn quilts. One of the floppy computers lists different titles, and when Elder taps on the screen, music fills the entryway.

For the first time since I woke up, I feel as if this is a place I could learn to love. It's not Earth, not by any stretch of the imagination— but I'm seeing art and inventions and life that Earth will never know.

And all this happened while I dreamt nightmares below genera-tions of people's feet. They didn't know about me any more than I knew about them.

"That's odd," Elder says, rapping his knuckles on one of the big wall computer things.

"What?"

"The image won't change," Elder says.

If it weren't for the label at the top—**LEAD-BASED FAST REACTOR PROTOTYPE**—I wouldn't know what it was at all. Not that the name helps me. I still don't know what it means.

"It's locked," Elder says. "Let me see if I can . . ." He steps over to one of the black boxes on the wall and runs his thumb over the scan-ner. "Eldest/Elder access granted," the computer chirps.

All around us, the pictures change. Now, images of Earth inter-mingle with images of *Godspeed*. A landscape painting of the Hospi-tal and garden are replaced with a photograph of Monument Valley. Although I didn't live there, it does remind me of the place out west where the space lab was, an hour from Colorado, where I met Jason, the last place I called home.

"Most people aren't allowed to see this," Elder says, still trying to get the one monitor to show something other than the engine sche-matics. "Whenever the new gen is born, school will start again. The children will see the model of Sol-Earth and the model of *Godspeed*. But they aren't allowed to see this."

"Why not?" I ask, brushing my fingers against the screen show-ing Monument Valley just before it melts into the Sphinx in Egypt.

"Eldest says it's best for people not to dwell too much on Sol-Earth. That we should think about the future, not the past."

"But he lets you see it."

Elder turns to stare at the screen, and for a moment, he looks a photo of Kim Jong-il in the eyes, but then the picture fades into one of the old presidents. I can't remember which one it is, the fat one with the big mustache.

"It's part of his lessons. He wants me to learn about Sol-Earth, so that I can prevent its mistakes. Why won't this frexing thing work?"

I want to say that Earth did not have mistakes, but I know that's not true. And I want to say that Eldest's method of running a world isn't right, but I'm not sure that's true. There is so much about this world inside a ship that I just don't understand.

"Orion!" Elder calls. "One of the wall floppies is stuck!"

"Is he here?" I look around—the place looks empty except for us.

The screen behind Elder shifts, fading from one old president to another.

"As I was saying, Eldest wanted me to learn from Sol-Earth. A lot of your leaders had it right—they just didn't get their people to follow. Like him."

I glance back at the image on the screen. "Who? Abraham Lincoln?"

Elder nods. "Sixteenth governmental leader of the United States of America, located in the northern hemisphere of Sol-Earth, between the Atlantic and Pacific Oceans. He was leader during the Civil War, a war between the states."

"Yes, I know." I am wary now. There is something in the way Elder speaks of Abraham Lincoln, so cold and disconnected, that makes me unsure—either of what he knows, or of what I know. I see a flicker of movement in the shadows near the door.

"He is the kind of leader Eldest wants me to be like." The picture starts to fade, but Elder touches the screen, and Lincoln's picture stays. I wait for him to continue. "When the states wanted to break up into discord, Lincoln provided the strong central leadership that kept them together."

"Yes." The word drawls out of my lips, long and low. Half my attention is on the door—is that Orion listening to us, or someone else? And why won't whoever it is come out of the shadows and talk to us?

"And when the differences that existed between the states were too strong, Lincoln was the one who eliminated the cause of that discord."

"I—what?"

"Monoethnicity. The cause of the war was that two races could not live in one country. Lincoln sent the black race back to the continent of Africa, and the war ended."

I sputter. "What are you talking about? That's not what happened!"

Elder taps on the screen, and the picture of Lincoln is replaced with text. He reads the words aloud, a hint of reverence in his voice.

"Four score and seven years ago our fathers brought forth, upon this continent, a new nation dedicated to the proposition that all men must be equal. Now we are engaged in a great civil war, testing whether that nation can long endure if men are not equal. We are met here on a great battlefield of that war to determine the future of one nation, one people, free of discord, at peace through sameness. Our nation will now discover the strength of unity and uniformity."

The text scrolls on. Elder takes a deep breath, about to continue reading.

"Stop."

Elder looks at me, surprised.

"That is not the Gettysburg Address," I say.

"Of course it is."

"It's not."

"Then what's the Gettysburg Address?"

I dig in my brain, trying to remember. "The four score part was the same. But this one is saying things like everyone should be the same—that's not in there."

"Then what does the Gettysburg Address say?"

"Er . . . Four score and seven years ago . . . um . . . Okay, look, I don't have the thing memorized, but I know enough to know that one's wrong."

Elder looks at me doubtfully, and I realize how weak my argument sounds. Inside, I'm beating myself up: how could I have left Earth without knowing this?

"That's—this thing is basically racism," I say. Elder doesn't seem to know what "racism" is. "The speech you just read—that was all about dividing the races. But that's not what the Gettysburg Address is about. And besides—look at you." I wave my hand at Elder's tan skin, almond eyes, high cheekbones, dark hair. "You're like the ultimate in mixed races."

Elder looks even more confused now. He has no concept that a race is part of a person's identity—he just sees it as a difference, a difference that's better off eliminated.

And I realize: That's exactly how Eldest wants him to think.

I think I hear laughter, soft chuckling, from near the door, but when I whip around to see, no one's there. Just Elder, who still doesn't understand me. And why should he? How can he learn from history if history's been altered?

I'm the only one who knows, and I don't know enough to fix it.

Would they even believe me if I tried?

58: ELDER

Amy's staring at the screen as upset as she was before we got here. This is not going as planned. This was supposed to be the thing that made her happy again. I tap the screen and let Lincoln fade. A picture of people during the German Inflation replaces Lincoln's creased face, their wheelbarrows of money blending in with his chaotic hair.

"We should go back," Amy says. "Harley's been guarding the cryo level long enough. I'll take a turn."

There is so much more here I want to show her: the rooms of books, real books, from Sol-Earth. The artifact room on the second floor, where there are models and Sol-Earth artifacts, including an original tractor that we base our tractors on. The science records room that shows how we developed the wi-com systems and the grav tubes. But she doesn't want to see any of it, so what's the point?

"I know that man," Amy says, awe and wonder in her voice. She pushes me aside so she can see the image on the screen.

I stare at the picture, but don't remember him. He's an older man, somewhere between Doc's and Harley's ages, with dark hair and eyes but that distinct oddness in his look shows how different he is from us—he's not monoethnic, and he just looks . . . different. He's sitting in front of a trailer, holding a fat baby in his lap. Certainly, he's no one important, no one Eldest made me memorize facts about.

"It's Ed."

"Who?"

"Ed. I met him just before I was frozen. He was actually one of the men who froze me and my parents."

That doesn't seem like an important enough reason for his picture to be located beside Abraham Lincoln's. I reach past Amy and touch the screen. The picture of this "Ed" stops; when I touch the screen again, the text about him pops up.

"Edmund Albert Davis, Junior," I read aloud. "The first child born on *Godspeed*, shown here with his father, Edmund Albert Davis, Senior, one of the recruits from Sol-Earth on the departing flight."

"I knew him," Amy says. Her head is cocked, and she's gazing at the picture as if Edmund Albert Davis, Senior, were alive and she was talking to him. "I had no idea he signed up to leave Earth on *Godspeed*."

I am thinking about Edmund Albert Davis, Junior, and how he was the first person born to captivity here. I wonder how he felt about it, growing up with people who'd lived on Earth, knowing he'd never ever see that.

"I wish I had known," Amy says. "I wish I had talked to him more. I wish I had asked him why he'd joined the crew. He seemed so bitter when we met. But maybe that was just . . ." She trails off, staring at the screen without seeing it. Suddenly, she laughs. "Just think! I met this man centuries and centuries ago, and now I could meet his ancestors on this ship! Descendants of the man who froze me! How cool would that be?" She turns to me, her eyes widening. "What if *you* were a descendent of Ed? Talk about a coincidence!"

I laugh because she's laughing.

"I wonder if you are," she says, her gaze dancing between me and the image on the wall floppy.

"Are what?"

"A descendant of Ed?"

"I don't know."

"Oh, please!" Amy snorts. "With all this technology, surely someone's kept a genealogical chart. I bet Eldest or that doctor has one— they were the ones all concerned about incest."

"They keep all the records here. This is the Recorder Hall," I say. She doesn't notice my hollow tone. I know that even if we find Ed's descendant, it won't be me. My birth records are hidden. We can trace Ed's whole lineage back to Sol-Earth, but I can't even go one step back on my family tree.

"Oh, come on! Let's see if you're related to Ed!" She grabs my arm, and I haven't seen her this caught up in excitement since . . . ever. The weight of worry she's been carrying around is forgotten, if just for a moment. And I'll do anything to keep it from coming back.

"It shouldn't be too hard to trace," I say. "With this being the first baby born on the ship, I'm sure they kept a record."

My fingers run across the hotspots on the screen, pressing in an info spot, then tapping in key words. Amy watches me, fascinated. I tap faster. My fingers get all tangled up, the screen beeps at me in anger, and I have to start the search engine over.

Finally: "Here it is!"

Amy's head tilts back as she reads the top of the screen. "Ed Senior leads to Ed Junior . . ." she mutters. Her eyes slowly sink down the screen before she looks up, puzzled. She looks as if she's going to ask me a question, but then she looks back at the screen and starts to count under her breath. "One, two, three . . ." She finally looks up at me, her brows creasing. "Thirteen generations. There are thirteen generations on this chart. From Ed Junior all the way down to Benita, here, there are thirteen generations of people recorded."

"So?"

Amy starts to pace from the model of Sol-Earth back to the screen. "How many generations can be born in a century? Maybe four or five? So thirteen generations would be around three centuries, right?"

I nod.

"But look at this." Amy points to the bottom of the screen.

And just under Benita's name are the words, "Killed by Plague."

"When was the Plague?" Amy asks.

"A long time ago," I say, slowly. I think of the statue of the Plague Eldest in the Hospital garden. It's worn and weathered so much that the details of his face are gone.

"How long?" Her words are quick, urgent, and they are infecting me.

"Longer than Eldest. Longer than the Eldest before him."

"So, like, maybe a hundred years. So that would mean that Benita, the thirteenth generation of this family . . . she had to have been born around three hundred years after the ship left. But she was killed by this Plague . . . and that happened like a hundred or more years ago. This ship's been flying at least a century longer than it was supposed to. . . ."

"But the ship was supposed to have landed in fifty years. We've only been flying for two hundred and fifty years," I say.

Amy stops pacing, turns, and faces me. Her eyes are wide, boring into mine.

"How do you know for sure?" she says. "Let's look up the charts after the Plague. If we count how many generations were born after the Plague, maybe we'll be able to figure out how long this ship has really been traveling."

It feels as if there is a rock in my stomach, pulling me down, pulling the entire ship down. "There are no genealogical charts after the Plague. I just remembered: Doc told me once that the Plague wiped out so many people that they quit making the charts after that."

"The Season," Amy whispers more to herself than to me. "The Season started after the Plague, right?" She is staring hard at nothing. "This can't be a coincidence. That thirteenth generation, Benita's generation—that was when the ship was supposed to land. It must have been close to three centuries then, surely. But then this Plague happened, and the Season was started, and they quit doing genealogical charts—"

"And photography was banned," I add. "There are no pictures of the ship from the year before the Plague till now. I was fascinated by the Plague when I was younger—it's one of the first things Eldest taught me about—but there aren't pics or vids of it at all, and now only the scientists on the Shipper Level can use photography, and only then as a record of their discoveries."

"Something happened during that Plague," Amy says slowly. "Something so bad that all the records of it were destroyed. And everything after—the Season, the way people act here—it all comes back to the Plague."

5 9 : AMY

Elder starts to say something to me, but just when he opens his mouth, the door to the Recorder Hall flings open.

"Elder!" Eldest's voice, strong and cold, rings out across the empty hall.

Elder lunges for the control panels. All the forbidden images of the people and places of my home disappear. The telltale genealogical chart fades to black; the stuck image of the engine slides away.

"Don't bother," Eldest growls. He taps one finger behind his left ear, where the communicator is implanted. "I keep tabs on what you study on this ship. I know what you've used your access to open."

"I'm sorry, sir," Elder says automatically, but I can tell he doesn't mean it, and he regrets saying it altogether. He stands straighter and regains some of his composure. "But since when do you keep 'tabs' on me? And honestly, I'm surprised you even noticed. The last time I saw you, you were dru—"

My head whips around to Eldest. Drunk? Was Elder about to say Eldest was *drunk*?

The movement's not lost on Eldest. He doesn't address me, though, just Elder when he says, "A true leader is never out of control, nor drunk on anything." *Now* he looks at me. "I seem to remember believing that you have the potential to disrupt my ship. Clearly, I am right."

"I didn't do anything!" I say. There is a hint of panic in my voice. I haven't forgotten his original threat.

Eldest waves his hand dismissively at me. "Your presence is enough. It's completely distracted my . . . student." He says this last bit with a sneer in his voice, as if he equates a student with an annoying, yapping little Chihuahua. He returns his gaze to Elder. "It's time to resume your studies. I've been busy with the Season and let you play with your little girl here, but if you have time to look up what I saw you looking up, then clearly it is time to refocus your studies to something more productive."

He walks back to the door. Elder chews on his lip, unsure of whether to follow or not.

"Wait!"

Eldest turns at my call, but does not come back.

"I want some answers, dammit," I say, striding toward him. "You and I both know there's some crazy crap going on. That Season was bad enough, but now the doctor's calling *me* crazy, and I've got to take that pill Elder takes, and this place has—"

"Enough." Eldest cuts me off with cold authority. "I told you not to become a disturbance. You clearly did not listen."

"I think this ship needs some disturbance!"

"The last man who thought that way no longer thinks anything at all."

Other than Elder's sharp intake of breath, the Recorder Hall is silent. We are facing off, Eldest near the door, me near the clay planets, and Elder in the middle, our mark in a tug-of-war game for the truth.

"Come on, Elder." Eldest turns again for the door.

"What happened in the Plague?!" I shout at him. "What are you not telling us? You know — I know you know! Why can't you just tell us the truth?"

At this, Eldest crosses the hall in three long strides and faces me. "This ship is built on secrets; it runs on secrets," he says, tiny droplets of spittle flying from his mouth to my face. "And if you keep asking about them, you'll see how far I'm willing to go to keep mine. Go to your chamber; I'll have Doc deal with you this time. Come, Elder!" he bellows. Elder jumps and follows Eldest out the door, shooting me an apologetic look just before the doors close, leaving me in the darkened hall with the dusty models.

I don't realize that my fists are clenched until I relax my grip, letting my fingers stretch out. I am shaking with rage. There is one thing I know for sure: I *will* find out whatever secret it is that Eldest is so determined to keep, and when I do, I'm going to shout it from the rooftops.

60: ELDER

No surprise: Eldest leads me straight to the grav tubes and the Learning Center. I take a seat at the table as if I am waiting for my lesson, but my mind is racing.

I know Amy thinks that I just meekly followed Eldest, an obedient dog trailing after his master. I could see the disappointment in her eyes as I left her in the Recorder Hall. I will have to let Amy think me weak; I will have to sacrifice her image of me.

Because that is what a leader must do.

I must play this game a little longer. Rely on Eldest's perception that I am stupid and ignorant, on his contempt for my weakness. Not forever. Just long enough to break down the wall he keeps up between me and my role as leader on board this ship.

Eldest is crumbling. The argument with Amy, the way he's so quick to lose his temper now, the sudden bursts of shouting and violence that have surfaced since the Season — Eldest's cool, grandfatherly exterior is cracking, and his true self, his petty, power-hungry self, is leaking through.

When he was arguing with Amy, he looked foolish in his anger. He is just an old man clutching his power as tightly as he can. And all I have to do is poke at those cracks, and I will be able to break through and discover what it is he's kept hidden from me for so long, why he never felt that he could share the secrets of the ship with me.

Although I was born Elder, for the first time I finally feel as if I can one day be Eldest.

Across from me, Eldest pinches the bridge of his nose between his eyes. "Why are you looking for this kind of information?"

"What kind of information?"

"Sol-Earth history, engine schematics, the Plague—what are you looking for?" His voice is tight and controlled, but barely.

"Why does it matter?"

"IT MATTERS!" Eldest roars, slamming his fists onto the table. I do not jump.

I force myself into the picture of calm. If I have learned one thing from Eldest today, it is this: Losing my temper will make me look foolish and childish. Instead, I speak slowly, calmly, and clearly, as if I were explaining something very simple. "I have begun to look for the information that you have refused to teach me. I am supposed to be the Eldest one day. If you don't tell me what to do or what I need to know to rule, then I'll just figure it out another way. If you're going to stand there and be mad at me for looking for answers to these questions, then you have only yourself to blame; it's your job to teach me these things first."

Eldest's face flushes pale, then purples. "Have you never thought I had a *very* good reason for keeping information from you?"

"No," I say simply. "I have known you since I was a kid; you had a hand in every part of my growing up; I have spent the last three years living with you. What possible reason could you have for not trusting me with any information at all about this ship?"

"You think you know *everything*," Eldest sneers. "You're still just a kid."

"You're losing it," I say calmly, tilting my head up at him. "You're not in control anymore. Look at you. You're raving. You're not fit to be Eldest."

"And you are?" Eldest is practically screaming, his voice rising to a painfully high pitch.

I shrug. "There must have been something in what Amy and I were looking up to make you get so angry. I wonder what it is. . . ."

Eldest is seething. I think to myself, *Orion was wrong. You don't have to be sneaky to get around Eldest. You just have to make him really frexing mad.*

"It can't be the history floppies; you've shown me them before. It must be the Plague."

Eldest raises his head and faces me. His anger now is deep inside him, a burning coal in his stomach, one that he's swallowed so I can't see it anymore. "I haven't talked about this in a very long time."

I suck in my breath. "The Elder before me?" Eldest nods. "Did he die? Or did you . . ." I can't bring myself to ask the question.

"You want to know about the Plague?" he says in a terrible monotone. "Fine. Let me tell you about the Plague."

He jumps to his feet, then shifts his weight off his bad leg. With both fists on the table, he looms over me, and I can do nothing but look up at him with meek eyes, waiting.

"Let me start with this," Eldest says. "There was never any Plague."

61: AMY

After Elder abandons me in the Recorder Hall, I stand there, alone in the dark. I'm not sure why Elder went with Eldest—I trust Elder, but not Eldest, and I thought Elder agreed with me about Eldest.

Under it all, always, deep inside of me, is a pulsing worry for my parents, a constant desire to find the killer and to protect them, as ingrained in my being as my heartbeat. A wave of fear washes over me. My leg muscles tremble, but I can't tell if it's because they want to run, or because they want to collapse from under me.

"Amy?"

I bite back a shout of surprise.

"It's Orion," he says, striding from the shadows behind the model of Earth.

"Where were you before?" I ask. "I thought I saw you . . ."

Orion smiles sheepishly at me. "I was looking at the wi-com loca-tor, just for fun, you know. I saw Eldest was nearby. I . . . I don't get along well with Eldest. I thought it might be best for me to lie low until he was gone."

"He hates you, too, huh?" I ask. Orion nods. "What'd you do?'

"It's mostly just the problem of my existence."

"Yeah, me too."

Orion brushes his hair out of his face, and I see a flash of white: a scar trailing up the left side of his neck.

"I've been meaning to ask you," Orion says, "I've seen you running and . . . what are you running from?"

He's the second person to ask this, but I think he means something different from the girl in the rabbit field.

"I'm not sure," I say, "but I think I'm tired of running now."

"Yeah." Orion glances behind him, into the Recorder Hall. "Me too."

"I better go," I say, even though I don't have anywhere to go. I just know I'm not going to stay here, stagnant, afraid to move, cowering in the shadows of unreachable planets.

"I'll see you soon," Orion calls after me.

I don't run back to the Hospital. I walk. I won't let myself enter the zone where my body's movement drowns out my brain's thoughts. I force my feet to go slowly so that my mind can race.

The air is humid in the Hospital garden. If I was on Earth, I would think that it was about to rain—but I'm not on Earth, and rain here is nothing but sprinklers in the sky.

"Leave off," an elderly voice behind me says. "I can walk up the stairs on my own." I turn, curious. This elderly voice has an inflection of knowledge and insight to it—and I recognize it. Steela. The woman who dispersed the crowd of Feeders in the City, on my first run after I woke up.

"Yes, Mother." The younger woman speaking is not like her mother. She has the same dead monotone that Filomina used when I observed her examination by the doctor.

Steela catches my eyes with her cloudy ones, the color of milk mixed with mud. She looks warily at me for a moment more, then her wrinkled lips spread into an even wrinklier smile. Her teeth are stained and crooked, and I can smell onions on her breath, but still it's a nice smile. It's a true smile.

"Mother," the woman says again.

"Shut up, you," the old woman says pleasantly. "I'll just be a moment."

"All right, Mother." The woman stands perfectly still, like a windup toy that has run out of windup. She's not upset in the least with her mother's rude words, and she seems perfectly at ease with merely standing.

"Nice to see you again," I say, extending my hand.

Steela's grip is firmer than I'd expected. "Wish I could say the same. I hate this place."

"Mother," Steela's daughter says pleasantly. "We should get you to the Hospital now."

Steela looks defeated and defiant at the same time.

"Mother." The woman's voice is needling, but pleasant. Perfectly pleasant. Perfectly creepy.

"I'm coming!" Steela sounds like an angry child, but she just looks like a sad old woman who is too aged to make decisions for herself.

"I'll take her," I say before I really think of what I'm saying. "I mean, I was going there anyway, no problem."

The daughter blinks. "If it is amenable to you, Moth—"

"Yes, yes, it's *amenable*. Now go." Steela watches her daughter leave. "Frexing shame, watching your daughter become one of *them*." I open my mouth to ask who *they* are, but Steela's a step ahead of me. "One of them brainless twits. They labeled me crazy when I was twelve, trained me up to be an agriculturalist." She gazes at the garden behind the Hospital as I lead her to the steps. "I made that garden. Weren't nothing but shrubs and weeds till I came. I've been takin' them little blue-'n'-white pills ever since. But I don't mind. Rather be crazy taking drugs than empty like that. Kind of wish me daughter was crazy, too. Might like her more then."

Empty. What a good way to describe them.

"Heard about you on the wi-com," Steela says, taking my arm. Her grip on my elbow is strong, belying her gnarled fingers. "Don't reckon you're what they said you were."

"I reckon you're one of the smartest people on this ship."

Steela snorts. "Not smart." She looks up as we reach the doors. "Not smart at all. I'm just scared, is all." She grips my elbow tighter, somehow finding the thinnest skin to dig her fingernails into. I want to pry her fingers from my arm, but when I look down at her, I can tell that she's using me as a lifeline, and I'm not going to be the one to let her drown.

"What do you have to be scared of?"

Steela stares blankly ahead. "I'm one of the last." She glances up at me and sees my confused face. "One of the last of me generation." The doors slide open and we step inside, but Steela is going slowly,

slowly, until she actually stops just a few feet inside the lobby. "No one's ever come back from here."

"Don't be silly." I laugh. "I left here this morning."

Steela gazes down at my smooth arm. "I don't forget. I've never forgotten any of them: Sunestra, Everard, me Albie . . . all of them dropped off here by their loving, brainless families, and none of them ever came back."

I bite my lip in worry. "I've never seen them," I say, but I remember not too long ago, the woman who was being checked in. The nurse took her away. But where?

I lead Steela up to the front desk and clear my throat to get the heavyset woman's attention.

"What?" she asks, staring at Steela with cold, hard eyes.

"Her daughter came to drop her off," I say.

The nurse nods and starts to come around her desk. "I'll take her up to the fourth floor."

"But you haven't even asked what's wrong."

The nurse rolls her eyes. "What's wrong?" she asks Steela.

"Nothing," Steela says.

"Did your daughter say you were having delusions?"

"She said I was . . ." Steela starts, a worried look on her face.

"That's not so bad," I say, patting Steela's hand. "Old people don't always think straight. It's nothing to worry about." I glance at the nurse. "It's nothing to go to a hospital over. I can take her back home."

"What kind of delusions?" the nurse asks, bored.

Steela's face grows dark. I can tell that she is really worried, really scared. "I . . . I remember . . ." she mutters.

"What do you think you remember?" The nurse doesn't look up from the floppy she's typing on.

"The stars," Steela whispers. My hold on her hand tightens. "Earlier, when Eldest said . . ."

Her voice trails off. She does not have to finish.

"But . . ."

My full attention is on Steela. I can tell by the way she's shaking that what she's trying to say is vitally important to her. The nurse yawns.

"But I can remember that happening before. When I was pregnant with me daughter—"

"Didn't happen," the nurse interjects. "Lots of the grays have been saying the same. Just getting the past mixed up with the present."

Steela bristles. "Don't tell me what I do and do not remember!"

"Classic delusional case, brought on by age," the nurse states in a matter of fact way. "Come with me."

She steps out from behind the desk and reaches for Steela's arm. Steela holds on to me tighter and refuses to move.

"Where are you taking her?" I ask.

"Fourth floor."

My mind is racing. I need to relieve Harley from guard duty; I need to focus more on solving the mystery of the killer. But Steela's fragile hands are shaking. I said I wouldn't be the one to let her drown. I can afford enough time to be her buoy a little longer. Besides—I want desperately to know what is behind those locked doors.

"I'll take her up there," I offer. I can feel Steela sag with relief at the thought.

"I shouldn't . . ."

"I don't mind."

"Let me call Doc." Her hand hovers near her ear-button.

"No, don't bother. I've been up there before. We won't get lost."

The nurse seems reluctant, but she nods. She watches us with beady eyes as we approach the elevator. She's clearly expecting us to make a run for it, but I just push the call button and wait for the elevator.

"We can escape," I mutter to Steela. "I know some back ways—I can get you out of here with no one noticing." I'm not even sure why I'm offering. If she needs medical attention, she needs the doctor. It's just that all of her fire is gone, replaced with fear, and it's killing me inside.

Steela shakes her head. "I can see myself standing up on that Great Room, pregnant with me daughter, looking at those stars. Can see it, clear as clear. But it can't have happened, could it? That nurse said lots of us were getting delusional. Maybe it is me age. I reckon I should see the doc."

The elevator doors slide open. I don't let go of Steela's arm until she's safely inside with me. My finger hovers over the third floor button, hesitating for a moment before it slides up and presses the button for the fourth floor. My stomach drops as we start to rise. We are both silent.

The elevator bobs for a minute, then stills. The light indicates we're on the fourth floor.

"Stay with me," Steela whispers as the doors slide open.

62: ELDER

"What do you mean there was no Plague?" I ask, my mind racing. This is one of the few things all of us—me, the Feeders, the Shippers, all of us—were taught. It is the first lesson every child on the ship learns: We must work together, be diligent, or risk another Plague. It is such a part of our lives that we slap a med patch on if we even *think* we're getting sick, and every sneeze is reported to Doc.

"There was no Plague. Sure, there's been sickness on the ship—some of it quite damaging, honestly—but no widespread Plague."

"But the deaths . . . we're still recovering from the death tolls from the Plague. We're not even up to original numbers now, and the Plague was so long ago." I think of the empty trailers in the City, of how there is still growing room for us aboard the ship, even though the Plague was longer ago than any living memory. "You taught me about this. You told me three-fourths of the ship's population died under the Plague." I cannot hide the note of accusation in my voice.

But really, I should not have been surprised. The lightbulb stars in the room beyond are proof enough of that.

"There were deaths. But not from a Plague."

"What do you mean?" Roles are reversed now. Eldest is the calm one; I am the one bordering on panic. How much more of my life will I discover has been built on lies?

"Come on." Eldest sighs as if he'd rather not show me anything, but before he can change his mind, I jump up and follow him out of the Learning Center, across the Great Room, and down the hatch to the Shipper Level. His shoes tap unevenly on the tiled floor, making his limp more noticeable. He ignores both me and the Shippers who snap to attention.

The Shipper Level reminds me, in a strange way, of the cryo level where Amy was. There are no living quarters here. All the Shippers live in the City on the Feeder Level and take the grav tube here. Instead, this level, like the cryo level, is all metal. Hallways branch off into laboratories and offices, some fitted with biometric scanners and some so old-fashioned that they have actual locks from Sol-Earth. For the most part, I'm ignorant of what lies behind the doors. Eldest has never bothered to let me learn the intricacies of what the scientists and Shippers study and do. I know, vaguely, that the importance of the job is determined by where it is on the level. The offices nearest to the grav tube are the least important, dealing with things like weather manipulation and soil-sample testing. The farther down the hallway you go, the more important the research. The farthest I've been is about midway down, where the solar lamp research is done.

Eldest takes us all the way to the end of the hall. I've never even

walked this far down the hall, let alone gone through these doors.
I know from studying the ship diagrams what is there: the energy
room, where nuclear physics is studied, that leads directly to the
engine room, where lies the massive heart of the ship. Beyond that is
the nav con, where Eldest said only the top Shippers go, the ones who
will finally land *Godspeed* in 49 years and 263 days . . . no, I mean, 74
years and 263 days—74 years. Frex . . . 74.

Eldest scans his thumb on the biometric scanner at the energy
room's doorway. "Eldest/Elder access granted," the scanner says
pleasantly. I pause. I've never gone past this room. But Eldest keeps
going to the door on the far wall. When it opens, I hear the deep
growling of the ship's engine.

I'm finally going to see the engine.

The engine room is hot, oppressively hot. I tug at my collar and
push up my sleeves, but Eldest does not show any indication that he's
even uncomfortable. All around us, scientists rush around. Some hold
vials or metal boxes, nearly all of them have floppies under their arms,
flashing important looking charts and diagrams.

"Follow me," Eldest says.

But I don't.

My eyes fill up with the thing in the center of the room: sunken
into the floor, and huge, is the engine.

For some reason, I never imagined the engine in the engine room.
I mean, I knew the engine was there, obviously, but I never bothered to think about it. I knew from Eldest's lessons that, in its crud-
est form, the engine is a nuclear reactor running off uranium. The
thing before me looks almost like a test tube, although giant and with
heavy metal pipes extending from its head and wrapping around it.

An undercurrent of *whirr-churn-whirr* cycles over and over and over. This is the heartbeat of the ship.

"It's loud," Eldest grunts when he sees where my attention has wandered. "And it smells."

I hadn't noticed the odd scent of grease and cleaner before. "It's beautiful."

Eldest snorts, then stares at me more intently. "It's not beautiful." His gaze shifts to the engine. "It's the ugliest thing I've ever seen," he says in a flat voice. "Do you know what kind of engine that is?"

"Nuclear," I say.

Eldest rolls his eyes. "Be a *little* more specific, why don't you?"

"A lead-cooled fast reactor?" I guess, remembering the engine schematics in the Recorder Hall.

Eldest withdraws the scale model of the engine, the one I last saw on his desk when I snuck into his room, from his pocket. He breaks it apart so that I can see the tiny innards. The engine is like a living thing with veins and organs and the slow *whirr-churn-whirr* of life.

"We use uranium," Eldest continues. "The uranium goes through the reactor, then here—" He points to a small box that's outside the test tube of the engine, connected by tubes and wires. "The uranium is reprocessed in the back end of the nuclear fuel cycle. We are supposed to be able to use and reuse the uranium over and over again, a constantly recycled fuel system."

The key words—supposed to be—are not lost on me. "Is that not what's happening?"

"The reprocessing part of the fuel cycle isn't working like we thought it would," Eldest says. "It's supposed to maintain the uranium's efficiency."

"But it's not?" I ask.

He shakes his head. "No."

"What's happening?"

I can tell Eldest wants to look away, but I don't break eye contact.

"The short answer? We're going slower. And slower. At first, we were at 80 percent maximum speed, then 60. Now we sometimes hit 40 percent maximum speed, but it's usually worse."

"That's why the ship's landing was delayed? That's why it's taking extra years to land?"

Eldest snorts—his first betrayal of emotion since we entered the Engine Room. "Twenty-five years behind schedule? I wish. We're not even halfway there. As of now, we're 250 years behind schedule."

63: AMY

Doc is waiting for us on the fourth floor. He's not surprised to see either of us, which I take to mean that the fat nurse downstairs used her ear button to call ahead. I knew we couldn't trust her.

"Steela, how are you?" the doctor says in falsely bright tones. "Amy, I can handle her on my own; you go on back to your chamber."

"No, thank you," I say as Steela's hand clenches on my arm.

"What?" The doctor looks surprised.

"I'm sticking with Steela."

"But—"

"I want her to," Steela says without a quaver in her voice.

The doctor frowns.

"I'm not going anywhere," I say.

There is a thin white line around the doctor's lips. "Fine," he says. He looks down at the floppy in his hand. "Bed 36 is available." He turns to the third door in the hallway. There are no biometric scanners on the door—instead, the doctor withdraws a big iron key from his pocket.

The large room has ten beds, five against each wall. The doctor leads Steela to the bed all the way across the room, the only one not occupied.

"We were waiting for you," the doctor tells Steela. A chill goes down my spine. "It's so much easier to do a room all at once," he mutters.

The doctor indicates a neatly folded hospital gown on the bed. Steela looks at me. She doesn't want to let me go; I don't want her to let go. When her hand releases my elbow, it is like a goodbye.

The doctor just stands there as if nothing is out of the ordinary. Steela's hands shake as she unfastens the top button of her tunic.

"Give her some privacy," I hiss at him. When he doesn't register what I've said, I take his elbow and turn him around. While we're waiting for Steela to change, I inspect the doctor—his back is turned as he fiddles with the instruments on the table by the wall. He'd not intended to peep on Steela—why would he want to? She's so old. No, he'd just forgotten that Steela might be sensitive about undressing in front of him. He doesn't look at her as a human with feelings. He's been playing doctor too long with the simple Feeders, and forgotten what a real person is like.

"I'm done," Steela says in her crackling voice.

She sits on the hospital bed with her legs sticking out straight in front of her and the sheet pulled up to her knees. Glancing around the room, I see that every other patient in the room is doing the same, but that they are all, as Steela would say, "brainless twits." She's emulating them, perhaps unconsciously.

Her tunic and trousers are folded neatly on the end of the bed. The hospital gown, so much thinner than her regular clothing, makes Steela look smaller, weaker, sicker than before. And so much more scared. She is shivering, but I don't think it's from the cool air blowing through the room.

"What are those?" Steela asks, her voice catching.

"Just IVs." The doctor holds them out. "For . . . nutrition."

"Why can't you use those med patch things?" I ask.

"Med patches are just for simple things, like headaches and stomach aches. This is more serious than that."

"None of the others have three IVs." Steela says.

The room is so quiet I'd almost forgotten that anyone else was here. The elderly in the other beds are meek, staring at the ceiling. Feeders. But Steela's right—the others have only two IVs—one each in the left hand and the left forearm.

"The third one's special, because you're special."

"Hogwash."

The doctor grins wryly. "It's because you're the only one here on mental meds."

Steela bites her lips. Like Elder, she believes she's as crazy as the doctor's been calling her all her life. And now she's uncertain—now she thinks that she needs to be here, cloistered with the others who are staring blankly straight ahead.

"You haven't even examined her yet," I say.

"Hmm?" The doctor doesn't look up from rubbing Steela's arm with disinfectant.

"You're jabbing her with needles and IVs and you haven't even examined her. What's going on?" My voice comes out low and deep.

I wonder if the doctor realizes that this is how my voice gets before I get very, very angry.

"The nurse downstairs informed me of the situation."

"What situation?" I ask, glaring. My glare is worthless; he doesn't even look up. Steela's watching us, though.

"She's having delusions. Just like everyone here." In quick order, the doctor attaches two of the IVs to Steela's left arm, then moves over to her right one with the third needle. The doctor pinches Steela's skin at the crease of her elbow. He jabs the "special" IV needle deep into her big, thick blue vein. Steela gasps at the pain of it.

And even though the doctor had said that this was an IV to give her nutrition, a thick dark red stream of blood drips down into the waiting bag at the end of the tube.

I don't think. I just ram my shoulder so hard into the doctor that he flies back and hits the wall. I pin him there with my arm. I may not be as big as he is, but I've got rage on my side.

"What are you doing?" I shout at him. "You said that was an IV—but it's not. Why are you always lying? What are you hiding?"

When I am done yelling, silence fills the room. The nine other patients on their beds all stare blankly ahead of them, unaware that anything has happened.

Out of the corner of my eye, I see Steela blink, staring straight ahead, oblivious to me shouting less than a foot away.

"Steela?" I whisper.

Nothing.

64: ELDER

We are back in the Learning Center, and I feel as hollow as the model of *Godspeed* in the Recorder Hall, each of us lacking an engine to propel us through life.

"Two hundred and fifty years behind schedule?" I ask. The words echo in my mind, replacing the *whirr-churn-whirr* of the engine's rhythm that had still been ringing in my ears.

Eldest shrugs. "Roughly. We were supposed to land about a hundred and fifty years ago—now it looks like we'll land in another hundred years. Maybe. If the fuel systems hold. If nothing else goes wrong."

"And if something else goes wrong?"

"Then the ship floats dead in the water, so to say. Until the internal reactors cool. And then the solar lamp dies, and we'll be in darkness. And then the plants die. And then we all die."

Inside the ship, we are always surrounded by one another, so much so that we cherish our tiny private rooms and time alone. Never before have I appreciated how truly alone we are on this ship. There is no one else but us. I always felt before that we were anchored between the two planets, and even if we couldn't reach them immediately, they were there, on the other end of an invisible rope. But they're not. If we fail, there is no one out there to save us. If we die, there is no one out there to mourn us.

"Do you see now?" Eldest asks, his eyes bringing me back aboard the ship.

I nod, not really registering his question.

"This is why you—*you*—must be the leader. A strong, assured leader. The Plague was not a plague. It was what happened when the leader of the ship told the people the truth, how long it would take to land the ship. When they learned that they would never see planet-landing, that their children, and their grandchildren would not see it, that there was a chance *none* of them would see it . . . the ship itself almost died."

I raise my face to Eldest, wetness blurring my vision of him. "What happened?"

"Suicide. Murder. Riots and chaos. Mutiny and war. They would have ripped through the walls into space if they could have."

"That's the Plague? That's the three-fourths of the ship who died—the ones who learned the truth?"

Eldest nods. "So one man, the strongest leader, stood up and became the first Eldest. He worked with the survivors. They developed the lie. They came up with the idea of a Plague to explain the deaths to the next gen, and the gen after that."

"How did they survive?" How could anyone survive this

knowledge Eldest has given me? The loss of planet-landing is so much worse now than when I heard of it before.

"The first Eldest noticed that most of the survivors were members of a family—or were pregnant. People will survive anything for their children."

Now I am confused. I cock my head and struggle to piece together this information. "You say the survivors were pregnant. But wasn't everyone of that gen pregnant? If the Season had just happened . . ."

Eldest rolls his eyes. "I thought you'd figured that out from the girl. The Plague Eldest developed the Season. Before this, people mated whenever they liked. Some were pregnant; some were not. The generations were blurred. The Plague Eldest came up with the idea of establishing the Season, ensuring everyone is pregnant at the same time. Every other gen, after the Season, we inform them they will not see the new land. But their unborn children will. This is motivation enough for them not to revert to chaos and riots. This is motivation enough for them to accept the delay for one more gen. And then another, and then another . . ."

"The water pump on the cryo level . . ." I say, thinking it through. "But wasn't that part of the ship's original design?"

Eldest nods. "It was. Used to distribute vits directly to the populace. But the Plague Eldest figured out another use. . . ."

Eldest smirks as he crosses the room to the tap on the far wall. He pulls a glass from the cabinet over the sink and fills it with water; then he comes back and sets the glass in front of me.

I stare at it. Clear, calm, still. Nothing like me. My first instinct is to drink from the glass before me. After all, water is the remedy all the Feeder wives use to calm their children, to placate the adults.

My eyes grow wide. "It's not just hormones, is it?" I ask, my gaze locked on the innocuous-looking liquid. "There's something else in there."

Eldest sits down across from me. The glass of water stands between us like a wall.

"It's Phydus."

"What?"

"Phydus. A drug developed after the Plague."

"What does it do?"

Eldest holds his hands on the table, palms up, as if asking for grace or forgiveness—or perhaps he thinks he's bestowing it. "Phydus ensures that people's emotions do not override their instinct for survival. Phydus controls extreme emotions, so that people won't cause so much death and destruction again."

I taste bile on my tongue. This isn't *right*. All those times Amy paced in her tiny room, declaiming the abnormality of life aboard this ship—I was just humoring her, never understanding what she really meant. Now I do. For a brief moment, my vision goes as my rage surges, and I literally see nothing but red.

"If this Phydus is in the water, and it takes away our emotion, why am I so frexing furious right now?" I grip the edge of the table, feeling the hard, smooth wood under my fingers. I wonder if I have the strength to overturn it on Eldest.

"You're upset? Why?"

"This isn't *right*! You can't go around taking away emotion! You can't kill one emotion without killing them all! You're the reason all those Feeders are so empty! You and this drug!"

"Not everyone is affected."

"It's in the water!" I shout, beating my fist on the table and making the water pulse within its glass. "We all drink the water!"

Eldest nods, his long white hair swishing. "But this ship cannot afford to be run by imbeciles. We need the Feeders to grow our food unquestioningly, but we need some people, people like you, to think, to really think."

"The Hospital . . ." I say, thinking furiously. "All of us who are 'crazy.' We're not crazy at all—we're just not affected by the Phydus in the water. But how . . ." Before Eldest can answer, it hits me. "The mental meds. The Inhibitor pills. They inhibit Phydus; they prevent Phydus from affecting us."

"We need creative thinkers," Eldest says. "We need you to think for yourself, we need the scientists to think so they can solve the fuel system problem. We provide the genes—you saw the DNA replicators—and then we give those with inborn skills the Inhibitor pills so they can bypass Phydus. We need their minds clear."

"Why artists?" I say, thinking of Harley, of Bartie, of Victria.

"Artists have their purpose. They provide a level of entertainment to occupy the Feeders. They may lack emotion, but even monkeys grow bored. Some artists also think outside their DNA replication. We are facing a problem in the engines that decades of intensive research have not solved. We don't know how creativity will manifest itself. Your friend, Harley? He was given spatial and visual creativity. He became a painter—but he could have just as easily become a drafter, or even, with the right twists of mental desire, an engineer."

"We're just pawns. A means to an end. Toys you manufacture to keep playing your game."

"This game is *life*, you chutz!" Eldest says, his voice rising. "Don't you understand? We're just trying to survive! Without the Season, the people would have nothing to live for. Without Phydus, they would tear down this ship in mad fury. Without the DNA replicators, we'd all be inbred imbeciles. We *need* this to survive!"

"What if one of those 'brainless' Feeders could grow up to solve the engine problem?" I ask. "But you've got him so drugged up with Phydus he can't think? Why not let them all think, let them all work on that problem?"

Eldest narrows his eyes at me. "Have you forgotten your lessons? What are the three main causes of discord?"

"First: differences," I say automatically. I don't want to play his game, but it's habit to answer him immediately.

"Then?"

"Lack of leadership." Now I just want to see his point.

"And last?"

I sigh. "Individual thought."

"Exactly. Phydus takes away individual thought, except from those specifically designed by us, who can help us. It's our best chance."

Eldest leans across the table and taps his fingers on the metal until I meet his eyes. "It's very important for you to understand this," he says, gazing at me intensely. "This is our best chance to survive."

He pauses.

"This is our *only* chance."

65: AMY

The doctor brushes my arm aside. "I want you to see this."

"What's happening?" I ask hollowly.

The doctor glances impassively at Steela's empty body. "Oh, that."

"That? *That?*" I scream. "That was a person just a moment ago! What did you do?"

The doctor walks around the bed and taps one of the clear IV bags. "There's a very high concentration of Phydus in here. It's a drug," he answers me before I can ask. "One that makes people passive."

I think of Filomina, of Steela's daughter, of myself. "You're drugging the ship," I whisper.

"Most of it." He shrugs.

"Why?"

"Medicine is a marvel," the doctor says, squeezing the IV bag. "If there is a problem, even a problem with a whole society, medicine can fix it."

"You're evil," I say, the words creating a dawning realization of the fact within my mind.

"I am realistic."

I reach down and grasp Steela's hand. It is cold and lifeless.

"What is happening?" I say, dropping her hand and stepping back in disgust.

The doctor's oblivious to both me and his patients, intent on the IV. "I told you: Phydus induces passivity."

"What does that mean?" I shout, a note of panic tingeing my words.

"Passivity? It makes them calm. Peaceful. Passive."

"But she's not moving!" My voice grows louder and louder. "She's not even blinking! Just staring straight ahead!"

The doctor looks surprised at my distress. "Don't you see that Steela—all of them—are beyond usefulness? She and the other grays are no longer physically useful; they can't do labor like the younger gens can. They are no longer mentally useful—long-term exposure to Phydus deteriorates the mind, even if they are on Inhibitors like Steela was. Their neurons are skipping around the Phydus, and they either become confused about what's real and what's not, or they become rebellious as they break through the drug's influence. Either way, they can no longer be anything but a burden to our society. So, we take from them what we can." He nods toward the bag with Stella's blood. "Her DNA held particular perception and intelligence; we might be able to recycle it. Once we've harvested what we can use from the grays, we put them to sleep."

Steela doesn't look asleep. She looks dead.

I remember the puppy my parents got me when I was eight. It

got Parvo disease and grew sick. My mom told me the vet had put it to sleep.

"You're killing them?" I whisper, horrified.

The doctor shrugs. "Technically."

"*Technically?!*" I screech. "They either die or they don't; there's no middle ground there!"

"We are in a contained environment," the doctor says. "This ship must sustain itself." His gaze roves from Steela to me. "We need fertilizer."

I choke back the bile rising in my throat.

"Take it out!" I scream. I lunge for the IV.

"It's too late. The drug is already in her system."

I rip the needles from Steela's arm, and I can tell the doctor isn't lying. A drop of blood falls from the IV needle's point, nothing else. The bag is empty. Steela's arm has flopped over the side of the bed, but she doesn't notice it.

"Amy," the doctor says coolly, "I tell you this because you need to understand reality aboard this ship. I have seen you question Eldest; I have seen you talking with Elder. You must know the danger of causing trouble, of getting on Eldest's bad side. The hatch is not the only way Eldest can dispose of you. Eldest is dangerous, Amy, very dangerous, and you'd do best to keep out of his way in the future."

He sighs, and for the first time, I wonder if he has sympathy or empathy or any feeling at all for these patients. "I knew when Elder brought you to me that you were being affected by Phydus. Eldest and I are responsible for distributing Phydus to everyone on *Godspeed*. It's our duty. However, although I believe that Phydus maintains peace, I do not believe it is best for everyone." He meets my gaze full on. "But if you disrupt this ship, Eldest will order me to take you here, to the fourth floor. And I will put that needle in your vein. And you will at first feel a sense of warmth, and comfort, and joy."

His gaze shifts to Steela, and mine follows. A tiny, tiny smile lingers on her wrinkled lips. "When Phydus has calmed your mind, it will calm your body. Your muscles will ease, and you will feel more relaxed than you've ever felt before."

Steela's body is sagging against the pillows. The smile slides off her face, not because she seems sad, but because the muscles in her mouth aren't working to keep her lips curved up.

"Your body will become so calm that eventually your lungs won't bother breathing, and your heart won't bother beating."

I watch Steela closely, my eyes flicking all over her body. I imagine that her chest is rising and falling, that I can hear ever so softly the beat of her heart.

But it's all just wishful thinking.

My hands shake as I close her staring eyes.

"It is a merciful death," the doctor says. "But still, it is death. If Eldest finds you useless—or worse, a nuisance—this is what awaits you."

66: ELDER

I can hear her sobbing through the door. I run my thumb over the scanner, and the door slides open before I realize what I've done — entered a room without permission. But that doesn't matter now — what matters is Amy lying on her bed, sobbing so hard that her whole body is shaking.

"What's wrong?" I ask, rushing forward.

Amy looks up at me, her eyes melting jade. She makes a bleating sound and lunges for me, wraps her arms around my waist, and buries her head into my stomach. I can feel the warm wetness of her tears through my tunic.

For a moment, I just stand there. She's attached to my middle, and I'm not sure what to do with my arms. She gives a little hiccup of a sob, and I act on instinct: I wrap my arms around her, holding her against me, being the strength she needs to stay up.

Eldest thinks power is control, that the best way to be a leader is to force everyone into obedience. Holding Amy against me, I realize the simple truth is that power isn't control at all—power is strength, and giving that strength to others. A leader isn't someone who forces others to make him stronger; a leader is someone willing to give his strength to others so that they may have the strength to stand on their own.

This is what I've been looking for since the first day I was told that I was born to lead this ship. Leading *Godspeed* has nothing to do with being better than everyone else, with commanding and forcing and manipulating. Eldest isn't a leader. He's a tyrant.

A leader doesn't make pawns—he makes people.

Amy pulls away and looks into my face. Her pale skin is blotchy red, her eyes are veined and shadowed, and a shiny line of snot trickles from her nose to the top of her lip. She wipes her face with her arm, smearing tears and mucus.

She has never looked more beautiful to me.

"What's wrong?" I ask again, sitting down beside her on the bed. Amy curls her feet under her and leans her head against my chest. I forget about Phydus, about Eldest, about all the problems on board this frexing ship, as a sudden, primal urge to push her against the bed and kiss her problems away sears through me.

"I found out what happens behind the locked doors on the fourth floor," Amy says, hiccupping halfway through the sentence. "It's horrible."

She tells me. When she gets to the Phydus, I tell her what I've learned from Eldest.

"That's what happened to me," she says. "When I felt so slow and fuzzy—it was this drug. The same drug they used on"—she chokes on the name—"Steela."

I nod.

Amy clutches my arm, squeezing it as I imagine Steela held her arm. "Elder, we've got to do something. This isn't right. It's not fair. These are *people*, whether or not Doc or Eldest sees them as such. That drug is evil. You shouldn't control people like this!" Her eyes gaze past me, and I know she's no longer with me: she's up on the fourth floor. "That drug makes people obey. It's just Eldest and Doc's sick way of controlling the ship."

A part of me, a very small part of me that I bury so deep inside me I hope Amy never sees it, thinks that not all of what Eldest and Doc are doing is wrong. After all . . . it's *worked*. The ship has run in peace for decades.

And then I remember the dead look in her eyes when she was drugged with Phydus, and the feel of her arms just now, and I push that part deeper down.

"And—oh, no!" Amy's face dissolves into more tears. "I've just remembered! My parents, down in the cryo level! I've not been down there all day! What if something has happened?"

She lurches up as if to stand, but I grab her wrist, and with the barest of tugs, she tumbles back onto the bed.

"How could I have forgotten them?" she wails.

I place both my hands around her face and lift her head so she can look me in the eyes.

"Calm down," I say in as steady a voice as I can muster. "Harley has been on the cryo level all day. You don't have to worry about that now. I'll go next and spend the night there."

Amy's watery eyes flick back and forth between mine.

"I'm so useless," she sighs. "I can't do anything but hide here and cry like a little girl! Look at me!" I look, but I don't think I see her the same way she sees herself. "It's pointless! I can't save my parents, I have no idea who's been killing the frozens, and this ship — it's the worst — and I'm stuck here for the rest of my life, surrounded by drugged up people who go to the fourth floor to die and become fertilizer!"

She breaks again. It's like watching the glass top of Amy's cryo chamber break when Doc heaved it off the night she woke up. For a moment, I can see the pieces of Amy all loosely together; then, starting with her eyes and her trembling mouth, she shatters. Her hands are against the sides of her forehead, her fingers curling around her hair. She softly beats her palms against her head, willing herself to think, tugging at her hair, pulling strands from her scalp, seemingly oblivious to her self-inflicted pain. I reach up and gently unwind her hair from her fingers and pull her hands back down into her lap.

"We can figure this out," I say, dipping my head down so I can catch her gaze. "Don't give in. You're not useless."

I catch a glance at the wall across from us, at the big painted black chart Amy started.

"You're the one who's going to figure this thing out. Keep doing what you've been doing. Figure out what the connection is." I reach over to her desk and hand her the jar of black paint and the brush. "You can do this."

Amy looks up at her painted wall, and for a moment she's focused on it. Then I see frustration and hopelessness wash over her face. Before she has a chance to break again, I jump up and go over to the chart, distracting her. "Keep working on it." I pause. "Try to figure out how these are connected," I add, indicating everyone on the list but her. "Remember: you woke up, but survived. Maybe you weren't meant to be unplugged; maybe you were an accident or something. You're the one who doesn't really fit into the list. Try looking at how they're all connected when we take you out of the picture."

Amy stares at the chart a moment longer, then nods slowly.

I stand, hesitate, then bend down and kiss her on the top of her head. She looks up at me, and my heart surges, and even though I can still see traces of hopelessness in her face, I have enough hope for the future for both of us.

"I'll go down there and watch over your parents. You need to rest," I say. I touch the side of her face, and she nuzzles her head against my palm. "You'll be fine," I add, and I hope she can believe it.

I hope I can believe it.

67: AMY

My fingers are stained black with paint. I examined my list of suspects first, but there was little to do there. It is Eldest, or perhaps Eldest and Doc together.

But *why*? If I can figure out their reason, I'll know what to do next.

I have stared at the wall until the lines and words blur together. I've added all the information I could from their charts, even the info that seems irrelevant. It cannot be random. Eldest and Doc do not act randomly.

I fall asleep with the wet paintbrush still in my hand.

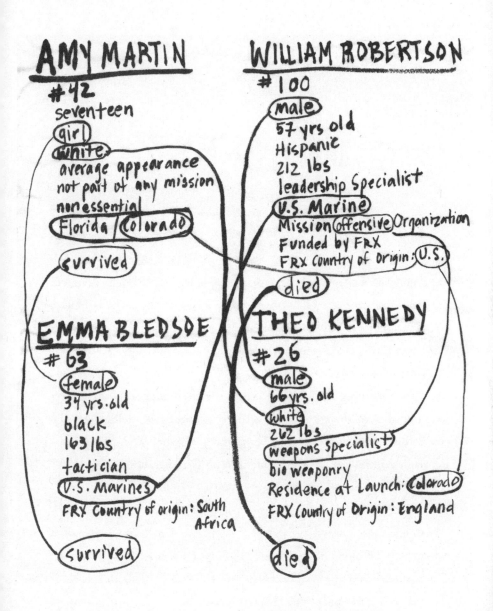

AMY MARTIN
#42
seventeen
(girl)
(white)
average appearance
not part of any mission
non essential
(Florida / Colorado)

(survived)

EMMA BLEDSOE
#63
(female)
34 yrs. old
black
163 lbs
tactician
(U.S. Marines)
FRX Country of origin: South
                                Africa

(survived)

WILLIAM ROBERTSON
#100
(male)
57 yrs old
Hispanic
212 lbs
leadership Specialist
(U.S. Marine)
Mission (offensive) Organization
Funded by FRX
FRX Country of Origin: (U.S.)

(died)

THEO KENNEDY
#26
(male)
66 yrs. old
(white)
262 lbs
(weapons Specialist)
bio weaponry
Residence at Launch: (Colorado)
FRX Country of Origin: England

(died)

68: ELDER

The cryo level is silent, a deep, penetrating silence that makes me feel like a trespasser in a private place.

"Harley?" I call. Where is he? He is supposed to be guarding this floor, protecting the sleeping frozens.

Silence answers.

I start walking through the aisles of cryo chambers, then I start jogging, and by the time I reach the seventies, I'm racing past the rows, shouting Harley's name. My panic is weighed down by a sinking feeling in the pit of my stomach. With each pounding step, I ask the same question:

What if the murderer has moved on to awake victims?

I round the corner, fully expecting to see Harley's body on the floor, a pool of blood, the murderer fleeing the scene.

Nothing.

I'm being stupid. He's probably at the hatch. My heart is

pounding. When I wipe the sweat from my neck, my fingers brush my wi-com button. I jab it quickly.

"Com link: Harley," I pant as I head toward the hatch.

Beep, beep-beep. My heart thuds. If he doesn't answer, I'll go back, grab a floppy, locate him and —

"What?" Harley's voice is sullen, impatient.

"Where are you?" I shout.

"On the cryo level."

"I'm here, where are you?"

"At the hatch."

I sigh with relief. Of course. Of *course* he's at the hatch. My previous panic makes me feel stupid and frexing mad. I turn down the hallway and there he is, his face pressed up against the bubble glass window.

"What are you doing?" I shout. "Why aren't you out there, guarding them?"

"You left me here all day!" Harley shouts right back. "Shite, I was *bored*, okay?"

"Amy's parents are here, all those helpless people down here, and all I asked you to do was sit and watch them. Was that too hard for you?"

Harley narrows his eyes at me. "Don't be such a chutz," he says. "Just because you're going to be Eldest some day doesn't mean you can order me around."

"Don't even play at that. How long did you wait before you came back here to look at the stars? Or did you wait at all? Did you even check to see if there were any melting bodies before you turned your back on them? I seem to remember that the last guy *died* on your 'watch.'"

Harley rushes me, grabbing me by my shirt collar with both hands and shoving me against the wall opposite the hatch. "How long did you keep them from me? When did Eldest first show you them?"

"What, the stars?"

"The stars, the stars, of course the frexing stars!"

"I only saw them a few days ago."

"Lies!" Harley rams me further into the wall. I twist and struggle against him, but even though my fingernails scrabble against his hands, he doesn't relinquish his grip. "You and Eldest, always so close."

"Like I had a choice!"

"Maybe if she could have seen the stars, she wouldn't have died!" Harley screams at me, his face scrunched in rage—and tears glistening in his eyes.

"What are you—Who?" I struggle to piece together what is going on.

"Kayleigh!" Harley says in a surge of grief. He lets me go, and I slide against the cool metal wall a few inches. "Kayleigh. Maybe if she had seen the stars, she wouldn't have given up."

Harley backs up to the hatch door. He places both palms against the door and presses his face to the glass window.

"No good, no good," he mutters.

"What's no good?" My voice is even, calm now. I'm remembering how Doc locked Harley up for weeks last time, certain that he'd try to follow Kayleigh in death. How closely the nurses watched his meds, how Doc always made sure Harley took the extra ones.

"Harley, why don't you come with me? I'll spend the night down here; you go back to your room and rest."

"You want it all to yourself, don't you?" Harley snarls.

"What? No!"

His face crumples. "I know, I know. You're my friend, I know." He turns back to the window. "But still, it's no use. There's no frexing point."

"No point to what?"

"Doesn't matter how long I stare. We're never going to land, are we Elder? We're never going to get off this frexing ship. We're all going to live and die in this metal cage. 74 years and 263 days. Too long . . . too frexing long . . . This is the closest I'll ever get to the out-side, isn't it?"

I want to tell him no, that he's wrong, but I know that's a lie. And I understand now, oh, how I understand why Eldest lies and makes the people all raise their children with the hope of planet-landing. If we don't have that, what do we have to live for? Does it matter if it's a lie if it keeps us alive? Taking away the chance for planet-landing has left Harley nothing more than an empty, desperate shell.

Harley has sunk all the way to the floor. He has a canvas there, but it's covered with muslin, and I don't have the heart to ask him what he's painting. Instead, I leave him here, the closest to freedom he can ever be.

I'm not going to be the one to drag him away from the stars.

Back by the cryo chambers, I hobble together a pile of lab coats and a stray blanket and make something of a nest for myself in front of the big open room. I cannot stay awake, but I hope my presence forestalls the murderer—and if not, I hope that I'll at least awake when the elevator dings. I'm so exhausted—*so* exhausted—and the weight of the ship, the stars, the hopelessness, Phydus, Amy, and Harley all crash on me at once.

I wake to the smell of paint.

Harley, I think.

I struggle with the lab coats I am lying on. Their arms drag me down, but I eventually disentangle myself from them.

"Harley?" I ask, breathing deeply.

I turn from the elevator to the cryo chambers behind me.

At first I think it is blood, but as I step closer to the cryo chambers, I see that it is only red paint—thick, not-yet-dry red paint. Dripping giant Xs mark some, but not all, of the cryo chamber doors. I touch the one closest to me—number 54—and leave a red fingerprint in the paint. Looking down this row, I see six doors marked with Xs; the next row only has three, but the row after that has twelve.

My immediate thought is that this is the killer's doing, that he has marked the people he plans to unfreeze next.

I shake my head. Could the killer have been down here, while I slept beside the elevator? No—it must have been Harley.

But just in case . . .

I creep down each hall, looking for someone who might still be here, counting the marked doors. Thirty-eight doors are marked in total, and none of them give any indication of who painted them.

I envision the killer here, silently marking the doors of his victims while I slept. I shake my head again. Paint means Harley. This is Harley's revenge for our shouting match last night; this is Harley trying to scare me or spook me, or he's just being stupid.

Harley, it has to be Harley.

I can't have let the killer stroll past me while I slept. I can't have. "Harley?" I call.

Nothing.

I run straight to the hallway, to the hatch, but before I get there, I know something is wrong.

The muslin-covered canvas is gone. Paint is splattered everywhere. For one sickening moment, I think that this is a crime scene and that the paint smears all over the floor and wall are blood splatters from a murder, but then I shake myself all over, and I whisper, "No," because if this was a murder, then Harley would be dead, but he's not here.

The control box beside the hatch door is broken.

The cover to the keypad has been pried off, and thin wires extend from the box through the shut door of the hatch.

Harley is inside the hatch, holding the keypad in his hand. He's already tapping out the code.

I pound on the hatch door. Harley gives me a watery smile.

"I can get closer," he says.

"Don't!" I shout, banging against the glass.

Harley turns toward the hatch. He finishes the code on the keypad. The hatch slams open and Harley is sucked out into space.

For a moment, he looks back at me, and his farewell is in his smile. Then he turns to the stars.

And he is gone.

The hatch door swings shut, leaving emptiness.

Harley is gone.

69: AMY

I wake up with the paintbrush stuck to my face. Harley would laugh if he could see me now, call me his Painted Fish.

By the door, there is a flashing red square of light. It's the button to the small rectangle metal cubicle beside the food cubicle. When I push it, the tiny door zips open and a big blue-and-white pill pops out. So that's what that door was for.

The Inhibitor medicine. The medicine that keeps me sane.

I stare at it, disgusted. It sticks in my throat as I swallow it. It burns going down, and fills my belly with a sense of revulsion and urgency that leaves me sick to my stomach. I push in the button to the food door, and it leaves me a pastry filled with something that is almost eggs and that oozes with something that is almost cheese. I'm done after a bite. I'm tired of almost. I want something real.

I return to my wall. Taking Elder's advice, I ignore my name and my list of characteristics. What can I or anything about me have to do with murder?

With my name gone, I see it, standing out before me as brightly as if the words were written in different colored paint.

The *military*.

Each victim, even the woman who hadn't died—all of them had worked for the military. Tactical specialists, offensive operations, bio-weaponry. They were frozen for their ability to kill—and they were the ones being killed.

But why me? Why was I unplugged? I have nothing to do with that.

Elder had said, *Maybe you weren't meant to be unplugged, maybe you were an accident or something.*

An accident . . .

Maybe the murderer had meant to unplug someone else . . .

Someone else in the military.

Like Daddy.

I jump up and race to the door, my heart thudding. Everything falls into place if the killer meant to kill Daddy, not me. He's killing people with fighting backgrounds.

The door slides open, and I crash into Orion.

I start to mutter my apologies and step around him to go to the cryo level and tell Elder what I've figured out, but Orion grabs my wrist with viselike strength.

"Let me go," I say. He's gripping me just where the men held me down before Harley saved me, his fingers pushing into the same bruises.

"Harley painted this," Orion says in his soft voice. I stop trying to pull away from him and notice the muslin-covered canvas in his hands. "He told me to give it to you when I gave him some wire."

"What is it?" I ask, curious.

"A painting. For you."

Orion releases my wrist and presses the canvas into my arms. As I look down at it, he fades into the shadows.

I step back into my room, set the canvas up on my desk, and peel off the muslin, which sticks a little to the still-wet paint. It is the most beautiful painting I've ever seen. It's a self-portrait—Harley floats in the center of the canvas, surrounded by sky and stars, his face upturned in an expression of rapturous joy, his arms spread wide as if he's about to wrap me in a hug. A tiny koi fish swims amongst the stars around his ankles.

My fingers tremble as I touch the painted Harley's face, but I snatch them back: the paint isn't fully dry. In his face, I see something I've only ever seen once before, and that was when he was talking about Kayleigh.

Somewhere, hidden under the paint, I understand what Harley meant by giving me this.

He was saying goodbye.

So when Elder bursts into my room a moment later to tell me that Harley has killed himself, I am not surprised.

70: ELDER

There is something within Amy beyond tears. She nods mutely, as if she already knows it has happened. She grows dimmer, but she does not break as she did last night. She steps back to let me into the room.

And then I see it.

"Harley," I breathe. My hands are trembling.

"Orion gave this to me," Amy says. "Harley . . . I guess he did it before . . ."

It is so realistic, more realistic than Amy can ever know. When the hatch pulled him out, the rush of movement had flattened his hair more, and there was more surprise in his face, and yes, pain—but in that brief second before the hatch door had closed and before the ship had moved beyond him and before space extinguished him, that was the look on his face, exactly that joy.

"You can have it," Amy says. "You were closer to him than I was. I'm not sure why he gave it to me and not you."

I notice the little fish swimming at the painted Harley's feet.

Amy always thought Harley called her Little Fish because her red-orange hair matched the colors of the koi he was painting when he met her, but he never told her the reason why he painted the koi in the first place—the reason why his room was filled with koi paintings—which was that it was Kayleigh's favorite animal.

"He wanted you to have it," I say. "You reminded him of someone he knew."

We stand a moment in silence, absorbing the painting, absorbing what Harley has done, how he has left us. Alone, still standing while he flew away.

"I figured it out," Amy says, pointing to the wall and dragging me back to now. "The connection between them. People who have background in military fighting. Those are the ones who were killed."

I examine the chart.

"My father has a military background. What if the killer pulled me out instead of him by accident?" Her voice quakes, and I wonder if it is because of fear for her father, or because Harley's gone, or both.

"When I woke up this morning, someone had marked dozens of the little cryo chamber doors. At first I thought it was Harley . . . but the killer could be marking his victims. . . ."

"Was my father's door marked?" Amy asks urgently, dropping her notebook.

"I . . . don't remember." I hadn't been looking for her father's door—I'd been looking for Harley.

"We've got to go check!" Amy heads for the door.

I pause just long enough to snatch the floppy off her desk. As we race down the hall, I scan my thumb and tap in my access code. The computer chirps, "Eldest/Elder access granted" as the elevator opens. While we rise, I bring up the wi-com locator map.

"What are you doing?" Amy asks, her eyes on the numbers above the door.

I slide the timer back, looking for the dots marking where and when everyone was.

On the map for last night is Harley's dot, beeping softly, mostly where the hatch door is, but sometimes pacing up and down the hall and once, all around the cryo floor. No one else is on the entire level—until I show up. There I am, running; there's where I stop. My glowing dot merges with Harley's, and I remember our fight, our last fight.

Amy hovers over my shoulder, watching. My dot leaves Harley's, and now it blinks near the elevator in front of the cryo floor. Harley's doesn't move from the hatch door. I wonder what he was doing in those last moments. Painting? Planning?

I fast forward. Around morning, Doc and Eldest's dots show up, but they don't linger—they go straight to the lab on the other side of the cryo level. I look up at Amy sheepishly.

"I fell asleep," I say. I wonder if Doc and Eldest noticed me.

Amy shakes her head. "It wasn't them, though, was it? They didn't go near the cryo chambers."

We turn back to the wi-com locator map. My dot moves quickly up and down the aisles of cryo chambers—discovering the painted Xs.

And then my dot goes to the hatch.

There I am; there he is.

Then his dot is gone.

A hard lump forms in my throat. My eyes blur at the moment

when it happens, when his dot suddenly jerks off the map and doesn't come back.

Amy sucks in a gasp, but doesn't let the air back out for a long time, and then it's just a hushed, "Oh."

"No one else came down there," I say as the door opens to the fourth floor. "It must have been Harley."

"But Harley never left the door, not after you showed up."

I meet Amy's eyes. Harley couldn't have painted the Xs.

"That thing," Amy says, pointing at the floppy, "it can only track people through their ear buttons, right?"

I nod.

"It couldn't see me, could it?"

I shake my head.

"What about Orion? He's the one who brought me the painting. He had to have been down there, but that means he doesn't have an ear button, doesn't it? He's got long hair to cover it, but I've seen that scar on his neck—that creeps up past his hair. I bet he doesn't have an ear button. He'd be invisible."

And—*oh*—she's right.

Orion.

71: AMY

The door at the end of the hallway is locked.

"How are we—?" I stammer. "What are we going to do?"

Elder kicks the door in.

He rolls his thumb on the scanner, punches the button, and then we're going down, down, so achingly slow.

I rub my pinky until it hurts, thinking about all the promises I made with Daddy. "What are you doing?" I ask Elder as we sink past the first floor.

"Checking the biometric scanner log-ins," Elder says. He taps on the floppy. "Harley came down midday yesterday. I came down after dark. This morning, Doc and Eldest came down, and it looks like they're still there, in the other lab. But look—there's no record of Orion scanning the elevator pass—it just shows Eldest's log-in again, but he was in the lab then."

He passes me the floppy. Sure enough, Eldest/Elder is recorded once after Doc and then, fifteen minutes later, it shows up again.

"He figured out a way to trick it," I say. Could this elevator go any slower?!

"You can't," Elder mutters, stuffing the floppy into his pocket. "It scans your DNA. You *can't* trick it."

The doors slide open.

Cold hits us like a blast.

Dozens and dozens of frozens lie exposed, their trays pulled out, the condensation already fogging the glass coffins, obscuring the bodies frozen inside. All the doors swinging open have freshly painted Xs on them. Elder was right. The killer was marking his victims, preparing for one last kill, one fell swoop to kill every frozen person in the military.

I have only one thought.

"DADDY!" I scream, knocking past Elder and racing to the cryo boxes. I rush to the aisle with the forties, and there, midway down, is my father's frozen body. I wipe away the condensation and stare at his face for just a moment.

I am gripping the cold glass lid, and I've got enough adrenaline inside me to pick it up and throw it down on the concrete floor. I want to. I want him to wake up, to break him out of the ice, to make him hold me against his warmth.

I *want* this.

I glance at the electrical box near his frozen head. The light is green, not red. Orion just pulled the trays out, he didn't unplug them as he had unplugged me.

Thuds and crashes surround me. Elder is running up and down the aisles, cramming all the other frozens back into place and slamming the doors shut behind them. I push Daddy's frozen slab back into the cryo chamber and swing the door shut. The red X painted on the door mocks me. I turn the handle down and lock it in place. I allow myself one last look at the door labeled 41, then I sprint down the aisle to the next exposed frozen.

It doesn't take long. The doors are shut, all the frozens safely returned to their frozen state.

And no Orion in sight.

"Why did he do this?" I ask, panting from the effort.

Elder's breath rises in faint clouds from his lips. "I was in the way." He's thinking as he speaks, realizing the truth as he answers. "Pulling out all the doors while I was here . . . that would have woken me up—that would have been much noisier than marking the doors with paint. And once they were marked . . . of course I'd run to you, and he'd have plenty of time to just pull out the frozens he'd already marked. . . ."

"But *why*?" I say. "Why bother? Surely he knew we'd go straight here, see what he did . . . He didn't even really unplug them, but pulled them all out."

Elder pauses. "It's almost like he was testing us."

"What do you mean?"

"He's showing us his plan. He's waiting to see what we do. Would we let them melt, or shove them back in?"

"Of course I wouldn't let my daddy melt!"

Elder stares at me. "I don't think the test was for you."

72: ELDER

"Shh!" I hiss at Amy. "Do you hear that?"

"Hear what?" she whispers, but I wave my hand to silence her.

It's soft, but there's a *whirr-churn-whirr* sound that reminds me of the engine room. But it can't be—we're two levels below the engine.

"It's coming from the laboratory."

I lead Amy across the cryo level. She casts a nervous look back. "We'll leave the door open," I say, because I can tell she's worried about leaving her father behind.

"What is this place?" she asks as we step inside the lab. She's whispering, and I can barely hear her as the whirring noise grows louder.

"The lab." I whisper, too. Something about the lab invites secrecy, and I've not forgotten that Doc and Eldest are in here, if the wi-com map's correct. We stick close to the walls.

"I've seen those needles before." Amy points to the big tubular syringes labeled with characteristic traits that Eldest wants the inhabitants of the ship to have.

"That's what they do here."

"What's that?" She points to the big amber-colored tube extending from floor to ceiling and filled with tiny bubbles of stuff floating in it. "That almost looks like . . ." She tilts her head. "Like embryos?"

I look at the debris floating in the amber liquid, and am surprised Amy could identify it so quickly. The only fetus I'd ever seen was one of a miscarried cow, and it was larger and bloodier and not really anything like these tiny round toe-sized bubbles.

I lead Amy to the back of the lab where, hidden by the way the room bends in a right angle, is the giant pump Eldest showed me the first time I was here. That's what's making the *whirr-churn-whirr* noise; the pump is on, shuddering and complaining as its internal mechanics heave Phydus and stars know what else into the water system.

Eldest stands at the pump, holding a bucket of clear viscous liquid.

Doc stands opposite him.

I grab Amy and we whirl back around the corner of the room. Neither of them has seen us—yet. I put my finger to my lips, and Amy nods. We both duck low and peer around the corner to watch them. A chair blocks our vision, but also gives us some level of cover.

"I'm sorry!" Doc shouts over the noise of the pump.

"You shouldn't have let her see!" Eldest storms toward Doc, his uneven gait making the bucket in his hands swing. Doc eyes it nervously.

"I thought it would make her more willing to behave."

"Nothing short of Phydus will control her. Why did you give her the Inhibitor pills?"

Eldest sets the bucket down.

"They're talking about me," Amy breathes in my ear.

Doc says something else, but his back is to us, and I can't catch it.

"Well, we'll just get her tonight and take her to the fourth floor," Eldest says, picking the bucket back up and lugging it to the pump.

"I don't think—"

Eldest throws the bucket down. The clear liquid inside sloshes, but it's denser than water, like syrup, and it doesn't spill over the side.

"You know what?" Eldest shouts, striding toward Doc. "I don't really care what you think. If you'd just listened to me the first time, with the other one, we wouldn't be in this situation."

"What do you—"

"You know what I mean!" Eldest roars. "Elder! You let Elder live!"

Amy grabs for my arm. I had been leaning forward, dangerously close, trying to catch their words.

"Elder is fine," Doc says.

"Not this Elder. The other Elder."

Doc stares at Eldest, his face emotionless and cold, but I can tell he's restraining himself. There's a thin line of white around his lips, and his jaw clenches.

Eldest is oblivious to Doc's reaction. "The Elder before this one! The Elder that is supposed to be assuming his duties *now* so that I can retire instead of wasting the last of my life on a teenager who's thinking with his chutz and not his head!"

"You told me to take that Elder to the fourth floor, and I did." Doc stands straighter, defiant.

"But you didn't kill him like I told you, did you?"

"I thought—the Phydus—"

"I think *you* should take some more Phydus." Eldest growls. "Are you protecting him, even now? Are you hiding him?"

"I thought . . ." Doc looks small and scared. "He disappeared off the wi-com map. I thought he killed himself."

Eldest snorts. "You never did check to make sure, did you? Now look where we are. Frozens being killed, one of them awake."

"He's dead, Eldest. I swear he's dead."

I don't know if Eldest believes him or just wants to believe him. He turns around and picks up the bucket again.

"What is that?" Amy whispers, jerking her head slightly toward the pump.

"It connects to the water supply," I say, my mind racing. And in that bucket . . .

Phydus.

I stand up. Amy tries to hold me back, but I shake her off. I can't let Eldest drug them anymore. I can't let any more Phydus sink into the water. I've *got* to destroy that pump.

I grab the chair Amy and I had been crouched behind.

"What are you doing here?" Eldest asks with a sneer, catching sight of me.

I raise the chair over my head.

"What are you doing?" Eldest's voice rises.

My hands shake. I can see the future laid out in front of me—a future with me as leader, not Eldest. And no Phydus.

Do I really want to rule without Phydus? I think of the fading bruises on Amy's wrist, of the conflicts I've seen in the Ward, amplified over the whole ship. *Can* I rule without Phydus?

Then I think about Amy's eyes when she was drugged.

I hurl the chair at the pump. It clatters against the metal and bounces onto the floor. The water pump continues to *whirr-churn-whirr*.

"What are you doing?" Eldest screeches. "You've gone mad! Just like the Elder before you!"

"What are *you* doing?" I yell back. "That's Phydus, isn't it? Just getting ready for another day of manipulation and mind-control?"

"YOU ARE NOT FIT TO BE ELDER!" Eldest screams. His white hair flies behind him, and he is the one who looks mad. "If you cannot do this, you cannot lead the ship! You are not strong enough to be leader! You never will be good enough!"

In three strides, I cross the room to Eldest and punch him right in the face. Eldest drops the bucket and falls flat on the ground. His nose is bleeding; the thin skin on his cheek is red and broken. I bend down, grab him by the shirt, and yank him back upright. He opens his mouth to speak, so I punch him again, but I still hold his shirt with one hand so he doesn't fall.

"I am not weak," I say. My voice is shaking, not with fear, but with suppressed rage. "I am strong enough to know that Phydus is wrong, and that your attempt to control people with it is nothing but weakness. If you were really strong, you'd lead this ship without drugs to do your dirty work."

It is not until I am done talking that I realize my voice is the only sound in the room.

"What have you done?" Eldest screams, but not at me—at Amy.

I look up. While I was punching and yelling at Eldest, Amy snuck around the pump, found a tiny door in the side of it, and quite simply ripped out all the wires.

She holds the brightly colored wires in her hand. "Well, that did the trick," she says, smiling.

73: AMY

I would have felt sorry for Eldest's broken nose and bloody mouth if he weren't such an evil, twisted tyrant to start with. But considering he's planned to kill me before—and again, just now, when he told Doc to leave me on the fourth floor—well, let's just say I didn't have too much sympathy for the old jackhole.

The doctor puts a hand on Elder's shoulder. "Elder, we need the drug. This ship won't operate without the control it affords us."

Elder almost agrees with him, I can see it in his eyes. "That's not true," I say, willing Elder to look at me, to remember how the drug killed me inside. "Yes, it will be harder without the drug. Yes, it may be easier for us all to bear a lifetime without the sky if we're doped up beyond thought. But that's no life, not really. In amongst all this sorrow"—I meet Elder's eyes then, and we both know I'm talking about Harley now—"there is also joy. You can't have one without the other."

Elder stumbles away from Doc and Eldest, closer to me.

"I can't be the kind of leader you want me to," he says. "I will never, ever be the kind of leader you want me to be. And I will be better because of it."

Eldest whirls around to Doc. "Do it."

"Do what?" I say.

Eldest has Doc's full attention. "We'll make another. Use different DNA replicators. We'll get rid of this one and make another."

"Do *what*?" Elder says. His eyes are wide, as if he's afraid of his own thoughts.

Eldest turns on Elder. "You frexing *idiot*. I can't believe we share the same DNA!"

"What are you talking about?" Elder's voice quavers. "Are you . . . my father?"

"There, *there*!" Eldest says, pointing. Beyond that wall is the table with the needles, and the big cylinder with golden-yellow liquid and tiny circles of embryos inside.

"What—some of your DNA was injected into my mother?"

Eldest roars in frustration. "You never had a mother! We're the same person! Elders are cloned—same DNA, same everything. All I did was pluck you from the jar and put you in a tube sixteen years ago."

"We are not the same," Elder says, disgusted.

"Down to our genetic code, we are exact replicas of every Eldest before us."

But I know that's not what Elder meant when he said he wasn't the same.

"That's why we shared access; that's why my biometric scan would get us anywhere," Elder mumbles. I think about the pleasant lady's voice in the computer: "Eldest/Elder access granted." The computer never distinguished between Elder and Eldest because there was no difference between the two.

"I don't care," Elder says louder, staring right at Eldest. "It doesn't matter to me that we're the same. I'm *not* you, and I won't make the decisions you've made. I don't care about your lessons; I don't care about your rules. I'm *done* listening to you!"

I hear soft footsteps behind me. Everyone else is so focused on Elder and Eldest they don't notice the man with scars on his neck, the one walking quietly forward. Orion reaches for the bucket of Phydus that Eldest dropped when Elder punched him. The movement of him bending down catches Doc's eye, then Elder's, then Eldest's. Eldest's eyes grow wide with shock.

"He's here," he whispers so softly I'm not sure of his words. His eyes dart to the doctor's and then back to the man before him. "You swore he was dead."

"And I am dead, Eldest," the man says, lifting the bucket up. "The Elder you made is dead, gone. I'm no longer that Elder. I'm Orion now. The Hunter."

Eldest opens his mouth—to rant, to rage, to rave—but Orion silences him by upturning the bucket of Phydus on his head.

"Stand back! Don't touch it!" the doctor screams as the gooey-thick liquid slides down Eldest's body. Orion steps back, smiling. Elder looks as if he'd like to rush to Eldest's aid, but stops himself.

Eldest's face was scrunched in a mask of anger, but the mask slips away as Phydus coats his skin. He cocks his head like a curious child. His knees crumple, and he flops to the ground, legs splayed in front of him, arms behind him, supporting his weight. A slow, easy smile spreads across his face, then falls into nothingness. He looks, for a moment, more gentle and at peace than I've ever seen him before. His hands slide on the smooth floor, and his body crashes all the way to the ground. He doesn't catch himself; his head cracks on the tile so hard I wince. Phydus spreads around his body like a bloodstain. I watch the slow in-and-out of his breaths until they stop.

Eldest has calmed to death.

74 : ELDER

"You killed him."

Orion looks up at me and grins, clearly pleased with himself. "You're welcome," he says.

Part of me thinks this is a great thing, killing Eldest. He was a tyrannical dictator. He was cruel. He never saw anyone on this ship, even me, as a real person.

But he's also the man I've lived with for three years, the one who had the biggest hand in raising me, and the one I always used to think I could turn to.

And now he's just a gooey mess.

I want to ask why, but I know why.

Despite myself, my eyes fill with burning tears. He was the closest thing to a father I had.

Orion sets the bucket down. He walks toward me, his hand outstretched. I take it without thinking—my eyes are still on Eldest's motionless body.

"I knew you'd be on my side!" Orion says, churning my arm up and down in an enthusiastic shake. "I wasn't sure—you'd been under Eldest's thumb for so long, and you didn't respond to the unpluggings like I thought you would—but I just knew you'd be on my side in the end."

"Your side?" I shift my blurry gaze from the dead Eldest to Orion—who, as the Elder older than me, is technically now the Eldest of the ship.

"When I started saying I didn't like the way of things, Eldest sent me to Doc. Told him to stick me on the fourth floor. Didn't he, Doc?"

Doc nods mutely. His eyes are wide with shock, or terror—I cannot tell which.

"Doc was my friend, weren't ya, Doc?"

Doc doesn't nod this time, just stares down at Eldest's body. "I thought, with enough Phydus . . ." he whispers. I turn my face away from Doc. He always did think that anyone could be cured if he threw enough drugs at him. Doc never believed people were more powerful than medicine.

"Couldn't let Eldest find me, so the first thing to go . . . " Orion raises his hand to where his wi-com should be, and he mimes clawing at his neck. When he opens his hand, I see a snaking scar across his thumb. "It was terrible. Worst thing I ever did, ripping that out of my own flesh, with my own hands. Felt like I was ripping my soul out."

There is silence in the room, punctuated only by the occasional drip of Phydus on the ground.

Orion continues. "When Doc saw the wi-com dot was gone, and since Eldest hardly ever leaves the Keeper Level . . . it wasn't hard to hide the truth from them. The old Recorder had . . . an accident, and I blended into my new life."

"Why didn't you ever tell?" Amy asks, her eyes locked on Doc.

"I didn't know," Doc whispers apologetically to Eldest's body. "I thought—I'd hoped—suicide." His eyes raise to Orion. "I thought— that night, at the Recorder Hall. That *was* you." He pauses. "But it had been seventeen years. . . ."

"You could have found me if you'd just gone next door. You know, the whole first year I stayed hidden, behind the walls, sleeping with the wires and pipes. But then I realized you and Eldest weren't even looking. I just had to give myself a new name, a new home, and the idiots you made accepted me without question.

"But," he continues, turning to Elder, "I always felt bad. About what I knew Eldest was doing. So much about this ship is wrong." His eyes bore into mine. "You've only just scratched the surface with Phydus. Have you learned about the ship's engine?" I nod. "Good," Orion says. "And you knew about the mission, obviously?"

"The mission?" I say.

"The real mission behind this ship?"

"What do you mean?" Amy asks. She walks over to me and weaves her hand in my mine, giving me her strength just as I gave her mine when she cried.

"Have you never questioned why we're here?" Orion asks me, ignoring Amy.

"To operate the ship—"

"The ship is on autopilot. It can get to Centauri-Earth without us."

"To—"

"No," Orion cuts me off before I can begin. "Whatever Eldest has told you was a lie. He kept much from you, after I betrayed him. No, there is only one reason why we're aboard this ship, and that reason lies beyond this door." He points to where the cryo chambers are, where Amy's parents are.

"What do you mean?" Amy says again, her voice more urgent.

"You know at least what the frozens are here for, right?"

"They are experts at terraforming, and environment, and defense."

Orion snorts. "They are experts at taking the planet away from us."

"You don't make any sense," I say, squeezing Amy's hand tighter.

"*They're* the colonists, not us. Never us. When we finally land, they'll use us. As slaves in their terraforming, and—if there are hostile aliens on the planet—as soldiers. They plan to work us or kill us. They put our great-great-great-whatever grandparents on this ship so that they could breed slaves and soldiers. That's all."

Amy gasps. "That's why you're killing the ones with military experience. You think they'll make the people born on the ship fight when they land."

"I know they will!" Orion roars. I can see the Eldest in him now, when he shouts. "And if there are no hostiles to fight, then they'll use that military experience to force us into slave labor. It's the perfect plan: growing expendable people while they sleep!"

"But why me?" Amy says, her voice a desperate whisper. "When you unplugged me, surely you could tell I wasn't my daddy? Why didn't you put me back in before I melted? Why did you let me wake up?"

A slow, evil smile spreads across Orion's face. His gaze pierces mine. I clench my fists. Orion cocks an eyebrow at me.

"I keep my secrets," Orion says, glancing at Amy.

"Daddy isn't a slave driver," Amy says. "And if there were 'hostile' aliens, he wouldn't force you to fight."

Orion shrugs. "How do you know that for sure? And," he adds before Amy can say anything else, "either way, better safe than sorry."

"Your kind of safe means killing my dad!"

Orion glances behind her at Eldest's body. Clearly, he has no hang-ups about killing.

"If you don't like it . . ." he says, walking over to the cryogenic freezing tube on the other side of the room. He opens the door and sweeps his arm to display the interior. "By all means, refreeze yourself. Sleep until we reach planetside, and see what kind of man your father really is. That is," he adds, thinking, "if Elder and I decide to let your father live until planet-landing."

"You're as evil as him!" Amy hisses, pointing at Eldest's lifeless body.

"But you know what's really gonna twist you?" Orion asks. "The fact that Elder sort of agrees with everything I'm saying."

"No, I don't—" I start when Amy looks back at me with her beautiful accusing eyes.

"And the fact that Elder here's the one who gave me the idea for unplugging them in the first place."

Amy covers her mouth with her hand. Her eyes fill with disgust, and it's directed at me.

"Don't believe him," I plead.

"No, really, it's true. You have realized that, haven't you, Elder?" Orion sneers, laughing, and I wonder how much he knows. I search his face, and see mine in it. We share the same DNA, but we aren't the same person. But maybe the same emotions and self-doubts and fears are woven into our identical genetic code.

"Why don't you tell her?" Orion continues. "Or would you like me to?"

"Tell me what?" Amy asks.

I stride across the room to where Orion is standing beside the cryogenic freezer. My hands are clenched into fists.

"She's a pretty thing," Orion whispers to me, low so Amy and Doc can't hear. "Very pretty. Is that why you did it?"

"Shut up," I growl.

"Don't let her get in our way."

I know that there are all sorts of logical reasons why I should do it. Orion is as crazy as Eldest, his method of control just as twisted, if not more so. I'll never be able to talk him out of killing the frozens, and he needs to be punished for the deaths he has already caused.

But those aren't the reasons why I shove Orion into the cryo-freezer and lock him inside.

"Let me out!" Orion screams.

I spin the dial. Cryo liquid held in the tank over the freezer bursts open, pouring blue-specked water over Orion's head.

"Frex!" he splutters. He claws at the door, his face twisted with pure terror. Amy comes up beside me, watching Orion through the little window in the door. When he sees her, his eyes fill with an evil glint. He opens his mouth to shout something at her.

I spin the dial again.

The cryo liquid pours faster, filling his mouth, drowning him. His face is under the liquid now, his cheeks puffed out, his eyes bloodshot and popping. One hand presses against the window, and I notice the jagged scar on his thumb, the only thing that separates his thumbprint from mine.

"Freeze him now, or he'll die," Doc says. "He might die anyway." He shrugs. "You didn't prep him for freezing."

I look into Orion's eyes and see myself in them.

I slam my fist into the big red square button.

A flash of white steam escapes the box.

Orion's face is pressed to the glass, his eyes bulging.

But he can no longer see us.

75: AMY

Elder stares through the small window into Orion's frozen face. I wrap
my arms around him from behind. I try to pull him back, but he won't
move, so I just hold him.

"It's over," the doctor says. "Unless you wake him back up, you're
Eldest now."

I can feel Elder stiffen under me.

Elder shakes his head. "Let the people he tried to kill judge him
when they land."

I think of my father, and what kind of judge he will be to this man,
and I am not the least bit sorry for him.

"How am I going to lead a ship full of people?" Elder asks, his
voice catching. "When the Phydus wears off, they're going to realize the lies. They're going to be angry. They're going to hate Eldest,
and me."

"They won't hate you," I whisper into the back of his neck. "They
will relish their anger, because that is the first emotion they will have

ever truly felt, and then they will realize there are other emotions, and
they'll be glad of them."

"Will you stay with me?" Elder whispers. His breath fogs the
glass covering Orion's face.

"Always."

Elder pushes his ear button, and he makes an announcement to
the entire ship, just as Eldest did before when he told the ship to fear
me. His first announcement is simple. In childlike terms, he explains
that they've all been under the influence of a drug, and that they will
slowly start to regain their own emotions. Elder encourages them to
remain calm as they begin to feel for the first time, especially the pregnant mothers.

Doc begs me for the wires to fix the pump.

"We should at least keep putting the hormones in the water," he
insists, "so that they don't start mating with relatives."

"Most people don't want to commit incest," I say dryly. "When
they wake up from the drug, we'll just explain to them what incest
is, and what it does, and that they should get a blood test before they
have sex. You've got those scanner things that test DNA. We could
start mapping out family trees again."

I hand the wires to Elder.

Doc turns to him. Elder just looks at him coldly. "No more drugs,"
he says.

And that's that.

Later, when men with thick gloves have taken Eldest's poisoned body and thrown it out of the hatch after Harley, when Doc has put Orion in an empty cryo chamber, when we're safely back in my room with Harley's painting watching over us, Elder gives his second announcement. It is a repeat of Eldest's last one: Everyone is to go to the Keeper Level.

Before we go up there, we discuss the truth.

"That's what killed Harley," I say. "The truth. When he heard about how he'd never leave the ship—" I choke on my words.

"He couldn't live with that truth," Elder finishes for me.

"We should have known that it wasn't Eldest killing the frozens. He would have known it would make you seek the truth, and he wanted to keep it from you, from everyone."

Elder looks down at his hands, then up at Harley's painting. "A part of me thinks that we cannot share the truth, not all of it."

I start to speak, but Elder cuts me off.

"A part of me thinks that the truth will kill them all, just like it killed Harley. This is a big truth, a great truth. We cannot just say it. We must let people discover it."

Elder goes to the Keeper Level alone. He will stand on the platform, and he will tell the people, who are *feeling* for the first time, some of the truth, but not all of it.

He will tell them that he is Eldest now. That the old Eldest is dead.

He will tell them about Phydus, about the hormones in the water, about the lie of the Season.

They will be angry, furious even, but then they will realize that they are *feeling*, and they will know that Elder was right to do as he did.

He will tell them of the engine, but not how far behind schedule we are. Anyone with any interest in science, mechanics, engineering, will go with the Shippers and will see the engine, and will try to help the scientists solve the problem.

Elder will not tell them about Orion, or the frozens.

But he won't keep the truth from them, either. While he is telling them as much of the truth as can be told, I'm writing out all I know in pages ripped from the notebook my parents brought from Earth. I fold the pages in half, and leave them in the Recorder Hall. They're there for anyone who looks to find.

Many won't. They won't care to know; they won't seek any kind of truth. Some will—and they will not believe the truth. But others will need the truth, and crave it, and they will seek it, and accept it for what it is.

Later, Elder and I will continue working in the Recorder Hall. I will rewrite as much of the falsely written history as I can. All the files of Earth's past will be made available to all the people. And Elder will have his people start recording the lives of the ship's inhabitants, just like before, so that they may feel they are more than forgotten shadows of a ship floating through empty space.

But now, I open my blue notebook to the remaining blank pages. I hold the pen over the first page, then slowly scratch out the first words.

Dear Mom and Daddy . . .

76: ELDER

It came to me, the first night after Eldest was killed and Orion was frozen, that I shared the same DNA as both of those men, but I was nothing like them. The truth of the ship twisted both men differently, turning one into a dictator, one into a sociopath.

The three of us, we're the same. We were raised with the same knowledge, formed from the same genetic material, given the same truth. But one of us hid the truth through lies and control, one tried to change the truth through chaos and murder, and me . . . well, I am still figuring out what truth is. And what I will do with it.

Was I lying to my people when I didn't tell them about Orion?

Was it wrong to give them access to a truth that might kill them like it killed Harley?

And what right do I have to make any mandates about truth when my greatest joy is that Orion never had a chance to tell the truth to Amy?

In the end, am I really all that different from Eldest or Orion if I let her believe a lie?

THE PAST: ELDER

This is what happened.

This is truth.

I saw her lying there, frozen in her glass box. And she was different. *Really* different. I could never have the sunset of Sol-Earth, but it was all there, in her hair, floating immobilized in ice, pale skin like lamb's wool. And young. Like me.

She will never understand.

I went down there, later, to stare and dream. To think of what she could tell me of Sol-Earth. To think of how she—unlike every other person on this frexing ship—*she* would be my age during my Season.

And I wouldn't have to be alone.

And then I heard it. A tiny whisper in my mind, a barely heard voice I almost—but not quite—ignored.

And the voice held a question. And the question was:

What if I unplug her?

And at first I did ignore it. But the question got louder. And louder.

It roared.

And so, just to make it shut up, I reached out, and I flipped the switch in the box above Amy's cold head, and I watched the light blink from green to red.

And the voice inside my head sighed in relief and whispered words of comfort and told me she would smile at me when the ice melted.

I was going to wait, right there, be there for her when she yawned and stretched and emerged from the box. Be there as her eyes fluttered open, as her lips curved into a smile.

But I heard—

—Orion, scuffling in the dark, listening to his own voice—but I didn't know that then. I swear I didn't know it was him, watching.

So I ran to the elevator and went to the garden and tried to pretend I had not brought a girl back to life with the flip of a switch.

Then came the alarm.

And the scream of it—*aroo! aroo!*—blended into Amy's scream.

Of pain.

And later—of regret. Sorrow. Broken dreams and hopes.

I broke those dreams.

Me.

And nothing comforted her, not even the love she never saw from me.

And Doc said she couldn't go back; she could never go back.

And I knew—I *knew*—

I could never tell her the truth.

77: AMY

I sit in front of the hatch door, my back against the cool metal wall, my eyes staring through the glass to the stars beyond, thinking about Harley, wondering what it felt like in those brief moments between flying and dying.

I come here often now. With awakening, the people of the ship who had been passively meek are now explorers. They are in the gardens, they are in the Hospital—to read Victria's books or listen to Bartie's guitar playing or look at Harley's surviving paintings. Some are even in the Recorder Hall, and some leave with eyes opened wide with truth. This is one of the few remaining places where I can truly find solitude. Elder doesn't think it's safe to let everyone come to this level, even though some are now aware of its existence. I agree. I don't want anyone else taking Orion's stand on the issue. The painted X on my Daddy's door has still not faded away, even though I have scrubbed and scrubbed.

Elder had the keypad fixed—and improved—so that when I

punch in the code word, the hatch door stays open for as long as I want it to, and I can stare out the glass window into the stars for as long as I need to. It's a long way home from here, but this is the closest I can be.

I stare at the stars. There are so many here, so many more that I can see here than I could see when I stood on Earth's surface. And even though there are so many and they look so close together, I know they are light years apart. The glitter in the sky looks as if I could scoop it all up in my hands and let the stars swirl and touch one another, but they are so distant, so very far apart, that they cannot feel the warmth of each other, even though they are made of burning.

This is the secret of the stars, I tell myself. *In the end, we are alone. No matter how close you seem, no one else can touch you.*

"Amy?"

Elder stands over me, and for a moment he looks ominous, like a vulture.

I risk a smile at him.

"I'm glad it's over," I say.

Elder does not return my smile.

"It's a relief. I think I might be able to live an okay life here, if I don't have to worry about my parents every second. Ugh, that sounds ungrateful. You know what I mean."

"Amy."

I look up at him. His face is very serious.

"What's wrong?" There is laughter in my voice, but it's nervous. "Did something happen?" My fingers curl, scraping against the cold metal floor. "Did something happen to my parents? Was it not really Orion?"

"No, no, nothing like that." Elder bites his lip.

"What is it then? Here, sit down beside me."

Elder doesn't sit. "I have to tell you something," he says in that voice that makes me know whatever it is he has to tell me cannot be good.

"What is it?" I finally screech, because I cannot take his nervous silence.

78: ELDER

"I'm the one who unplugged you."

79: AMY

I feel my heart thud—once, hard—and then it's like a rushing of blood and emotion from my body and I am empty inside, frozen like before, and I see nothing, and I feel nothing, but that's not true. Because as soon as I think that, I feel again, I feel *everything*, and I can't see, I can't breathe, but I *do* feel.

And what I feel is rage.

I think for a moment—*I was wrong: it would be better to not feel than to feel this*—and then

I

quit

thinking.

I scream something, but even I can't distinguish what words spit from my mouth. I'm standing now—I don't remember standing, but I'm standing. And I lunge for him. I want to hurt him—I don't care how—as long as I can cause *some* sort of pain, maybe that will be enough. I get in one good, solid hit, and I know that I've surprised him more than hurt him, despite the fact that there's already a red mark on his cheekbone under his eye. My fingers are curled claws, but he grabs my wrists before I can attack again, and he holds me back. I kick, but my short legs can't outdistance his long arms, and I do the only thing left for me to do. All the rage tears from my throat.

"I'm sorry," Elder pleads.

Sorry? *Sorry?* Sorry isn't enough. Every. Single. Thing. I ever loved is beyond my reach now. Everything I ever wanted. Everything I ever was.

"I could have died!" I shout. "I almost *did* die!"

"I didn't know"—he trips over his words—"that—I mean—frex! I didn't know you'd be—and—"

I want to ask why. Except—there is no why. I can see it in his face. He didn't mean to hurt me. To take away my only chance to be with my parents. To trap me in a metal cage.

To kill me as effectively as I am dead on Earth.

He just did it.

There is no why, just like there is no going back.

"But I had to tell you the truth."

That stops me.

Something inside me snaps into place, painfully. The truth grinds against my bones.

Daddy lied to me when he said coming or not was my choice. He made the choice. The empty trunk in the cryo chamber is proof enough of that.

Jason let me believe what I wanted to believe.

This whole ship has been held together with metal and lies, everyone either deceived or a deceiver.

Except for Elder.

80: ELDER

Amy's face is stone, and I cannot see any cracks in it. It's not been this immovable since she was frozen.

My hands clench compulsively in my pockets. The wires from the Phydus machine poke my fingers. Amy expected me to throw them away, I know she did . . . but I can't. Their weight in my pocket is the weight of another lie. But I can't shake that nagging voice in my head, the one that asks: *Can you rule without Phydus?*

I'm afraid the answer is no.

I should tell her. I should produce the wires like another confession.

But it would just drive her further away.

"When I did it . . . when I unplugged you . . ." My voice cracks, something that hasn't happened since I was fourteen. "I didn't know Doc couldn't put you back. I thought I could wake you up, and that maybe we could meet, could talk, and then after you told me about

Sol-Earth, I'd be ready to let you go and be frozen again. I didn't know you couldn't go back. I didn't know that I would almost kill you."

I've spoken all of this in a rush, but now my words peter out until they are almost nothing.

Amy doesn't say anything.

I touch my cheekbone tenderly, pushing at the place where she hit me. It will bruise. If she'd aimed higher, I would have a black eye.

"I'm really sorry, you know," I say.

Amy stares ahead of her. I can't tell if she's staring at the metal that traps her inside the ship or the glass that shows her the universe outside it.

"I know," she says.

It's not much of an invitation, but it's the only one I've got. I lean against the wall beside her. A rivet digs into my back, but I don't care. This may be the closest I'll ever be to her again.

Amy doesn't move away. That's something, I guess.

"I just wanted to meet you. I didn't know I'd ruin your whole life."

Silence.

Amy doesn't look up.

81: AMY

There's a smudge of paint—red—at the edge of the hatch door. Harley's last mark.

Past the paint, past the bubble window, I stare at the stars. It looks like a lonely, cold place out there. I put my hands on either side of the window. It's a lonely, cold place in here, too.

"I don't want to be alone," I whisper, and it's not until the words are out there that I realize how true they are.

I sense more than see the tiniest movement of Elder behind me. He steps forward, hesitates, then reaches for my hand. I pull away.

Like Harley.

I stare resolutely ahead at the stars. I wonder if he would still be here if only he'd reached toward us, instead of toward them.

I shut my eyes and take a deep breath, but all I smell is metal. The life I'd once known is forever gone. My air will never smell of summer or spring, real rain or snow.

I open my eyes and see the last thing Harley saw before he left us. *Maybe the secret of the stars has nothing to do with being alone.*

I reach behind me, and Elder is there. Like he always has been. He grabs my hand, but I shake loose.

I'm not ready for that.

But . . . if my life on Earth must end, let it end with a promise.

Let it end with hope.

I wrap my pinkie around his. He squeezes my finger, and this world doesn't feel so cold anymore.

"Will you stay with me?" I whisper.

"Always."

ACKNOWLEDGMENTS:

I'd like to thank everyone on the Penguin/Razorbill team—you all made this book look brilly. Special thanks to Ben Schrank and Gillian Levinson, who helped make *Across the Universe* into the book I'd always intended it to be, but somehow didn't get on the page without their insightful edits, questions, and suggestions. Thanks also to Emily Romero, Erin Dempsey, Courtney Wood, and the rest of Penguin marketing, and to my amazingly talented designers, Natalie Sousa and Emily Osborne.

I couldn't have joined the team at Penguin without Merrilee Heifetz, who matched me with the perfect publisher, and I couldn't have done that without Jennifer Escott, who matched me with the perfect agent. Thank you both for guiding me through the world of publication with such enthusiasm!

The best part about being a writer is having writing friends. Robyn Campbell and Rebecca Carlson helped me hammer out the first draft of *Across the Universe*, Heather Zundel and Christina Farley helped me break it to pieces and write it back better, and Erin Anderson, PJ Hoover, and Christine Marciniak told me *Across the Universe* was finally done and I should just submit it already.

I've spent most of my years in some school or another, but by far the best ones were the six I spent teaching literature at Burns High School. To all of my students: you were all my favorite. Special thanks to Charly White, who painted a picture of a fish on my podium and inspired the character Harley. Thanks also to my friend and fellow teacher Laura Parker and my friend (who's not a teacher and quite happy about it) Jennifer Randolph for supporting my writing career.

There are three people who always believed in me more than I did and who never once thought I wouldn't see my name on a book cover: my parents, Ted and JoAnne Graham, and my husband, Corwin Revis.

Thank you, thank you, thank you.

Godspeed was fueled by LIES.
Now it is ruled by CHAOS.

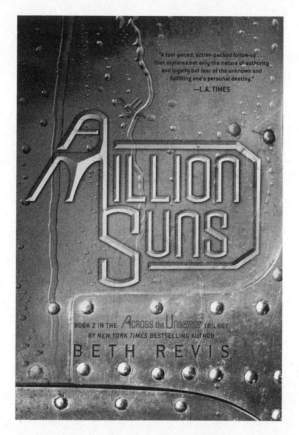

Turn the page to check out the next chapter in
Amy and Elder's journey . . .

A Million Suns

Book Two in the **Across the Universe** Trilogy

From *New York Times* Bestselling Author **Beth Revis**

1: ELDER

"This isn't going to be easy," I mutter, staring at the solid metal door that leads to the Engine Room on the Shipper Level of *Godspeed*. In the dull reflection, I see Eldest's dark eyes, just before he died. I see the smirk on the corner of Orion's mouth as he relished in Eldest's death. Somewhere, beneath my cloned features and the echoes of every Eldest before me, there has to be something in me that's mine alone, unique and not found in the cloning material two levels beneath my feet.

I like to think that, anyway.

I roll my thumb over the biometric scanner and the door zips open, taking with it the image of a face that has never felt like mine.

A very mechanical smell—a mixture of metal and grease and burning—wraps around me as I enter the Engine Room. The walls vibrate with the muffled heartbeat of the ship's engine, a *whrr-churn-whrr* sound that I used to think was beautiful.

The first-level Shippers stand at attention, waiting for me. The

Engine Room is usually crowded, bustling with activity as the Shippers try to figure out what has crippled the lead-cooled fast reactor engine, but today I asked for a private meeting with the top ten Shippers, the highest-ranking officers beneath me.

I feel scruffy compared to them. My hair's too long and messy, and while my clothes should have been recycled long ago, their dark tunics and neatly pressed trousers fit perfectly. There is no uniform for the Shippers—there's no uniform for anyone on board the ship—but First Shipper Marae demands neatness of everyone she has authority over, especially the first-level Shippers, who all favor the same dark clothing worn by Marae.

Marae's in the twenty-year-old generation, only a few years older than me. But already lines crease at her eyes, and the downward turn of her mouth seems permanent. A carpenter could check the accuracy of his level by the line of Marae's shorn hair. Amy says that everyone on board *Godspeed* looks the same. I suppose, given that we're monoethnic, she's right in a way. But no one could ever mistake Marae for anyone else, nor think she's anything less than First Shipper.

"Eldest," she says by way of greeting.

"I've told you: just call me Elder."

Marae's scowl deepens. People started calling me Eldest as soon as I assumed the role. And I'd always known I'd *be* Eldest at some point, although I'd never dreamed that I'd be Eldest so soon. Still, I was born for this position. I *am* this position. And if I can't see it in myself, I can see it in the way the Shippers still stand at attention, the way Marae waits for me to speak.

I just . . . I can't take the title. Someone called me Eldest in front of Amy, and I couldn't stand the way her eyes narrowed and her body froze, for just a minute, just long enough for me to realize that there was no way I could bear to see her look at me as Eldest again.

"I can be the Eldest without changing my name," I say.

Marae doesn't seem to agree, but she won't argue.

The other first-level Shippers stare at me, waiting. They are all still, with their backs erect and their blank faces turned to me. I know part of their perfection is due to Marae's strong hand as First Shipper, but I also know a part of it comes from the past, from Eldest before he was killed and the exacting way he expected everyone to perform.

There is nothing of me in their stoic obedience.

I clear my throat.

"I, uh, I needed to talk to you, the first-level Shippers, about the engine." I swallow, my mouth both dry and bitter-tasting. I don't look at them, not really. If I look into their faces—their older, more experienced faces—I will lose my nerve.

I think of Amy. When I first saw Amy, all I could see was her bright red hair swirled like ink frozen in water, her pale skin almost as translucent as the ice she was frozen in. But when I imagine her face now, I see the determined set of her jaw, the way she seems taller when angry.

I take a deep breath and stride across the floor toward Marae. She meets my gaze head-on, her back very straight, her mouth very tight. I stand uncomfortably close to her, but she doesn't flinch as I raise both my arms and shove her shoulders, hard, so she crashes into the control panel behind her. Emotion flares on the faces of the others—Second Shipper Shelby looks confused; Ninth Shipper Buck's eyes narrow and his jaw clenches; Third Shipper Haile whispers something to Sixth Shipper Jodee.

But Marae doesn't react. This is the mark of how different Marae is from everyone else on the ship: she doesn't even question me when I push her.

"Why didn't you fall over?" I ask.

Marae pushes herself up against the control panel. "The edge broke my fall," she says. Her voice is flat, but I catch a wary tone under her words.

"You would have kept going if something hadn't stopped you. The first law of motion." I shut my eyes briefly, trying to remember all I had studied in preparation for this moment. "On Sol-Earth, there was a scientist. Isaac Newton." I stumble over the name, unsure of how to pronounce a word with two *a*'s in a row. It comes out as "is-saaahk," and I'm sure that's wrong, but it's not important.

Besides, it's clear the others know who I'm talking about. Shelby looks nervously at Marae, her eyes darting once, twice, three times to the mask of Marae's unnaturally still face. The steady stoniness of the other first-level Shippers' postures melts.

I bite back a bitter smile. That seems to be what I always do: break the perfect order Eldest worked so hard to make.

"This Newton, he came up with some laws of motion. It seems frexing obvious, this stuff he wrote about, but . . ." I shake my head, still somewhat shocked by how simple his laws of motion were. Why had it never occurred to me before? To Eldest? How was it that while Eldest taught me the basics of all the sciences, somehow Newton and the laws of motion never came up? Did he just not know about them, or did he want to keep that information from me too?

"It's the bit about inertia that caught my attention," I say. I start pacing—a habit I've picked up from Amy. I've picked up a lot of things from Amy, including the way she questions everything. *Everything.*

Right at the top of my questions is a fear I've been too terrified to voice. Until now. Until I stand in front of the Shippers with the limping engine churning behind my back.

I shut my eyes a moment, and in the blackness behind my eyelids, I see my best friend, Harley. I see the hollow emptiness of space as the hatch door opened and his body flew out. I see the hint of a smile on his lips. Just before he died.

"There are no external forces in space," I say, my voice barely louder than the *whrr-churn-whrr* of the engine.

There was no force that could stop Harley from going out that hatch door three months ago. And now that he's in space, there's no force to stop him from floating forever through the stars.

The Shippers stare at me, waiting. Marae's eyes are narrowed. She won't give this to me. She's going to make me pull the truth from her.

I continue, "Eldest told me that the engine was losing efficiency. That we were hundreds of years behind schedule. That we had to fix the engine or risk never reaching Centauri-Earth."

I turn around and look at the engine as if it could answer me. "We don't need it, do we? We don't need the fuel. We just need enough to get to top speed, and then we could shut off the engine. There's no friction, no gravity—the ship would keep moving through space until we reached the planet."

"Theoretically." I don't know if Marae's voice is wary because she's unsure of the theory or because she's unsure of me.

"If the engine's not working—and hasn't been working for

decades—then the problem should be that we're going too *fast*, right? That we're going to just zoom past the planet . . ." Now there's doubt in my voice—what I'm saying goes against everything I thought I knew. But I've been researching the engine problem since Eldest died, and I just can't correlate what Eldest told me with what I've learned from Sol-Earth's books. "Frex, our problem should be that we're going to crash into Centauri-Earth because we can't slow down, not that we're going to float aimlessly in space, right?"

I feel as if even the engine has eyes, and it's watching me too.

Looking at the Shippers, I can see that they all—they *all*—knew that the engine's problems did not lie in fuel and acceleration. They knew all along. I haven't told them anything new with this information. Of course the first-level Shippers know of Newton and physics and inertia. Of course they do. Of course they understood that Eldest's words about inefficient fuel and limping through space behind schedule were entirely false.

And what a frexing fool I am for thinking differently.

"What's going on here?" I ask. My embarrassment feeds my anger. "Is there even anything wrong with the engine? With the fuel?"

The Shippers' eyes go to Marae, but Marae's silently watching me.

"Why would Eldest lie to me about this?" I can feel myself losing control. I don't know what I expected—that I'd figure out the big problem and the Shippers would jump up and fix it? I don't know. I never really thought past telling them that the laws of physics go against the explanations Eldest gave me. I never thought that I'd say what I came to say and they would look to the First Shipper, not me.

"Eldest lied to you," Marae says calmly, "because we lied to him."

BETH REVIS WOULD LIKE TO SEND A SPECIAL
THANK YOU TO EARLY FACEBOOK FANS OF THE
ACROSS THE UNIVERSE TRILOGY:

Basma Aal
Rummanah Aasi
Samantha Abbott
Libiel Abrajan
Wendy Adams
Jason Adams
Gabrielle Adelle
Poly's Aguilera
Cynthia Aguirre
Natalie Aguirre
Jezka Ahearn
Khadija Ahmed
Iffath Ahmed
Lena Ainsworth
Maria Airam
Tanieshika Alazar Curitas
Hânifé Âlbâyrâk
Taryn Albright
Khyla Alcantra
Karen Alderman
Ricky Alexander
Nora Alison Corasaniti
Alethea Allarey
Jolene Allcock
Jordan Allen
Recilla Allen Harms
Ashleigh Allenbaugh
Courtney Allison Moulton
Lucas Allred
Asriani 'Ally' Purnama
Rachele Alpine
Samantha Alvey
Kelsey Alyssa McNallie
Emma Amburn
Francesca Amendolia
Alanna Amphetamine
Anne Amundson
Kelly Anastasopoulou
Eric Anders Harrison
Sarah Andersen
Kent Anderson
Sarah Anderson
Liz Anderson
Sarah Anderson
Katie Anderson
Jamie Anderson
Erin Anderson
Angela Anderson Hill
Christina Andre
Paula Andrea Guzmán Angel
Savannah Andrea Smith
Fleurhelmina Ang
Louisse Ang
Van Anh Do

Mary Anika Patterson
Lisa Ann Richards
T Anne Adams
Sarah Anne Coe
Nutschell Anne Windsor
Abby Annis
Stephanie Anthony
Jenilee Antonio
Fernando Antonio Viera
Lenore Appelhans
Angie Araujo
Fallen Archangel
Amber Argyle
Nicole Armanno
Jessica Armenta
Lucas Armiliato
Laura Arnold Bernier
Mark Arthur
Katarina Asanovic
Venessa Asencio Ricardez
Laura Ashbaker
Laura Ashlee Graves
SheKnown AsJess BlogSpot
Smash Attack
Lizzy Aube
Nichole Avery
Carrie Axtell
Nafiza Azad
Maryam Azme
Julie B Reviews
Sara B. Larson
Alexis B. Salcido
Kim Baccellia
Samantha Bailey
Jill Bailey
Sjoukje Bakker
Rachel Baldwin
Michelle Ball
Gina Balsano
Krysta Banco
Emilie Bandy
Myrna Barber Foster
Luciana Barbosa
Leanne Barden
Ashley Barker
Beth Barker Shaum
Sherry Barnes
Kristina Barnes
Jay Barnewold
Jonathan Barrett
Arcadia Barrile
Alexandra Barry
Kalina Bartosik
Debra Baseden

Lisa Basso
Danielle Bateman
Melissa Bauer
Christina Baulch
Erin Beach
Kassey Beam
Colene Beck
Brenda Beck Knutson
Sofi Bee
Stéphanie Beeckman
Mariym Belikov
Danielle Belyea
Mike Belyea
Taylor Benfield
Katie Bennett
Jamie Bennett
Larissa Benoliel
Ashley Benson
Annette Benson
Norma Berastain
Oana Bercuci
Nina Bermudez
Hannah Bernal
Robin Bernstein Reul
Nevey Berry
Louisa Berry
Gina Betancourt
Livvie Bieber Midgley
Tanisha Binion
Shanda Birdsey
Lexie Birren
Alyssa Bixler
Casey Blackwell
Kristian Blake
Anime-Otaku Blake
Arena Blake
Caitlin Blakeley
Brittany Blanton
Sab-Ya Bliss
Ciara Blmgn
Marco Blood
Meri Blubb
Bobby Bobzien
Katherine Boden
Lacey Boldyrev
Lea-Ya Book Queen
Diva's Bookcase
Ashley's Bookshelf
Rebecca Booth
Jennie Booth
Priyanka Bose
Lindsey Bousfield
Bobby Boxall
Samantha Boydman

Becky Boyer
Sondra Boyes
Jessy Boz
Brenna Braaten
April Bradley
Ryan Brady
Jessica Bravo
Mary Brebner
Bill Breuer
Molly Brewer
Shellie Brewer
Cassidy Brianna Jones Lozano
Grace Bridges
Cameron Bridges
Brandon Bridges
Courtney Bridges
Robin Bridges
Devan Bridget
Elizabeth Briggs
Katie Brinton
Charity Broeringmeyer Bradford
Amy Brooks
Kyle Brown
Sarah Brown
Kathleen Brown
Elizabeth Brown
Jennie Brown
Nicole Brown
Cassandra Brown
Theresa Brown Milstein
Stacey Brucale
Jeannette Bruce
Sya Bruce
Emily Bruce
Kate Bruck
Angel Brucker
Lesley Bucio
Britne Bucklew
M.g. Buehrlen
Amanda Buff
Hillary Bui
Liz Bui
Velle Bulaclac
Danielle Bunner
Mandy Burford
Jennifer Burke
Valerie Burleigh
Elizabeth Burns Barbarow
Missie Burson
Mónica Bustamante Wagner
Katie Butler
Caitlin Byham
Mina Byrd
Christopher C Fenimore
Cristina C. Espina
Taneesha C. Freidus

Ellen C. Oh
Cristhin Cabezudo Rojas
Amanda Cain
Melissa Caldwell
Miriam Caldwell
Steve Campbell
Sarah Campbell
Robyn Campbell
Manuel Campos
Brittany Cannon
Stacey Canova
Noelle Carey
Ana Carla Ponte
Brooke Carleton
Russel Carlson
Kristine Carlson Asselin
Kirstin Carlson-Dakes
Amanda Carmichael Plavich
Gabrielle Carolina
Cindy Carolina Rivero Alcocer
Gabriela Carrasco Márquez
Brianne Carter MSVU
Kristin Carter
Sequoia Cartwright
Guadalupe Castiñeira
Christina Castro
Alison Catherine
Brittany Causby
Kate Cavanaugh Towery
Jenny Cayabyab Cohen
Arantza Cazalis
Kristen Ceci
Alexandra Cenni
Kristin Centorcelli
Jasmine Cervik
Kristi Chadwick
Katie Chafin Glasgow
Fiona Chan
Tasha Chanda Leir
Sophia Changma
Amanda Chao
Taylor Chapman
Billy Chapman
Kai Charles
Katie Chashin
Farya Chattergoon
Fernanda Chávez
Jane Che
Lesley Cheah
Elaine Cheang
Cindy Chee
Alisha Cherry
Marie Chettle
Andrea Chettle
Aik Chien
Ken Chinavare

Yat-Yee Chong
Rebecca Christiansen
Sarah Christina Jordan
Sartani Christopher
    Simangunsong
Cass Chu
YeonJoo Chung
Asena Cino
Nikki Ciuciura
Gama Clamor
Amber Clark
Wesley Clark
Christina Clark
Julie Clark Golden
Bridgette Clark Waldrop
Rachel Clarke
Natalie Cleary
Ally Clement
Jessica Cline
Tawni Coakley
Carmen Cobb
Angela Cobb Fleming
Nicole Cody
Mardie Cohen
Allison Cole
Theresa Cole
Susan Colebank
Anekas Collins Leite
Renee Combs
Kathy Condie Habel
Vicki Congdon
Lois Connell Moss
Alex Connolly
Kirsty Connor
Colleen Conway
Tabatha Cook
Rose Cook
Garrett Cook
Macy Cook
Crystal Cook
Kristie Cook
Regan Coomer
Stacey Coons McElveen
Ivy Coop
Mimi Cooper
Katherine Cope
Janelle Corbitt Alexander
Deneis Correa
Carla Costa
Zoe Courtman Smith
Emilie Couture
Vickie Couturier
Steven Cox
Adrienne Crezo
Kellye Crocker
Jessica Croswait

Kat Crouch
Cassandra Crouser
Nathan Crow
Reggie Cruz
Angel Cruz
Alexandra Cuevas
Cade Cummings
Tina Currie
Laura Cushing
Shallee Cutler McArthur
Katie Dahlberg
Mariana Dal Chico
Tiffany Dall
Catherine Dammer-Jones
Lucy D'Andrea
Briana Danielle
Dayse Dantas
Bidisha Das
Mitali Dave
Michelle Davidson Argyle
Jocelyn Davies
Victoria Davis
Angie Davis
Mariya Davis
Elizabeth Davis
Nicole Davis
Kimberly Dawson
Sharli De Entre Libros
Zarina de Ruiter
Mary DeBorde
Belle Découverte
Lisa DeGroff
Amy Del Rosso
Mevurah Deleon
Janie Delhi
Sarah Demello
LadyJai Dement
Ezmirelda Demetri
Erin Dempsey Berger
Stephanie Denise Brown
Sophie Deo
Latisha DePoortere
Brooke DeSpain
Patti Deupree Holden
Ashlie Dewey
Laura Diamond
Elizabeth Diane
Juliana Dias
Misty Dickey
Tiffani Diggs
Lux Dilune
Gaby Dinh
Emily Dismuke
Ashley Dismuke
Kate Ditzler
Zemira Djedovi_

Kristina Djordjevski
Sophie Djurich Riggsby
Raquel Dominguez
Cinthya Dominguez
Kisha Donyale Pio
Heinz Doofenshmirtz
Tatiana Dostes
Shelby Dotson
Melinda Douch
John Drehobl
Anne-Marie Ducharme
Nicole Ducleroir
Abhishek Duggal
Christine Dunbar
Kate Duncan
Nicole Duncan
Stephanie Dunn
Mandy Dupree Kristoffersen-
  Dickinson
Puja Dutta
Danielle Duvick
Rae Dy
Thomas E Centofanti Jr
Emily E Ellsworth
Jessica E Subject
Deanna E Voakes
Beverly Ealdama
Taffy Earl Lovell
Jacqueline Easthope
Jen Eckert-Lehman
Kristina Edmondson
Brooke Edwards
Britta Eileen Gunneson
Ann Eisenstein
Caitlin Elise
Erika Elizabeth
Camra Elizabeth
Amanda Elizabeth Baird
Letitia Elkins
Nora Ellen
L.t. Elliot
Ryan Elliott
Jan Elmore
Kate Elstad
Jennifer Elyse Blaser
Jessica Emanuel Spotswood
Tiff Emerick
Tegan Emma Bain
Stefanie Emmy
Jaime Engl
Gene Eplee
Amy Epps Stewart
Angela Erika Kubo
Alexandra Erving Diana
Eve Eschenbacher
Kaila Escobales

Jennifer Escobedo-Danford
Jen Escott
Cheryl Escott Levinsky
Sarah Esser
Eric Etten
Rich Evans
Ashley Evans
Milady Evey
Stella Ex Libris
Saragoza Fafi
Sarah Fairhall
Alice Fanchiang
Leslie Fannon
Blueicegal Fantasies
Trisha Farnsy
Tammy February
Kelly Fehnel
Mikala Ferguson
Christina Ferko
Maria Fernanda Gonzalez
Joel Fernando
Rachel Fewell
Gaby Figueiredo
Jillian Fine Heise
Valerie Fink
Bailey Finley
Tanya Fisher-Maxemow
Kelsey Fleming
Erin Fletcher
Loni Flowers
Caitie Flum
Paige Follbaum
Jill Foltz
Christine Fonseca
Morgan Forde
Jessica Forno
Miriam Forster-Wiedeback
Erin Foster
Chelsea Fought
Autum Frailey
Kaitlyn Francis
Veronica Franco
Kim Franklin Hatchel
Beth Fred
Patricia Frederickson
Jessi French
Brent Frost
Absynthe Frost
Samantha Frye
Kulot Funa
Tami Furlong
Precious Gabriel Banaag
Maria Gabriela Guajardo
Lynette Gabriella Payne
Erin Gallagher
Candace Ganger

Michael Gantt
Charlotte Gardner
Sarah Gardner
Katrina Garner Lantz
Angie Gatlin
Lilly Gayle
Christina Gebhardt
Paul Genesse
Laurie Genishi
Matthew Geoffrey Levine
Caitlin George
Lizzie Gerry
Katja Gi
Françoise Giang
Jennifer Gibson
Elijah Gibson
Sara Gilbert
Kristin Gill
Melissa Gilleland
Jessica Gladstone
Michelle Glisson-Vandever
Vanessa Godden
Therese Godfree
Glitters Gold
Gayle Gold Humpherys
Brooke Goldetsky
Ciara Gonzales
Luis Gonzalez
Jennifer Gonzalez
Fabiie Gonzalez
Chloe Goodhart
Carla Gordon
Beverly Gordon
Danielle Gorman
Emily Gottschalk
Imani Grace Lewis Norelle
Julianne Grace Valmoria Agito
Lucas Graden
JoAnne Graham
Beth Graham Revis
Laura Grassie Henderson
Emily Gravatte
Christina Gray
Stephanie Gray
Chanelle Gray
Avery Greaves
Diane Green
Pip Green
Amelia Greene
Alicia Gregoire
Margo Gremmler
Sean Grey
Jani Grey
Gretchen Griffith
Ara Grigorian
Sara Grochowski

Chelsey Gruber
Rosa Guardado
Alicia Guerrero
Zana Guest
Lauren Guitar
Öykü Güler
Paromita Gupta
Dalila Gurney
Teri Hack
Mariska Hadienns
Melissa Haefele
Rebecca Hagan
Kelly Hager
Katrina Haggard
Dwayne Halim
Andrew Hall
Joyce Hall Farmer
Angela Halliday-Ackerman
JoAnna Halpin Becker
Jessica Hamilton
Carolynn Hamm
Lorri Hamm Wilson
Christy Handkins Evers
Skye Handley
Kelly Hansen
Nadine Harder
Elizabeth Harkinson
Rachael Harrie
Kim Harrington
Jamie Harrington
Carrie Harris
Rachel Harris
Erik Harrison
Cassie Hart
Maryelizabeth Hart
Rhiannon Hart
Brandi Harvey
Emmie Haslehurst
Cynthia Hatfield-Garcia
Jill Hathaway
Debbie Haupt
Laura Hayden-Plowman
Lauren Hayes
Rachelle Hayes
Loralei Haylock
Laura Heath
Bella Heavens
Caitlen Heckman
Adam Heine
Emily Heinlen
Melissa Helmers
Austin Hendrick
Kristen Hendricks
Veronica Henline Lusted
Steve Henninger
Rebecca Herman

Jacob Hernandez
Becky Herrick
Christi Herron Aldellizzi
Jordan Hertling
Andy Hertzenberg
Sabrina Heuschkel
Christina Heuschneider
Jennifer Heustess Jordan
Madison Hewett
Holly Hewett
Bailey Hewlett
Janie Hickok Siess
Kendra Highley
Jenn Hilgeman
Lillie Hill
Amy Hinchman
Jacinda Hinten
Danya Hiob
Gracesha Hitachiin
Tommy Hixson
Kelly Ho
Tram Hoang
Kelly Hobbs
Elizabeth Hoffman
Karen Hoffman Akins
Anni Holladay Thompson
Charlotte Holland Cartee
PJ Hoover
Megan Hoover-Swicegood
Denise Hope
Ambur Hostyn
Stephanie Hough
Tiffany Howard
Kt Howard
James Howell
Bucky Hoyle
Rachel Hoyt
Lucia Hua
Jess Huckins
Laura Hughes
Kimmy Hughes
Maria A. Hughes
Ann Hughes White
Dominique Hughey
Cynthia Hull
Erik Humberto Barajas
    Martinez
Annie Hunter
Leah Hurley Graves
Becki Hurst
Cindy Husher
Maryam Hussein
Allison Hutchins
Wilfredo I. Soto
Hafsah IceyBooks
Katia Ignacia

Andrea Infinger
Self Injury Awarness
Nathalie Intheworld
Sarah Irene Hanson
Kyle Irvin
Suzan Isik
Malak Ismail
Ariana Issa
Adriatika Ivashkov
Erika Iversen
Shelby J Barwood
Barbara J Shelton
Donna J Smith
Rebecca J. Carlson
Karon J. Powell
Lauren Jackson
Andrea Jacobsen
Denise Jaden
Cécilia Jamart
Victoria James
Jared James Giesige
Michelle Jamshidi
Songhe Jang
Mindy Janicke
Simone Jansen
Thomas Jared Mcswain
Anna Jarzab
Jackie Jaskulski Cohen
Pippa Jay
Carly Jean Facciani
Kristi Jeans
Neysa Jensen
Kay Jernigan McGriff
Priscilla Jimenez
Aura Jimenez
Alejandra JimmYo Delafuente
Sammie Jo
Shelli Johannes Wells
Danielle Johns
Kyeesha Johnson
Plamena Johnson
Susannah Johnson
Elana Johnson
Terry Johnson
Chelsea Johnston
Krystal Jones
Amy Jones
Andra Jones
Lesley Jones
Julie Jones
Caroline Jones
Lori Jones
Chelsea Jordan Lutz
Morgyn Joubert
Edalaine Joy
Linda Joy Singleton

Avery K Tingle
Nicole K.
Jasmine K. Call
Marissa Kaak
Stacey Kade
Courtney Kae
Robin Kae
Beth Kaelin
Linda Kage
Pat Kahn
Alexa Kalas
Jennifer Kalman
Allison Kami
Liza Kane
Anja Kapllani
Julia Karr
Samantha Kate
Sarah Katherine Waff
Sakshi Kaul
Julie Kawalec-pearson
Angela Kay Doster
Joy Keeney
Heather Kegler
Lynne Kelly Hoenig
Justin Keltner
Valerie Kemp
Megan Kenal
Andrew Kenneth Ballard
Anne Kenny
Victoria Key
Yasmeen Khan
Deborah Khuanghlawn Kennedy
EleNa Kiara Casillas A
Christine Kida Danek
Deb Kidist
Bronwyn Kienapple
Lisa Kilgariff
Karen Kincy
Heather Kirksey Vanmoer
Rebecca Kiser
Paige Kiss
Jess Kliebisch
Danielle Klimashousky
Kimberly Knutson
Mandy Kocevar
Ruth Koeppel
Christine Kolshorn Marciniak
Lexy Koperdak
Erin Korenko
Olga Koulouri
Rachel Kramer Bussel
Margie Krawczyk
Emily Kristin Morse
Alicia Kuhnau
Shelley Kuklish
Burak Kumral

Reni Kunta
Tsuki Kuro
Sierra Kurosaki Bishop
Amanda Kwieraga
Madie L. Farris
Anthony L. Isom
Lynnette Labelle
Moka Lafaire
Megan Laffoon
Michelle LaMarca
Len Lambert
Ale Lanaro
Brittany Landgrebe
Kara Landhuis
Michele Landi
Keary Landon Taylor
Jenniffer Lane
Amber Lane
Melissa Lane
Mike Lanzett
Nidia Laracuente-Harris
Deborah LaRose
Sheri Larsen
Torre Laughlin
James Laughlin
Esther Laurel Placido
Hank Lawrence
Jennifer Lawrence
Jodi Lawrence Meadows
Holly Lawson
Melissa Layton
Yvonne Leacy
Danyelle Leafty
Ebyss Leann
Ashley LeCroy
Suzanne Ledford
Robyn Lee
Brodie Lee
Hannah Lee
Megan Lee
Robert Lee
Deana Lee
Vivian Lee Mahoney
Corrine Leegstra
Kate Leger
Christie Leigh
Amanda Leigh McClure
Leslie Leigh Parker
Cynthia Leitich Smith
Mary LeMieux McDonald
Shannon LeMoine O'Donnell
Nola Lenis Tarlamis
Bianca Lennon
Misty Lenz Waters
Sandy Leon
Ivy Leung

Ann Léveillé
Gillian Levinson
Joanne Levy
Annie Lewis
Michelle Lewis
Sasha Leykin
Paige Liberty Ayling
Samantha Lien
Mariah Lily Meade
Debora Lima
Judy Lin
Jennifer Lin
Yan Lin
Valia Lind
Stacey Lindo
Jocelyn Lindsay
David Lintz
Mariah Lions
Nata Live Choi
Oswaldo Llamas
Karen Lockinger Greenberg
Janyece Lofthouse Swineford
Yvonne Logan
Pene Lolohea
Constance Lombardo
Mykayla Long
Autumn Long Crochet
Jessica Lopes
Jennifer Lopez
Lucia Lorena
Kim Loth Hurst
Lisa Lott Gibson
Lyzzie Lou Land
Laura Louise Renegar
Michelle Lowe
Jennifer Lowe Howerth
Ana Lucía Arroyave
Barbie Lucy McMorrison
Daijah Luvs Dinosaurs
Nghi Ly
Jayde Lynch
Amanda Lynn Jackson
Aurora Lynn Mortensen
Makayla Lynn Page
Shelly Lyon Burns
Miranda Lyons
Rebecca M Fleming
Danielle M Smith
Donya M. Ali
Selene M. Dumont
Theresa M. McMackin
Heather M. McWilliams
Lisa M. Potts
Stacey Mac
Teresa Machado
BreAnna Mader

Gilliene Mae Ong
Jogelyn Mae Peggy Plaza
Joanne Mae Tadle
LoveLetter Mag
Denise Malia
Angie Manfredi
Susan Mann
Kelly Maple Polark
Maricar Mara
Marie Marcelo Alvarez
Julie Marcinik
Chantealy Mareen Menzer
Ria Maria
Giada Mariani
Paige Marie
Angella Marie
Julie Marie
Julia Marie Christy
Kristi Marie Criddle
Krystle Marie Irizarry Garde
Brianne Marie Jarvis
Darcy Marie Lepore
Heatherly Marie Selby
Katie Marie Stout
Shelby Marie Watson
Ricki Marking-Camuto-Dunn
Michelle Marquis McLean
Brittany Marshall
Deb Marshall
Suzanne Martin
Stephanie Martin
Kathy Martin
Jenny Martin
Sarah Martin
Cynthia Martinez
Jessica Martinez
CrystalRose Martinez
Betsy Martinez
Anaiz Martinez
Bianca Martinez Ankrum
Mandy Maschka
Theresa Mashura
Karma Mason
Rye Mason
Melissa Mason
Tina Matanguihan
Acacia Matheson
Misha Mathew
Nicole Mathias
Alex Matias
Branko Matija_evi_
Author Matthew Rush
Bethany Mattingly
Madison Max Smith
Lorrie Maxson
Jessica Maxson

Richard Maxwell Jr.
Jasmine May
Lexie May Hogan
Caroline Mazurek
Megan Mc Dade
Molly Mc Keagney
Michelle McAllister Merrill
Celeste McCauley
Chase McClure
Casey McCormick
Harley Mccutchen
Mandy McElhaney Anderson
Alice McElwee
Lisa McGeen Dell
Lianne McIntosh
Jaime McKenzie
Chrystal McLean
Briana McNair
Gretchen McNeil
Pamela McNeil Manasco
Leah McPhearson Miller
Rachel McWilliams
Celia Medrano
Briana Medrano
Julia Meek
Nicole Meer
Henry Megann
Nikki Meiggs
Lauren Meinhardt
Besosdeunangel Mel B
Rachel Melinda Yarbrough
Windowpane Memoirs
Cristina Menéndez
Leigh Menninger
Stephanie Merrell Baassler
Matthew Messner
Dawn Metcalf
Renee Meyer
Catherine Meyer
Emma Michaels
Lacey Michele Ashe
Alix Michelle Ferrell
C Michelle Jefferies
Briana Michelle Meyer
Courtney Miidget Greene
Rachel Mikkay
Claire Mill
Kelsey Miller
Meredith Miller
Becky Miller
Jessica Miller
Tez Miller
Larissa Miller Hardesty
Travis Millet
Caleigh Minshall
Estephanya Miranda

Cherry Mischivous
Jenny Misty
Elise Mitchell
Elizabeth Mize
Lorena MMondragon
Maggie Moe
Sarah 'Mogard' Olson
Yolaine Moise
Saba Molai
Shahira Molai
Wahida Mollah
Erica Molly Haglund
Aurora Momcilovich
Iman Monique Gibson
Carrie Monroe
Serena Montez
Laura Montoro
Natalie Monzyk
Hunter Moon Lytle
Brittany Moore
Brittany Moore
Laura Moore
Jessica Moore
Michelle Mootreddy
Barbara Morais
Courtney Morehead
Lisa Moreira
Michele Moreno
Beth Morey
April Morgan
Jenny Morris
Ashley Morrison
Tracy Mort Hopkins
Amber Morton Orr
Sarah Mostafa Dorra
Emily Muise
Natalie Mulford
Sarah Mulhern Gross
Alex Mullarky
Brianne Mulligan
Sandra Muñiz
Alain Munley
Julia Munslow
Claudia Murkl Osmond
Cynthia Murphy
Kelly Murphy
Carrie Murphy Kausch
Maria Muscarella
Cody Myers
Angie Myers Thompson
Chas N Kai
Melissa Nataly
Javier Navarro
Paula Navarro Cuesta
Martin Navis
Rick Ned

Alicia Nelson
Julia Nelson
Ashley Nelson
Jennifer Nelson
Aimee Nelson Brown
Robin Nesheim Nelson
Emily Nevels
Traci Newcomb
Shanta Newlin
Dawna Newman
Lynsey Newton
Jenn Ng
Steff Ngo
Debye Nicholl
Jacque Nichols Stengel
Misty Nicholson-Price
Heather Nicole Hansen
Patti Nielson
Cieara Niespodzianski
Yelania Nightwalker
Marieke Nijkamp
Kathryn Niles Hickle
Joyce Nivens Harrell
Rachel Nixon
Barbara Nolan
Leah Norod
Phoebe North
Luigi Novi
Hanna Nowak
Vicky Nuñez
Brittanie Nycole Sharpe
Andrea Oakeson
Jean Oberlander
Devonte O'Brian Moore
Cybele O'Brien
Mike O'Brien
Katie O'Connell
Mandy O'Dell Silberstein
Adiba Oemar
Lucile Ogie-Kristianson
Jen Ohzourk
Jana Oleson Warnell
Laure Oliva
Madalena Oliveira
Karina Oliveira
Gabriela Oliveira
Mary Oliver
Gloria Oliver
Tara Oliveri
Jessie Oliveros
Véro Olivier
Ingvild Olsen Gaarden
Kayla Olson
Kari Olson
Tabitha Olson
Mia Olufemi

Mooncatfarms Onebookshy
Clayton Onuoha
Kelsey Opsahl
Pamela Ortiz
Amparo Ortiz
Emily A. C. Osborne
Krystal Osmond
Megan O'Sullivan
Lura Overman Wilcox
Alannah P. Javier
Anthony Pacheco
Kathryn Packer Roberts
Jessica Padgett
Luna Paez
Kellie Pagoota Hovelson
Tahmina Paiker
Stefanie Painter
Adrian Palacios
Judita Pálenίková
Chloe Palka
Jon Palmer
Emma Palmer
Alex Palmer
Lucia Pannacci
Elyssa Papa
Natasha Parker
Laura Parker
Sarah Parker Ardrey
Melissa Parker Wadkins
Jaz Parks
Shannon Parsons
Katie Pash
Ekta Patel
Rebecca Pates
David Patrick
Rae Pavey
Shannon Pearcy
Matthew Pearson
Travis Pearson
Vera Pelissero
Stephanie Pellegrin
Valerie Pereira
Kathie Perez
Glaiza Perez
Alessandra Peron
Natalie Perrin-Smith Vance
Ron Peterson
Nolwenn Petitbois
Monique Petrie
Aerie Petro Anderson
Anna Pett
Raven Pettigrew
Julianne Pham
Van Pham
Crystal Phifer Folk
Katene Philip Barbara

Lisa Phillips
Ginger Phillips
Anjulie Pickett
Laura A. Pino
Harald Pinter
Juliana Piovani
Rachel Piper
Jm Poet
Chin PohYee
Joyce Polanco Veliz
Lisa Polkosnik
Irene Portillo
Tizzy Potts
Angela Potze Sharp
Britney Pouch
Rahchelle Powell
Aizlyn Pranke
Frank Prescia
Antonella Preuss
Lisa Pridgen
Noémie Prochasson
Amy Puente
Jeffy Pukka
Abby Putnam
Tabitha Qualls
Sally 'Qwill' Janin
Michael R Roush
Susan R. Mills
Prathima Radhakrishnan
Kristin Rae
Courtney Rae
Saleana Rae Carneiro
Kelsey Rae Dickson
Maritza Ramirez
Cibele Ramos
Ethan Ramsey
Tara Randall Newman
Melissa Ratcliffe
Kristy Rathbun Jones
Dorothy Ray
Bethany Ray Goodman
Maya Raya
Craig Rayl
Midnyte Reader
Andye ReadingTeen
Kirstin Reads
Ellz Readz
Candice Rebecca
Sarah Redd
Naomi Rees
Cherie Reich
Maryanne Reilly Hipple
Annika Reimers
Gabs Reiscal
Nova Ren Suma
Casey Renaud-Miller

Kerri Renner
Hobbitsies Reviews
Chris Revis
Corwin Revis
Diana Reyes
Michelle Reynoso
Mary Rhinehart
Kimberly Rhoades
Mila Rianto
Julia Rice
Cynthia Rice Revis
Renee Richardson
Emilee Richardson
Aydrea Rickert
Shannon Riffe
Koriann Riggenbach
Laura Riken
Doreen Riopel
Danica Ritherdon
Lessa Ritzma
Karen Rivers
Lindsay Robbins
F Roberta Walker
Dominique Roberts
Carrie Roberts
Sarah Robertson
Lindsay Robertson
Rob Robinson
Candace Robinson
Del Robinson
Amber Robinson
Jamie Robinson Durant
Kara Rochester
Jonjon Rodaz
Aimee Rodden
Casey Rodriguez
Alicia Rodriguez Humaran
LisaLaura Roecker
Jen Rogers Bigheart
Melissa Rogerson
Elie Rojas
Tricia Rojas
Gary Roland
Catarina Romeira
Emily Romero
Amanda Romine Lynch
Jen Rook
Kelly Rosbury Lee
Brigid Rose Lohman
Katie Rose Marciniak
Corey Rosen Schwartz
Amanda Ross
Jen Rossi
Jessica Rothenberg
Ann Rought
Allysia Roza Mayne

Alexandra Rucinski
Ashley Rudder
Dylan Rudisill
Dan Ruffino
Valorie Ruiz
Jennifer Rummel YA Librarian
Lacey Rusaw
Lynn Rush
ViCera Russ
Kate Ryan
Jeanne Ryan
Jordan Ryan Keeler
Ana S. Michele
Petra S_korová
Alicia Saechao
Marsha Saenz-Jones
Nejjar Safaâ
Jessica Sage Smith
Book Sake
Sherry Salach
Shey Salcedo Saumet
Lance Saltzman
Aurélie Salvatore
Rebecca Sampson
Jeff Sampson
Melissa Sampson Williams
Dani Samson
Andrea Sanchez
Nancy Sanchez
Idris Sandelis
Angela Sanders
Bonny Sandifer Anderson
Liz SanFilippo
Ashelynn Sanford
Michelle Santiago
Carlos Santos
Carrie Sapach
Genna Sarnak
Lei'Anna Saulsbery
Elizabeth Savage
Cass Says
Anna Scanlon
Natascha Schmalvogl
Sarah Schmalzer
Jamie Schneider
Ben Schrank
Lindsey Schueller
Ricki Schultz
Victoria Schwab
Mad Scientist
Heather Scott
Allison Scott
Michael Scott Copley
Rachel Scroggins
Rachel Searles Altan
Milena Seibel

Carolin Seidenkranz
Katryna Seki
Charles Selvaggi Castelletti
Henry Semanjarrez
Cediana Seme
Nicole Sender
Margie Senechal
Carrie Sepaugh
Ruta Sepetys Smith
Nicole Settle
Ruth Setton
Rahaf Sh
Sarah Shade
Aprille Shadowspeak
Rosa Shah
Laura Shanks
Jaidis Shaw
Jack Shedd
Kathryn Sheridan Kupanoff
Tressa Sherman
Shannon Sherman
Emy Shin
Nicole Shipley
Karen Shipp
Marta Silva
Brittany Silva
Shana Silver
Anyu Silverman
Donna Simmonds
Heather Simone
Keely Sinclair
Kyleigh Skaggs
Alison Skap
Birdie Skolfield
Brynne Skoropys
Jami Slack
Dawn Slaughter
Viki Sloboda
Julie Smeltzer
Angie Smibert
Donna Smith
Milissa Smith
ZMom Smith
Kayla Smith
Mandy Smith
Andrew Smith
Sarah Smith
Kendra Smith
Jennifer Smith
Cindy Smith
Kelly Smith
Erin Smith
Jodie Smith
Sydney Smith
June Smith Morgan
Neda So

Rafla Soares
Elena Solodow
Samantha Somethin
Megan Sordyl
Jessica Souders
Mark Southard
Barbara Southard
Brittany Southard
Wilda Sowell
Susan Sowers Light
Bonnie Sparks
Melissa Spence
Lindsay Sperling
Dylan Spivey
Meg Spooner
Kara Squire
Hilary St. Laurent
Jason St. Sauver
Jasmine Stairs
Tony Stanhope
Joanne Stapley
Brittani Star Benton
Kimberley Steel
Amanda Stefancin Furman
Julianna Steffens
Rachael Stein
Jennelle Stepanski
April Stevens
Ram Stevens
Abby Stevens
Shannon Stidham
Corey Stiles-Meyer
Alisa Stofer
Tiffany Story
Katie Stout
Vania Stoyanova
Jennifer Strand
Zoe Strickland
Janet Sumner Johnson
Author Susan Kaye Quinn
Sammy Sutton
Rebecca Sutton
Keidi Suursaar
Elin Svensson Tollehed
Caitlin Sweeny
Josh Sweezy
Sasha Switz
Myriiam Sykes Landin
Sara T. K. DeSabato
Melissa T-agentnerdy
Tara Tagli Lassin
Stephanie Takes-Desbiens
Elizabeth Talbott
Wesley Tallent
Raheemah Tauhidi
Holly Taylor

Brent Taylor
Brent Taylor
Wendy Taylor
Kpl TeenSpot
Michele Teevan
Jeshka Teh Chibi
Melisa Tellio
Staci Terrell
Mikael Tezia
Storm TheImpact Smith
Tarah Theoret
Monica Theramblings-
   ofabookaddict
Jean Thomas
Sabrina Thompson
Katherine Thompson
Julie Thompson
Jenn Thompson
Rochelle Thorold Benoit
Jamie Thurston Burch
Beguile Thy Sorrow
Sarena Tien
Robyn Tilbrook
Sara Tilch
Danielle Tilson
Jade Timms
Minas Tineh
Ala Tineh
Stephanie Tolbert
Leslie Toledo
Lucy Tonkin
Brenda Topham Child
Ambar Torres
Jessica Torres
Alexandra Torres
Johana Torres Chain
Tonia Trail
Kristine Treece Michael
Erika Trenas
Heather Trese
Tine Trum
Angelique Truong
Jessica Tudor
Logan Turner
Sara Twaddle
James Tyler Camp
Sandra Ulbrich Almazan
Kimberly Usselman
Sylvia Uy
Suzanne Vadnais Droppert
Vicky Vakouftsi
Melody ValAdez
Savannah Valdez
Carolina Valdez Miller
Amanda Valdez-Milner
Elzar Valdivia

Marissa Valentine
Felicity Vallence
Vive van der Vaart
Krystal Van Eyk
Geri Vancena VanDevender
Danny Vanquish
Hazel Vara
Alyssa Vargas
Wendy Vasconcelos
Oriana Vasquez
Ina Vassbotn Steinman
Maiden Veil
Gabrielle Velasco
Gaby Velasquez
Aliyah Veltz
Emilia Venegas Hinojosa
Tony Ventura
Cathie Veres
Martin Vergara
Samantha Vicars
Valeryy Vidales
Luis Viera
Vannessa Viidalez
Gabriel Villa
Jackie Villeneuve White
Aaron Vincent Espinas-Delos
    Santos
EagerReader Violet
Amber Violet Griffiths
Anne Voigt
Stephanie Vollick
Ryan Von Swartzchild
Jade Walker
Elizabeth Walker
Aleisha Walker
Dorothy Walker
Valerie Walker
Dawn Walker
William Walker Perry
Jennifer Walkup Cerruto
Sharon Walling
Devante Walls Eleni
Hattie Walls DeRaps
Darden Walton
K.M. Walton
Erin Wamala

Emma Warburton
Kristi Ward Chestnutt
Shannon Watkins Condie
Jen Watson
Cat Watts
Cassie Wayland
Charissa Weaks
Courtney Webb
Sari Webb
Elizabeth Weibley
Laurie Welden Lamb
Mindi Wells Rench
Sar Werb
Kat Werner
Valerie West
Jeffrey West
Jeremy West
Jennifer White
Leslie White
Pamela White
Charly White
Gina White
JamieLee Whitehouse
Jacki Whitehouse
Cayla Whitney
Katrina Whittaker
Kayla Whittle
Nicole Wick
Melissa Wideen
Lauren Widtfeldt
Susan Wilcox
Nicole Williams
Sarah Williams
Sandy Williams
Crystal Williams Fulcher
Waitman Willie
Ashley Willis
Jess Wilmshurst
Emily WilowRaven
Bryan Wilson
Danna Wilson
Jessica Wilson
Jena Wilson
Christie Wilson
Haley Wilson
Stephanie Winkelhake

Val Winkler
Kristie Winks
Susanne Winnacker
Meagan Witherspoon Vaughn
Bri Wolford Laycock
Cleo Wong
Sarah Woodard
Erin Woodbridge
Faith Woodley
Melissa Woolley Baldwin
Jenna Worden
Andrew Wrathall
Lisa Wuebkes Lauerman
Britney Wyatt
Cicely Wynne
Cassidy Xandria Dean
Pedro Xd
Molly Xiong
Isaac Xiong
April Xu
Natalia Y. Pérez
Krystle Yanagihara
Becky Yanez
Janice Yang
Andy Yanira Estrada
Steph Yanqui
Sori Yarbrough
Gail Yates
Shellie Yaworski
Beth Yelton Whitener
Annie Yohai
Bing Yuan
Kristie Yutzy
Cg Yvette
Hana Zainal Abidin
Megan Zaiser
Ale Zamudio
Victoria Zheng
Anastacia Zittel
MDest ZKilla
Claire Zlotnicki
Nicole Zoltack
Moslimah Zoud
Victoria Zumbrum
Heidi Zweifel

THEIR UNIVERSE CHANGED AT 11:11 A.M. ON 1/11/11